THE INGERSOLL LOCKWOOD COLLECTION

Ingersoll Lockwood

EAST INDIA
PUBLISHING COMPANY
PREMIER CLASSICS

Published by the East India Publishing Company
Ottawa, Ontario.

© 2021 East India Publishing Company

Cover Design by EIPC. © 2021
9781774261620

CONTENTS

1900; OR, THE LAST PRESIDENT

CHAPTER I.

That was a terrible night for the great City of New York—the night of Tuesday, November 3rd, 1896. The city staggered under the blow like a huge ocean liner which plunges, full speed, with terrific crash into a mighty iceberg, and recoils shattered and trembling like an aspen.

The people were gathered, light-hearted and confident, at the evening meal, when the news burst upon them. It was like a thunder bolt out of an azure sky: "Altgeld holds Illinois hard and fast in the Democratic line. This elects Bryan President of the United States!"

Strange to say, the people in the upper portion of the city made no movement to rush out of their houses and collect in the public squares, although the night was clear and beautiful. They sat as if paralyzed with a nameless dread, and when they conversed it was with bated breath and throbbing hearts.

In less than half an hour, mounted policemen dashed through the streets calling out: "Keep within your houses; close your doors and barricade them. The entire East side is in a state of uproar. Mobs of vast size are organizing under the lead of Anarchists and Socialists, and threaten to plunder and despoil the houses of the rich who have wronged and oppressed them for so many years. Keep within doors. Extinguish all lights."

Happily, Governor Morton was in town, and although a deeper pallor overcame the ashen hue of age as he spoke, yet there was no tremor in his voice: "Let the Seventh, Twenty-second and Seventy-first regiments be ordered under arms." In a few moments hundreds of messengers could be heard racing through the silent streets, summoning the members of these regiments to their Armories.

Slowly, but with astonishing nerve and steadiness, the mobs pushed the police northward, and although the force stood the onslaught with magnificent courage, yet beaten back, the dark masses of infuriated beings surged up again with renewed fury and strength. Will the troops be in time to save the city? was the whispered inquiry among the knots of police officials who were directing the movements of their men.

About nine o'clock, with deafening outcries, the mob, like a four-headed monster breathing fire and flame, raced, tore, burst, raged into Union Square.

The police force was exhausted, but their front was still like a wall of stone, save that it was movable. The mob crowded it steadily to the north, while the air quivered and was rent with mad vociferations of the victors: "Bryan is elected! Bryan is elected! Our day has come at last. Down with our oppressors! Death to the rich man! Death to the gold bugs! Death to the capitalists! Give us back the money you have ground out of us. Give us back the marrow of our bones which you have used to grease the wheels of your chariots."

The police force was now almost helpless. The men still used their sticks, but the blows were ineffectual, and only served to increase the rage of the vast hordes now advancing upon Madison Square.

The Fifth Avenue Hotel will be the first to feel the fury of the mob. Would the troops be in time to save it?

A half cheer, a half cry of joy goes up. It is inarticulate. Men draw a long breath; women drop upon their knees and strain their eyes; they can hear something, but they cannot see as yet, for the gas houses and electric plants had been destroyed by the mob early in the evening. They preferred to fight in the dark, or by the flames of rich men's abodes.

Again a cheer goes up, louder and clearer this time, followed by cries of "They're coming, they're coming."

Yes, they were coming—the Twenty-second down Broadway, the Seventh down Madison avenue, both on the double quick.

In a moment or so there were a few bugle calls, and a few spoken commands rang out clear and sharp; and then the two regiments stretched across the entire square, literally from wall to wall, in line of battle. The mob was upon them. Would this slender line of troops, could it hold such a mighty mass of men in check?

The answer was a deafening discharge of firearms, a terrific crack, such as some thunder bolts make when they explode. A wall of fire blazed across the Square. Again and again it blazed forth. The mob halted, stood fast, wavered, fell back, advanced again. At that moment there came a rattle as of huge knives in the distance. It was the gallant Seventy-first charging up Twenty-third street, and taking the mob on the flank. They came on like a wall of iron, bristling with blades of steel.

There were no outcries, no cheers from the regiment. It dealt out death in silence, save when two bayonets crossed and clashed in bearing down some doubly-vigorous foe.

As the bells rang out midnight, the last remnants of the mob were driven to cover, but the wheels of the dead wagons rattled till daybreak.

And then the aged Governor, in response to the Mayor's "Thank God, we've saved the city!" made answer:

"Aye, but the Republic——."

CHAPTER II.

Great as has been the world's wonder at the uprising of Mr. Bryan's "struggling masses" in the city by the sea, and the narrow escape of its magnificent homes from fire and brand, yet greater still was the wonderment when the news was flashed across the land that Chicago did not stand in need of a single Federal soldier.

"Chicago is mad, but it is the madness of joy. Chicago is in the hands of a mob, but it is a mob made up of her own people—noisy, rude and boisterous, the natural exultation of a suddenly enfranchised class; but bent on no other mischief than glorying over the villainous and self-seeking souls who have ground the faces of the poor and turned the pitiless screw of social and political power into the hearts of the 'common people' until its last thread had been reached, and despair pressed its lupine visage hard against the door of the laboring man."

And yet, at this moment when the night air quivered with the mad vociferations of the "common people," that the Lord had been good to them; that the wicked money-changers had been driven from the temple, that the stony-hearted usurers were beaten at last, that the "People's William" was at the helm now, that peace and plenty would in a few moons come back to the poor man's cottage, that Silver was King, aye, King at last, the world still went wondering why red-eyed anarchy, as she stood in Haymarket Square, with thin arms aloft, with wild mien and wilder gesticulation, drew no bomb of dynamite from her bosom, to hurl at the hated minions of the law who were silent spectators of this delirium of popular joy.

Why was it thus? Look and you shall know why white robed peace kept step with this turbulent band and turned its thought from red handed pillage. He was there. The master spirit to hold them in leash. He, and he alone, had lifted Bryan to his great eminence. Without these twenty-four electoral votes, Bryan had been doomed, hopelessly doomed. He, and he alone, held the great Commonwealth of the West hard and fast in the Democratic line; hence he came as conqueror, as King-maker, and the very walls of the sky-touching edifices trembled as he was dragged through the crowded streets by this orderly mob, and ten times ten thousand of his creatures bellowed his name and shook their hats aloft in mad exultation:

"You're our Saviour, you've cleaned the Temple of Liberty of its foul horde of usurers. We salute you. We call you King-maker. Bryan shall call you Master too. You shall have your reward. You shall stand behind the throne. Your wisdom shall make us whole. You shall purge the land of this unlawful crowd of money-lenders. You shall save the Republic. You are greater than Washington. You're a better friend of ours than Lincoln. You'll do more for us than Grant. We're your slaves. We salute you. We thank you. We bless you. Hurrah! Hurrah! Hurrah!"

But yet this vast throng of tamed monsters, this mighty mob of momentarily good-natured haters of established order, broke away from the master's control for a few brief moments, and dipped their hands in the enemy's blood. The deed was swift as it was terrible. There were but four of them, unarmed, on pleasure bent. At sight of these men, a thousand throats belched out a deep and awful growl of hatred. They were brave men, and backed against the wall to die like brave men, stricken down, beaten, torn, trampled, dragged, it was quick work. They had faced howling savages in the far West, painted monsters in human form, but never had they heard such yells leave the throats of men; and so they died, four brave men, clad in the blue livery of the Republic, whose only crime was that

some months back, against the solemn protest of the Master, their comrades had
set foot on the soil of the commonwealth, and saved the Metropolis of the West
from the hands of this same mob.

And so Chicago celebrated the election of the new President who was to free
the land from the grasp of the money-lenders, and undo the bad business of
years of unholy union between barterers and sellers of human toil and the law
makers of the land.

Throughout the length and breadth of the South, and beyond the Great Divide,
the news struck hamlet and village like the glad tidings of a new evangel, almost
as potent for human happiness as the heavenly message of two thousand years
ago. Bells rang out in joyful acclaim, and the very stars trembled at the telling,
and the telling over and over of what had been done for the poor man by his
brethren of the North, and around the blazing pine knots of the Southern cabin
and in front of the mining camp fires of the Far West, the cry went up: "Silver
is King! Silver is King!" Black palms and white were clasped in this strange love-
feast, and the dark skinned grand child no longer felt the sting of the lash on his
sire's shoulder. All was peace and good will, for the people were at last victorious
over their enemies who had taxed and tithed them into a very living death. Now
the laborer would not only be worthy of his hire, but it would be paid to him in
a people's dollar, for the people's good, and now the rich man's coffers would be
made to yield up their ill-gotten gain, and the sun would look upon this broad
and fair land, and find no man without a market for the product of his labors.
Henceforth, the rich man should, as was right and proper, pay a royal sum for
the privilege of his happiness, and take the nation's taxes on his broad shoulders,
where they belong.

CHAPTER III.

The pens of many writers would not suffice to describe with anything like historical
fullness and precision, the wild scenes of excitement which, on the morning after
election day, burst forth on the floors of the various exchanges throughout the
Union. The larger and more important the money centre, the deeper, blacker
and heavier the despair which sank upon them after the violent ebullitions of
protest, defiance and execration had subsided. With some, it seemed that visions
of their swift but sure impoverishment only served to transform the dark and
dismal drama of revolution and disintegration into a side-splitting farce, and they
greeted the prospective loss of their millions with loud guffaws and indescribable
antics of horseplay and unseemly mirth.

As the day wore on, the news became worse and worse. It was only too
apparent that the House of Representatives of the Fifty-fifth Congress would
be controlled by the combined vote of the Populists and Free Silver men, while
the wild joy with which the entire South welcomed the election of Bryan and

Sewall left little doubt in the minds of the Northern people that the Southern Senators would, to a man, range themselves on the Administration side of the great conflict into which the Republic was soon to be precipitated. Add to these the twenty Senators of the Free Silver States of the North, and the new President would have the Congress of the Republic at his back. There would be nothing to stand between him and the realization of those schemes which an exuberant fancy, untamed by the hand of experience, and scornful of the leading-strings of wisdom, can conjure up.

Did we say nothing? Nay, not so; for the Supreme Court was still there. And yet Justice Field had come fully up to the eightieth milestone in the journey of life and Justice Gray was nearly seventy, while one or two other members of this High Court of Judicature held to their lives with feeble grasp. Even in due and orderly course of events, why might there not come vacancies and then?...

In spite of the nameless dread that rested upon so many of our people, and chilled the very blood of the country's industries, the new year '97 came hopefully, serenely, almost defiantly in. There was an indescribable something in the air, a spirit of political devil-me-care, a feeling that the old order had passed away and that the Republic had entered into the womb of Time and been born again. This sentiment began to give outward and visible signs of its existence and growth in the remote agricultural districts of the South and Far West. They threw aside their working implements, loitered about, gathered in groups and the words Washington, White House, Silver, Bryan, Offices, Two for One, the South's Day, Reign of the Common People, Taxes, Incomes, Year of Jubilee, Free Coinage, Wall Street, Altgeld, Tillman, Peffer, Coxey, were whispered in a mysterious way with head noddings and pursing up of mouths.

As January wore away and February, slipping by, brought Bryan's Inauguration nearer and nearer, the groups melted into groups, and it was only too apparent that from a dozen different points in the South and North West "Coxey Armies" were forming for an advance on Washington. In some instances they were well clad and well provisioned; in others, they were little better than great bands of hungry and restless men, demoralized by idleness and wrought up to a strange degree of mental excitement by the extravagant harangues of their leaders, who were animated with but one thought, namely, to make use of these vast crowds of Silver Pilgrims, as they called themselves, to back up their claims for public office.

These crowds of deluded people were well named "Silver Pilgrims," for hundreds of them carried in hempen bags, pieces of silverware, in ninety-nine cases of a hundred, plated stuff of little value, which unscrupulous dealers and peddlers had palmed off upon them as sterling, with the promises that once in Washington, the United States Mint would coin their metal into "Bryan Dollars" giving "two for one" in payment for it.

While these motley "armies" marched upon the capitol of the Republic, the railway trains night and day brought vast crowds of "new men," politicians of low degree, men out of employment, drunken and disgruntled mechanics, farmer's sons, to seek their fortunes under the Reign of the People, heelers and hangers-on of ward bosses, old men who had not tasted office for thirty years and more, all inspired by Mr. Bryan's declaration that "The American people are not in favor of life tenure in the Civil Service, that a permanent office holding class is not in harmony with our institutions, that a fixed term in appointive offices would open the public service to a larger number of citizens, without impairing its efficiency," all bearing new besoms in their hands or across their shoulders, each and every one of them supremely confident that in the distribution of the spoils something would surely fall to his share, since they were the "Common People" who were so dear to Mr. Bryan, and who had made him President in the very face of the prodigious opposition of the rich men, whose coffers had been thrown wide open all to no purpose, and in spite too of the satanic and truly devilish power of that hell upon earth known as Wall Street, which had sweated gold in vain in its desperate efforts to fasten the chains of trusts and the claws of soulless monsters known as corporations upon these very "Common People," soon to march in triumph before the silver chariot of the young Conqueror from the West.

CHAPTER IV.

There had been a strange prophecy put forth by some one, and it had made its way into the daily journals, and had been laughingly or seriously commented upon, according to the political tone of the paper, or the passing humor of the writer, that the 4th of March, 1897, would never dawn upon the American people. There was something very curious and uncanny about the prediction, and what actually happened was not qualified to loosen the fearful tension of public anxiety, for the day literally and truly never dawned upon the City of Washington, and well deserves its historical name, the "Dawnless Day." At six o'clock, the hour of daybreak, such an impenetrable pall of clouds overhung the city that there came no signs of day. The gathering crowds could plainly hear the plaintive cries and lamentations put up in the negro quarters of the city. Not until nearly nine o'clock did the light cease to "shine in darkness" and the darkness begin to comprehend it.

But although it was a cheerless gray day, even at high noon, its heaviness set no weight upon the spirits of the jubilant tens of thousands which completely filled the city and its public parks, and ran over into camps and hastily improvised shelters outside the city limits.

Not until the day previous had the President announced the names of those selected for his Cabinet. The South and Far West were fairly beside themselves with joy, for there had been from their standpoint ugly rumors abroad for several days. It had even been hinted that Bryan had surrendered to the "money-changers," and that the selection of his constitutional advisers would prove him recreant to the glorious cause of popular government, and that the Reign of the

Common People would remain but a dream of the "struggling masses."

But these apprehensions were short lived. The young President stood firm and fast on the platform of the parties which had raised him to his proud eminence. And what better proof of his thorough belief in himself and in his mission could he have given than the following:

Secretary of State—William M. Stewart, of Nevada.

Secretary of Treasury—Richard P. Bland, of Missouri.

Secretary of War—John P. Altgeld, of Illinois.

Attorney General—Roger Q. Mills, of Texas.

Postmaster General—Henry George, of New York.

Secretary Navy—John Gary Evans, of South Carolina.

Secretary Interior—William A. Peffer, of Kansas.

Secretary Agriculture—Lafe Pence, of Colorado.

The first thing that flashed across the minds of many upon glancing over this list of names was the omission therefrom of Tillman's. What did it mean? Could the young President have quarreled with his best friend, his most powerful coadjutor? But the wiser ones only shook their heads and made answer that it was Tillman's hand that filled the blank for Secretary of the Navy, left there by the new ruler after the people's own heart. Evans was but a creation of this great Commoner of the South, an image graven with his hands.

The inaugural address was not a disappointment to those who had come to hear it. It was like the man who delivered it—bold, outspoken, unmistakable in its terms, promising much, impatient of precedent, reckless of result; a double confirmation that this was to be the Reign of the Common People, that much should be unmade and much made over, and no matter how the rich man might cry out in anger or amazement, the nation must march on to the fulfillment of a higher and nobler mission than the impoverishment and degradation of the millions for the enrichment and elevation of the few.

Scarcely had the young President—his large eyes filled with a strange light, and his smooth, hairless visage radiant as a cloudless sky, his wife's arm twined around his, and their hands linked in those of their children—passed within the lofty portal of the White House, than he threw himself into a chair, and seizing a sheet of official paper penned the following order, and directed its immediate promulgation:

Executive Mansion, Washington, D. C., March 4th, 1897.

Executive Order No. 1.

In order that there may be immediate relief in the terrible financial depression now weighing upon our beloved country, consequent upon and resulting from the unlawful combination of capitalists and money-lenders both in this Republic and in England, and that the ruinous and inevitable progress toward a universal gold standard may be stayed, the President orders and directs the immediate abandonment of the so-called "gold reserve," and that on and after the promulgation of this order, the gold and silver standard of the Constitution be resumed and strictly maintained in all the business transactions of the Government.

It was two o'clock in the afternoon when news of this now world-famous Executive Order was flashed into the great banking centres of the country. Its effect in Wall street beggars description. On the floor of the Stock Exchange men yelled and shrieked like painted savages, and, in their mad struggles, tore and trampled each other. Many dropped in fainting fits, or fell exhausted from their wild and senseless efforts to say what none would listen to. Ashen pallor crept over the faces of some, while the blood threatened to burst the swollen arteries that spread in purple network over the brows of others. When silence came at last, it was a silence broken by sobs and groans. Some wept, while others stood dumb-stricken as if it was all a bad dream, and they were awaiting the return of their poor distraught senses to set them right again. Ambulances were hastily summoned and fainting and exhausted forms were borne through hushed and whispering masses wedged into Wall street, to be whirled away uptown to their residences, there to come into full possession of their senses only to cry out in their anguish that ruin, black ruin, stared them in the face if this news from Washington should prove true.

CHAPTER V.

By proclamation bearing date the 5th day of March 1897, the President summoned both houses of Congress to convene in extraordinary session "for the consideration of the general welfare of the United States, and to take such action as might seem necessary and expedient to them on certain measures which he should recommend to their consideration, measures of vital import to the welfare and happiness of the people, if not to the very existence of the Union and the continuance of their enjoyment of the liberties achieved by the fathers of the Republic."

While awaiting the day set for the coming together of the Congress, the "Great Friend of the Common People" came suddenly face to face with the first serious business of his Administration. Fifty thousand people tramped the streets of Washington without bread or shelter. Many had come in quest of office, lured on by the solemn pronouncement of their candidate that there should be at once a clean sweep of these barnacles of the ship of State and so complete had been their confidence in their glorious young captain, that they had literally failed to provide themselves with either "purse or script or shoes," and now stood hungry and footsore at his gate, begging for a crust of bread. But most of those making up this vast multitude were "the unarmed warriors of peaceful armies" like the one once led by the redoubtable Coxey, decoyed from farm and hamlet and plantation by some nameless longing to "go forth" to stand in the presence of this new Savior of Society, whose advent to power was to bring them "double pay" for all their toil. While on the march all had gone well, for their brethren had opened their hearts and their houses as these "unarmed warriors" had marched with flying banners and loud huzzas through the various towns on the route.

But now the holiday was over, they were far from their homes, they were in danger of perishing from hunger. What was to be done? "They are our people," said the President, "their love of country has undone them; the nation must not let them suffer, for they are its hope and its shield in the hour of war, and its glory and its refuge in times of peace. They are the common people for whose benefit this Republic was established. The Kings of the earth may desert them; I never shall." The Secretary of War was directed to establish camps in the parks and suburbs of the city and to issue rations and blankets to these luckless wanderers until the Government could provide for their transportation back to their homes.

On Monday, March 15th, the President received the usual notification from both houses of Congress, that they had organized and were ready for the consideration of such measures as he might choose to recommend for their action.

The first act to pass both houses and receive the signature of the President, was an Act repealing the Act of 1873, and opening the mints of the United States to the free coinage of silver at the ratio of sixteen to one, with gold, and establishing branch mints in the cities of Denver, Omaha, Chicago, Kansas City, Spokane, Los Angeles, Charleston and Mobile.

The announcement that reparation had thus been made to the people for the "Crime of 1873" was received with loud cheering on the floors and in the galleries of both houses.

And the Great North heard these cheers and trembled.

The next measure of great public import brought before the House was an act to provide additional revenue by levying a tax upon the incomes, substantially on the lines laid down by the legislation of 1894. The Republican Senators strove to make some show of resistance to this measure, but so solid were the administration ranks, that they only succeeded in delaying it for a few weeks. This first skirmish with the enemy, however, brought the President and his followers to a realizing sense that not only must the Senate be shorn of its power to block the "new movement of regeneration and reform" by the adoption of rules cutting off prolonged debate, but that the "new dispensation" must at once proceed to increase its senatorial representation, for who could tell what moment some one of the Northern Silver States might not slip away from its allegiance to the "Friend of the Common People."

The introduction of a bill repealing the various Civil Service acts passed for the alleged purpose of "regulating and improving the Civil Service of the United States," and of another repealing the various acts establishing National Banks, and substituting United States notes for all national bank notes based upon interest bearing bonds, opened the eyes of the Republican opposition to the fact that the President and his party were possessed of the courage of their convictions, and were determined, come good report or evil report, to wipe all conflicting legislation from the statute books. The battle in the Senate now took on a spirit of extreme acrimony; scenes not witnessed since the days of Slavery, were of daily occurrence on the floors of both the House and the Senate. Threats of secession came openly from the North only to be met with the jeers and laughter of the silver and populist members. "We're in the saddle at last," exclaimed a Southern member, "and we intend to ride on to victory!"

The introduction of bills for the admission of New Mexico and Arizona, and for the division of Texas into two States to be called East Texas and West Texas, although each of these measures was strictly within the letter of the Constitution, fell among the members of the Republican opposition like a torch in a house of tinder. There was fire at once, and the blaze of party spirit leapt to such dangerous heights that the whole nation looked on in consternation. Was the Union about to go up in a great conflagration and leave behind it but the ashes and charred pedestals of its greatness?

"We are the people" wrote the President in lines of dignity and calmness. "We are the people and what we do, we do under the holy sanction of law, and there is no one so powerful or so bold as to dare to say we do not do well in lifting off the nation's shoulders the grievous and unlawful burdens which preceding Congresses have placed upon them."

And so the "Long Session" of the fifty-fifth Congress was entered upon, fated to last through summer heat and autumn chill, and until winter came again and the Constitution itself set limits to its lasting. And when that day came, and its speaker, amid a wild tumult of cheers, arose to declare it ended not by their will, but by the law of the land, he said: "The glorious revolution is in its brightest bud. Since the President called upon us to convene in last March, we have with the strong blade of public indignation, and with a full sense of our responsibility, erased from the statute books the marks of our country's shame and our people's subjugation. Liberty can not die. There remains much to be done in the way of building up. Let us take heart and push on. On Monday, the regular session of this Congress will begin. We must greet our loved ones from the distance. We have no time to go home and embrace them."

CHAPTER VI.

When a Republican member of the House arose to move the usual adjournment for the holidays, there was a storm of hisses and cries of "No, no!"

Said the leader of the House, amid deafening plaudits: "We are the servants of the people. Our work is not yet complete. There must be no play for us while coal barons stand with their feet on the ashes of the poor man's hearthstone, and weeds and thorns cumber the fields of the farmer for lack of money to buy seed and implements. There must be no play for us while railway magnates press from the pockets of the laboring man six and eight per cent. return on thrice watered stocks, and rapacious landlords, enriched by inheritance, grind the faces of the poor. There must be no play for us while enemies of the human kind are, by means of trust and combination and 'corners,' engaged in drawing their unholy millions from the very life-blood of the nation, paralyzing its best efforts and setting the blight of intemperance and indifference upon it, by making life but one long struggle for existence, without a gleam of rest and comfort in old age. No, Mr. Speaker, we must not adjourn, but by our efforts in these halls of legislation let the nation know that we are at work for its emancipation, and by these means let the monopolists and money-changers be brought to a realizing sense that the Reign of the Common People has really been entered upon, and then the bells will ring out a happier, gladder New Year than has ever dawned upon this Republic."

The opposition fairly quailed before the vigor and earnestness of the "new dispensation." There were soon before the House and pressed well on toward final passage a number of important measures calculated to awaken an intense feeling of enthusiasm among the working classes. Among these was an Act establishing a Loan Commission for the loaning of certain moneys of the United States to Farmers and Planters without interest; an Act for the establishment of a permanent Department of Public Works, its head to be styled Secretary of Public Works, rank as a cabinet officer, and supervise the expenditure of all public moneys for the construction of public buildings and the improvement of rivers and harbors; an Act making it a felony, punishable with imprisonment for life, for any citizen or combination of citizens to enter into any trust or agreement to stifle, suppress or in any way interfere with full, open and fair competition in trade and manufacture among the States, or to make use of any inter-State railroads, waterways or canals for the transportation of any food products or goods, wares or merchandise which may have been "cornered," stored or withheld with a view to enhance the value thereof; and, most important of all, a preliminary Act having for its object the appointment of Commissioners for the purchase by the Federal Government of all inter-State railway and telegraph lines, and in the meantime the strict regulation of all fares and charges by a Government Commission, from whose established schedules there shall be no appeal.

On Washington's Birthday the President issued an Address of Congratulation to the People of the United States, from which the following is extracted:

"The malicious prognostications of our political opponents have proven themselves to be but empty sound and fury. Although not quite one year has elapsed since I, agreeable to your mandate, restored to you the money of the Constitution, yet from every section of our Union comes the glad tidings of renewed activity and prosperity. The workingman no longer sits cold and hungry beside a cheerless hearthstone; the farmer has taken heart and resumed work; the wheels of the factory are in motion again; the shops and stores of the legitimate dealer and trader are full of bustle and action. There is content everywhere, save in the counting-room of the money-changer, for which thank God and the common people of this Republic. The free coinage of that metal which the Creator, in His wisdom, stored with so lavish a hand in the subterranean vaults of our glorious mountain ranges, has proven a rich and manifold blessing for our people. It is in every sense of the word the 'people's money,' and already the envious world looks on in amazement that we have shown our ability to do without 'foreign cooperation.' The Congress of our Republic has been in almost continuous session since I took my oath of office, and the administration members deserve your deepest and most heartfelt gratitude. They are rearing for themselves a monument more lasting than chiseled bronze or polished monolith. They knew no rest, they asked for no respite from their labors until, at my earnest request, they adjourned over to join their fellow citizens in the observance of this sacred anniversary.

"Fellow citizens, remember the bonds which a wicked and selfish class of usurers and speculators fastened upon you, and on this anniversary of the birth of the Father of our Country, let us renew our pledges to undo completely and absolutely their infamous work, and in public assembly and family circle, let us by new vows confirm our love of right and justice, so that the great gain may not slip away from us, but go on increasing so long as the statute books contain a single trace of the record of our enslavement. As for me, I have but one ambition, and that is to deserve so well of you that when you come to write my epitaph, you set beneath my name the single line:

"Here lies a Friend of the Common People."

CHAPTER VII.

This first year of the Silver Administration was scarcely rounded up, ere there began to be ugly rumors that the Government was no longer able to hold the white metal at a parity with gold. "It is the work of Wall Street," cried the friends of the President, but wiser heads were shaken in contradiction, for they had watched the sowing of the wind of unreason, and knew only too well that the whirlwind of folly must be reaped in due season.

The country had been literally submerged by a silver flood which had poured its argent waves into every nook and cranny of the Republic, stimulating human endeavor to most unnatural and harmful vigor. Mad speculation stalked over the land. People sold what they should have clung to, and bought what they did not need. Manufacturers heaped up goods for which there was no demand, and farmers ploughed where they had not drained and drained, where they were never fated to plough. The small dealer enlarged his business with more haste than judgment, and the widow drew her mite from the bank of savings to buy land on which she was destined never to set foot. The spirit of greed and gain lodged in every mind, and the "Common People" with a mad eagerness loosened the strings of their leather purses to cast their hard-earned savings into wild schemes of profit. Every scrap and bit of the white metal that they could lay their hands upon, spoons hallowed by the touch of lips long since closed in death, and cups and tankards from which grand sires had drunken were bundled away to the mints to be coined into "people's dollars."

At the very first rumor of the slipping away of this trusted coin from its parity with gold, there was a fearful awakening, like the start and the gasp of the miser who sees his horded treasure melting away from before his eyes, and he not able to reach out and stay its going.

Protest and expostulation first, then came groans and prayers, from which there was an easy road to curses. The working man threw off his cap and apron to rush upon the public square, and demand his rights. Mobs ran together, processions formed, deputations hurried off to Washington, not on foot like the Coxey Army, but on the swift wings of the Limited Express.

The "common people" were admitted to the bar of the house, their plaints patiently listened to, and reparation promised. Bills for increased revenue were hurriedly introduced, and new taxes were loaded upon the broad shoulders of the millionaires of the nation;—taxes on checks, taxes on certificates of incorporation, taxes on deeds and mortgages, taxes on pleasure yachts, taxes on private parks and plaisances, taxes on wills of all property above $5,000 in value, taxes on all gifts of realty for and in consideration of natural love and affection, taxes on all passage tickets to foreign lands, and double taxes on the estates of all absentees on and after the lapse of six months.

There was a doubling up too of the tariff on all important luxuries, for as was said on the floor of Congress, "if the silks and satins of American looms and the wines and tobacco of native growth, are not good enough for 'my Lord of Wall Street,' let him pay the difference and thank heaven that he can get them at that price."

To quiet the murmurs of the good people of the land, additional millions were placed to the credit of the Department of Public Works, and harbors were dredged out in one month only to fill up in the next, and new systems of improvement of interstate waterways were entered upon on a scale of magnitude hitherto undreamt of. The Commissioners for the distribution of public moneys to farmers so impoverished as to be unable to work their lands, were kept busy in placing "Peffer Loans" where the need of them seemed to be the greatest, and to put a stop to the "nefarious doings of money-changers and traders in the misfortunes of the people," a statute was enacted making it a felony punishable with imprisonment for life, for any person or corporate body to buy and sell government bonds or public funds, or deal in them with a view to draw gain or profit from their rise and fall in value.

But try never so hard, the Government found itself powerless to check the slow but steady decline in value of the people's dollar. By midsummer, it had fallen to forty-three cents, and ere the fair Northland had wrapped itself, like a scornful beauty, in its Autumn mantle of gold, the fondly trusted coin had sunk to exactly one-third of the value of a standard gold dollar. People carried baskets in their arms, filled with the now discredited coin, when they went abroad to pay a debt or make purchase of the necessaries of life. Huge sacks of the white metal were flung at the door of the mortgagee when discharge was sought for a few thousand dollars. Men servants accompanied their mistresses upon shopping tours to carry the necessary funds, and leather pockets took the place of the old time muslin ones in male habiliments, least the weight of the fifteen coins required to make up a five dollar gold piece should tear the thin stuff and spill a dollar at every step.

All day long in the large cities, huge trucks loaded with sacks of the coin rolled and rumbled over the pavement in the adjustment of the business balances of the day. The tradesman who called for his bill was met at the door with a coal scuttle or a nail keg filled with the needful amount, and on pay day, the working man took his eldest boy with him to "tote the stuff home" while he carried the usual bundle of firewood. And strange to say, this dollar, once so beloved by the "common people," parted with its very nature of riches and lay in heaps unnoticed and unheeded on shelf or table, until occasion arose to pay it out which was done with a careless and contemptuous toss as if it were the iron money of the ancient Spartans, and Holy Writ for once at least, was disproven and discredited for the thief showed not the slightest inclination to "break in and steal" where these treasures had been laid up on earth, although the discs of white metal might lie in full view on the table, like so many pewter platters or pieces of tinware. Men let debts run, rather than call for them, and barter and exchange came into vogue again, the good housewife calling on her neighbor for a loan of flour or meal, promising to return the same in sugar or dried fruit whenever the need might arise.

And still the once magic discs of silver slipped slowly and silently downward, and ever downward in value and good name, until it almost seemed as if the people hated the very name of silver.

CHAPTER VIII.

The "Fateful year of '99" upon its coming in, found the Republic of Washington in dire and dangerous straits. The commercial and industrial boom had spent its force, and now the frightful evils of a debased currency, coupled with demoralizing effects of rampant paternalism, were gradually strangling the land to death. Capital, ever timid and distrustful in such times, hid itself in safe deposit vaults, or fled to Europe. Labor, although really hard pressed and lacking the very necessities of life, was loudmouthed and defiant. Socialism and Anarchism found willing ears into which to pour their burning words of hatred and malevolence, and the consequence was that serious rioting broke out in the larger cities of the North, often taxing the capacities of the local authorities to the utmost.

It was bruited abroad that violent dissensions had arisen in the Cabinet, the young President giving signs of a marked change of mind, and like many a man who has appealed to the darker passions of the human heart, he seemed almost ready to exclaim: "I stand alone. The spirits I have called up are no longer obedient to me. My country, oh, my country, how willingly would I give my life for thee, if by such a sacrifice I could restore thee to thy old time prosperity."

For the first he began to realize what an intense spirit of sectionalism had entered into this "revolutionary propaganda." He spoke of his fears to none save to his wise and prudent helpmate.

"I trust you, beloved," she whispered, as she pressed the broad, strong hands that held her enclasped.

"Ay, dear one, but does my country?" came in almost a groan from the lips of the youthful ruler.

Most evident was it, that thus far the South had been the great gainer in this struggle for power. She had increased her strength in the Senate by six votes; she had regained her old time prestige in the House; one of her most trusted sons was in the Speaker's chair, while another brilliant Southron led the administration forces on the floor. Born as she was for the brilliant exercise of intellectual vigor, the South was of that strain of blood which knows how to wear the kingly graces of power so as best to impress the "common people." Many of the men of the North had been charmed and fascinated by this natural pomp and inborn demeanor of greatness and had yielded to it.

Not a month had gone by that this now dominant section had not made some new demand upon the country at large. Early in the session, at its request, the internal revenue tax which had rested so long upon the tobacco crop of the South, and poured so many millions of revenue into the national treasury, was wiped from the statute books with but a feeble protest from the North.

But now the country was thrown into a state bordering upon frenzy by a new demand, which, although couched in calm and decorous terms, nay, almost in the guise of a petition for long-delayed justice to hard-pressed and suffering brethren, had about it a suppressed, yet unmistakable tone of conscious power and imperiousness which well became the leader who spoke for "that glorious Southland to which this Union owes so much of its greatness and its prestige."

Said he: "Mr. Speaker, for nearly thirty years our people, although left impoverished by the conflict of the states, have given of their substance to salve the wounds and make green the old age of the men who conquered us. We have paid this heavy tax, this fearful blood money unmurmuringly. You have forgiven us for our bold strike for liberty that God willed should not succeed. You have given us back our rights, opened the doors of these sacred halls to us, called us your brothers, but unlike noble Germany who was content to exact a lump sum from "la belle France," and then bid her go in peace and freedom from all further exactions, you have for nearly thirty years laid this humiliating war tax upon us, and thus forced us year in and year out to kiss the very hand that smote us. Are we human that we now cry out against it? Are we men that we feel no tingle in our veins after these long years of punishment for no greater crime than that we loved liberty better than the bonds of a confederation laid upon us by our fathers? We appeal to you as our brothers and our countrymen. Lift this infamous tax from our land, than which your great North is ten thousand times richer. Do one of two things: Either take our aged and decrepit soldiers by the hand and bless their last days with pensions from the treasury of our common country, for they were only wrong in that their cause failed, or remove this hated tax and make such restitution of this blood money as shall seem just and equitable to your soberer and better judgment."

To say that this speech, of which the foregoing is but a brief extract, threw both Houses of Congress into most violent disorder, but faintly describes its effect. Cries of treason! treason! went up; blows were exchanged and hand to hand struggles took place in the galleries, followed by the flash of the dread bowie and the crack of the ready pistol. The Republic was shaken to its very foundations. Throughout the North there was but a repetition of the scenes that followed the firing upon Sumter. Public meetings were held, and resolutions passed calling upon the Government to concentrate troops in and about Washington, and prepare for the suppression of a second Rebellion.

But gradually this outbreak of popular indignation lost some of its strength and virulence, for it was easy to comprehend that nothing would be gained at this stage of the matter by meeting a violent and unlawful demand with violence and unwise counsels. Besides, what was it any way but the idle threat of a certain clique of unscrupulous politicians?

The Republic stood upon too firm a foundation to be shaken by mere appeals to the passions of the hour. To commit treason against our country called for an overt act. What had it to dread from the mere oratorical flash of a passing storm of feeling?

It is hard to say what the young President thought of these scenes in Congress. So pale had he grown of late that a little more of pallor would pass unnoted, but those who were wont to look upon his face in these troublous times report that in the short space of a few days the lines in his countenance deepened perceptibly, and that a firmer and stronger expression of will-power lurked in the corners of his wide mouth, overhung his square and massive chin, and accentuated the vibrations of his wide-opened nostrils. He was under a terrible strain. When he had caught up the sceptre of power, it seemed a mere bauble in his strong grasp, but now it had grown strangely heavy, and there was a mysterious pricking at his brow, as if that crown of thorns which he had not willed should be set upon the heads of others, were being pressed down with cruel hands upon his own.

CHAPTER IX.

When the last embers of the great conflagration of the Rebellion had been smothered out with tears for the Lost Cause, a prophecy had gone up that the mighty North, rich with a hundred great cities, and strong in the conscious power of its wide empire, would be the next to raise the standard of rebellion against the Federal Government. But that prophet was without honor in his own land,

and none had paid heed to his seemingly wild words.

Yet now, this same mighty North sat there in her grief and anxiety, with her face turned Southward, and her ear strained to catch the whispers that were in the air. Had not the sceptre of power passed from her hand forever? Was not the Revolution complete? Were not the Populists and their allies firmly seated in the Halls of Congress? Had not the Supreme Court been rendered powerless for good by packing it with the most uncompromising adherents of the new political faith? Had not the very nature of the Federal Government undergone a change: Was not Paternalism rampant? Was not Socialism on the increase? Were there not everywhere evidences of an intense hatred of the North and a firm determination to throw the whole burden of taxation upon the shoulders of the rich man, in order that the surplus revenues of the Government might be distributed among those who constitute the "common people?" How could this section of the Union ever hope to make head against the South, united, as it now was, with the rapidly growing States of the Northwest? Could the magnificent cities of the North content themselves to march at the tail of Tillman's and Peffer's chariots? Had not the South a firm hold of the Senate? Where was there a ray of hope that the North could ever again regain its lost power, and could it for a single moment think of entrusting its vast interests to the hands of a people differing with them on every important question of statecraft, pledged to a policy that could not be otherwise than ruinous to the welfare of the grand commonwealths of the Middle and Eastern sections of the Union and their sister States this side of the Mississippi? It were madness to think of it. The plunge must be taken, the declaration must be made. There was no other alternative, save abject submission to the chieftains of the new dispensation, and the complete transformation of that vast social and political system vaguely called the North.

But this revolution within a revolution would be a bloodless one, for there could be no thought of coercion, no serious notion of checking such a mighty movement. It would be in reality the true Republic purging itself of a dangerous malady, sloughing off a diseased and gangrened member; no more, no less.

Already this mighty movement of withdrawals from the Witenagemote of the Union was in the air. People spoke of it in a whisper, or with bated breath; but as they turned it over and over in their minds, it took on shape and form and force, till at last it burst into life and action like Minerva from Jupiter's brain—full-fledged, full-armed, full-voiced and full-hearted.

Really, why would it not be all for the best that this mighty empire, rapidly growing so vast and unwieldy as to be only with the greatest difficulty governable from a single centre, should be split into three parts, Eastern, Southern and Western, now that it may be done without dangerous jar or friction? The three republics could be federated for purposes offensive and defensive, and until these great and radical changes could be brought about there would be no great difficulty in devising "living terms," for immediately upon the Declaration of Dissolution, each State would become repossessed of the sovereign powers which it had delegated to the Federal Government.

Meanwhile the "Fateful year '99" went onward toward its close. The whole land seemed stricken with paralysis, so far as the various industries were concerned, but, as it is wont to be in such times, men's minds were supernaturally active. The days were passed in the reading of public prints, or in passing in review the weighty events of the hour. The North was only waiting for an opportunity to act.

But the question that perplexed the wisest heads was: How and when shall the Declaration of Dissolution be made, and how soon thereafter shall the North and the States in sympathy with her withdraw from the Union, and declare to the world their intention to set up a republic of their own, with the mighty metropolis of New York as its social, political and commercial centre and capital?

As it came to pass, the North had not long to wait. The Fifty-sixth Congress soon to convene in regular session in the city of Washington, was even more Populistic and Socialistic than its famous predecessor, which had wrought such wonderful changes in the law of the land, showing no respect for precedent, no reverence for the old order of things. Hence all eyes were fixed upon the capital of the nation, all roads were untrodden, save those which led to Washington.

CHAPTER X.

Again Congress had refused to adjourn over for the holidays. The leaders of the Administration forces were unwilling to close their eyes, even for needful sleep, and went about pale and haggard, startled at every word and gesture of the opposition, like true conspirators, as they were, for the Federal troops had been almost to a man quietly removed from the Capital and its vicinage, lest the President in a moment of weakness, might do or suffer to be done some act unfriendly to the Reign of the Common People.

Strange as it may seem, there had been very little note taken by the country at large of the introduction at the opening of the session of an Act to extend the Pension System of the United States to the Soldiers of the Confederate Armies, and for covering back into the various treasuries of certain States of the Union, such portions of internal revenue taxes collected since the readmission of said states to the Federal Congress, as may be determined by Commissioners duly appointed under said Act.

Was it the calm of despair, the stolidity of desperation, or the cool and restrained energy of a noble and refined courage?

The introduction of the Act, however, had one effect; it set in motion toward the National capital, mighty streams of humanity—not of wild-eyed fanatics or unshaven and unkempt politicasters and bezonians—but of soberly-clad citizens with a business-like air about them, evidently men who knew how to earn more than enough for a living, men who paid their taxes and had a right to take a look at the public servants, if desire so moved them. But very plain was it that the mightier stream flowed in from the South, and those who remembered the Capital in antebellum days, smiled at the old familiar sight, the clean-shaven faces, the long hair thrown carelessly back under the broad brim felts, the half unbuttoned waistcoats and turn down collars, the small feet and neatly fitting boots, the springy loping pace, the soft negroese intonation, the long fragrant cheroot.

It was easy to pick out the man from the Northland, well clad and well-groomed, as careful of his linen as a woman, prim and trim, disdainful of the picturesque felts, ever crowned with the ceremonious derby, the man of affairs, taking a business-like view of life, but wearing for the nonce a worried look and drawing ever and anon a deep breath.

The black man, ever at the heels of his white brother, set to rule over him by an inscrutable decree of nature, came forth too in thousands, chatting and laughing gayly, careless of the why or wherefore of his white brother's deep concern, and powerless to comprehend it had he so desired. Every hour now added to the throng. The broad avenues were none too broad. The excitement increased. Men talked louder and louder, women and children disappeared almost completely from the streets. The "Southern element" drew more and more apart in knots and groups by itself. Men threw themselves upon their beds to catch a few hours sleep, but without undressing, as if they were expecting the happening of some portentous event at any moment, the event of their lives, and dreaded the thought of being a moment late.

If all went well, the bill would come up for final passage on Saturday, the 30th day of the month, but so fierce was the battle raged against it, and so frequent the interruptions by the contumacy both of members and of the various cliques crowding the galleries to suffocation, that little or no progress could be made.

The leaders of the administration forces saw midnight drawing near with no prospect of attaining their object before the coming in of Sunday on which the House had never been known to sit. An adjournment over to Monday of the New Year might be fatal, for who could tell what unforeseen force might not break up their solid ranks and throw them into confusion. They must rise equal to the occasion. A motion was made to suspend the rules, and to remain in continuous session until the business before the House was completed. Cries of "Unprecedented!" "Revolutionary!" "Monstrous!" came from the opposition, but all to no purpose; the House settled down to its work with such a grim determination to conquer that the Republican minority fairly quailed before it. Food and drink were brought to the members in their seats; they ate, drank and slept at their posts, like soldiers determined not to be ambushed or stampeded.

It was a strange sight, and yet an impressive one withal—a great party struggling for long deferred rights—freemen jealous of their liberties, bound together with the steel hooks of determination that only death might break asunder.

Sunday came in at last, and still the struggle went on. "The people know no days when their liberties are at stake," cried the leader of the House. "The Sabbath was made for man and not man for the Sabbath."

Many of the speeches delivered on that famous Sunday sounded more like the lamentations of a Jeremiah, the earnest and burning utterances of a Paul, or the scholarly and well-rounded periods of an Apollos. The weary hours were lightened by the singing of hymns by the Southern members, most of them good methodists, in which their friends and sympathizers in the galleries joined full throated and fuller hearted; while at times, clear, resonant and in perfect unison, the voices of the staunch men of the North broke in and drowned out the religious song with the majestic and soul-stirring measures of "John Brown's Body," the "Glory, Glory Halleluiah" of which seemed to hush the tumult of the Chamber like a weird chant of some invisible chorus breaking in upon the fierce rioting of a Belshazzar's feast.

Somewhat after eleven o'clock, an ominous silence sank upon the opposing camps, the Republican leaders could be seen conferring together nervously. It was a sacred hour of night, thrice sacred for the great Republic. Not only a New Year, but a New Century was about to break upon the world. A strange hush crept over the turbulent House, and its still more turbulent galleries.

The Republican leader rose to his feet. His voice sounded cold and hollow. Strong men shivered as they listened. "Mr. Speaker: We have done our duty to our country; we have nothing more to say, no more blows to strike. We cannot stand here within the sacred precincts of this Chamber, and see our rights as freemen trampled beneath the feet of the majority. We have striven to prevent the downfall of the Republic, like men sworn to battle against wrong and tyranny, but there comes a time when blank despair seizes upon the hearts of those who struggle against overwhelming odds. That hour has sounded for us. We believe our people, the great and generous people of the North, will cry unto us: Well done, good and faithful servants. If we do wrong, let them condemn us. We, every man of us, Mr. Speaker, have but this moment sworn not to stand within this Chamber and witness the passage of this act. Therefore we go—"

"Not so, my countrymen," cried a clear metallic far-reaching voice that sounded through the Chamber with an almost supernatural ring in it. In an instant, every head was turned and a thousand voices burst out with suppressed force:

"The President! The President!"

In truth, it was he, standing at the bar of the House, wearing the visage of death rather than of life. The next instant the House and galleries burst into a deafening clamor which rolled up and back in mighty waves that shook the very walls. There was no stilling it. Again and again it burst forth, the mingling of ten thousand words, howling, rumbling and groaning like the warring elements of nature. Several times the President stretched forth his great white hands appealing for silence, while the dew of mingled dread and anguish beaded on his brow and trickled down his cheeks in liquid supplication that his people might either slay him or listen to him. The tumult stilled its fury for a moment, and he could be heard saying brokenly:

"My countrymen, oh, my countrymen——"

But the quick sharp sound of the gavel cut him short.

"The President must withdraw," said the Speaker, calmly and coldly, "his presence here is a menace to our free deliberation."

Again the tumult set up its deafening roar, while a look of almost horror overspread the countenance of the Chief Magistrate.

Once more his great white hands went heavenward, pleading for silence with such a mute majesty of supplication, that silence fell upon the immense assemblage, and his lips moved not in vain.

"Gentlemen of the House of Representatives, I stand here upon my just and lawful right as President of the Republic, to give you 'information of the state of the Union.' I have summoned the Honorable the Senate, to meet me in this Chamber. I call upon you to calm your passions, and give ear to me as your oath of office sets the sacred obligation upon you."

There was a tone of godlike authority in these few words, almost divine enough to make the winds obey and still the tempestuous sea. In deepest silence, and with a certain show of rude and native grandeur of bearing, the Senators made their entrance into the Chamber, the members of the House rising, and the Speaker advancing to meet the Vice-President.

The spectacle was grand and moving. Tears gathered in eyes long unused to them, and at an almost imperceptible nod of the President's head, the Chaplain raised his voice in prayer. He prayed in accents that were so gentle and so persuasive, they must have turned the hardest heart to blessed thoughts of peace and love and fraternity and union. And then again all eyes were fixed with intensest strain upon the face of the President.

"Gentlemen of the House of Representatives, this measure upon which you are now deliberating"——

With a sudden blow that startled every living soul within its hearing, the Speaker's gavel fell. "The President," said he with a superb dignity that called down from the galleries a burst of deafening applause, "must not make reference to pending legislation. The Constitution guarantees him the right 'from time to time to give to the Congress information of the Union.' He must keep himself strictly within the lines of this Constitutional limit, or withdraw from the bar of the House."

A deadly pallor overspread the face of the Chief Magistrate till it seemed he must sink then and there into that sleep which knows no awakening, but he gasped, he leaned forward, he raised his hand again imploringly, and as he did so, the bells of the city began to toll the hour of midnight.

The New Year, the New Century was born, but with the last stroke, a fearful and thunderous discharge as of a thousand monster pieces of artillery, shook the Capitol to its very foundations, making the stoutest hearts stand still, and blanching cheeks that had never known the coward color. The dome of the

Capitol had been destroyed by dynamite.

In a few moments, when it was seen that the Chamber had suffered no harm, the leader of the House moved the final passage of the Act. The President was led away, and the Republican Senators and Representatives passed slowly out of the disfigured Capitol, while the tellers prepared to take the vote of the House. The bells were ringing a glad welcome to the New Century, but a solemn tolling would have been a fitter thing, for the Republic of Washington was no more. It had died so peacefully, that the world could not believe the tidings of its passing away. As the dawn broke cold and gray, and its first dim light fell upon that shattered dome, glorious even in its ruins, a single human eye, filled with a gleam of devilish joy, looked up at it long and steadily, and then its owner was caught up and lost in the surging mass of humanity that held the Capitol girt round and round.

TRAVELS AND ADVENTURES OF LITTLE BARON TRUMP AND HIS WONDERFUL DOG BULGER

CHAPTER I.

I come from one of the most ancient and honorable families of North Germany—famous for its valor and love of adventure.

One of my ancestors, when just entering the twenties heard at his father's table one morning, that England's great King Cœur de Lion was about to lead an army against the infidels.

"Gracious parent," cried the young man starting up from his seat, his eyes on fire, his cheeks ablaze, "May I join the Crusaders and aid in the destruction of the enemies of our holy religion?" "Alas, poor boy!" replied his father, casting a pitying glance at the youth, who, through some strange freak of nature had been born armless, "thou wert not intended for terrible conflicts such as await our cousin Cœur de Lion. Thou lackest every means of wielding the battle sword, of couching the lance. 'Twould be murder to set thy defenceless body before the uplifted cimeter of the merciless Moslem! My dear son, banish such thoughts from thy mind and turn thee to poesy and philosophy, thou shalt add new lustre to our family name by thy learning." "Nay gracious parent, hear me!" urged the youth with eloquent eye: "true, nature has denied me arms, but she has not been so cruel as might be supposed for, as compensation, she has given a giant's strength to my lower limbs. Dost not remember how last month, I slew a wild boar with one blow from the heel of my hunting-boot?" "I do," answered the grim old Baron with a smile, "but—" "Pardon my interruption noble father" came from the young man, "I shall go into battle doubly armed, for to each stirrup shall I affix a sword and woe betide the Mussulman who dares meet me on the battle-field."

"Go then my son!" cried the old Baron as the tears trickled down his battle-scarred cheeks, "go, join our royal cousin Cœur de Lion and if thou, armless, canst withstand the fury of the infidel, another glory will be added to the name of Trump, and in this ancestral hall shall hang a portrait of the 'Armless Knight,' upon which for all time the lovers of valiant deeds shall rest their wondering eyes."

The joy of my young ancestor knew no bounds.

Scarcely staying to make needful preparations for his journey, with a handful of trusty retainers, he rode from the castle yard amid the plaudits of thousands of fair women who had gathered from the neighboring city to wish God speed to the "Armless Knight."

'Twas not until the famous battle under the walls of Joppa that my ancestor had an opportunity to give an exhibition of his bravery, his extraordinary strength, and the resistless fury of his onslaughts.

Not one, not five, not ten common soldiers dared face the "Armless Knight."

Whole squadrons recoiled in terror before this mysterious avenger of the wrongs of Christendom, who, without hands, struck down the Moslem warriors, as the grain falls before the blast.

Again and again, Saladin sent the flower of his men against the "Armless Knight," whose strength and valor had already made his name a terror to the superstitious soldiery. Little realizing the terrible fate awaiting him, the Moslem warrior would rush upon my ancestor with uplifted cimeter, when with one blow of his sword-armed stirrup the "Armless Knight" would cleave the breast of his foeman's horse, and then trample the infidel to death as he rolled upon the ground.

It was now high noon.

Upon an eminence, Saladin, watching the tide of battle, saw with anxious eye the appalling slaughter of the very flower of his army.

Already the name, rank, and nationality of my young ancestor had been made known to the Moslem leader.

"La, il la! Mahomed ul Becullah!" he cried, stroking his beard. "Blessed is the man who can call that Christian warrior his son! How many of the Prophet's children has he slain this day?"

"Six hundred and fifty-nine!" was the answer given.

"Six hundred and fifty-nine," echoed Saladin, "and it is but noonday!" When nightfall came the number had been increased to one thousand and seven.

Upon hearing of the terrible day's work of the "Armless Knight," Saladin's great heart bled, and yet he could not withhold his admiration for such wondrous skill and bravery.

"Go!" cried the magnanimous infidel Chieftain, "go, take from my household that beauteous slave Kohilât, her with orbs of lustrous black, the very blossom of grace and flower of queenly beauty. Lead her to the "Armless Knight," with royal greeting from Saladin; his valor makes him my brother, Giaour though he be! Away!"

When the beautiful Kohilât was led into the presence of my young ancestor, and the announcement made to him that Saladin had sent her as a present to him, the "Armless Knight," with royal greeting as a token of his respect for one so young, and yet so valiant, the first thought of the Christian youth was to wave her indignantly from his presence.

At that moment, however, Kohilât raised her large and lustrous eyes, and fixed them full upon the young man's face.

It was more than human heart could stand.

Motioning her retinue to leave his tent, he advanced to her side, with respectful mien, and said:

"Kohilât, a strange fate has sent thee to me. The messenger of the great Saladin imparts to me knowledge of thy goodness, thy amiability, and thy gifted mind, which holds within its store most delightful imagery and useful knowledge as well. He informs me that thou standest in the direct line of descent from that famed princess of your land, Scheherezada, who for a thousand and one nights held the thoughts of the Sultan of the Indies so enthralled by the play of her brilliant fancy, as to turn him aside from his terrible project of vengeance. Dost think, Kohilât, that thou canst forget thy false god and love only the true one?"

"Ay, my lord," murmured the gentle Kohilât, "if such be my lord's pleasure."

A smile spread over the handsome face of my young ancestor. He would fain have met with more resistance in converting the fair infidel to the true faith, but though he searched that beautiful face long and closely for any sign of subtility, yet saw he none.

"'Tis well, Kohilât," he continued, "and now answer me, and speak from thy heart. Art thou willing to become my wife, according to the rites of the Christian church and the laws of my native land?"

Again the beautiful Kohilât replied:

"Ay, my lord; if such be thy pleasure."

The following day a truce was proclaimed, and in the presence of the two great leaders of the opposing armies, Cœur de Lion and Saladin, both surrounded by the most glorious retinue, my young ancestor and the princess Kohilât were joined together as man and wife by the royal confessor, the "Armless Knight" towering above the surrounding multitude in his glittering coat of mail like a column of burnished silver. When he advanced to meet his dark-eyed bride, with the marriage ring held between his lips, a mighty shout went up from both armies.

Saladin stroked his beard. Cœur de Lion made the sign of the cross. In a short half hour the leaders had returned to their camps, and war had resumed its awful work of destruction.

To this union of my renowned ancestor, the "Armless Knight," with the Moslem maid, I attribute my possession of an almost Oriental exuberance of fancy.

CHAPTER II.

While it lies within my power to gratify the curiosity of my readers as to what part of the world it was in which I first saw darkness—for I was born in the night— yet, as to the nature of the immediate spot on which I was born, unfortunately I am able to do more than repeat my father's words when questioned as to this point.

"My son, if I were on my death-bed I could only say that thou wert either born in the centre in a great lake, on an island, upon a peninsula or on the top of a very high mountain, as I have often explained to thee."

Let it suffice, then, gentle reader, for the present, for me to inform you that at the time of my birth, my parents were traveling in Africa; that my father had just successfully accomplished one of the most wonderful feats in mountain climbing, namely, the ascent of the loftiest peak of the Mountains of the Moon; that his guides had abandoned him upon his reaching a particularly dangerous spot in the ascent; but that he had pushed forward without them, and reached the summit after several days of terrible privation, suffering both hunger and thirst,—it being a peculiarity of the atmosphere after passing a certain height that the muscles of the face and throat became paralyzed and the unfortunate traveler either perishes from hunger or thirst while in the very presence of delicious fruit and cool, limpid water.

Upon rejoining my mother, who had accompanied him as far up the mountain side as the best-trained and most surefooted mules could find a foot-hold, they proceeded to make their way, as they supposed, to the valley from which they had first set out.

An impenetrable fog now shut them in and they soon found themselves hopelessly and helplessly wandering about.

On the morning of the third day the fog had even increased in thickness, closing around them like a pall, almost shutting out the light of day.

While groping about my father had come into contact with the two beasts of burden which had served him in the easier parts of the ascent. They were quietly and unconcernedly browsing upon the sweet and tender shrubs which grew on the mountain side.

Suddenly an idea came to my father. It was born of that desperation which makes a man think long and hard before lying down to die.

It was thus he reasoned: If these animals are permitted to eat their fill whenever their appetites demand, they will be quite willing to stay where they are, especially when they find themselves surrounded by such excellent pastures, and, in addition thereto, quite relieved from all toil. Let them, however, feel the pangs of hunger, or better yet, starvation's tooth at their vitals and their thoughts will at once revert to their homes, their masters, their feeding-troughs and they will lose no time in setting out for the village where they belong. With the energy of despair, my father hurriedly bound a piece of canvass over their mouths so that they could neither graze nor drink and awaited the results of his experiment, with bated breath, for the tears and groans of my poor mother, whose strength was fast ebbing away, smote him to the very soul.

After a few hours the animals rose to their feet and became very restive, and in another hour their hunger had so increased that they were making frantic efforts to feed, as my father could easily tell from the jerking of the line which he had been careful to attach to their headstalls.

After the fourth hour there was a long silence, during which the animals seemed to be deliberating as to what course they should pursue.

The fifth hour came.

My mother had sunk to rest, weak and weary, in my father's arms. Suddenly there was a tightening of the guiding lines. Gently my father aroused his sleeping mate, whispering a few words of comfort.

Again the lines tightened.

My parents were now on their feet, peering into the depths of the impenetrable fog which shrouded them about and made them even invisible to each other.

Hist! the animals move again! with a sudden impulse, as if their minds had at last solved the problem which had been bewildering them for several hours, the beasts, with violent snortings turned from the spot, pushing through the shrubbery and causing my parents to face quite about.

Evidently there was a complete accord between the conclusions reached by their intelligence or instinct, for not once did they pull apart or come to a halt, except when restrained by my father. And thus my dear parents were saved! All that day and part of the next did they pursue their dreary way. The fog at last lifted, and it was at once apparent to my father that, although the animals were guiding them towards human habitations, yet it was not the land he had quitted upon starting out upon the journey to the mountain peak. The path now became so plainly visible that my father removed the improvised muzzles from the two animals and allowed them to satisfy their hunger, which they proceeded to do with the keenest relish. So worn out was my mother that she sank helpless to the ground. Refreshing her with a draught of spring-water and the juice of some wild grapes, my father hastily prepared a bed of soft foliage, upon which they were both glad to throw themselves after their long and weary tramp.

They had soon fallen into a deep and most delightful sleep. How long they lay on their leafy bed, wrapt in their refreshing slumber, they knew not.

It certainly was for many a long hour; for when they awoke, hunger was gnawing at their stomachs. Fain would they have at once proceeded to gather fruit, had not their ears been suddenly saluted with most extraordinary noises. They rubbed their eyes and looked about and at each other, deeming themselves the sport of some merry jack-a-dreamer.

But, no; they were wide awake and in full possession of their senses. Again the strange sounds are heard and this time they are nearer and clearer.

There is a rise and a fall, a swelling out and then a dying away.

The sounds are jerky and snappy like and there is a singular music in them.

Nearer and still nearer they come. Louder and still louder they grow. "Wild beasts?" whispered my mother half inquiringly.

"Nay!" falls from my father's lips. "Not unless human beings may be so wild as to merit the name of beasts."

"Hark again!" murmured my mother.

There was no mistaking the sounds any longer, for, like a chorus of many voices, shrill and piping, deep and grumbling, soft and musical, harsh and guttural, yet all in a sort of rude and wild harmony, mingling in one mighty strain, now low and scarcely audible and now breaking out with a fierce and seemingly threatening vigor, the singers, chanters, howlers or what they might be, rushed into the valley below us in a wild and yet half regulated disorder.

They were human beings in savage garb, with painted faces and clubs swung lightly across their shoulders. Whether pausing or advancing they still kept up their wild and mysterious chant, choppy, jerky and snappy for all the world like a thousand people who had just drawn plentifully from a thousand snuff boxes.

"Save me, husband!" cried my mother with pallid face. "We shall be put to some awful torture by these wild children of the forest." A smile so gentle, and yet so calm, that it could not fail to be reassuring spread over my father's features.

"Never fear!" said he, "I know them, I've been seeking them! What has been denied many a traveler stronger and bolder than I, has been accorded to a member of the Trump family in the most miraculous manner. When we return to Europe every Monarch, every learned society, will hasten to bind a medal on my breast, for, dear wife, your husband is the first white man to enter the land of the—"

"The—?" echoed my mother leaning forward and grasping her husband's arm.

"Melodious Sneezers!"

"Melodious Sneezers?" repeated my mother with wide-opened eye, and amusement seated in every feature.

"Melo—"

But she could get no further. To my father's infinite amusement, she fell a-sneezing most violently. In such rapid succession did the sneezes flow that it sounded exactly like a diminutive engine under full headway.

At last the fit seemed to have passed. "Melo—" but in vain; she could not reach the second syllable.

And now, in his turn, my father started off, slow at first but going faster and faster.

Strange to say their sneezing soon began to catch the ways of the country and blended thoroughly, keeping time in spite of their efforts to check it.

"Know then, dear wife," cried my father pantingly when his fit was over, "that those strange people stretched on the greensward below are the "Melodious Sneezers;" that they are not only perfectly harmless, but gentle, kind and peaceable to an astonishing degree. Fear them not! Their clubs are only for game." "But why—?" asked my mother warily lest another fit should take her.

"I understand thee," was the reply. "Listen. Know, that in this valley and in the greater ones below, the air is always filled with myriads upon myriads of insects of infinitesimal size; only the strongest microscope can give proof to your sight of their actual existence. For countless generations, these peaceable barbarians here have been subjected to the tickling sensations which you and I have—"

Again my poor parent fell a-sneezing in regular and musical cadences, up and down, deep and shrill, now fast and faster, now slow and slower until silence reigned again.

"Just experienced," resumed my father, "until it has rendered the effort of sneezing quite as easy as breathing, and taking advantage of results which they soon discerned could not be avoided, these children of nature were not slow to lay aside their usual speech and literally talk by sneezes!"

"With them, a sneeze is capable of so many intonations, so many inflections, that they find no difficulty in expressing all the necessary feelings and sensations,—at least necessary for them in their simple lives, as you shall see later on."

Fain would my poor mother here express her passing wonder but she dare not open her mouth. "Come, dearest mate," cried my father gayly. "Courage! Let us descend into this beautiful valley, for as yet we are only standing upon the borders of the "Land of the Melodious Sneezers" called in their soft and musical tongue Lâ-aah-chew-lâ."

The pronunciation of this word again threw my poor parents into a perfect whirlwind of sneezes; but nothing daunted, they advanced to meet the natives, who at first sight fell prostrate on their faces and for several moments kept up a low plaintive hum of sneezes, with their noses thrust into the grass.

By degrees however, my father succeeding in convincing them that he was quite as peaceably inclined as they were.

Whereupon the Melodious Sneezers performed a most singular and withal pleasing dance of joy, their feet keeping perfect time with their chorus of sneezing.

As my father afterwards learned, the dance was to express their intense gratitude to the "white spirits" for not having eaten them alive.

The march homeward was now entered upon, my father walking hand in hand with the King Chew-chew-lô, and my mother escorted by a score or more of his wives, the favorite of the royal house being named Chew-lâ-â-â-â and each successive one according as she occupied a less lofty place in the King's affections having a shorter name until at last Chew-lâ signified little better than a mere serving maid.

My father found that the villages of the Melodious Sneezers, on account of the frequency and the violence of inundations from the network of rivers which completely shut in their land, consisted of houses or habitations built in the trees or upon lofty piles.

He and my mother were lodged in one of the most commodious of the royal dwellings and so many slaves and attendants were assigned to care for their wants that there was little or no room to move about.

To their great sorrow, my father proceeded to dismiss several hundred in order that he might get close enough to my mother to converse without holloaing and then sent word to King Chew-chew-lô that both he and my mother would need at least a week of perfect rest and quiet to regain their health and strength after their terrible sufferings on the slopes of the Mountains of the Moon.

CHAPTER III.

At this point my hand trembles and the ink flows unsteadily from my pen.

I am about to record certain events which, I feel assured the reader will agree with me in considering to be the most interesting of my strange and varied life. Possibly I should say interesting to me; for, gentle reader, one of these "certain events" above referred to is a no less important occurrence than my birth into this grand and beautiful world—a world which has proven to be full of wonderful things and of more wonderful beings, as you shall see as I go on with my story.

I was born in midsummer. It was the night season.

Ten thousand stars twinkled over the cradle of that wretched, little, helpless, lump of clay; but brighter than all, like a crimson torch flaming in the skies, Sirius, the dog star, shone down upon me!

My father looked up at the heavens and smiling, murmured: "Little stranger, thou shalt ever be a lover of dogs. Thy smile shall be joy to them, thy words music and in some four-footed beast of their race shalt thou find thy best, thy faithfulest, thy truest friend."

As if to set the very stamp of truth upon my father's words at that very instant a cry of a mother dog was heard in an adjoining room and one of the Royal household Chew-lâ-â came running into my presence with a basket of tiny puppies. My father laughingly seized the wicker cradle of this newly arrived family and holding it up to me, cried out:

"Choose, little baron, choose thee a friend and companion." I put out my tiny baby hand and it rested upon one with a particularly large head. "Ha! ha!" laughed my father, "thou hast well chosen, little baron, for him thou hast chosen hath so much brain that his head doth fairly bulge with it."

And when my infant tongue came to wrestle with that word, it was twisted into "Bulger." And thus it was that Bulger and I started out on life's journey at almost the same moment! Upon the following day my father made discovery that the waters had begun to recede in the night, and as he looked down from our lofty dwelling, he saw that it now stood apparently in the centre of quite an extensive island. After breakfast, in accordance with the custom of the country, my father put on a pair of King Chew-chew-lô's wooden shoes which were worn by all of the Melodious Sneezers when attempting to move about on the surface of the soft mud occasioned by the inundation.

These wooden shoes are extremely light although quite as long and as broad as snow shoes. The soles being polished, the wearer is enabled to glide over the mud which, from the nature of the soil is very oily, with the same rapidity as a runner upon snow shoes.

After an excursion of several hours up hill and down dale my father returned with this piece of strange intelligence, namely, that their habitation had undoubtedly, prior to the falling of the waters been situated in a lake; but that by degrees, as the waters had receded, an island had been formed, which somewhat later had been transformed into a peninsula, which in its turn by a still further sinking of the waters, had been changed into the crown of a mountain with gently sloping sides so that, as he reported to my mother, to his dying day it would be impossible for him to say whether his son had been born in a lake, on an island, upon a peninsula or on a mountain top, a fact which pained him extremely, for, like all the members of his family, he took the greatest pride in recording important events with scrupulous exactitude, even to the smallest detail.

Unlike most babes, who seem content to pass the first half year or so of their lives eating, sleeping and crying, I from the very outset displayed a most astonishing precocity.

When only a few weeks old, although I could not talk, yet I had learned to whistle for Bulger, whose development in mind and body seemed to keep even pace with mine and who passed most of his time looking up into my childish face with an expression which meant only too plainly:

"Oh, I shall be so glad when that little tongue is unloosed so that you may call me Bulger and bid me do your will."

Nor had he long to wait.

The one thing, which, at this early period of my life gave me most joy, was the sunlight.

Within doors, I was fretful, peevish, irritable, but once out in the open air, my whole nature changed. I drank in the soft, balmy atmosphere with a vigor and a satisfaction that delighted my father. My face brightened, my eyes traveled from valley to hill, from mountain-top to sky.

Into such an ecstacy of pleasure did this sight of the great world throw me, that my mother became anxious lest it presaged some great evil that was to happen unto me.

But the stately Baron only smiled. "Fear nothing, wife, it only means that within that little head dwells a most wonderfully active mind for a child of its months."

Whenever Bulger heard his little master crying out in joyful tones at sight of the beautiful world, he was sure to be seized with a fit of violent barking, during which he sprang around about me with the wildest and most extravagant manifestations of sympathy.

Without a doubt, there was a wonderful bond of affection between us.

To my mother's-I had almost said horror, I, one day while she was walking with me in her arms, upon the broad veranda, which encircled Chewchewlô's palaces, attempted to throw myself from her arms, crying out in German: Los! Los! (Let me go! Let me go!) I was but two months old and the loud and vigorous tone in which I pronounced this first word which I had spoken in my mother's tongue fairly startled her.

I had, up to that time, apparently been more interested in the soft and musical language of my royal nurse, Chewlâ, in which I could make myself understood very easily. About this time an accident happened to me which, although it did not bring about, it greatly hastened the release from parently restraint, so ardently desired, both by Bulger and by me, for from my very entrance into this world something told me that I should be a famous child, not a mere, precocious youth who is made use of by his parents at social gatherings to bore people already in poor spirits, by mounting upon chair or table and declaiming verses, parrotlike, with half a dozen woodeny, jerky gestures; but a genuine hero, a real traveler, not afraid to brave a tempest, face a wild beast or bully a barbarous people into doing as he wanted them to do.

It was my mother's custom in the cool of the day to sit with me on the broad veranda while she darned my father's stockings; for, although of gentle birth, she had been so accustomed when a girl to exercise German thrift in all things that now, even though she had become the wife of a real baron, she could not forego the pleasure of doing things in those good old ways.

And thus she saved my father many a pfennig which the good man bestowed upon the worthy poor and went down to the grave loaded with their blessings.

At such a time it was that a sudden fit of sneezing seized my mother and to her unspeakable horror she let me slip from her arms. Down, down I fell, striking in the soft mud and disappearing from sight.

The poor woman dropped to the floor like lead.

The stately baron rose to his feet and the color fled from his manly cheek.

But Chew-chew-lô, who fortunately was paying a visit to my father, only smiled.

"Unfeeling barbarian!" roared the great baron, "hast no respect for a father's tears, a mother's anguish? Out upon thee! Would to heaven I had never entered thy domain!" Chew-chew-lô spake not a word. Turning with imperious mien and right royal manner towards a crowd of retainers, he waved his hand.

Quicker than thought the band of Melodious Sneezers sprang to their wooden shoes.

Away, away, they darted like black bats on the wing.

The baron saw that in his terrible grief he had let his better judgment slip away, and with pallid face and bended head stood supporting the fainting form of his wife.

He felt, he knew, that his presence among the Melodious Sneezers at this moment would only disconcert them, impede their progress, and possibly so confuse them that all their efforts might be in vain. They, from their childhood, were so accustomed to wear those huge wooden shoes, to move about on the surface of this treacherous mud, that if it were possible for human hands to restore his son to his arms, theirs would do it.

And so he spoke a few words of encouragement in my mother's ear, and continued to stand like a statue, with his gaze riveted upon the long files of Melodious Sneezers, as they wound around the crest of the mountain to gain the spot where, as they judged, I had disappeared.

Armed with their light, broad, wooden shovels, their dusky arms rose and fell with wonderful precision and regularity, keeping time with the musical notes of their sneezing; now soft and low, now breaking out into a wild and galloping measure.

Down! Down! Down!

And yet they delved in vain!

No sign of me was there to gladden the hearts of my poor, grief-stricken parents.

But hark!

What is that shrill cry?

It is not human!

No; for it is Bulger's bark, or rather it is Bulger's yelp.

He had been watching the band of Melodious Sneezers, as their white shovels rose and fell all in vain, with his head thrust through the railings of the veranda.

No one was there with mind and heart enough to catch the meaning of that poor yelp.

Chew-chew-lô saw that his men were standing, leaning on their shovels, with looks of doubt and hesitation in their eyes.

The King was silent.

It was the great baron who spoke:

"Oh, let them not give o'er! My life, my wealth, my all, are thine, good, kind Chew-Chew——"

A fit of sneezing cut short his appeal.

Again Bulger's cry was raised, and this time the King heeded it.

An attendant saw the royal nod, and hastening to bind broad wooden cups upon the dog's feet, he was turned loose upon the surface of the mud.

What is man, with his boasted intelligence?

They were ten paces or more distant from the point where I had disappeared.

Yelping, barking, and whining by turns, my dear Bulger hurried to the spot where his unerring scent told him that his beloved little master had gone down.

Again the band of Melodious Sneezers set to work with renewed vigor, their white shovels flashing with strange effect against the inky blackness of the mud.

Bulger encouraged them with loud and joyful barkings.

Suddenly a clear, ringing, melodious "chew" rent the air.

They had caught sight of me!

With rare foresight for one of my months, I had closed my nostrils with one hand before reaching the mud, and had thus saved my lungs from filling up.

But how useless would have been this precaution, had not my faithful Bulger come to my rescue!

His joy now knew no bounds.

I thought that I caught a glimpse of a smile on the old baron's tear-stained cheek, as his boy was borne to the veranda, more like an animated lump of earth than aught else, for the air had revived me. My eyes were not only wide open, but they were the only clean place on my whole body.

Utterly regardless of my filthy condition, my fond mother clasped me convulsively to her breast, and I verily believe that she would have pressed her lips upon my mud-covered head and face, had she not seen the baron's broad palm held in suspicious proximity, while her mother's heart was emptying itself out in words. A few basins of warm water, and I was myself again.

No, I was never myself again. My bath in the warm mud of I.â-aah-chew-lâ effected a most remarkable change in me; it checked the growth of my body and turned all my strength upwards into my head and brain.

In one short month my head almost doubled in size.

My baby face and expression were gone!

And ere another moon had filled her horns I had grown to be a living wonder!

Not only was the size of my head something remarkable, but from my eyes beamed an astonishing intelligence.

The poor women of Lâ-aah-chew-lâ Land crouched in front of me as if I were a being from another world and then tapping their foreheads they approached my mother and whispered:

"Most gracious Chew-lâ-â-â-â-â-â the Great Spirit has made a mistake and put two souls in there instead of one!"

And then they bent their graceful bodies till their foreheads touched my mother's feet and withdrew, going out backwards like the best regulated court ladies, each leveling her finger at me and opening wide her eyes as she disappeared through the door.

The whole scene was so grotesque that I burst out into a shout of laughter.

Upon hearing which, the poor creatures tumbled headlong over each other in their mad efforts to get outside of the house, shrieking at the top of their voices:

"Save us! save us! He will bewitch us!"

"Little Baron!" said my father in a tone of mock anger, "you should not have frightened the ladies of King Chew-chew-lô's Court!"

Chew-pâ! Chew-pâ! (Idiots! Idiots!) I replied, looking up from my slate upon which I was working out an example in arithmetic, for I was very fond of figures.

In fact, my father had already taught me addition by showing me how to trade off worthless glass beads for valuable ivory, and division, by taking away ninety cents from every dollar I made. Long before I could read or write, I knew the letters of several languages by name, and could spell any word which had no silent letter in it. No one took more delight in my wonderful accomplishments than Bulger.

He seemed to know instinctively that his little master was no ordinary being and respected him accordingly. We now bade adieu to the Land of Lâ-aah-chew-lâ and the Melodious Sneezers.

King Chew-chew-lô with a mighty band of retainers accompanied us to his frontier, making the forests resound with their melodious chew-chew-a-ing. Standing on the old baron's shoulders, I waved them a last goodbye to which they answered with such a perfect whirlwind of Chew-chew-â's that Bulger fairly howled with delight.

Any special honor paid to his master was always a personal matter to him. The elder baron had intended to penetrate still further into the heart of Africa; but the fact is, that the continual growth of my mind was so wonderful that it engrossed his attention from morn till night. He endeavored to hide this from me; but all to no purpose.

Before I was two years old my brain had grown so heavy that my mother was obliged to sew pieces of lead in the soles of my shoes to keep me right end upwards, and yet, in spite of this precaution, I was often found standing upon my head working out difficult mathematical problems by making use of my toes, as the Chinese do their counting machines.

The first thing which my father did upon reaching home was to take me to a phrenologist in order to have a chart made of my head.

The examination lasted a month.

At length, upon the completion of the chart, it was found that I possessed thirty-two distinct bumps.

Well-developed ones, too!

It was, therefore, at once determined to engage thirty-two learned tutors, each tutor to have charge of a separate bump and to do his utmost to enlarge it even if it grew to be a horn.

My father was resolved to leave nothing undone in order to develop my mental powers to the utmost limit. I said nothing either for or against the scheme.

In one short year I had learned all that the thirty-two tutors could teach me, and, what is more, I had taught each one of them fifty things which he had not known before, and which I had learned while traveling in foreign lands with my parents.

One fine morning to the great surprise of my thirty-two tutors I discharged the whole of them.

The elder baron at my suggestion now sent a bill to each tutor for services rendered him by me.

Each tutor refused to pay.

The elder baron, at my suggestion, now caused legal process to be served upon each one of them.

The court upon hearing my testimony rendered an opinion which covered five thousand pages of legal cap paper and required a whole week to read, in which they held that each thing which I had taught to each one of my thirty-two tutors was so remarkably strange and peculiar that in the eye of the law it was worth at least one hundred dollars. That made the bill of each tutor amount to five thousand dollars, or one hundred and sixty thousand dollars in all.

The court then adjourned for a year, all three judges being so worn out mentally and physically as to need a twelve months' rest before taking up any other business.

CHAPTER IV.

The question which now occupied my father's mind to the exclusion of all other thoughts was how to invest this large sum of money, so that upon my attaining my twenty-first year I would be provided with a sufficiently large income to live as a baron should—particularly when he belonged to so famous a family as ours.

The fact of the matter is, my father permitted this question to prey upon his peace of mind to such an extent that he lost flesh perceptibly.

My mother, too, seeing his lamentable condition began to fret and worry to such a degree, that she likewise became greatly emaciated. With their loss of flesh naturally their appetites dwindled and little or no food was provided; or, anyway, no more than was just sufficient to satisfy Bulger's and my wants.

Whereupon the servants began to lose flesh, both the indoor and outdoor ones; and in their desperate attempt to keep body and soul together, the horses and cattle were fed upon short rations, and the consequence was, they, too, soon began to fall away.

So it grew to be quite a serious sight to see my poor father and mother reduced to mere skin and bones, driven about the country by mere shadows for coachman and footman, and drawn by four horses whose bones fairly rattled under their skins when they were coaxed or beaten into a lazy trot.

Bulger and I alone retained our plumpness and good spirits. At length I determined to interfere and put a speedy end to this deplorable state of affairs. I exacted from the elder baron a solemn promise that he would follow my directions to the letter and not raise any objections, no matter how wild or unreasonable they might appear to him, or to my mother.

Then bidding him to partake of some good, succulent food, retire early and get a nice long sleep, I saluted him respectfully and said:

"Baron, until to-morrow morning!"

I had scarcely finished my breakfast when my door opened and the elder baron walked into the room.

He looked much refreshed. The color had returned to his cheek, the gleam to his eye.

He was already a different man.

"Here, gracious Sir," I began, handing him a parchment roll, "is a list of all the best known almanac makers in our land. Have interviews with them at once and purchase from them the right to furnish weather prognostications for the coming year!"

The elder baron began to expostulate. "Baron!" I remarked sternly, raising my hand, "a true Knight has but one word to give!"

He was silent and motioned me to continue.

I did so as follows:

"Respected parent, when you have secured this right from each of them, return to me."

In a few days my father had accomplished his mission.

He entered my room and put into my hands the needful concessions from every noted almanac maker in the land.

Again I bade him refresh himself thoroughly, get a good night's rest and see me in the morning.

As Bulger and I were returning from breakfast the elder baron presented himself at the door of my apartments.

He looked strong and well. His face had filled out again and his step had recovered its old-time elasticity.

Again I placed a roll of parchment in his hands, and said to him:

"Scatter the contents of that parchment evenly and plentifully throughout each almanac, on the pages devoted to the months of November, December, January, and February."

He looked at me inquiringly, and his lips began to move.

"Noble Sir!" said I, ere a sound had issued from his mouth, "in our family, knights have always been without fear and without reproach." He bent his lofty form in silence and withdrew.

Possibly the reader may have a little curiosity to know the contents of the parchment roll which I placed in the hands of the elder baron on this occasion.

If brevity be the soul of wit, it was witty. If a fair round hand be the garb of truth, it was truthful. Be this as it may choose to be, the words which my pen had traced on that parchment roll, read as follows:

"All signs point to an extremely cold Winter." "Indications are that the coming Winter will be the severest for half a century." "Forecasts all give the same answer—a Winter of exceptional length and bitter coldness." "Most skilled prognosticators agree in predicting a degree of low temperature rarely reached in these latitudes." "About this time expect unusual cold." "Protect plants." "Now look well to your winter vegetables." "Secure them from the extreme frost." "Double your supply of winter fuel." "Now look for fierce snow-storms." "Expect bitter cold weather during all this month." "Prepare for most unusual hail storms." "Be on your guard for sudden and penetrating north winds." "House cattle warmly for all this month." "Beware of deadly blizzards, they will come with a furious onset."

After a few days' absence, my father returned to the manor house. His arrival was duly announced to me by Bulger, to whom I said: "Go, good Bulger, and conduct the Baron to my apartment."

Away he bounded with many a sportive leap and bark, and soon returned, ushered in the elder baron with the joyous manner so common to him when active in serving me.

"I have obeyed thee, my son!" murmured the elder baron with a stately arc in his bending form.

"'Tis well!" I replied, motioning him to be seated.

"And now honored guide of my childhood's uncertain feet, give heed to my words: Our task is almost done. In a few days the investment of this money, which has occasioned thee so much anxiety, fairly robbing thee of thy heart's service, will be complete; ay, complete; and, what is better still, so fortunately invested that thou shalt be enabled to call thyself the father of one of the richest children in the Kingdom."

"Hearken, Baron. Go now into the leading markets of the land and put every fur merchant under written contract to deliver unto thee in early Autumn all the pelts, dressed, undressed, or on the backs of the owners, of which they will guarantee the delivery under their hands and seals."

The words had scarcely fallen from my lips ere the elder baron had risen from his chair and caught me warmly to his breast.

"My son!" he cried as he stroked my protuberant brow, "it is a master stroke! It is worthy of a governor of a province! I long to begin the good work. Permit me to set out this very night!" "Wait baron!" said I, leading him to his chair and gently constraining him to be seated. "Wait, Baron; there is somewhat yet to be said. When thou hast completed the purchase of all the pelts, which are expected to enter the Kingdom this year, expend the rest of the money in purchasing all the wood, coal and peat thou canst find, not that I would draw profit from the poor man's slender store; but simply to keep others from wronging him by combining against him, as they would surely do upon the first publication of the weather predictions." "Ah, little Baron!" exclaimed my father, "how thoughtful; for, as thou sayest, we must not lay a burden on the poor man's shoulders!"

Such was the diligence with which my father carried my plans to completion, that in a single month I had bought and sold again the entire product of the fur market, at a small advance, it is true, but large enough to make me an extremely rich man.

It was so gently and skillfully done, that no one ever suspected the clever ruse by which I was enabled to acquire riches enough to set out upon my travels just as my inclination might prompt, and to know that were I to be captured and held for ransom by the most grasping freebooters, my bankers would have gold enough to ransom me.

Upon the completion of my eighth year I was seized with an uncontrollable desire to enter at once upon the fulfillment of my long cherished plans, to visit far-away lands inhabited by strange and curious people. My own home, my own language, my own people, wearied me and wore upon me.

In my sleep I paced the deck of staunch vessels, shouted my orders, crowding sail in calm and reefing in threatening weather. I passed my time from morn till night, packing cases with suitable articles for traffic with the savages, so that I might be able to penetrate into interiors never visited by civilized man, and ascend rivers closed since the world began to the white-winged messengers of trade and commerce. But, strange to say, my father urged thereto, possibly, by the entreaties of my mother, firmly and resolutely set his face against my project of leaving home.

I was beside myself with disappointment. I entreated, I implored, I threatened. For the first time in my life—it pains me even now to make the confession—I was guilty of a certain disrespect to the authors of my being.

Bulger, after studying the situation for several days, reached the conclusion that the elder baron was in some way the cause of my unhappiness, and it required, at times, my sternest command to restrain him from setting his teeth in the calves of the elder baron's legs as he quitted my apartment after some stormy interview.

"What!" cried I, in tones tremulous with grief, "am I doomed to waste the splendid gifts with which nature has endowed me, shut within the walls of this petty town, whose most boisterous scenes are the brawls of its market places, whose people never witness a grander pageant than the passing of a royal troop of horse? It must not, it shall not be. Thou hast said, thyself, that I am no ordinary child to be amused with ball and top, and entertained with picture books."

But the elder baron had hardened his heart, and all my pleading was to no purpose.

And yet I did not despair of gaining my point in the end.

The continual dropping of water finally wore away the rock. I made up my mind now to move the elder baron to acquiesce in my project of leaving home by resorting to entirely different tactics. Said I to myself:

"He wishes me to be a child: I'll be one!" And forthwith I set about making friends with every mischievous little rogue in the town.

Not a single juvenile ne'er-do-well escaped my attentions.

The more rampant, active, and tireless his power of mischief, the closer I wrapped him in my affections.

From gray dawn to dewy eve these chums and boon companions of mine flocked about the castle. They worshipped me as their leader and yielded an implicit obedience to my commands as were I possessed of some mastery over them.

The elder baron saw the gathering cloud and bent his head as if to meet the coming storm with better chance of resisting it.

Came there a dinner party, the choicest Burgundy was found to have been spirited away and the bottles filled with common claret. Did the elder baron meet his friends in the fields for a trial with the hawks, it was only to discover that they had been so overfed as to sit stupidly placid when the hood was removed. Let the cook be told that guests were expected, and that he must be careful to have the little dumplings of his soup extra delicate, to the elder baron's horror, a cherry stone would be found in the centre of each little dumpling.

One of my coadjutors was venturesome enough to pilfer the elder baron's snuff box and fill it with pepper. The result may be imagined. Another took good care to pour water into all the tinder boxes before the guests called for their pipes. Upon attempting to rise from the table, here and there a queue would be found securely tied to the back of the chair.

One of my favorite exploits was to station myself on the first landing of the stairway and "hold the bridge like Horatius Cocles of old," my wild band of two dozen young barbarians rushing madly up the staircase with screams, yells and vociferations which would have done credit to any horde of real savages I have ever visited, while I, with my wooden sabre, beat down their sticks, occasionally rapping too bold a youngster on the knuckles and sending him bawling to the foot of the stairway, to Bulger's infinite amusement, as he always insisted upon taking part in the fray and gloried in my prowess.

At last to my great joy, I noticed that the elder baron showed signs of surrender.

Like a prudent general I ordered an attack all along the line.

There was to be a fox hunt the next day. I directed one of my trusted lieutenants to feed the hounds all the raw meat they could swallow, about an hour before the start.

Ten others, most fleet-footed and glib-tongued, I dispatched to the houses of the ten leading physicians and surgeons of the town and its immediate neighborhood, with the same message to each, namely, that every man, woman and child at the manor house had been taken violently ill, and that the greatest haste must be made to come with their medicine chests so that the epidemic might be checked.

The ten doctors galloped into the courtyard at nearly the same moment, only to find the elder baron and his friends gathered on the platform and holding a whispered consultation over the strange actions of the hounds. The angry disciples of Galen refused to prescribe for the poor animals, and galloped away again with their well-filled holsters thumping against their legs.

Meanwhile I had not been idle.

To the claws of a score or more of the elder baron's fowls I tied a kind of fuzee of my own invention, so inflammable that the slightest friction would cause it to burst into flame, and then I turned them loose in the fields and garden adjoining the family hall.

They had been cooped up all the Summer, and were overjoyed at the prospect of a good, comfortable scratching time 'mid the dry leaves and stubble of the open fields.

The gamekeepers by this time had succeeded in arousing the hounds somewhat from their stupor, when the cry of "fire! fire!" went up. The hunting party hastily dismounted and joined the servants in the mad rush for buckets of water.

I was sitting calmly in my apartment, with Bulger by my side, when the alarm was raised.

The elder baron at first was inclined to think that although my workmanship was plainly visible in the fabrics of mischief, which consisted in overfeeding the hounds and summoning the ten doctors to the manor house on a wild goose chase, yet the breaking out of the fire in the neighboring gardens and fields was really something with which I had nothing to do. The return of a venerable old Dominick rooster, which had been either too feeble or too lazy to explode the fuzees attached to his claws, settled the matter, however.

The elder baron's mind was now clear as to who had conceived the crime in which his poor fowls had so unwittingly become the accomplices.

That night Bulger and I went to bed with light hearts.

The elder baron had at last consented to let us set out on our first journey in quest of strange adventures among the curious people of far-away lands.

CHAPTER V.

I threw myself now heart and soul into the task of making ready for my first voyage.

Bulger was not slow to understand what all the hurry-skurry meant.

He was delighted at the prospect of a trip to distant lands where life had less monotony about it. By the hour he would sit and watch me at my labors and, from time to time, to please him, I pointed out articles lying here and there about the room and bade him fetch them, which he invariably did, with many manifestations of pleasure at being permitted to help his little master.

In fact, everybody lent a hand most kindly, so that, to my great satisfaction, I was left more time for the study of navigation.

My poor mother, the gracious baroness, would not permit anyone else to mark my clothing. With her own slender, white fingers she worked the crest and initials of my wardrobe.

There was a matter which I turned over in my thoughts for several days, to wit: What national garb I should adopt.

After long and mature deliberation I resolved to attire myself in Oriental dress. I did so for several reasons. It had been a favorite garb of mine.

Its picturesque grace appealed to my love of the beautiful, while on the other hand, its ease and lightness made it very agreeable to one of extreme suppleness of limb and elasticity of step. While the old manor house was being literally turned topsy-turvy and everybody, from cook to chambermaid, set by the ears, the elder baron was by no means idle. He took good care, among other things, that I was well provided with wholesome reading matter, and brought me several books of maxims, precepts, reflections, thoughts and studies, which he requested me to thrust into the empty corners of my chests, "for," said he, and that, too, with a great show of reason, "thou wilt have many idle hours on thy hands in calm weather. It behooves thee to feed thy mind lest its wonderful development be checked and thou become as an ordinary child, with no thoughts above games and picture books." My poor mother, the gracious baroness, added to this stock of good literature by presenting me with a small volume entitled: "The Straight Road to Good Health; or, Everybody His Own Doctor." As to my medicine chest, I gave that my personal supervision, for I was always skilled in the art of reading all kinds of symptoms and was gifted with the rare faculty of knowing almost instinctively what remedy to give for a certain ailment, without first experimenting upon the patient by trying one thing after another, as is the custom with most people who pretend to heal sickness.

Everything was going well now, and I was in the best of spirits, when the elder baron came to me with a proposal which, for some reason, I can hardly tell why, displeased me, although it would seem that it ought to have had the opposite effect. He proposed to precede me, by a week or ten days, to the North Sea, in some port of which I intended to purchase and fit out a swift, staunch vessel, purchase the vessel himself, give his personal attention to fitting her out and shipping a crew of picked men.

What could I do?

If I refused his offer, it would have been tantamount to a confession of distrust on my part.

Can he have in mind any project to thwart my scheme?

O, perish the thought!

But I must confess that I did not accept his proffered services without serious misgivings.

This sudden anxiety on the part of the elder baron to hurry my departure, after having opposed it so long and so vigorously, made me a little uneasy in my mind.

Before setting out for the North Sea to purchase a ship for me, the elder baron entered my apartment, and spoke as follows:

"Pardon me, little baron, for interrupting thy labors, for I perceive that thou art deep in the study of navigation."

"Speak, Baron," said I, looking up, with a mischievous smile, "that right belongs to thee."

"I have a last request to make," he continued, in his usual calm manner, "nor is it a matter of very great importance. Rather is it a whim, more than aught else. Thou knowest from my lips, and from the perusal of our family chronicles, that we were in ancient time very large land owners on the coast of the North Sea. We controlled several ports, were extensively engaged in trade, sending out at least a score of ships in a twelvemonth. One of the ports of our domain was a famous one, famous for the extraordinary character of its inlet and outlet currents, channel, etc. It was said of this port that it was more dangerous than the open sea, that vessels were really safer out of it than in it. I know not how much of truth may be in all this, but I do know that one man, an ancestor of ours, not only sailed into it, but safely out again, for thou must know that the channel by which a vessel gained admission to this port could not be used to leave it again, as the irresistible current always flowed the one way, namely, from the sea into this mysterious basin. To leave it, the bold mariner must trust his bark to another channel, and therein lurked the danger.

"It would gratify me greatly, little baron, if thou couldst prove to the world that, no matter how difficult, other captains once found, and now find it, to sail out of this port, yet to thee it offered no insurmountable obstacles, and therefore, am I come to ask thee to set sail from this port!"

"It is called?" I asked carelessly, as I turned to a chart of the North Sea.

"Port No Man's Port," replied the baron.

"I like its name," said I. "Order my ship to await me there!"

The elder baron arose, and bending his body with stately grace, withdrew. I accompanied him to the door and dismissed him with most respectful obeisance.

"Port No Man's Port," I answered. "Ah, here is the chart!" The descriptive text reads as follows:

"Abandoned for many years; ingress easy; egress so dangerous as to mean fatal injury, if not destruction, to sailing craft; outer channel blocked by a fearful whirlpool and swinging rock called "Thor's Hammer;" inner basin extremely dangerous from constantly shifting sands; closed by order of the Royal Ministry of Commerce and Marine." Upon finishing the reading of these words I sprang up and began to pace the floor, wildly and half unconsciously.

The blood rushed in upon my brain. I was obliged to halt and cling to the back of a tall oak chair, or I should have staggered and fallen to the ground.

Bulger was greatly alarmed and sent up a suppressed howl of grief. I spoke to him as calmly as I could to comfort him.

After a few moments the vertigo passed off and my mind cleared up completely.

"Nay, it is impossible," I whispered, "the elder baron could not be guilty of bad faith to me! Away with such a thought! He errs through thoughtlessness and lack of experience. He little knows the terribly dangerous character of the task he is setting me. To him, the talks of shipwreck and death within Port No Man's Port are but the legends of old-time sailor-life. He has not the faintest suspicion that his request, so lightly made, exposes his only child, son and heir to a princely fortune and honored name, either to be engulfed by these shifting sands, sucked down to destruction by this fearful whirlpool, or crushed by a blow from Thor's Hammer.

"And yet why murmur?

"It is too late to protest. Already the elder baron has proclaimed to the world the, to him proud piece of news, that his son was about to renew the old-time glories of his family! I must do one of two things: Face these dangers like a man of cool, calm courage, or condemn myself to a life of dull and listless activity, the magnate of a province and not the hero of two worlds!

"No! the die is cast!

"I have said it and it is as good as done!

"My ship sails from Port No Man's Port, or this little body feeds its fish that day!"

Doubtless my eyes brightened, and my cheeks took on a glow of crimson hue, for Bulger, who had been listening to my soliloquy with a most pained expression on his face, as he vainly tried to get at the meaning of my words, now broke out into a very lively succession of barks, bounding and springing about the room in the wildest merriment. He knew only too well that some terrible struggle had been going on in my mind.

Now he realized that all was well. Faithful creature, if he could only tell his love, how he would put all human lovers to blush!

As the hour drew near for me to bid adieu to the baronial hall, that good lady, the gracious baroness, my mother, suddenly thought of a thousand and one things which she deemed of the very greatest importance to me. She warned me that I was not to sleep in a draught; not to partake of freshly-baked bread; not to drink cold water while overheated; not to cut my finger nails too short; not to sleep with my mouth open; not to wear my underclothing longer than one week; not to neglect to brush my teeth; not to fail to have my hair cut with the new moon; not to strain my eyes reading by a poor light not to swallow my food without thoroughly chewing it; not to laugh while I had food in my mouth; not to attempt to stop a sneeze; not to neglect to pare my corns; not to pick my teeth with a metal point; not to examine the end of my nose without a looking-glass; not to eat meat without pepper, or vegetables without salt; not to exert myself after a hearty meal; not to stand upon my leg while it was asleep; not to walk so fast as to get a pain in my side; not to go to sleep until I had first rested on my right side; not to fail to take a pill if I saw flashes in the dark; not to neglect to tie a stocking around my neck in case my throat felt sore, etc., etc., etc. When the moment came to take leave of the gracious baroness, my good mother, I was deeply moved. All the servants and retainers, from indoors and out, filed in front of me, kissed my hand and showered blessings on me.

I may safely say that the only being present not moved to tears was Bulger. He was so anxious to get under way that he passed an hour or so racing from the manor house to the carriage and back again in a piteous endeavor to get the procession started.

Start we did, at last.

A hundred hands waved us a fond farewell.

The stately trees that shut in the baronial hall swayed solemnly. I was glad when we rolled out of the court yard for I needed rest and quiet.

My nerves had been on such a stretch for the past month that a change of scene brought me balm and relaxation.

My journey to the North Sea was quiet and uneventful.

I found my ship safely anchored in Port No Man's Port, and the elder baron there in charge of her. He introduced me to the sailing-master, pressed me in his own loving arms, and with a gracious smile and stately wave of the hand, seated himself in the family coach. His only adieu was:

"My son, thy wisdom comes to thee by inheritance. Thou couldst not have acquired it. Therefore, make a noble use of so noble a gift. Farewell!"

I bent my head in silence. The carriage rolled away. I stood alone. Nay, a true and loving friend was there. He looked up with his large, lustrous eyes, as if to say:

"Don't be sad, little master. No matter who goes, I'll stay by thee forever!"

Turning to my sailing-master, I ordered the ship's launch to be manned, and began at once a survey of the mysterious port in which my ship lay anchored.

I found it to be a roomy basin, shut in by a rock-bound shore. In places the waters slept beneath black and glassy surfaces; in others, all was movement and commotion. Its waves came boiling and bubbling against the launch with swirling masses of white sand, shifting hither and thither, as if condemned to perpetual unrest.

The fact that my men, while fishing in different parts of the bay, often caught deep-sea fish, proved to me that Port No Man's Port was traversed by a channel from four to six fathoms in depth.

The only difficulty would be to fix the boundaries of this constantly shifting path long enough to sail across the basin.

I next turned my attention to the whirlpool. It marked the junction of the outer channel with the basin of Port No Man's Port.

Having purchased a number of condemned hulks for the purpose of testing the strength and fury of the whirlpool, I caused a strong hawser to be rigged to a capstan on shore, and was in this way enabled to let the launch approach within a ship's length of the whirlpool with perfect safety. In truth, it was, when roused to the full measure of its fury by the intrusion of any large floating body, a sight to strike terror to the stoutest heart!

With a deep booming and rumble, its waters rose in tumultuous commotion, boiling, bubbling, seething, till snow-white foam covered the pool like a mantle of bleached linen, then lifting the intruder, which in this case was one of the hulks that I had ordered to be launched upon them, these angered waters whirled it completely around. In an instant, as if exhausted by this tremendous effort, a mysterious calm sank upon the pool. The foam-sheet, broken in shreds, danced gently on the rippling bosom of the waters. All was peace, save that the hulk still lay trembling like an affrighted being in the lap of this resting monster!

For, look! It is aroused again. Faster and faster it whirls its prey. Deeper and deeper its now wide-opened jaws draw down the ill-fated hulk!

A terrible roar tells that the end is near!

'Tis gone!

Ay, but wait! It will give up its prey again!

Even now bits of plank float seaward, dancing on the rushing waters.

Soon the crumpled, broken, crushed remnants of that strong hulk will follow.

This watery monster doth not feed upon what he swallows! He destroys for the mere love of destruction. Night had come now. I returned to my ship. The shifting sands and the whirlpool had uncovered their horrors. But I feared them no more! Like the horse-tamer when he has at last succeeded in thrusting the steel bit between the champing and gnashing teeth of the wild young steed, I now felt that they were conquered.

"And now for Thor's Hammer!" was my cry, as I sat down beside Bulger for a brief moment's reflection.

The first streak of gray light in the east found me on deck.

"Thor's Hammer" was a huge shaft of black, flinty rock, projecting about twenty feet out of the water and ending in a hammer-shaped head. It guarded the channel where it reached the sea, standing exactly in the middle, thus forcing a vessel to pass on one side or the other of it.

Beneath the waters, this dread sentinel must have ended in a gigantic ball, which, in the flight of time had worn a socket for itself in the bed rock of the channel; for it swung loose and free, moved by every powerful billow from side to side, threatening swift destruction to any passing craft.

To speak frankly, the sight of this terrible engine of destruction appalled me! How shall I escape the vigilance of this gigantic sentinel, who knows no sleep, no rest, whose blows fall with like fury on friend or foe? How shall I lull him to repose for a few brief moments?

Determined to study closely the strength, the rapidity, and the character of the blows struck by "Thor's Hammer," I caused several huge structures of plank and timber to be erected near the position of this mighty sentinel of rock. One after the other I ordered them to be thrown into the channel.

At first, I was fairly paralyzed upon discovering that even the slight vortex caused by the drifting by of one of these wooden structures set the swinging rock in violent vibration and always towards the passing object.

Judging from the effect of Thor's Hammer upon these floating masses of plank and timber, a single blow would suffice to crush the very life out of my ship in spite of her unusual staunchness.

I stood transfixed with dread forebodings. I could feel the beads of perspiration break from my forehead and trickle down my cheeks. Must I give up and return home, broken in spirits, humiliated, the butt of ridicule, the target of village wit, the subject of mirth and laughter in every peasant's cottage?

Oh, no! It can not, it must not be!

Like a flash of lightning, a thought flamed across the dark horizon of my mind.

Am I not dreaming? Was it really so?

One of the wooden structures still remained. Controlling my emotion with great difficulty, I ordered it thrown into the channel and took up a favorable position to watch once again the wrath of the towering sentinel! In a few moments "Thor's Hammer" felt the coming of the craft and bent itself in impotent rage beating the air with blows which fell faster and faster! Ay, I was right! When once Thor's Hammer had begun its labor of death and ruin, it turned not from its task, so long as there remained any object for it to spend its fury upon!

Nor was there any escape for the ill-fated craft until it had been pounded into flinders! Hanging over it, blow followed blow with fearful clash and clamor. Not until the poor remnant had drifted seaward, did that black and flinty shaft cease its furious swinging.

Turning to my sailing-master, who stood with his wondering eyes fixed full upon me, I called out in a calm and careless tone: "In three days, skipper, if the weather is clear, we leave Port No Man's Port!"

A lump rose up in his throat, but he gulped it down, and cried out merrily: "Ay, ay, sir."

And what three busy days they were, too! My men were not long in catching something of the indomitable spirit of their new commander. I worked them hard, but I fed them well, served out grog with a liberal, but wise hand, and saw that all their wants were satisfied. In turn, their wonderment became admiration, and their admiration affection.

The first day all the hands that could be spared were set to work making fishing lines, with a good, stout hook at one end and a cork float at the other. The lines were cut about three fathoms in length, and the floats were painted a bright crimson. I then gave orders to rig three jury-masts, one midships, and one fore and aft.

My men set to work with a will, but I caught them several times in the act of tapping their foreheads and exchanging significant glances. But if this last order threw them into a brown study, my next had the effect of a bombshell exploding in their midst.

Sailing-master and all, they stood staring at me as if they were only waiting for me to annihilate them.

My order was to rig a steering gear under the figure-head. A coasting vessel, which I had sent for, now came sailing leisurely into Port No Man's Port. I directed the skipper to pay her crew three months' extra wages, and discharge them.

This done, my men were ordered to lash the coaster on our starboard side.

I verily believe that my whole plan, so carefully studied out, was at this point only saved from utter failure by the wisdom of my faithful Bulger.

The coaster had no sooner been lashed to our side than he sprang lightly over the railing, and began to amuse himself by gamboling up and down the clear deck. Suddenly he paused near one of the hatches and broke out into a most furious barking. I called to one of my officers to look sharp and see what the matter was. He reported in a few moments that one of the discharged seamen had been found concealed in the hold. When I threatened to put him in irons, he confessed that his design had been to cut the coaster loose as soon as our ship had drawn near to the whirlpool.

It was a narrow escape.

Dear, faithful Bulger, how much we owe thee for that discovery!

The third day dawned bright and fair.

The wind was most favorable, blowing strong off shore.

At the first glimmer of light, my men were astir and on the lookout for my appearance.

They greeted Bulger and me with three hearty cheers.

They had made up their minds that what I didn't know, Bulger did! At last all was ready!

I nodded to the sailing-master, and in a moment or so the capstan began to revolve, and the merry "Yo, heave O!" of the men told me that the anchor had been started. Hundreds of the lines and floats, well-baited, were now cast overboard. Standing on the taffrail, glass in hand, I watched them closely and anxiously.

Imagine my joy at seeing several of these crimson floats disappear like a flash, rise again, and again vanish for an instant.

"The first point is gained," I cried out. "I have found the channel!"

Passing word quickly to the sailing-master who was in charge of the steering gear, my good vessel moved slowly out of Port No Man's Port, stern first. Again and again the baited lines with their crimson floats were thrown overboard. The deep water fish that swarmed the ever-shifting channel kept steadily at work. As our ship advanced, they tugged at the lines and thus kept the tortuous course plainly marked out. Glass in hand, I watched the successful working of this part of my plan, with tingling veins and a bounding heart. A loud huzza from my men tell me that we have cleared the shifting sands. Ay, true it is! We have crossed the basin of Port No Man's Port! Its dreaded quicksands swirl and roll in vain. It was not fated that they should engulf the Little Baron's ship!

But see! The channel narrows! The waters grow black, and troubled. And hark!

Didn't you hear that dull roar? I spring down from the taffrail! I pass among my men and drop here and there a word of encouragement. My perfect calmness impresses them. No merry "ay, ay, Sir!" goes up, but I see a response in their faces. It is: "We trust you little captain, speak!" The dull roar grows louder and louder.

The rapids catch us up and bear us along like chips on the foaming tide of a mountain stream. Our staunch vessel rocks like a toy boat. The coaster lashed to one side creaks and groans in its wild efforts to break away.

Calling Bulger to me I pass the line around him and lash him firmly to the main-mast, for I was fearful lest a sudden lurch might hurl him overboard. On, on, we speed through the frightened waters. The roar is deafening. I glance at my seamen. Their bronzed faces are blanched. They cling to the shrouds and stays. Their eyes are riveted upon me.

Look! the fearful whirlpool is dead ahead of us. It opens its foam-flecked jaws like some terrible monster. We leap into its very mouth. Are we lost? How can it be otherwise? As if our staunch vessel were a nutshell, the swirling, raging, whirling, battling, boiling waters catch her up in their encircling arms, lift her high above the sea level, turn her completely around and drop her with such terrific force that great walls of water rise on all sides and threaten to engulf the frail wooden thing. But most wondrous change; mark how she floats upon a glassy pool! The foam dances in the sunlight on the rippling waves. All is peace where but a moment before nature raged with demoniac fury. Quick as thought I leap into the mizzen shrouds: "Cut away the jury-masts!" They fall overboard with a crash. My men work with a mad earnestness. They know too well that every instant may be their last. Our mainsail already hoisted is sheeted home without a word or a cry. We are too near death to sing! See! See! The wind fills the great sail! We move. The waters seem to scent our escape. They are awaking to new fury. A deep rumble from the very bowels of the earth calls upon them to arouse from their lethargy.

They reach out for us.

Too late! too late!

We sweep out of their reach. We are saved! We are saved! A shout goes up from two score throats, from which Fear now takes her hand!

Look back! As if robbed of its prey, the whirlpool awakes with redoubled fury.

A hundred arm-like streams of water gush forth and pour around our good ship in vain effort to draw her back into that terrible vortex.

We are drenched with clouds of spray and mist, as we slowly but steadily keep on our course. Would that we were safe upon the swelling tide of the open sea, for there is still another danger to be met.

Our channel suddenly narrows. I could toss a biscuit to the rocky wall, which shuts us in on both sides.

Again a deep silence falls upon ship and crew, broken only by a strange sound of rushing waters, bursting out and dying away as regularly as the swing of a pendulum. 'Tis Thor's Hammer, beating the frightened waters into foam, as it sways from side to side.

In spite of my effort to appear calm, I can feel my heart beat faster.

A cold chill benumbs my hands. A glance ahead startles me like a blow from an unseen hand. There, with the morning sun resting on its hammer-shaped crest, swings that dreaded shaft of flinty rock, threatening instant destruction to any ship bold enough to attempt to pass it.

In accordance with my orders, every sail on the coaster had been set, and her helm lashed, so as to pass to the right of Thor's Hammer.

"Courage, men!" I cried. "Stand by, all! Cut away the lashings! Cast off the tender!"

Then waving my hand to the skipper, our mainsail came down with a run. Everything worked like a charm. Our ship slowed up, while the coaster shot ahead to her destruction. See, how gallantly the doomed craft speeds on her way; for the breeze had freshened, and several gay streamers and flags, which my men had run up to the topmast, fluttered in the crisp morning air.

There! Did you not hear that crash?

Thor's Hammer has struck her!

Blow follows blow!

Crash! Crash! Crash!

Now is our time, or never!

I was not caught napping. The moment we were clear of the coaster, I had ordered sails enough to be set to hold our ship steady on her course.

Already we drew near to Thor's Hammer, which is fast battering the coaster to a shapeless mass. The sea is filled with bits of plank and broken timber. Thor's Hammer bends to its dread work of destruction, unmindful of our presence.

What could withstand its terrible fury?

Those sturdy timbers yield like twigs.

Another minute, and we have the monster and his victim in our wake!

Now, now, we're passing him! Our sails tremble from the very force of his breath! Our deck is strewn with splinters! The roar and crash are deafening. Thor's Hammer bends for one last blow at the ribs and keel of its broken and disjointed victim!

Hurrah! Hurrah!

Our good ship dips to the deep roll of the ocean's breast! We are on the open sea! Port No Man's Port, farewell!

As my men looked back at the rocky gateway and the grim sentinel of Port No Man's Port, they tossed their caps into the air and sent up cheer after cheer.

Bulger bounded about the deck, doing his best by most vigorous barking, to testify his admiration for his little master.

The sailing-master drew near; and, touching his cap and scratching the deck with the toe of his shoe, cried out gayly:

"Bravo! little Baron. That was splendidly done! I was sure we should never get through the shifting sands. And when they were passed, I was ready to swear the whirlpool would make short work of us. But when we sailed safely out of that, I drew near the tail rail ready to jump overboard, for I felt that nothing could save us from a blow from Thor's Hammer. I've grown wrinkled and gray facing the storms of Neptune's domain, but I never felt I had a master until now."

I nodded and smiled, and quickly turned the conversation to some other topic.

"By the way, skipper," said I, "remember, the very moment we clear the English Channel, turn her head southward!"

"Ay! ay! little Baron!" was the reply. Calling Bulger to me I now went below. I wanted to be alone. The fact of the matter is, I needed rest. The terrible strain on my nerves caused by the hopes and fears of the past few days, began to tell upon me.

Throwing myself upon a canopy, I fell into a deep sleep from which I was awakened by Bulger's whining and crying.

The sailing-master was anxiously feeling my pulse.

I had slept three days and three nights. All this time Bulger had absolutely refused to leave my side or partake of food, although the skipper had tempted him with the daintiest morsels.

His joys knew no bounds as I sprang up and shook myself into shape.

"Where are we, master?" I cried.

"On the broad Atlantic, headed dead south, little Baron!" was the answer.

"Good! send me a rasher of bacon and some hard-tack. The Atlantic breeze has given me an appetite and, skipper," I added, "a little broiled fowl for Bulger."

"And now, for the land of warmth and sunshine!" I murmured, "now for the home of the orange and the palm! Cold winds like me not, I am a child of the tropics, born in a land where nature works and man plays. No chill blast ever whistled its sad tune over my cradle! Let those who will, spend one-half their lives waiting for mother Earth to wake from her Winter sleep! Freeze the body and you freeze the brain. I am of those who love flowers better than snowflakes. Glorious South land! I greet thee, thy child comes again to thy arms, oh, take him up kindly and lovingly!"

Southward, ever southward my good ship sped along. By day I paced the deck to watch the dolphins at play or to observe Bulger's amazement when a stray flying fish fell fluttering on deck; by night, with my eyes fixed upon the blazing Southern Cross, I longed for the time to come when I should set foot upon some beautiful strand decked out with coral branch and shells of pearl, in whose limpid waters golden fish nestle mid sea plants of not less brilliant hue.

It was now three weeks since the last murmur of Thor's Hammer had fallen on our ears.

My chronometer marked high noon. Every sail was set and our good ship careened as gracefully as a swallow that bent in its flight to touch the cool waters of some glassy lake. All of a sudden the wind fell, our ship stood still on the motionless sea, my pennant hung like a string. There was not air enough to lift the smoke from our galley fire. A strange mysterious stillness weighed upon the ship and sea. I knew too well what it betokened. One of those dreaded calms, more feared by the seamen that the buffeting gale, had overtaken us.

Our ship stood like one moored to a marble wharf!

And as the thought flashed across my mind that days, ay even weeks might pass ere the winds would lift themselves again to bear us on our way, a feeling of utter listlessness came over me. It required a great exertion for me to throw it off.

I dared not let my men see aught of discouragement in my face.

And yet, it was a hard task. Had I not been made of stern stuff, I would have wept to see my progress stayed at the very moment victory was almost within my grasp.

Again, as was the case, when the terrors of Port No Man's Port rose, like demons of malignant might, to shut me forever in that rock-encircled basin, did my thoughts revert to home—to the elder baron and his gracious consort, my dear mother; to the servants and retainers of the baronial hall; to the villagers and tenantry. How, oh how should I be able to face them all, if I were forced to return home with the humiliating confession that my voyage had been a failure?

Bulger was the first to catch a glimpse of the shadow on my brow. He turned his dark lustrous eyes full upon me so pleadingly as if to say: "Oh, little master, what aileth thee? May I not do aught to drive the dark melancholy from thy face? Thou knowest how I love thee. Teach me to help thee. My life is thine. Thy grief weighs like lead on my heart. Speak to me little master!" Tenderly and lovingly I stroked his head, and spoke in softest tones to him. He was rejoiced, but still he sat and watched me, for it was impossible to deceive him by feigning to be lighthearted and unconcerned.

The second week found us lying like a log in a millpond, our sails unvisited by the faintest breath of air; the sea sunken into a sleep that seemed like death. Despair sat on the faces of my men. "Rouse thee, little baron!" I murmured to myself as I paced my cabin floor, "where is thy boasted cunning? Where is thy vaunted wisdom? Nevermore say that thou art a man of projects, quick to devise, and quick to perform! Thou hast lost thy hold on the spoke of fortune's wheel!"

"Thinkest thou so?" cried I in answer to my own thoughts.

"Follow me, we shall see!" With a bound I cleared the gang way. The sailing-master lay asleep on the deck. The men in groups, here and there, looked the very picture of despair. Rousing the skipper with a vigorous tug at his belt, aided by Bulger's frantic outburst of barking, I called out:

"Avast! there, skipper. Asleep from overwork? Pipe all hands on deck!" The men came up in lively fashion, greatly amused by my cut at the sailing-master, who stood rubbing his eyes, half dazed by my sudden outburst. "Send me the ships carpenter!" I continued; and catching up a piece of chalk I drew the plan of a large box or chest, nearly as long as our ship's breadth of beam, and gave the carpenter directions to build it of the strongest planks to be had on board. He and his assistants were soon at work.

Turning then to the cook I ordered him to kill the pigs and fowls we had shipped for our own supply of fresh meat, bidding him to be careful and not lose a drop of the blood.

These orders fairly drove my men wild with curiosity.

The sailing-master drew near and attempted to get some explanation from me but in vain. I was too deep in thought to speak.

The long box was ready in a few hours. Word now went up that I was about to abandon the ship and strive to reach land by rowing, and that this long box was to hold the provisions.

The sailing-master again fixed his gaze inquiringly upon me. I pretended not to notice his beseeching looks. The cook by this time had the fresh meat in readiness. Under my directions it was all transferred to the long chest, the blood poured over it, and the box securely closed with a heavy plate-glass lid, made up of several pieces shipped for the purpose of restoring broken lights. By this time the men had grown so excited over this mysterious box and its still more mysterious contents, that I was obliged to order them to fall back so that the carpenter and his assistants might go on with their work without interruption.

The next step was to weight the long chest with lead and to attach hoisting tackle to each end by strong iron rings. When all was ready I called out to my men to stand by and lower it over the stern rail. Stationed so that I could watch the lowering of the long box, I was careful to sink it about three feet under water and then lash it firmly to the ship's stern. I had scarcely given the word to lower away on all the sails when the ship began to move! The effect on my men was indescribable. Some turned pale and stood as if transfixed with fear. Others laughed in a wild maniac-like way. Others, who had their wits about them, rushed to the stern taffrail to fathom the mystery.

A glance was enough!

It was a simple thing after all.

Gradually the others recovered their reason, and hastened to join their companions and gaze down into the waters where I had lashed the long box, with its glass lid and strange contents. Meanwhile our good ship moved faster and faster through the sluggish, listless waters. A ringing cheer, three times repeated, went up when the mystery was fully solved.

Mystery?

Hear then what this mystery consisted of!

In the first days of this dead calm, which settled like a terrible blanket spread over us by the hands of some unseen monster, to check our advance, I had noticed that the waters swarmed with sharks of extraordinary length; that these fierce demons of the deep hung about our vessel in shoals of countless numbers, attracted by the garbage thrown overboard, and, doubtless, too, by the odor of the many living beings on board the ship.

When, at times, a particularly large supply of garbage fell into the water, so fierce was the onslaught of these ravenous monsters, that they actually jarred the ship as they struck against its sides or stern, locked together like advancing cohorts of trained soldiery.

Upon this hint I acted. If, as I reasoned, I can only control this now wild force, why may I not make use of it to rescue my ship from a worse danger than raging storm? For far better would it be to face the howling blast and foam-crested wave than to perish from thirst, chained to the open sea by this breathless calm.

Now, however, all was changed.

On, on, our good ship went, with ever-increasing speed, gliding noiselessly and swiftly through the mirror-like waters. My device worked far better than I had dared to dream, for, as the fresh blood began to trickle through the crevices of the long box, the ravenous sea monsters were almost maddened by its smell and taste. The largest and fiercest pressed forward in serried ranks, tossing their smaller companions high in the air, as they took up their places with wild and eager search for prey which lured them on, ever so near them, and still ever beyond their reach.

No sooner did the foremost ranks of this army of myrmidons of the deep show signs of fatigue than long lines of fresh and eager recruits darted forward, hurling their exhausted fellows right and left, like bits of cork, and took up the task of following the ever-retreating prey, which, although giving out its life blood, and plainly visible to them, yet seemed to know no tiring, and sped onward, and ever onward before the wild, tumultuous attack of their pushing, plunging cohorts!

The moon now shone like a plate of burnished silver on the blue walls of heaven, and the deep silence of the sleeping waters was broken by the splash of those mighty bodies, glistening in her light, as they toiled and struggled to urge our vessel on its way.

I could not sleep.

Wrapped in a woolen cloak, to shield me from the insidious dews of the tropics, I threw myself on deck, with Bulger's head pillowed on my lap.

Something whispered to me that if those hunger-stricken marauders of the deep would only keep to their task till the morning sun streaked the east, my cheek would feel the breath of coming winds.

And so it turned out. With the first glimmer of daylight I caught sight of a ripple on the lake-like bosom of the ocean. At that very moment, too, I noticed that our ship was slowing up. I sprang up on the taffrail. Lo! our allies had abandoned us. Not a single follower of that riotous camp was in sight! Ah, little did they dream how they had saved ship and crew! How limitless is man's selfishness! The beasts of the field, the monsters of the deep must minister to his pleasure, obey his commands. I had pointed out the ripple in the water and when the first sturdy breath of wind reached us we were in readiness to receive it. Every sail was set.

My heart leaped with joy as our ship drew up to the wind, obeying her helm like a thing of life!

And that was the way I saved my ship and crew from a worse danger than storm-lashed billows. From this time on, all went well. Scarcely a week had gone by when I was startled by a cry which sounded sweeter to my ears than voice of monarch to courtier.

"Land ho! Dead ahead!"

Seizing my glass I sprang up into the main-shrouds, and turned my gaze in the direction indicated. Ay, true it was! There it lay before us, rising from the ocean with gentle slope, its heights crowned with trees of many-colored foliage, its shores ending in long stretches of snow-white beach.

Above the unknown land hung a purple mist of a deep rich tint, like the cheek of a ripe plum. As we drew near a landlocked harbor seemed to welcome us. Not a sound or sign of life, however, came to break the deep repose which enveloped the bay and shore.

Slowly and in stately bearing our good ship sailed into the harbor and cast anchor. The radiant beauty of the land now burst upon me. Ten thousand shells of pearly tints and hues glistened on the white sands, while in the limpid waters, sea-flowers and foliage of deepest crimson swayed gently with the tide. Up the sloping banks nature seemed to be holding high carnival. No shrub or bush or tree was content to wear simple green. Each waved some blossom of richest radiance in the soft and balmy air. Here and there, a brooklet came tumbling down the hillside, rippling, purling and splashing over the moss-grown rocks in its bed. The air was heavy with the fragrance of this vast garden so beautiful and yet so silent and deserted.

The next day, leaving my sailing-master in command, I set out on a tramp, accompanied solely by my faithful Bulger. My idea was to see if this island, for such I thought it to be, contained anything quaint and curious. The further I advanced into the interior of this fair land of bright flowers, purling brooks, clear skies and perfumed air, the more was I astonished to find that neither vine, shrub, brush, nor tree bore any berry or fruit to feed upon; and though it was just such a land of brooks, flowers and balmy air as some dweller of the far-away North might dream about; yet was it untrodden by the foot of man, for, rare indeed is it that the people of the tropics are willing to prepare any other food for themselves than that which nature spreads before them.

I now began to be thankful that I had supplied myself plentifully with dried fruits before leaving my ship to set out for a tour of the island, for such it seemed to me to be.

At this moment Bulger halted, and raising his nose in the air, sniffed hard and long, and then fixed his dark eyes on me as much as to say: "Take care, little master, some sort of living creatures are approaching!" I had hardly time to draw one of my pistols and give a hasty glance at its priming when with strange cries and stranger movements a dozen or more beings of the human species sprang out of the thicket with noiseless steps, and surrounded us. I raised the fire-arm, which I held grasped in my right hand, ready to stop the advance of this band of most curious creatures, by slaying their leader; for, judging by the forbidding aspect of their faces and the terrible condition of their bodies, apparently reduced by the dread pangs of hunger, to mere sacks of skin hung on frames of bone, which methought rattled at every step they took, I anticipated an instant attempt on their part to strike us down and eat us.

But I was very quickly reassured. First, by the fact that they bore no weapons of any kind; and second, by the softness of their voices and the walkingbeam-like motions of their bodies, which I interpreted to mean a sort of welcome mingled with a desire to make friends with a human being so different from themselves. Although I gave them to understand, or tried to do so, by imitating the ducking motion of their heads, followed by an attempt to equal their performance in making a large number of very low bows, so graceful and easy that they would have done credit to a French dancing master, that they had nothing to fear, yet they continued to back away from me as fast as I advanced. Bulger was somewhat surprised at my eagerness to make friends with such a starved-out looking set of creatures and kept up a furious growling, eying them suspiciously as they continued the walkingbeam motion of their bodies all the while backing away from me.

I now found myself in front of a group of umbrella shaped bamboo huts into which most of them had retreated. With no little difficulty was it that I finally succeeded in coaxing them forth and convincing them that my intentions were perfectly peaceful. For a quarter of an hour or more, they circled about me in silent wonder, while I, on my part, gazed in speechless astonishment at these extraordinary looking specimens of our race. What they thought of me, you will learn as my story goes on, but how shall I ever describe them to you so as to give you even a faint idea of their wonderful appearance.

Imagine skeletons of rather small stature walking about, with collapsed meal bags hung upon them, skin hanging down in folds everywhere, flapping about at every step and you'll have some faint conception of the utterly ridiculous and grotesque look of these beings.

Almost every bone in their bodies was visible beneath this thin covering. Their cheeks hung like two empty pouches on each side of their faces, their noses stuck out like knife-blades. Deep wrinkles and creases crossed and criss-crossed their faces, giving them a look of terrible melancholy and utter wretchedness.

With their skeleton fingers ever and anon they grasped a fold of skin and smoothed it out or pushed it elsewhere as one might a loosely fitting garment. And yet, utterly wretched and melancholy as these creatures seemed to be to the eye of the looker-on, their voices were light and gay, and soft as flute notes. They chatted and laughed among themselves, were full of mischief and pointed their pencil fingers at different parts of Bulger's and my body with evident enjoyment at the sight of things so new and strange to them. Several times while gazing upon these mournful and woebegone looking faces and at the same time listening to their happy and childlike chatter, I broke out into a peal of laughter which was not only very ill-bred, but which invariably had the effect of causing them to fall back in disorder.

Gradually, however, they grew bolder, and by means of a kind of sign language, gave me to understand that they desired to touch me. By recourse to the same common language of mankind, I informed them that I should be only too happy to gratify their requests and proceeded to lay bare my breast and roll up the sleeves of my coat. They half repented of their foolhardiness, and crowding together, interlocked their arms and legs in such a manner that, to save my life, I couldn't tell where one commenced and the other ended.

But after a few moment's coaxing, I succeeded in persuading them to advance and lay their hands upon me.

Loud outcries followed exclamations of wonder and astonishment. As I afterwards learned the words they uttered meant: "Lump!" "Chunk!" "Stone!" "Hard!" "Solid!" At this moment, feeling a little bit hungry, I opened my sack of dried fruit and thrust several pieces into my mouth.

And now came a still more furious outburst of wonder, mingled with cries of horror and disgust. Again they retreated and tied themselves into a knot.

Can it be, I asked myself, that these creatures never touch solid food?

Observing now that they were consulting among themselves as to what course to pursue in regard to me, and being afraid that they might take it into their heads to escape into the thicket, for they were as quick in their movements as sprites and phantoms, I lost no time in making them understand that I desired to be led into the presence of their King or ruler.

This seemed to please them. But with many duckings of their heads, they withdrew a short distance, and held a sort of pow-wow. After which, one of their number, who seemed to be a sort of leader among them, and whose name, as I afterwards learned, was Go-Whizz, advanced toward me with numerous low-bendings of his body, and succeeded in informing me that their chief lived at a great distance from where we were, and that it would be necessary for me to remain here while they returned to their ruler to ask his permission to conduct me to him.

I readily consented to such an arrangement.

Go-Whizz then led me to one of their dwellings, pointed out a bed of nice dry rushes, and invited me to make myself comfortable until he should come again to conduct me into the presence of their chief, Ztwish-Ztwish, as was the name he bore.

Bulger and I didn't wait for a second bidding, for we were tired to the bone after our long tramp. With half a dozen or more bows, quite as low as those made by Go-Whizz and his companions, I began to make ready for a night's rest.

For a moment or so, I stood watching the retreating figures of these extraordinary people who, in single file, swiftly and noiselessly, like so many phantoms, had flitted away from the spot. Then throwing myself down on the bed of rushes, called out to Bulger to lie down by me. But he was not so trustful as I, and after caressing my hands, took up his position at the door of the dwelling, so as to save his little master from any treachery on the part of the phantom people.

Day now went out suddenly, like a lamp quenched by the wind.

Bulger refused to sleep.

But I, sheltered from the night dews by this thickly-thatched roof, soon fell into a deep and refreshing sleep, out of which Bulger found it difficult to arouse me, for I have a faint recollection of having felt him scratching at my arm for several moments, ere I could shake off the fetters of sleep, which held me bound so tightly.

Sitting up hastily, I discovered that Bulger was patrolling the floor in a state of great excitement, pausing ever and anon to sniff the morning air, which, it was plain to be seen, brought him a warning of some kind. Instantly it occurred to me that wild beasts were prowling about in the neighborhood. I examined the priming of my fire-arms. Bulger looked well pleased to see that I was thoroughly aroused as to the threatening danger.

He now grew bolder, and springing out into the open air, made a circuit of the dwelling, only to return with bristling hair, and growling out his suspicion that all was not right.

His ever-increasing anxiety now began to cause me genuine alarm. I was upon the very point of making a hasty retreat to my vessel, when the thought flashed through my mind: "What! escape these swift-footed phantoms? It were idle to attempt it!" So I determined to take my chances, come what might.

The hut was strongly built and its roof would at least protect us from a flight of poisoned arrow's.

While I was occupied in making a hasty survey of the place, a loud outcry from Bulger startled me. I gave one look and a shiver of fear zigzagged through my body.

An armed band was full in sight.

With fierce shouts, deep and rumbling, they came nearer and nearer. Their massive forms swayed from side to side. Their huge limbs, moved like walking oaks. Their arms seemed the sturdy branches ending in hands which, in the dim morning light, took the shape of gnarled and knotted knobs; terrific strength was shadowed forth by their broad and heavy shoulders. One blow from a hand of such sledge hammer weight would lay a frail creature like me helpless in the dust!

Bulger, brave as he was, quailed at the sight. In an instant I collected my thoughts and breathed a last goodbye to the elder baron and to the gentle baroness, my mother, in their far-away home beneath the northern skies.

Now they had reached the very doorway, and stood beating their huge chests and giving forth deep rumbling sounds.

Instinctively I unsheathed my poniard and brandished it in the air.

The effect was astounding!

With terrific cries, groans and shouts they fell back in the wildest terror, rolling over each other, bounding asunder like gigantic footballs, striking the earth and bounding into an erect position.

When at last these human air-bags settled down into something like rest, one of their number broke out into the most plaintive and beseeching speech which, I afterwards learned, had about the following meaning: "O, Master: O, Magician! O, Mysterious Lump! O, Impenetrable Chunk! put away that dread instrument! Prick us not with its awful point, pierce not our delicate skins. The slightest touch from that frightful blade would cause our bodies to burst like pricked balloons! Fear us not. We are thy friends. We come to conduct thee to our great chief, Ztwish-Ztwish. I am Go-Whizz, thy slave."

Suddenly the truth broke in upon my wondering mind. There was no falsehood in the speaker's words. It was Go-Whizz! The others were his companions—the wretched woebegone bags of bones who had parted with me only the day before.

With a smile and gentle wave of the hand, I hastily returned my dagger to its sheath and gave Go-Whizz to understand that he had nothing to fear from me. Half crazed with curiosity I now advanced to take a closer look at Go-Whizz and his companions. Sober fact is it when I tell you that they were, man for man, the self same beings I first fell in with on my starting out to explore the island.

But this wonderful change you ask? How had they in one short night grown to such herculean build—arms and limbs as massive as those of Japanese wrestlers.

I reply it was all air! When I first met these gentlemen they had not dined. Now they had just come from a hearty meal. For, you must know that I was now in the land of the wonderful Wind Eaters! When the air is calm and the winds asleep, these curious people are obliged to fast, and, their skins hang in wrinkled bags as I have described; but when the wind starts up for a mad frolic or even a gentle puff and blow, these strange creatures at once begin to increase in size, and not long is it before every wrinkle and crease disappear like magic.

As Go-Whizz and his companion stood before me, I was struck by the ridiculous contrast between their voices and the expression of their faces. Yesterday, with their fierce and forbidding faces their voices were soft and flute-like; to-day, their voices were terrible, deep and rumbling, while their faces now puffed out smooth and round seemed wreathed in smiles and good humor.

As I stood lost in wonder at the sight of these strangely-transformed beings, Go-Whizz rumbled out something which I easily understood to be a request that I should permit him to conduct me to the residence of his great chief, Ztwish-Ztwish.

I smiled assent and set about gathering up my traps.

Bulger was completely nonplussed and fixed his lustrous eyes upon me as much as to say:

"Dear little master, how canst thou trust thyself to these huge mountains of flesh, a single one of whom could crush thy frail body as easily as I would a mouse?"

I gave him a few caresses and stroked his silken coat, to let him know I was sure that I was right. Go-Whizz and his band, clumsy as they seemed, were by no means slow of pace. They moved forward at a brisk rate for the air was calm and they had little to carry. Now and then, upon bumping together, they bounded apart like rubber balls. It was a difficult thing for me to keep from laughing, especially when I saw Bulger's look of utter perplexity. He rolled his eyes up at me in the most comical manner. However, at last we entered the village of the Wind Eaters, where the great chief, Ztwish-Ztwish held his court.

He too was puffed out pretty round, although, as I afterwards learned, the laws of the land did not allow him to eat as heartily as his subjects. Here and there a wrinkle was visible. His face and arms didn't have that look of puffy tightness common to his people after a hearty meal. He had already been fully informed of my arrival on his island, and of my extraordinary weight and hardness for my size.

It took about fifteen of the Wind Eaters to balance me in the scales.

Chief Ztwish-Ztwish received Bulger and me with the greatest kindness. I was at once presented to his ministers of state and to the members of his family. Queen Phew-yoo was a very stately dame, dignified and reserved in her manners; but the little princess Pouf-fâh charmed me with her childlike curiosity.

Their excellencies, the ministers of state, stood behind their master and seemed intent upon giving him far more advice than he was willing to listen to. Their names were Hiss-sah, Whirr-Whirr and Sh-Boom.

You may well imagine the excitement created in the home of chief Ztwish-Ztwish by my arrival. From the highest to the lowest, from chief to serving-man, everyone begged and implored to be allowed to feel of me.

Anxious to make a favorable impression upon the strange people so that I might have a good opportunity to study them at my ease, I submitted good-naturedly for an hour or more, to being patted, pinched, prodded, rubbed, and stroked.

It were vain for me to attempt to give you any idea of the thousand and one outcries of surprise, delight, wonder, fear, anxiety, and dread which went up from this multitude of strange beings, who were, although they didn't seem to think so, quite as great curiosities to me as I to them.

My stock of dried fruit was now quite exhausted and I began to feel the gnawings of hunger.

I was always blest with a splendid appetite and the pure bracing air of this island only added to it. Bulger, too, I could see, was casting inquiring glances about in search of some signs of kitchen arrangements. I made known to chief Ztwish-Ztwish, as well as I could, the state of affairs, and he at once summoned Hiss-sah, Whirr-Whirr and Sh-Boom to his side for a consultation.

They held a most animated discussion and one too, which ran from quarter hour to quarter hour without any sign of coming to an end.

All this time my poor stomach was wondering what had cut off the customary supplies.

Like rulers the world over, chief Ztwish-Ztwish was impatient and self-willed. Finally he lost his temper completely and moved about so vigorously that his three ministers were kept continually on the bounce, so to speak.

If you can only wait long enough every thing comes to an end. I was finally bidden to approach the chief, who asked me whether I had, since my arrival on his island, seen anything which I could eat?

I was obliged to confess that I had not. Whereupon there was another consultation, which ended in Ztwish-Ztwish seizing his corkwood club and sending each one of his ministers in a different direction, with three quick smart blows. The sight was so ludicrous that I would willingly have let my dinner go for a chance at the bat myself.

Suddenly an idea came to me. I could see that this settlement of the Wind Eaters was not far from the seashore. So, as best I could, I made chief Ztwish-Ztwish comprehend that I could eat the oysters and other shell fish, of which I had noticed vast quantities lying on the white sands of the ocean.

When the thing was made thoroughly plain to them that I proposed to satisfy my hunger by devouring such horrid and disgusting creatures as lived between these shells, I was really alarmed at the consternation it caused.

Queen Phew-yoo and princess Pouf-fâh were taken ill and withdrew to their apartments in great haste, while one and all, even including the fierce Go-Whizz, were seized with symptoms of nausea. By degrees, however, they recovered and orders were issued to half a dozen serving-men who, not being gorged, were in good marching condition to set out for the shore, and bring a supply of the shell-fish to appease my hunger, which, by this time had really set its teeth in my vitals.

Meanwhile Bulger and I were conducted to a neat bamboo dwelling with an umbrella-shaped roof, and left to ourselves until the supply of food should arrive.

I was too hungry to sleep. And, Bulger, too, was in the same condition. But he was patience itself, as he always is, when he knows that his little master is suffering.

I threw myself down on a heap of dried rushes and my loving companion came and pillowed his head on my arm.

After a tedious wait of an hour or so a great outcry told me that something unusual had happened in the village of the Wind Eaters.

It was the arrival of the serving-men bringing the supply of oysters.

I could hardly restrain myself until chief Ztwish-Ztwish should summon me to break my long fast.

When I reached the chief's quarters I found a vast crowd of people assembled to see the "Lump Man" put solid things down his throat.

Chief Ztwish-Ztwish and his court occupied front seats.

As you know by this time the voice of a Wind Eater depends upon the condition he is in. If he has just eaten and his body is rounded out like a well-filled balloon, his voice is deep and rumbling; if, on the other hand, he has not taken food for a day or so and his skin hangs in folds and wrinkles on his framework of bones, he speaks with a soft, flute-like tone.

As I stepped to the front, followed by Bulger, and took my place beside the heap of oysters, a deafening outcry went up, in which the deep roars of the inflated Wind Eaters were mingled with the soft flute-like tones of the fasting ones. Not noticing any instrument at hand with which to pry the shells open I thoughtlessly drew my poniard from its sheath. In an instant a terrible panic seized upon the assembled multitude. Queen Phew-yoo and princess Pouf-fâh fell into a swoon. Chief Ztwish-Ztwish being in a fasting condition darted away to his apartments like a phantom. The ministers of state, Iliss-sah, Whirr-Whirr and Sh-Boom, being puffed up to their fullest capacity, struck the ground with their feet and rolled out of the way like huge footballs.

Quick as thought I sheathed my dagger, the sight of whose glittering point had brought about all this consternation; and, profiting by the lessons given me at our first meeting by Go-Whizz and his companions, I began a series of head-duckings and walkingbeam motions of my body, which soon restored confidence in my peaceful intentions and brought my scattered audience back to their seats. Go-Whizz, who had run the farthest, was now loudest in his boasts that he had not been the least frightened. Chief Ztwish-Ztwish resumed his seat with considerable nerve, but I noticed that he kept his eyes fastened on the place where I had hidden my dagger in my belt. Although the sight of the toothsome oysters only served to whet my appetite, yet was I now terribly perplexed to know how I should pry the shells open, for the laws of the land of the Wind Eaters visited the death penalty upon any one found with a sharp-pointed instrument in his possession.

In earliest childhood the finger-nails are kept pared down to the flesh, until they lose their power to grow hard, and their place is taken by a piece of tough skin.

Teeth—the Wind Eaters have none; or, more correctly speaking, their teeth do not grow above their gums. Nature seemed to have gradually ceased taking the trouble to supply these people with something for which they had absolutely no use.

You must bear in mind that these curious people had not always been satisfied with such thin diet. In ancient times—so chief Ztwish-Ztwish informed me, their ancestors had been fruit-eaters; the fruits, however, failing, they had been forced to have recourse to the gums which flowed from the trees, and as these gradually dried up, they made discovery that the various winds which blew across the island were filled with some invisible germs or particles, which had the power of sustaining life.

To resume: Observing a flint hatchet lying on the ground, I laid hold of it and set to work opening one of the largest oysters. A deep silence settled upon the assemblage. With a skilful twist, I wrenched the upper shell off, and, raising the lower one, upon which the fat and luscious creature lay unmindful of his impending fate, I opened my mouth and gracefully let the dainty morsel slip out of sight! A hundred cries of half horror, half wonder broke like a great chorus from the surrounding crowds of Wind Eaters. Again and again this outburst died away, only to break forth once more with redoubled vigor.

Many of the lookers-on were made so seriously ill by this—to them—most extraordinary spectacle, that they hastily left the place before I was able to take a second mouthful.

You may fancy how they felt. About as you would were I to begin gulping down bits of stone and iron.

Queen Phew-yoo clung timorously to her husband's arm; but the princess Pouf-fâh stepped boldly nearer to me, so that she might have a better view of the "little man solid all through." Again I raised one of the largest shells and let its occupant slip noiselessly down my throat, not forgetting each time to loosen the white muscle which held the shells together for Bulger's share of the feast.

Gradually the qualms of the Wind Eaters, at sight of a human being swallowing food in lumps, gave place to a devouring curiosity on their part to draw nearer and get a better view of my manner of satisfying hunger.

I could understand enough to know that many of the Wind Eaters had serious doubts that I really swallowed the oysters.

To them, I was little less than some sort of a sleight-of-hand man or doer of tricks.

The little princess Pouf-fâh mounted upon one of the benches, and the instant the oyster disappeared down my throat insisted upon my opening my mouth to its greatest width, in order that she might take a look for herself and see if the oyster were not hidden away under my tongue or in my cheek somewhere.

A sudden scream of terror startled the lookers-on as much as it did me.

The little princess was carried away in a swoon.

It was my teeth! They had frightened the gentle Pouf-fâh half to death.

For a moment all was confusion. Encouraged by Go-Whizz, many of the Wind Eaters seized their clubs and pressed forward with murderous intent. The reappearance of princess Pouf-fâh, bright and smiling, set everything right again.

Now the crowd was seized with unconquerable curiosity to draw near and take a look for themselves at the terrible thing which had thrown Pouf-fâh into a swoon.

My jaws soon began to ache from stretching my mouth wide enough open to give each one of them a glance at my double row of ivory cutters and grinders, and if I do say it myself, I had in those days one of the finest sets of teeth that ever cut their way through a slice of Nienburg biscuit, or ground up a piece of German roast goose.

From now on, these childlike and simple-minded people became pretty thoroughly convinced that the "Little Man Thick All Through" was a kind and peaceful creature and every way perfectly harmless.

The children flocked about me, and encouraged by my smiles and head-duckings soon made friends with me.

I was glad of this, for I was anxious to make a close study of the Wind Eaters young and old.

You may judge of my surprise when I saw a bevy of these children—animated puff-balls that they were—engaged in the to them, novel sport of rushing full tilt at me and bouncing off like rubber balls from a board fence.

Well, I suppose you are bursting with curiosity to hear something more definite about these strange people.

To me they were not entirely unknown. I had read here and there ancient books of travel by Arabian authors, of some such a race; whose bodies were so frail that they were unable to partake of any stronger and heavier food than the sweet gums which flowed from the trees and whose skins were so transparent that they were called "glass-bodied," the beating of their little hearts being plainly visible to the eye of the beholder. I have no doubt that these authors referred to the dwellers of this wonderful island, on which no fruits, berries or edible roots were to be found, and whose ancestors, as I was informed by chief Ztwish-Ztwish, did, in former ages, thus sustain their lives. But I must confess that the fact that there were in existence human beings who literally lived upon air; or, more correctly speaking, upon winds laden with some invisible particles of life-sustaining matter, was a little more than I had ever dared to dream out, even in the most active workings of my imagination. You may judge then of my delight upon finding myself among these extraordinary people, and upon discovering them to be such true children of nature, mild-mannered and peacefully-inclined.

And yet I was not long in making a discovery which proved to be quite an important one to me.

It was this. I learned that although the truth was as I have stated it, that the Wind Eaters are as a rule, a race of peace-loving creatures, gentle in their dispositions and averse to wrong-doing, yet there were exceptions to this general rule. Strange to say, it depended on what wind they fed upon.

All the women, for instance, were gentleness itself. They fed upon the soft zephyrs of the south. But the great majority of these people contented themselves with satisfying their hunger by resorting to the strong and wholesome west wind; while a goodly number, from some idea that it had a sweeter and more delicate flavor, a sort of heavy, nut-like taste, preferred the fitful, irregular east wind. It was however not considered wholesome diet by the best physicians of the nation and they contended that those who made a habit of feeding upon this wind were never as hale and hearty as those who restricted themselves entirely to the nutritious and bracing west wind.

A few there were—as in every land there are those who delight in strong, rich food, who insisted upon feeding on the rugged, gusty north-west wind, claiming that it was best suited to their wants, and that nature had intended man to partake of a wind powerful and strong-bodied, in order to fit them for the battle of life. There were even some—a very few, be it said to the honor of these mild-mannered and peace-loving people, who, contrary to the laws of the land and the express commands of chief Ztwish-Ztwish, welcomed the blowing of the angry whistling, boisterous north-wind, and drank in the dangerous fluid until their better natures were completely changed; and from being gentle, timorous and peace-loving, they became rough, and quarrelsome.

To this ilk belonged Captain Go-Whizz. In fact, as I was told by Whirr-Whirr, chief Ztwish-Ztwish himself showed signs of fear when he saw Go-Whizz come swaggering into the village, his eyes inflamed, his steps unsteady, his speech indistinct after a heavy meal upon the rude and buffeting wind of the north. While in this condition Go-Whizz lost the slight control he had over himself and had, upon one occasion, so far forgotten himself as to breathe out threats and defiance against chief Ztwish-Ztwish, driving that ruler out of his own apartments, by advancing upon him with a bit of flint which he had ground to a dangerously sharp point.

Such were the curious people among whom I now found myself sojourning and on terms of pleasant intimacy with their ruler.

A few days after my arrival at the village of the Wind Eaters, I was, unfortunately the innocent cause of rather a grave accident, which, for a while had the effect of making me somewhat unpopular at the court of chief Ztwish-Ztwish.

It all came about in this way:

I've already told you how quick the children were to discover the solidity of my body and what delight they took in throwing themselves against me full tilt, in order to have the sport of bouncing off again like so many rubber balls.

Now you must keep in mind the fact that even after a hearty meal, a whole dozen of these babies weighed about one good pound.

I used to encourage them to play about me, in order the better to observe their curious tricks and ways, one of which was to lock arms and legs and thus form a chain of human links, one of which being fastened to a peak of the roof and the other possibly to some high staff or pole, at times even extending across the street and ending on the roof of the opposite dwelling. Thus festooned they spent hours swaying to and fro in the cool of the day, often swinging themselves to sleep. And it was not at all an unusual thing to see one of the mothers in search of her child come bustling along, halt, take down the line of living links, unhook her baby, replace the line and hurry away home.

While seated, one day, on the balcony of one of chief Ztwish-Ztwish's cottages, a dozen or more of the children set to work to form such a chain, one end of it being fastened to one of my earrings which, like a good sailor, I took pleasure in wearing at times, and the other reaching nearly to the ground, passing over the high rail of the balcony.

Scrambling, pushing and squirming, uttering the queerest cries, shouts and squeals, these tiny Wind Eaters were half wild with joy, when suddenly one of those nearest me swung against the point of a needle which I had, doubtlessly, thrust into the lapel of my coat the last time I had been doing some mending, for, like a true sailor, I was skilled in the use of needle and thread.

I was aroused from my dreamy contemplation of these fantastic beings by a sharp crack like that made by the bursting of a toy balloon.

Again and again the same sharp noise rang in my ear.

A glance was sufficient to explain it all. I could feel my hair bristling up with horror as I saw the living links of this chain snap asunder, one after the other, and disappear into thin air. Exploded by coming into contact with the needle point, the force of the explosion of the first of these tiny puff-balls of humanity had been sufficient to burst the baby next in the line and so on to the end of the chain!

A dozen of them gone in less than as many seconds and not so much as a lock of hair to carry home to the heart broken mothers!

In a few moments, the news of the accident had spread to every quarter of the village. The weeping, shrieking mothers, howling for vengeance, gathered quickly about the dwelling into the interior of which Bulger and I had retreated.

Now you may believe me when I say, that I would not have stood in the least dread of an army of the Wind Eaters, when they were fully inflated after a hearty meal, but it so happened that the air had been calm for a day or so, and that many of them were now shrunken to the living skeleton size in which I had first met them. In this condition they were foes not to be despised, for, moving as they did, with almost lightning rapidity, their mode of fighting was to entangle their enemy in fine nets, woven of bamboo fibre and then beat them to death with their clubs.

True, these clubs were made of corkwood, and a score of them weighed less than a pound; yet, this fact would only make death slower and more painful; for, while a few blows might suffice to put one of their own kind out of his misery, it would, most surely, have required a whole day for them to beat the life out of such a solid enemy as I was.

Before I had chance to collect my thoughts, Go-Whizz was at the door with his band, their nets coiled to throw over me, while behind the net-throwers stood a row of club-bearers, anxiously awaiting their turn to begin proceedings. Thought I to myself: "This is serious business. If chief Ztwish-Ztwish is not at hand, they will entangle me in their nets and try to beat the life out of me before he returns, for they well know his affection for me." But, worse than all, was the fact that Go-Whizz had just returned from a distant part of the island, whither he and a few of his chums had made a secret journey, in order to gorge themselves on the rude and boisterous north-west wind. He was full of swagger and ire! I had never seen him swollen to such a size. His voice sounded like the deep bellowing of some fierce animal.

He whirled his net in the air, and called out in thundering tones for his men to follow him.

I felt now that the moment had arrived for me to make a desperate effort to save my life and Bulger's, too, for, with his four feet twisted up in one of their nets, he would fall an easy prey to Go-Whizz and his band. I felt, too, that it would be worse than useless to appeal to Go-Whizz for mercy, influenced, as he was, by long and deep draughts of the fierce and raging north-west gale.

There he stood, puffing, blowing, blustering, swaggering, as round and round his head he swung the fatal web, which, the moment I should attempt to take my back from the wall, he intended to cast over me as a fowler would entrap a bird.

Suddenly I bethought myself of the little instrument which had brought me to this dangerous strait.

Before drawing it, however, from its hiding-place, I determined to play the bully and swagger a little myself.

Now, the heaviest Wind Eater weighs about six pounds; and, as you may imagine, my weight, nearly a hundred pounds, was a source of great dread to them. They stood in constant fear that I might accidentally tread upon one of the toes of a Wind Eater and explode him.

Before they would allow me to venture out upon one of their balconies, or to inhabit an upper story of one of their dwellings, they proceeded to strengthen it with the stoutest bamboo poles they could find. So, I now began to give the valiant Go-Whizz a few gentle reminders of my weight and solidity.

Leaping high into the air, I landed upon the bamboo flooring with such a thump that everything creaked and trembled.

At first there was a general stampede of Go-Whizz's followers, and that blustering leader was the only one left to face Bulger and me.

He stood his ground pretty bravely, although I could see that he was half inclined to heed the cries of his men and make his way out of the dwelling before I succeeded in wrecking it. But, after a few more of my jumps, seeing that the flooring withstood all my efforts to break it down, Go-Whizz succeeded in rallying his band.

Again, and now more furious than ever, they surrounded us, shrieking and howling like mad, their uplifted right hands bearing the dangerous nets, with which they hoped to entangle Bulger and me, and then dispatch us.

Now, it was high time for me to fall back on my reserves.

I did so. The effect was simply astounding. The needle proved to be one of the kind used for darning; very long and bright, and exceedingly sharp-pointed. My dagger point was bad enough. It had thrown them into a wild and panicky fear. But, this little instrument, as I brandished it in front of them, threw them into fits of rigid terror.

They stood rooted to the ground, their bulging eyes riveted upon the needle-point as if they, one and all, expected it to prick them to death if they stirred an inch.

At last, making a mighty effort, Go-Whizz broke away from the spot, uttering a deep and rumbling cry of horror, his men rolling after him, in the wildest terror. When they saw the tumultuous manner in which the valiant Go-Whizz and his followers retreated from my presence, the assembled men and women, with frightful cries, took to their heels as if a legion of demons were pursuing them.

In a few moments Bulger and I stood alone on the battle field. He had not budged from my side during the time that death threatened me.

"Come!" said I, as I stooped and stroked his head. "Come, thou faithful friend and companion, let us go to chief Ztwish-Ztwish and lay the matter before him!"

The chief had just awoke from a noonday nap. He had calmly slept through the whole conflict, and so it was necessary for me to give him a full account of the unfortunate accident which resulted in exploding an entire string of babies, and of Go-Whizz's attempt to slay me. He listened with great calmness and most patiently too. He then begged to be excused for a few moments as an attendant had just informed him that a very soft and sweet south wind had begun to blow.

He stepped out on the balcony; and after he had taken about a dozen mouthfuls of the pure, refreshing breeze, returned looking a little plumper and, like all men after enjoying a meal of favorite food, was still more amiable and kindly in his manner than before.

The news that a dozen of the smallest subjects had been so unceremoniously popped out of existence didn't seem to worry him very much. What moved him most of all, was the fact which, apparently, up to that hour had never entered into his mind, namely, that a point so fine, so delicate, so deadly, so nearly invisible, could be created by the hand of man!

I assured him that it was that very moment hidden in the stuff of my garb, right in front of his eyes.

He trembled.

I strove to reassure him, by explaining to him that I would as soon think of plunging my poniard into my own heart as of turning this almost invisible and yet deadly point against his life.

He tried to smile, but it ended in a shudder.

"Thinkest thou, little man thick-all-through," asked chief Ztwish-Ztwish with a trembling tongue, "that I may look upon it and not fall into a swoon?"

"O, most assuredly, great chief:" was my reply. "In fact, most light and buoyant Ztwish-Ztwish," I continued, "I can rob this dreaded instrument of all its power to injure thee and place it in thy hand like any harmless bit of wood. Is it thy will that I should thus deliver to thee this dreaded point?"

With a slight shiver, chief Ztwish-Ztwish made answer:

"Ay, great and learned little master, I think I can bear the sight of it now. I am, indeed, very brave, but thou knowest a single prick of that deadly point would instantly end the life of the sturdiest Wind Eater."

I again assured him that there was really nothing to dread so long as he followed my directions. So saying I drew the darning needle from its hiding place.

Chief Ztwish-Ztwish closed his eyes at first, but gradually grew bold enough to gaze upon the glittering point.

Stooping down I picked up one of the cork clubs and breaking off a bit of the smaller end thrust the needle point into it.

Chief Ztwish-Ztwish watched my movements with a sort of painful curiosity.

"There, great chief of the Wind Eaters," I exclaimed, "now thou mayest toy with it, hide it in the rushes of thy bed, it cannot injure thee! It is as harmless as a pebble rounded by the sportive, sparkling waters of one of thy mountain brooks. Take it! it may serve thee some day, in case of a sudden attack upon thy illustrious person."

"At such a moment, fear naught! seize it firmly, draw its dreaded point from its hiding place in this bit of cork. So small is it that it will be invisible in thy hand, and while thine enemy stands before thee in fancied safety, pierce him to death; for, thou are ruler and it is fitting that death should strike him who attempts to rob thy people of their chief!"

Chief Ztwish-Ztwish took the needle with trembling hand, and hid the bit of cork which held it under the thatch of the roof. Then, calling out, he summoned one of his serving-men and bade him bring from a neighboring apartment a certain small bamboo chest, from which he drew a string of rare jewels somewhat of the nature of amber, only a thousand times more brilliant. With this beautiful gift he dismissed me, issuing orders to his ministers that no harm should be allowed to come to me for the accident which exploded the string of little Wind Eaters.

Go-Whizz could with difficulty hide his anger at seeing me once more an honored guest at the court of chief Ztwish-Ztwish.

I did not relax my vigilance in the least, however. Every night I barred the windows with my own hands, and placed Bulger's mat of rushes in front of the door, so that it would be impossible for the wrathful leader to surprise me.

Now that the explosion of the babies was quite forgotten, my sojourn among the Wind Eaters would have continued to be extremely pleasant, had not a new difficulty arisen to cause me anxiety.

The rather thin diet upon which I had been existing, since my arrival among these curious people, while it appeased my hunger, robbed me of that plump and well-fed look which I had always had, I found myself losing flesh at an alarming rate. Chief Ztwish-Ztwish and queen Phew-yoo were delighted, for as they expressed it, "the little man thick-all-through was rapidly becoming in appearance at least, a genuine Wind Eater."

Bulger, too, fell away dreadfully.

Now and then I surprised him with his dark, lustrous eyes fixed upon me with as much as to say: "O, little master, what is the matter with us? We eat, and yet we grow thin. Are we really turning to Wind Eaters?"

And another bad phase of the matter was, that while my ever-increasing leanness was causing me so much anxiety, it was carrying joy to the heart of queen Phew-yoo who, it seems, had formed the plan of keeping me for the rest of my life in the service of her lord and master by bestowing upon me the hand of the fair princess Pouf-fâh.

Queen Phew-yoo's explanation of my ever-increasing thinness was, that it was the effect of the wonderful atmosphere of their island; that it mattered very little how thick and solid a man might be, if he lived long enough among them, he would gradually lose it and become, if not a genuine Wind Eater, at least almost as light and airy a being as they were.

As I learned of these views from others before hearing them from the queen's own lips, it was not at all a surprise for me, one day to receive a message from the stately Phew-yoo summoning me to present myself before her.

She accorded me a very gracious reception, and princess Pouf-fâh too, showed great delight at seeing me under her mother's roof. She bounced hither and thither like a toy balloon, now shaking perfume from dried flowers, now holding up strings of the curious gems, which I have already mentioned, and making them glisten in front of my face.

I amused her by holding her out on the palm of my hand and tossing her up and catching her, as I would a rubber ball.

Queen Phew-yoo looked on in mute satisfaction.

When Princess Pouf-fâh had grown weary of play, the queen spoke as follows:

"O, little man thick-all-through, I have to say to thee that which will gladden thy heart. The great chief, my husband, and I have noticed with joy that day by day thou art growing thinner and thinner. Know then, that this is the magical effect of the air thou breathest. When our forefathers landed on this island, they, like thee were solid all through. Therefore, be not alarmed when, a few months hence, thou findest thyself completely changed. Thou wilt, ere long, lose this heavy load of useless flesh, which thou hast been for so long a time condemned to carry about with thee, and become light and buoyant, like us. And, O beloved Lump, that thou mayest hasten the change from thy present solid form and become a graceful and hollow being like one of us, I do, with the chief Ztwish-Ztwish's counsel and consent, accord thee permission to eat with us each day. This very hour shalt thou make thy first meal upon the sweet and wholesome wind of the South. The very moment, little Chunk, that thou hast become thin enough to suit the great chief, he will give thee the fair princess Pouf-fâh for thy wife."

At these words, the princess, who really seemed to be very fond of me, clapped her hands joyfully, and bounced between her mother and me like a toy football.

"But, little Man-Lump," continued queen Phew-yoo, "before we set out to dine on the sweet wind which blows over Banquet Hill, there are two things which the great chief Ztwish-Ztwish said I must be very particular to mention to you, the two conditions upon which he is willing to honor you above all men, by bestowing the hand of the beautiful princess Pouf-fâh upon thee."

"Name them, gracious queen!" I cried, for I was too wise to raise any objections at this point. I knew only too well that a single word from chief Ztwish-Ztwish would hand me over to the tender mercies of the fierce Go-Whizz.

"They are," resumed queen Phew-yoo, puffing out her cheeks and tapping them playfully with the backs of her thumbs, "they are, little man thick-all-through, that thou shalt file thy teeth down even with thy gums and keep thy nails always pared down to the flesh."

"It shall be, gracious queen, as thou desirest," I replied, with several low bendings of my body.

"Then," answered queen Phew-yoo gayly, "there remains nothing for thee to do but to begin at once to accustom thyself to our food; so let us set out for Banquet Hill without delay, for the sweet south wind is blowing fresh and strong!"

I accompanied queen Phew-yoo and princess Pouf-fâh to the place indicated. It was a beautiful knoll, from which I could look far away to southward over a valley, enchantingly fair.

She and the princess at once began to inhale the soft, sweet air, and encouraged me to do the same.

They were delighted with my efforts. In fact, the motherly Phew-yoo seemed a little bit anxious lest I should overeat myself.

After the princess had taken a few deep draughts, I was surprised to see an attendant approach her and place about her throat a necklace of beads, strung upon an elastic cord. This was a precaution to prevent the princess from eating too heartily, were she so inclined. Well, as you may imagine, I returned to my apartments from dining with queen Phew-yoo and princess Pouf-fâh on Banquet Hill a very hungry man; if that were possible, hungrier than I was before, for the pure, fresh air and many deep breaths had fairly made me ravenous.

Once more alone with Bulger, I set to work thinking out some scheme to get hold of more food; and, by checking my alarming loss of flesh, put an end to queen Phew-yoo's plan of transforming me into a genuine Wind Eater and giving me the princess Pouf-fâh for a wife.

It occurred to me that possibly I might catch some fish in one of the arms of the sea nearest to the village and broil it on live embers, for I had my tinder box in my pocket.

This plan worked to a charm. I soon succeeded in teaching several of the serving-men to rig up a number of their war-nets as a sort of seine, and was overjoyed the first time I cast it to make a haul of a dozen or more fine sea-bass.

Bulger entered into the sport with great zeal, seizing a rope in his mouth and tugging away for dear life, as we began to haul in.

The next thing was to gather some dry leaves and wood, and start a suitable fire to make a bed of embers. Crowds of the Wind Eaters gathered about me and watched my movements with a sort of mixture of wonder, fear and pleasure.

When at last the smoke began to curl up, and the flame showed itself, cries of consternation broke forth, and a wild stampede ensued.

Chief Ztwish-Ztwish was hastily summoned; but, I had no difficulty in convincing him that I intended no injury to anyone, that the red tongues which he saw darting forth were perfectly harmless if they did not come in contact with one's flesh; that it would only be necessary for him to issue a command forbidding the people to approach too near to the tongues of crimson which darted from the black clouds of smoke.

By the time the live embers had formed I was ready with a dressed sea-bass of about two pounds' weight, and the cooking began.

It is needless for me to assure you that Bulger and I sat down to a delightful meal, really the first satisfactory one since my arrival among the Wind Eaters.

From this time on all went well. Every day my oyster gatherers and my fishermen made their visit to the shore to keep my larder supplied. Upon their return, I was always in readiness with a fine bed of embers. So things went on for a week or so. I was delighted to find Bulger and myself gaining flesh in splendid style. And still, every now and then I was obliged to accept queen Phew-yoo's invitation to dine with her and the princess Pouf-fâh at Banquet Hill, where I pretended to enjoy a meal on the soft and perfumed south wind quite as much as they did themselves. Queen Phew-yoo insisted that my complexion was growing clearer and more transparent every day, and that, beyond all doubt, in a few months I would be able entirely to give up a "swallowing stones" as she called it.

While I was quietly pursuing my studies of these curious people, another unfortunate occurrence took place, and this time it turned out to be a very grave and serious matter.

The Wind Eaters were not long in getting accustomed to the, to them, at first, startling sight of "crimson tongues darting from the mouths of black clouds." In fact, they soon learned to like the odor of the delicate morsels as they lay broiling on the embers, and when the air was chilly, didn't hesitate to form a circle around Bulger and me as we sat eating our dinner and enjoy the warmth, and to them, curious spectacle at the same time. It so happened that one evening, I had left a deeper bed of embers than I had imagined. The ashes collected over them and they continued to glow till nightfall. A band of roysterers belonging to the Go-Whizz faction, by the merest chance, returned homeward that night from a trip to the north shore of the island, where they had gorged themselves upon the boisterous wind of that quarter. Attracted by the glow of the remaining embers, they made haste to gather a lot of wood, threw it upon the smoldering fire, and, as the flames began to thrust out their red tongues here and there, ranged themselves in a circle to enjoy the warmth, for the night was damp and chilly.

So pleasant did they find the effects of the warmth that they resolved to pass the night there and threw themselves down on the ground as close to the fire as they deemed it prudent to go.

About midnight a gentle scratching on my arm from Bulger's paw, told me that something unusual had happened, for he never awakened me unless he was quite sure that the matter was serious enough to warrant him in disturbing me.

I found the village in the wildest state of alarm. Ear-piercing screams from the women mingled with the deep rumbling outcries of the men.

You have no doubt, already guessed what had happened. The facts were simply these: In the night, the cold had increased, and several of the Wind Eaters, half asleep, and half stupefied by the deep draughts of the boisterous north-west wind, had approached closer and closer to the fire, when suddenly the vast quantity of cold air which they had swallowed began to expand and four of them exploded with a terrific noise.

In quicker time than it takes to tell it, my dwelling was surrounded by a screaming, shrieking, howling mob of Wind Eaters, demanding my instant death.

It required all of chief Ztwish-Ztwish's influence with his people to save me from being entangled in their fatal nets and beaten to death on the spot.

To make matters a thousand times worse, the bully and swaggerer, Go-Whizz, entered the village at this very moment, with a pack of his quarrelsome hangers-on at his heels. He had been away on a secret trip to the farthest northern point of the island, where the north wind howls and roars its maddest. I had never seen him puffed up so to the very bursting point with his favorite food.

When he heard of the fate which had overtaken his four comrades, his fury knew no bounds. He and his followers pounded their chests until the air quivered with deep and rumbling sounds, while ever and anon they broke out into the wildest lamentations for their dead companions. He openly and boldly charged chief Ztwish-Ztwish with having betrayed his people and given over their once happy island to certain ruin at the hands of the "little monster thick-all-through," who, by his dread magic and foul mysteries, would soon bring their people to feed upon stones like himself.

Day now began to break; and with the coming light, the confusion in the village seemed to take on new strength. So sure was I that death was about to strike me that I wrote out several messages to the elder baron and to the gentle baroness, my mother, on the leaves of my note-book, and left directions with one of the chief's serving-men that, in case of my death, it was my wish that he should send them to my people, whom he would find on my ship in the beautiful bay on the distant shore of the island.

I said nothing about Bulger, for I knew only too well that he would die by my side.

I prepared for the worst. I examined the primings of my pocket-pistols, and concealed my dagger under my coat at the back of my neck, where I would be better able to reach it, if it came to close quarters.

This done, I proceeded to cut my finger-nails to as sharp points as I could, for I was determined to sell my life as dearly as possible.

While I felt confident of chief Ztwish-Ztwish's affection for me, yet I couldn't tell at what moment he might lose courage and turn me over to the mob, in order to save himself.

Bulger watched all my preparations with wide-opened and intelligent eyes, occasionally giving utterance to a low, nervous whine, as the howling, shrieking, roaring mob surged back and forth in front of chief Ztwish-Ztwish's dwelling.

By the law of the land, the common people were prohibited from entering the inner enclosure of the chief's abode, but Go-Whizz, being one of the nobles or minor chiefs, was entitled to advance into the chief's presence and state his wrongs or make his requests.

So now, the raging Go-Whizz, parting from his followers, who never ceased crying out for vengeance upon the "little demon Lump," who, on two different occasions, had spread death and destruction among their people, strode into the presence of chief Ztwish-Ztwish.

The chief was calm. He had not partaken of food for four and twenty hours, and stood up, wrinkled, creased and seamed, as the Wind Eaters always look when fasting. Near him sat queen Phew-yoo and princess Pouf-fâh, while directly behind him were ranged his three councillors, Hiss-sah, Whirr-Whirr, and Sh-Boom. They were well-rounded out by recent draughts of the strong and wholesome west wind, and hence, looked as contented and smiling as Ztwish-Ztwish looked sad and solemn. I stood in an adjoining apartment, concealed behind a bamboo screen, with my faithful Bulger by my side. I was so placed that I could see all, without being seen myself. Chief Ztwish-Ztwish knew of my presence there.

As Bulger caught a glimpse of the raging and bellowing Go-Whizz, he grew so nervous that I was obliged to stoop and stroke his head to let him know I feared nothing. But the fact of the matter is, great dangers always exert a subduing influence upon me.

I face them cooly, but sadly, for my thoughts in such moments go back to the elder baron and to the gentle baroness, my mother, in the far-away home 'neath the skies of the beloved fatherland.

Like a huge football impelled by the kick of some gigantic foot, Go-Whizz landed in the audience chamber of chief Ztwish-Ztwish. He shook his arms violently, and bounded up and down with inward fury, for he was still too much beside himself with rage to utter any other sound than a deep rumbling growl or mutter.

From my place behind the bamboo screen I followed, with all the keenness of sight for which I am so justly famous, every movement of the furious Go-Whizz, as well as the actions and demeanor of chief Ztwish-Ztwish and of his councillors, for I was determined not to be caught napping in case any signs of treachery should be visible. At the very first glance I saw that the rebellious Go-Whizz had something hidden in his girdle, and from the shape and length I knew at once that it was a flint knife. Quick as thought, I beckoned a serving man to my side and sent a message to the chief, telling the attendant to appear to be engaged in waving the branches of perfumed leaves as was his duty while he whispered it in the chief's ear.

It was as follows:

"Be on thy guard! O, Chief. The brawler hath a flint knife hidden in his girdle. He will attempt to slay thee. Be careful! Be calm!"

Go-Whizz had now quieted down a little; but, with a voice of thunder, he began his tirade. He pictured the long years of peace and happiness on their island, the blessings they had enjoyed under the long and glorious line of rulers of which Ztwish-Ztwish was the worthy descendant. He thundered out defiance against all the enemies of the Wind Eaters and as softly as possible roared his own praises telling of the many deeds of valor he had performed in Ztwish-Ztwish's service and ended by declaring himself ready and willing to die for his beloved chief.

When Go-Whizz had spoken, the chief bowed his head for a few moments in silence and then made answer: "Thou hast spoken truly and wisely, O Go-Whizz! Thou art brave. Thou hast the right to demand favor at my hands! Speak, Go-Whizz, what may Ztwish-Ztwish do for thee?"

At these words of Ztwish-Ztwish, all the former fury of Go-Whizz broke forth once more. Pounding his chest and striding up and down the audience chamber, he roared out:

"That thou givest into my hands this very hour, the 'Solid Demon,' the dreaded 'Man-Lump,' the monster 'Thick-All-Through' who hath brought all this death and ruin into our peaceful land!"

Chief Ztwish-Ztwish was silent for a few moments.

Need I tell you that my very heart listened for the reply?

I could hear nothing but the deep, coarse, grating sound of Go-Whizz's breath as I leaned forward to catch the first word which should fall from the chief's lips.

It seemed a lifetime. At length Ztwish-Ztwish spoke:

"My brother, thou art inflamed with the deep draughts of the fierce and raging north wind! Thou art beside thyself. Thou seest not clearly! I must not adjudge death except when the decree will rest on the laws of our fathers. True, the 'Little Man-Thick-All-Through' hath been the cause of great misfortune to our people, but the innocent cause. He hath not striven or desired to harm us. He is a lover of peace, a friend of his kind. My followers were warned of the danger of the crimson tongues. The 'Man Lump' did not seek their death. And full well too, thou knowest that the laws of our fathers bid us to hold the lives of our guests as sacred as the texture of our skin. Go thy way, therefore, Go-Whizz, I cannot doom the 'Man Lump' to death."

"Is this," roared the disappointed leader, "the kind of justice which thou givest to my people?"

"Ay, is it, thou brawler!" replied chief Ztwish-Ztwish, now fast losing control over himself. "Hold thy peace and depart, lest in my wrath at thy frequent wrong doing I give thee over to merited punishment!"

"Have a care, Ztwish-Ztwish!" roared Go-Whizz, boiling over with rage, "have a care lest thy people rise in their might and cast thee out, thou unjust ruler!"

"Begone, I say!" was Ztwish-Ztwish's calm but stern reply.

"Go thou first, then, traitor to thy people!" thundered out Go-Whizz, springing forward with the flint knife raised high in the air.

Cries of terror burst from those gathered in the audience chamber. But chief Ztwish-Ztwish calmly put forth his hand and touched the would-be assassin.

With a deafening crack the body of the raging Go-Whizz flew into a thousand pieces, like a huge balloon seized by the hands of the tempest and whirled against the spear-like branches of some shattered oaken monarch of the plain.

Queen Phew-yoo and princess Pouf-fâh, bewildered and terror-stricken, clung to each other, while silent fear sat on the faces of those around the chief. But he was calm, and spoke a few words in a mild and steady voice to the queen and the princess.

When the people learned of Go-Whizz's attempt to slay their ruler and how the brawler, at the very instant he lifted the flint knife to strike, had been mysteriously stricken dead at Ztwish-Ztwish's feet, they sent up loud huzzas, for the fierce Go-Whizz was more feared than loved, even by his followers.

It required several days for the village of the Wind Eaters to quiet down and take on its every-day look, after the mysterious death of Go-Whizz; but, with his disappearance vanished all opposition to chief Ztwish-Ztwish's rule.

The people firmly believed that it was the avenging spirits of the air who had touched the brawler with their sword points when he raised his hand against their ruler.

I need hardly tell you that the chief's gratitude to me knew no bounds. No gifts were too beautiful or too costly to be offered me. And the fact that I declined them all, only seemed to strengthen his affection for me.

But how could I, how dared I reject the gift of the hand of the fair princess Pouf-fâh?

To do this would be to undo all that I have done, to make Ztwish-Ztwish my enemy, to transform his love into hate, his confidence into suspicion—possibly to write my own death warrant.

There was but one course left for me to pursue. And that was escape!

And escape, too, it must be at once, before I had lost the chief's confidence. One of Ztwish-Ztwish's first acts after his rescue from the flint knife of the murderous Go-Whizz, was to restore to me the tiny instrument with the invisible point.

This done, a terrible load seemed to be lifted from his mind. He became himself again. And with his returning happiness and content, came a still stronger desire to hasten my marriage with the princess Pouf-fâh.

With the greatest caution, I made this and that excuse, in order to gain time to collect my thoughts and settle upon some sure plan of escape, for recapture I knew meant death, or worse than death—imprisonment until I should consent to give up all desire to leave the island of the Wind Eaters, and pledge myself to become, so far as nature would permit, one of their people.

Cautious as I was, my excuses awakened suspicion.

The first proof of this was to find that orders had been given to cut off my supply of fish.

Queen Phew-yoo was afraid that so long as I was permitted to have all the solid food I wanted, I would not grow thin enough to be content with air diet, and, therefore, not satisfied to make my home among them for the rest of my life.

The next thing to happen to me was to find my supply of oysters and mussels reduced one-half by orders of Phew-yoo. This meant yield or starve!

It struck me like a bolt out of a clear sky!

But it has always been just such blows as this which have, throughout my life, aroused me to calm, quick, intelligent action.

I hesitated no longer. My plan reached perfection in a single moment. When nightfall came I hastily scrawled a few lines addressed to my sailing-master, telling him of the fate which threatened to overtake me and bidding him arm a few trusty men and hasten to my rescue. This I tied to the collar of my loved and faithful Bulger. He covered my hand with caresses and I held him clasped in my arms for an instant while the tears fell hot and fast. Then I softly opened the door of my bamboo lodge.

The night was bright and glorious. "Away, my beloved Bulger!" I whispered, stooping and pressing my lips for the last time on his silken ears and shapely head. "To the ship! Away!" He paused, looked into my face, gave a low whine as if to say: "Ay, ay, little master, I understand!" And away he sprang like the wind. For an instant I could follow him as with a long and sturdy bound he sped along! And then he was gone!

The next morning, to my utter astonishment, I was informed that all the preparations for the marriage of the princess Pouf-fâh and the "little man thick-all-through," were completed and that the feasting and merrymaking would begin the day following.

This piece of news, startling as it was, I received with perfect calmness. I completely disarmed all suspicion by my apparent satisfaction with the bright prospect of becoming the son-in-law of the great chief Ztwish-Ztwish. I searched my pockets for trinkets to bestow upon the light and airy Pouf-fâh.

Queen Phew-yoo was not visible. So great had been the joy of her mother's heart that in a moment of weakness she had partaken too greedily of the rich, but unwholesome east wind and was now suffering from a fearful attack of dyspepsia.

This was a most fortunate thing for me, for I am quite certain that queen Phew-yoo would never have consented to allow me to return to my own apartments that night. There was now but one thing left for me to do and that was to make for the distant sea-coast, where I had left my ship and crew.

And start, too, that very night. As ill luck would have it, chief Ztwish-Ztwish, noticing that a delightfully strong west wind had begun to blow insisted upon having a sort of preliminary feast about sundown.

I was invited to join the party.

Not daring to refuse, I set out with the merry-makers and not only tired myself out by making frantic efforts to fill myself with their invisible food but it was nearly midnight before the village grew perfectly quiet and everybody seemed to have closed the doors and windows of his dwelling. But, after all, the rioting of the Wind Eaters was a fortunate thing for me. They went to bed so gorged with many and deep draughts of the hearty and filling west wind, that they slept like logs, if you will allow me to compare puff-balls to solid wood.

I waited until the rumbling of the voices had died away as the last group of roysterers broke up and the solitary Wind Eaters, scattered along the streets, disappeared one by one into their bamboo dwellings.

Leaving my door fastened on the inside, I sprang lightly through the window, and under cover of the deep shadows made my way unnoticed to the outskirts of the town. Here I broke into a sharp run, for at very most I would have but six hours' start of the Wind Eaters and that was far too little; for, as I have already told you, they flit along like phantoms when in a fasting condition, and even when pretty well filled, are very swift of foot—more especially if the air be quiet so as not to impede their advance.

On, on, I sped with a desperate resolve to make such a good use of my start as to make it impossible for them to overtake me.

To my horror, after about an hour's run I noticed that my legs were beginning to tire.

This was a terrible blow to me. For a few moments I staggered along half unconscious of where I was, whither I was hastening and of the awful danger threatening me. All at once the truth of the matter broke upon me.

I was but the wreck of my former self. The long months of fish diet had robbed my muscles of that wonderful strength and elasticity which was once my pride and my chief dependence in moments of peril.

Frail as I had grown, my legs now bent beneath me.

Slower and slower grew my pace. My heart seemed to swell and shut out the very breath of life.

On, ever onward, I toiled with a desperate effort to escape my pursuers, whose rumbling voices it half seemed to me were faintly booming in the distance.

But Nature would do no more!

I reeled, I staggered, I stopped, I fell!

How long I lay there I know not. But when I came to myself, I could plainly feel that change in the air which tells of the coming day. The rippling of a brook fell on my ear. I dragged my aching body in the direction the sound came from. A deep pull at the cool, clear water of the brook refreshed me somewhat. I attempted to rise; but, O, new loss of hope—to discover that my joints had stiffened while sleeping on the ground, uncovered, yes, even ill-clad, for I had left one piece of my clothing hanging on the window-sill of my lodge in the village, to quiet any suspicion which might arise in the minds of the serving-men.

Thoughts of home, however, of the elder baron, of the gentle baroness, my mother, of my loved Bulger, flitted through my fevered brain, and prompted me to make one more effort to regain my feet and escape death at the hands of chief Ztwish-Ztwish's enraged people, who would soon be bounding along, up hill and down dale, like spirits of the wind, as they were.

A groan escaped my lips as I rose to my feet, so like knife-points in my joints were the pains which shot through my frame.

But I must try to be up and away, even though the effort cost me a thousand agonizing twinges.

I owe it to the loved ones at home to push on till I fall utterly broken, till, like a stricken beast, robbed of the power to stand, I should topple and fall at the feet and at the mercy of my pursuers.

Such were the thoughts which oppressed my poor, reeling brain.

A terrible mystery, a torturing dream weighed me down.

I still had my mind. I could see. I could feel. I could hear. And why should I not rise and move onward, and away from the certain death which hovered over me?

Crazed by such thoughts, I struggled to my feet and staggered along, sending forth a groan with every step!

But I had steeled myself to the task, and dragged myself along, still oppressed by some strange and mysterious power, which gave to every pebble the rock's size, and widened every gully to a yawning chasm, on the brink of which I paused in sickening fear of plunging into some black abyss. And yet, oh joy! gradually the films faded from my eyes, the mysterious power lifted its spell from my brain. I felt more like myself.

I saw clearer. My step grew firmer. Now, at last, thought I, all is going well!

When, suddenly, a long, blue-gray streak of light flashed along over the heads of the hills in the far distant eastern sky. It was the signal of morning!

Again, with a groan I sank on my knees, caught myself, rose half-dazed, pressed on again, slowly, slowly, every step jarring on my heated brain like a hammer's blow; but still onward, onward!

A terrible grip as of some giant hand—palm of iron and fingers of steel—set itself on my very vitals. The thought that even now my escape was known to my enemies, that the phantom Wind Eaters, armed with their nets and clubs, were flitting out of the streets of chief Ztwish-Ztwish's village, charged to carry me back alive to a worse death than death itself, or slay me for having broken faith and set the face of honesty over my fraud and deceit, seemed to paralyze my limbs and rob me of the little strength I had left.

Still on and ever onward I struggled, like one in the dull stupor of the wine cup. Fast! ah, too fast that streak of gray dawn lengthened and widened and the orb of day shot up through the morning shadows a messenger of light here and there, now weak and fitful, now stronger and farther reaching.

I saw them, ay, I felt them, for in my dread of them they seemed to flash toward me and strike my half closed eyes, as if knocking at the windows of my soul and rousing me to move out of death's harm.

For a brief moment I halted as if expecting some fond, familiar voice to ring in my ears.

It came.

It was the gentle baroness, my mother! Gently, softly, sweetly, that well-known voice came floating on the morning air bidding me take heart, calling me by name just as in childhood's days, and saying: "My baby! my boy! my son! my darling! Rouse thee! Press on! Press on quickly!" And then I took heart.

The fearful clamp set on my breast relaxed its hold.

I could feel my strength returning. But oh, so slowly, so slowly! Still, it was on its way back at last! I could feel my feet grow lighter. With some effort I quickened my pace almost to a run.

On, on, I sped, now every instant giving me new strength, every motion sending the warm blood tingling to my fingers' ends.

The spell had been lifted! I was myself again!

Swifter, and swifter my pace quickened until I flew along as in days of old, when with ease I left all comers far behind me!

Methought I could almost hear the plash of the waves on the snow-white sands of that beautiful harbor where my good ship lay.

On, and ever onward, I sped with a new and mysterious strength. I was astounded at my own deeds. I was almost afraid, so fast I was bounding along, lest again some demon of the air should touch my limbs and stay my course.

But hark! Didn't you hear that deep rumble?

The sky is clear. It cannot have been the voice of the storm fiend.

Ha! again, deeper and clearer than before, that hoarse, low, muttering rumble, half-roar, half-growl comes borne along on the wings of the awakened breeze.

Lost! Lost! Lost!

It is the cry of the pursuers, it is the voice of the enemy!

Those children of the air are on my track. They follow me with leap and jump. What madness to think to outrun them. Let me halt and die like a man! Look how they bound along over the plain!

Swift and noiseless are their steps, phantoms that they are!

I halt. I turn. I grasp my fire-arm! Too late! A score of entangling nets envelope me! I struggle only to entwine myself the more, arms, hands, legs, feet, are twisted in wretched confusion.

I sway, fall, roll over, wrapped 'round and 'round in that dreadful tangle!

And now down upon my defenceless body comes a rain of sharp, stinging blows. Deep rumbling cries fill the air and keep time in a wild way with the showers of blows rained on my face and head and hands.

As they continue they seem to increase in strength.

The pain, bearable at first, now becomes excruciating.

The light goes out of my eyes, swollen shut as they are beneath this cruel pelting.

A thousand ringing sounds assail my ears.

My brain reels—I am going—going—dying—

When, hark again!

You can not hear it! Your ears would not know it! But mine do! Mine do!

'Tis Bulger's bark and I am saved! Faster and faster the Wind Eaters ply their clubs.

I do not heed them. I do not feel them now, for nearer and nearer comes that joyous music.

'Tis here!

I'm strong again. I rise half up—my lips move—I speak—I cry out: "Quick, good Bulger, or all is lost!" A single glance at the terrible plight of his little master tells him all. With a howl of rage, his dark eyes shooting flame, he throws himself upon the heels of the Wind Eaters. His sharp teeth pierce like needles!

Crack!

Again and again he sends his fangs through the skin of a Wind Eater.

Crack! Crack!

Their clubs cease swinging. A cry of horror goes up, as for the fourth time good Bulger's teeth pierces the heel of a Wind Eater and sends his body with a loud report to vanish into thin air.

They turn; they break away in wild dismay; they fly for their lives, casting away their clubs and abandoning their victim. I could see no more.

It grew black, a vertigo seized me. I tried to free my hands to touch my loved Bulger, for death, I thought, had come!

When life came back Bulger was licking my hands and face and whining piteously. He had gnawed the netting free from the limbs of his little master.

With a cry of joy and a brust of tears, I caught that faithful, loving creature to my breast.

At that instant, distant shouts came floating over the hills. They came from my sailing-master and his relief party.

I could not answer. But Bulger raised his head and sent forth a few sharp barks to tell them where we were.

In a short half hour they were at my side.

After my bruised face and hands had been bathed in cool water and I had swallowed a few mouthfuls of wine, I felt strong enough to get on my feet and move slowly forward.

Bulger walked proudly by my side, pausing ever and anon to look me in the face, meaning to ask:

"How goes it with thee, little master?" Once on shipboard, strengthened by good food and cheered by the comforts of my cabin, I was not long in getting my health back again. After a week's rest, I gave orders to weigh anchor and turn our good ship's head northward, for I was anxious, very anxious to see the elder baron and the gentle baroness, my mother, and tell them all about the wonderful things I had seen.

CHAPTER VI.

Upon my return from my first journey to far away lands, the elder baron and his faithful spouse, my beloved mother, followed by all the retainers of the household, met Bulger and me at the outer gate and welcomed us home with that wild and boisterous joy which only German hearts are capable of.

The elder baron threw his arms around my neck, and, forgetful of the fact that I was only half his size, lifted me completely off the ground in the unreasoning joy of a father's heart, nearly throttling me.

I kicked vigorously, but, the soft felt soles of my oriental shoes prevented me from giving him to understand that he was fast choking me to death.

At last my thoughtful mother noticed that I was growing black in the face, and laying hold of my legs, pulled me downward out of the dangerous embrace in which the elder baron had wrapped me. Not, however, until my father's Nuremberg egg had bored painfully into my protuberant brow, adding another bump to that already bumpy territory. Upon noticing which the elder baron dispatched an attendant to his apartment with orders to search his medicine chest for a bottle of volatile liniment. In his eagerness to undo the harm he had inflicted, he poured a stream of acrid liquid into my eyes, causing me intense suffering. This red and inflamed condition of my eyes, however, the tenants, and retainers attributed to my emotion upon entering the baronial hall once more, after so long an absence.

I didn't regret this little accident at all, for while I am opposed to that ready-made style of emotion which some people always keep on hand, I have no objections to a noble and dignified use of tears.

It is needless to say that every body was delighted to see Bulger. They all found that he had increased in size, beauty and intelligence.

He received all this homage with a dignity that was charming to behold.

To impress the crowd with a due sense of that discipline and self-control which he acquired as the constant companion and confidant of his master, he absolutely refused to touch the many tid-bits and dainty morsels which the retainers offered him, and gazed with the utmost indifference at the other dogs in their mad scramblings for the food which he had declined.

I was very proud of him.

In a few days everything had settled down to its wonted quiet again beneath the baronial roof. Evenings I passed giving accounts of the many wonderful things I had seen while abroad.

To these sittings, a few of the older and more confidential household servants were admitted.

My good mother arranged them in a semi-circle behind the chairs of the elder baron and his guests. I, with Bulger by my side, occupied a dais, either seated by the side of a table holding my curiosities or standing in front of my auditors in an easy position, while I held them spell-bound by my narration.

There was one thing that worried me, and it was this: How will the elder baron receive the announcement of my intention to leave home again, ere many moons?

To my great surprise and delight he didn't even wait for me to make known my intentions.

While seated in my library, one day, poring over a very rare book of travels which I had just purchased, a gentle tap at the door caused Bulger to raise his head and give a low growl.

"Come in!" said I.

It was the elder baron.

"I disturb you!" he began.

"You have that right, baron," I replied, with a gracious smile; "be seated, pray."

And saying this, I arranged the pelt of a very beautiful and rare animal which I had killed while abroad, so as to make a comfortable seat for the elder baron on the canopy.

"My son!" said the baron, "I come to bring thee this little token from our gracious master, the Emperor."

I looked up.

He held in his hand the insignia of the Grand Cross of the Crimson Cincture.

I laid the bauble on the table.

"Little baron," continued my father, "I am well pleased with thee."

I made a low obeisance.

"Thy marvelous adventures fill all mouths. Thou hast set a new lustre on the family name, and I come to rouse thee from thy apparent sloth. Thou must be up and doing. Thou must shake off this indolence which will gain an increased power over thee each passing hour. New triumphs await thee. Go forth once more. Turn aside out of the beaten paths. Seek the wonderful and marvelous. But ere thou settest forth, ponder the contents of this parchment roll. Many years ago, when the down of manhood first came upon my cheek, and before life's burdens had come to lie heavily on my soul, I found it in the damp and noisome vaults of an ancient Roman Convent, which the pestilential air of an encroaching marsh had emptied of its inmates. It may turn thy footsteps toward something strange and interesting!"

Concealing with difficulty the joy occasioned by my father's words and my earnestness to know the contents of the parchment roll, I returned the elder baron's salutation with marked respect, and he withdrew.

I need not assure the reader of the almost breathless anxiety with which I unrolled the volume.

It was in the Latin tongue, and was the work of a scribe.

The ink had faded somewhat, but, even in places where it had entirely disappeared, I could by the aid of a strong lens readily trace out the words by the lines scratched into the parchment by the point of the reed pen.

It was a copy of an ancient Roman newspaper or Acta Diurna, and bore a date corresponding to our forty-fifth year before the present era.

Cæsar was at the height of his power.

Peace reigned, the arts flourished. Rome, the centre of the world, was the home of a glory and magnificence far beyond anything the eyes of man had yet gazed upon.

The contents of this copy of the Acta Diurna were largely made up of detailed accounts of a famous trial just completed at Rome, in which seven noted sculptors had been found guilty of poisoning a beautiful maid named Paula, after they had each completed a statue of her, in order that no other sculptors should ever be able to make use of her for the same purpose.

The judges had pronounced the sentence of death upon them, but in consideration of their splendid services in beautifying the imperial city, Cæsar had changed their punishment from death to life-long exile.

The seven sculptors had been transported in an imperial galley to a far-away island in the Southern Seas. As stated in this copy of the Acta Diurna it was the most remote piece of land belonging to the Roman Empire lying to the Southward:

"Ad insulam remotissimam imperii romani medianorum."

As an additional act of the imperial clemency the wives and children of the condemned sculptors had been graciously accorded permission to follow their husbands and fathers into their terrible exile.

When I had finished reading all the minute details of this strange crime and its awful results, I found that my blood was coursing through my veins with a mad violence. I paced the floor with such a quick and nervous step and with agitation so plainly visible in my looks, that I was aroused from my reverie by the anxious whining of Bulger, who was following me about the room close upon my heels.

Why not go in quest of this far-away isle to which these seven sculptors and their families were transported by command of great Cæsar?

Perchance in that far-distant isle dwells a race of beings who, forgetting the world, and forgotten by it, will, by their strange habits and peculiar customs so interest me as to repay me for all the dangers I may run in crossing untracked seas and turning aside from ocean paths.

Perchance their descendants may be living yet?

This idea now took possession of my whole being.

Sleep was impossible.

Far into the night I pored over ancient charts.

While deepest silence enwrapped the baronial halls, I worked out in my mind, or, rather, let my mind work out, the course which I should pursue.

For it was always a custom of mine never to attempt to solve the unsolvable. In fact, I early made the discovery that any interference on my part with the mysterious workings of my mind tended rather to impede its action.

So I waited calmly for light.

It came at last.

Closing my eyes, with my inner sight I could see a map of the eastern world traced in glowing, shimmering lines upon an inky background.

And there, too, could I see my course marked out in dotted lines of fire.

With a loud, ringing cry of joy I sprang to my feet and exclaimed: "I shall find this wonderful isle! I shall unlock the portals of the Southern seas! I shall gaze upon the descendants of Paula's murderers!

"Come, Bulger! Away! Away!"

Hastily bidding adieu to my parents, I swung myself into the saddle, and, with Bulger securely strapped en croupe, dashed madly away towards the shores of the Mediterranean.

"The baron's mad son is off again!" cried the peasants, as I galloped past their farm houses.

In three days I stood upon the deck of my vessel.

In obedience to my orders, the captain's hand literally rested upon the helm.

All that day he had been standing with his eyes riveted upon the shore, for something told him that I could not be far away.

Everything was in readiness, even to the last biscuit.

As Bulger and I leaped over the rail, my good ship rounded to the wind, and darted away like a thing of life.

The blood tingled in my veins at sight of the blue waves and white bellying sails.

Bulger gave vent to his satisfaction in mad gambols and ear-piercing barks.

It was certainly an auspicious beginning.

Leaving the command of the ship to the mate, the captain joined me in the cabin, where I unfolded to him my project of sailing in the Southern seas in quest of a long-forgotten island.

He made haste to unroll his chart and adjust his spectacles, in order to fix the location of the island when I should give him the latitude and longitude.

Fancy his almost consternation when I told him that the only proof I had of the existence of such an island was the brief mention in the ancient Roman newspaper.

Was I mad?

Did I care no more for life than to throw it away in such a foolhardy undertaking?

Had I no idea of the rage of the terrible typhoon, the treachery of the hidden reef, the weight of the watery mountains which would topple on our deck?

Could I expect seamen to go where there was no record that the most adventurous sailors of past centuries had ever ploughed the water?

I smiled.

"Master," said I, after a moment's silence, "this ship is mine, and you have sworn to serve me like a true seaman, but if your courage has failed you, you shall be put ashore at the first port we make. Go!"

"Nay, little baron," cried the skipper, "I was only testing your resolution. If you have the courage to sail into unknown seas, I have the courage to follow you, come bright skies and calm waters or come storm clouds and thunderbolt!"

I shook the old man's hand, and bade him go on deck, for at last sleep had come to my wakeful eyes—the first time in three whole weeks—and I wanted to be alone.

In a few days we passed the Straits of Gibraltar and turned southward, keeping the African coat in sight.

I passed my time perfecting myself in the Latin language, and often called forth very vigorous protestations from Bulger by addressing him in that tongue, and making use of him as a sort of audience before which I delivered my speeches after I had rounded them and polished them.

The only stops we made now were for water or provisions.

By daylight and starlight my staunch ship bounded along on her course as if some friendly nereids were pushing at her stern. In the long watches of the night I lay in my hammock and pictured to myself that Roman galley as it bore those seven exiles with kith and kin away from their beloved land forever.

Ere another moon had bent her crescent in the evening sky we had reached the Cape, and came to anchor with intent to overhaul our ship most thoroughly before going farther southward.

This occupied several days.

I chafed under the delay.

Ten times a day I summoned the ship's master to my cabin and urged him to make greater haste. He bore with me most patiently. My heart gave a leap, when, at last, I heard the master order the crew to set the sails.

The seamen were singing and tugging away at the main-sheets as I stepped upon the deck.

"How shall I head her, little Baron?" asked the master, raising his hand to his cap.

"Dead to the southward!" I replied.

He stood transfixed.

He had thought that we would round the Cape and follow the usual course to the Indies.

His lips move as if to protest.

I cut him short, however, with an imperious wave of the hand.

Several of the sailors, noticing the pallor which had overspread the captain's face, drew near and stood gazing upon us, half wonderingly, half inquiringly.

"Captain!" said I calmly, but quite loud enough to be overheard by the men standing in a group near by, "my pistols were made by the Emperor's armorer. They never miss fire. Let me find you changing this vessel's course a single point east or west of south and I'll kill you in your tracks!"

Saying this I walked away.

From that moment all went well.

The ship's master saw that I was determined to have my way, even if I lost my life in consequence, and he yielded.

Turning around to the group of sailors, I called out:

"A thousand ducats to the man who first sights land!"

A hearty cheer rent the air, and calling to Bulger to follow me, I went below to think.

That night I not only took the precaution to hang a lanthorn so that I could lie in my hammock and see a ship's compass at any time I might awake, but, fearful lest some treachery might be attempted, I ordered my faithful Bulger to sleep with his back against the door so that the least vibration would arouse him.

Night after night these precautions were followed out most strictly. During the day, too, my pistols were always in my belt.

Bulger felt the danger I was in, and he, by his vigilance gave me the advantage of eyes in the back of my head.

A low growl warned me of the approach of the master or one of the crew.

Thus protected and guarded, I felt that nothing save a general mutiny need be feared. And this I knew to be almost impossible, for a number of the crew were too devoted to me to listen to any traitorous proposals. They would have slain the master in cold blood had he dared to breathe the word mutiny!

Things went very well for about ten days when I saw that a terrible struggle was going on in the captain's mind.

I began to fear that he might lose his reason and throw himself into the sea.

His face took on a yellow-greenish hue.

He was literally dying of fright.

One morning he threw himself upon his knees in front of me, and with tear-stained cheeks implored me to put back to the African coast again.

I did all I could to quiet him, but in vain.

His reason was slowly but surely giving way.

Calling the mate to me, I put him in command of the vessel, and directed him to confine the captain in his cabin and place a guard over him.

It cut me to the heart to be obliged to do this, for the poor fellow begged like a dog to be left in command of his ship.

But I was deaf to his entreaties.

I felt that now all trouble was at an end.

The wind was blowing fifteen knots an hour.

Every stitch of sail had been crowded on.

We fairly leapt out of the water like a thing of life, half flying half swimming.

Ever and anon I glanced at the compass.

She was headed dead south.

My cheeks tingled and I could feel the flow of warm blood through every vein in my body.

The moon went up like a shield of burnished gold. The sea glittered like liquid fire. Anon, a porpoise leaped into the air and sent a thousand ripples circling away as he plunged into the water again

Our good ship cleft the glassy bosom of the sea like some huge black monster of the deep, and left a trail of fire in her wake as far as the eye could reach.

Towards midnight I went to rest.

But neither rest nor sleep was possible.

Half undressing, I threw myself into my hammock, and Bulger took his accustomed place at the door.

The lanthorn was not strong enough to overcome the light of the full moon. It streamed through the bull's eyes in weird, fantastic rays, and crowded my cabin with strange and mysterious forms.

They were seven!

Their faces and figures were godlike, so white, so beautiful were they.

There was an indescribable sadness in their full dark eyes.

They spake not a word.

Suddenly the paneling of the cabin ceiling parted, and disclosed a staircase wrapped in dim, uncertain light.

Adown these steps came a most gracious being, so white and fair and lovely that I gazed with bated breath.

Down, down it came, nearer and nearer.

She needed but wings to be an angel!

But, oh! her fair face was so filled with sorrow!

Her lips were parted, her long black hair fell in confused tresses on her shoulders.

She stepped into the cabin. And then, with a quick, dread look, her gaze fell upon the seven bowed figures.

"Paula!" they cried, and drew their white robes over their heads.

"Land ho! Land ho!"

What! Could I believe my ears?

"Land ho! Land ho!"

With a bound I sprang from my hammock and rushed upon deck.

Ay, it was true! There, half a mile ahead of us, was a sight that stunned me like the blow of a bludgeon.

Land it was, but not such a land as in my wildest dreams I had hoped to find.

Ten thousand lights glimmered on that mysterious shore, and illumined the front of a Roman temple whiter than milk. A marble staircase of the same hue led down to the very water's edge.

A sacrifice was in progress.

From the highest terrace a column of black smoke curled slowly upward.

No sound reached my ear.

I stood almost bereft of my senses.

At last, my power of speech returned. I ordered anchor to be cast, and clinging to the shrouds of my good ship, gazed long and joyfully upon the entrancing scene.

The land rose in natural terraces from the seashore, and no matter in what direction you looked, your eye caught glimpses of a graceful statue or group of statuary gleaming in the white moonlight, amid the dark foliage, like white-robed figures astray in a wood.

"It must be!" I murmured to myself.

"I have found it! This Roman temple, this marble stairway, these groups of statuary, all point to the glorious success of my voyage of discovery. This is the Sculptors' Isle!"

How long I stood there gazing upon this beautiful shore I know not. Some one pulling gently at my sleeve roused me from my reverie.

It was Bulger.

I stooped and stroked his head for a few moments.

Suddenly I awoke to a sense of great weariness, and casting another glance toward that mysterious shore, I turned and descended to the cabin.

I soon fell into a deep sleep.

The terrible strain upon my nerves since leaving the Cape, caused by the half mutiny of the crew, the insanity of the ship's master, and the long watches through which I had lain and listened for the cry of land, had at last told upon me.

The sun was several hours high when I sprang out of my hammock and rushed upon deck.

Could it all have been a dream? Should I find the noble temple, staircase of marble, and all the towering statues melted away into thin air?

Ah no!

That beautiful shore was still there, unrolled before my wondering eyes like some fair picture full of light and grace and delicious coloring.

"Man the launch!" I called out and in quicker time than it takes to tell it, I was on my way to the shore of the Sculptors' Isle.

Faithful Bulger sat beside me, his eyes bright and expressive as he gazed into my face.

Landing at the foot of the marble stairway, I sprang lightly out of the launch, followed by Bulger, and bounded up the marble steps.

There were three landings before I reached the level of the temple, from each of which the outlook grew more and more delightful. In truth, it was a glorious approach to produce which art and nature had fairly outdone themselves. At length I cleared the last flight of steps, and with a throbbing heart crossed the tessellated court and paused in front of the entrance to the temple.

The embers were still smouldering on the altar, around which stood several white-robed priests with low-bowed heads and averted faces. Unwilling to break in upon their solemn office, I turned and followed a broad way, paved with marble and shaded by most graceful trees and trailing vines.

At every step my eyes fell upon some statue of ravishing beauty—now nymphs; now goddess; now Jove himself; now the great Cæsar; now the fair Graces; now terrible Pluto; now smiling Ceres; now the crescent-crowned Diana, accoutered for the chase; now dancing satyrs; now goat-footed Pan; now some Roman hero or statesman; and ever and anon, came the figure of a maiden, wondrously fair, but with an unutterable look of sadness upon her beautiful face. So often did the same figure meet my gaze that I was led at last to approach its pedestal in hopes of finding some explanation. I gave a cry of pleasure as my eyes fell upon the name sculptured there.

It was Paula.

Now every doubt was dissipated.

I had indeed found the Sculptors' Isle

Broad winding paths, leading right and left, now lured my footsteps. No fairy land could be more beautiful.

Golden fruit glistened 'mid the dark green leaves.

Flowers of countless hues bloomed on every side, sending forth the most delicate perfumes. Trailing vines hung in graceful festoons or twined around the pedestals of the statues, carrying their white blossoms to the whiter hands of these silent and motionless inhabitants of this region of loneliness. I say inhabitants, for as yet my eye had seen no living creature, save the priests grouped about the altar.

Have I landed upon the shores of an island, upon which nature, with a lavish hand, has bestowed stately forests, placid lakes, purling brooks, trees laden with delicious fruits, plants waving their flowery tassels and plumes in the perfumed air, vines trailing their richly variegated foliage from tree to tree, a radiant sky above, a soil clad with velvety verdure beneath, only to find it abandoned, deserted of man; a thing of beauty and yet loneliness, a mere polished and painted shell, out of which all life has gone forever?

Such was the train of thought which busied my mind as I strolled along through these winding paths paved with marble shut in by a leafy roof, through which ever and anon the sunlight burst to light up the masterpieces of the sculptor's art, around whose pedestals climbed and clambered scores of flowering vines, some carrying in their curved laps clusters of berries, brighter in hue than burnished gold, others holding out to the passer-by bunches of grapes deeper in purple than the Lydian dye.

As I pursued my way through this enchanted garden, in which the swaying lily stalks bent their perfumed-filled cups down to my cheeks and the trees dropped their gold and purple fruit at my feet, while deep in the bosky thicket of red-leaved shrubs and silken-tufted pine, the melancholy nightingale warbled his liquid melody in slow and plaintive measure, my heart yearned for the sound of a human voice.

"Would that some living being," I cried, "no matter how bent and twisted in figure, or how discordant in voice, might come forth to meet me in this beautiful solitude."

I noticed now that my path was ascending a gently sloping hillock. I quickened my pace, for I was anxious to stand upon some elevation, so that I could command a more extensive view of the outlying country.

As I gained the summit of the hillock, a scene of indescribable beauty met my gaze.

As far as the eye could reach I saw unrolled beneath me a landscape of such surpassing loveliness that I paused spell-bound. Imagine a valley shut in by wooded heights, through which a silvery stream courses tranquilly; here a forest giant spreads its far-reaching limbs, and there a clump of fruit trees display their load of golden treasures in the sunlight; on this side flowering shrubs shine white as ivory against the dark greensward, on that with trailing vines and trimmed copses, man's hand has built many a shady bower of fantastic outline; to this add scores of statues posed in every conceivable attitude of grace and beauty—here a group, there a single figure, and farther on by twos and threes, standing, reclining, sitting, at play, in meditation, listening, reading, thrumming stringed instruments, in attitudes of the chase, casting the quoit, or reaching up to pluck fruit or flowers.

"Is this a dream?" I murmured. "Am I not the sport of some mischievous spirit of the place?"

From this deep reverie the loud barking of Bulger aroused me with shock-like violence.

I looked in the direction of the sound.

Poor, foolish dog, he was gamboling about one of the statues and amusing himself in waking the echoes with his voice.

I was a little nettled by the interruption, and called to him to cease his barking.

It seemed to me almost a sacrilege to disturb the deep repose of this fair valley.

Again the barking broke forth. This time Bulger's strange antics were wilder than before.

He seemed fairly beside himself bounding around and around the statue which was that of a young man in the act of reaching aloft for fruit or flowers—and giving vent to a sort of half anger, half mischief, in a series of barks, growls and whinings. Rare indeed was it that Bulger did not give heed to my wishes, no matter how faintly expressed, but now, not even a threatening tone of voice seemed to have the slightest effect upon him.

He continued his mad gamboling and sharp, angry barking. Determined to reproach him most severely for his disobedience, I strode angrily toward him.

I drew near.

I looked! I saw!

Ashes of my forefathers, what? The statue had wide-opened eyes. The statue had the blush of life on its cheeks.

Motion, movement, even to a hair's breadth, there was none! And yet these fair blue eyes were bent upon Bulger in half-inquisitive, half-wondering gaze.

I rubbed my eyes and looked again.

I took a step forward.

Suddenly a wave of fear crept over me like the flow of icy water. Would the living marble, as it warmed to life, moved by some long pent-up passions, raise its hand and strike me dead?

Gathering myself together, I glanced toward a group of maidens at play beneath the shade of a leafy roof of arched branches and interlacing vines.

Quicker than it takes to tell it, I sprang forward and fixed my gaze upon their faces.

Death could not hold the human form in attitude more motionless than theirs.

And yet their eyes were filled with strange light.

Upon their fair faces the red tint of life glowed, bright and warm!

Where was I?

A strange feeling of half dread, half delight, now swept over me.

And still I dared not speak. My voice will break the spell by which all these breathing children of earth's flinty breast keep their hold on life, and they will fade away to nothingness.

And now the eyes of her nearest me—of deeper black than polished coal, appeared bent full upon me. I could see, I thought, the glisten of those ebon orbs, as if a tear had broken over them.

Her hand was outstretched.

What if I touch it, thought I, to see if it have the warmth of life within it, or whether it be not in truth a thing of stone, and I the sport of some mischievous spirit of the island?

I'll do it, if I'm slain like a poor worm, which, warmed by an approaching flame crawls to meet it.

I touched its finger-tips!

O, wondrous thing!

They were not of stone, but of softest, warmest flesh!

I staggered back, expecting to see the group vanish in thin air.

But no; it moved not.

It stood as motionless as before!

And now I felt my limbs grow strong beneath me.

I determined to speak, come evil or come good!

Fixing my gaze upon their fair young faces, I uncovered and addressed them thus:

"O, strange and mysterious beings, resent not this bold intrusion of a puny mortal upon your sacred repose! Speak to me! If ye so will, let me take my feet off the soil of your fair island. But ere I go, speak to me, let me know whether ye be not the creations of some spirit of this isle, or whether ye are really living, breathing beings!"

No sound issued from those rosy lips, parted as if in the very act of speaking.

No movement, no tremor, came to break the marble-like pose of these fair figures.

A whole minute elapsed.

To me it seemed an eternity.

I stood riveted to the ground in most anxious suspense.

The minutes dragged their heavy bodies along one after another.

But joy unutterable!

Their lips begin to move.

A smile, almost imperceptible at first, spreads slowly, slowly, over their faces.

The crimson of their cheeks takes on a deeper hue.

Their eyes bend a most sweet and friendly look upon me.

The word "we" falls gently on my ear.

Another pause!

I lean forward, in most painful suspense, to catch the next faint syllable.

It came at last.

"Live!"

"They live!" I cried in a loud and joyous voice, "they live! I am not the sport of any strange divinity. These figures are not cold and senseless marble, but warm-blooded, breathing, thinking, living beings!"

I cannot tell you the depth of my satisfaction that this discovery was made by my loved Bulger. He saw the terrible perplexity which had come upon his master, and hastened to his rescue; not frowning face, not threatening voice was sufficient to turn him from his purpose of letting light in upon my darkened mind. In my deep contrition, I could scarcely bring myself to speak his name.

I felt how unworthy of his love I was.

But he pardoned me with a nobility of character more than human and spake his forgiveness by covering my hands with caresses and uttering a series of soft low barks.

With Bulger by my side, I now mingled with these flesh and blood companions of the island's marble dwellers, passing from one group to another in speechless wonderment. Ay, in good faith they were alive, but not more so than the flowers, the shrubs, the trees, the vines which helped to make up the lovely scene of which they were the brightest and fairest ornaments.

The vines moved from place to place more rapidly than they, the flowers oped their buds more quickly than the maidens did their lips. Like beautiful figures of wax, moved by the slow uncoiling of some hidden spring, these living statues passed hours, nay days, in rising to their feet or sinking down upon the velvety greensward.

For several hours I stood watching the white hand of a maiden as it reached forward, with imperceptible motion to pluck a red-cheeked peach which hung beside her. A full hour went by ere those delicate fingers were clasped around the peach, another ere it had been carried to her lips. There, all day long, she held it pressed, but as the sun went down behind the wooded hills, it fell from her loosened grasp and rolled towards my feet. I slowly stooped, for I was not long in discovering that my quick movements pained these animated statues, and picked it up. I could feel that some of the pulp had been drawn from the luscious fruit, but the skin was hardly broken, so gently had she fed upon it.

At this moment, seeing a smile upon the face of one of the maiden's I turned to find upon whom she bent her gaze.

It was a handsome youth, who stood, perhaps fifty feet distant, with his eyes fixed beamingly upon the maiden's.

"Surely" thought I, "affection will, as in other lands, quicken their movements; they will advance toward each other somewhat rapidly now."

But no, the long twilight yielded little by little to the deeper shadows; night came; the moon set her glowing disc in the heavens, and yet that youth was not near enough to clasp the hand of the maiden he loved.

From the first coming of the twilight, smiles had been slowly gathering upon the faces of the other youths and maidens, whose eyes were turned upon the lovers.

At this moment a gentle "ha!" fell upon my ear, and, after the lapse of half an hour, another and louder "ha!" followed it, to be, after a still longer pause, followed by still another "ha!" This last "ha!" was lengthened out into a clear and ringing note which lasted several seconds. Then it grew fainter and fainter, and died away like a spent echo. Their mirth was over.

As I was threading my way among these living statues, one morning, I came upon a group of children at play.

At first I could not see that they had noticed my coming at all, but after the lapse of a quarter of an hour I discovered that their large beautifully clear eyes were slowly turning toward me, so I determined to sit down near by and observe them. Fancy my delight upon finding that a delicate thread-like flowering vine had twined around and around the body of a little golden-haired maid of about seven, encircled her neck with its many colored leaves and coral berries, and coiled itself like a crown of gold and crimson upon her soft ringlets, dropping its blossoms and tendrils gently down around her head and shoulders.

Seeing my astonishment, and hearing my words of delight, a mild-faced woman seated near me slowly, slowly raised her hands and extended her fingers to make me understand that these little cherubs had been ten days at play there upon the ground.

"This beautiful vine," thought I, "has joined in their sport. As much alive as they, it is in truth one of their playmates, and has wound itself lovingly around the child seated nearest to it."

I looked again. Lo! a tree loaded with delicious nuts was swinging in the breeze and shaking them into the laps of these children at play, while on the other side, a tall, graceful plant bearing cup-shaped flowers of sunny whiteness, each of which I noticed was filled with limpid water, drops of which sparkled in the sunlight like polished gems, gently brushed against the cheek of a smiling boy, as if to say:

"Drink, dear little brother!"

"Wonderful!" cried I, "these happy creatures, these trees and flowers, these fruits and vines are all children of the same family. No storms ever come to darken these fair skies. Eternal spring reigns here. By daylight, starlight and moonlight their lives flow gently along like some broad, silvery stream, whose motion is too slow for human eye to note it. Mysterious people! How shall I fathom the wonderful secret of your existence? How shall I read the history of a people whose only books are speechless brooks and silent groves, whose tongues have so lost their power to interpret thought that months might go by and yet the mystery remain unsolved!"

After a sojourn of a few days among the "Slow Movers," as I shall call them, I made a discovery which alarmed me greatly.

I found that this mysterious silence, this strange fate which cast me among living creatures with whom converse was next to impossible, this utter inability to distinguish the living statues from the marble ones, was beginning to prey upon my mind.

Bulger noticed my ever-increasing melancholy, and exerted himself to amuse and comfort me.

I responded but poorly to his thousand and one cunning tricks and laughable antics.

In fact, I felt that my mind was gradually yielding to some dread influence which pervaded the very air, and which, even hour by hour, so gained in strength that I realized the necessity of making a superhuman effort to break away from the power it had already acquired over me, or else become myself a living statue and brother to the forms of flesh and marble which inhabited this wonderland.

I will not weary my readers with minute details of the plan which I had conceived to end the danger which threatened me, to snatch myself from the living death which I could already feel creeping over me.

In my despair I determined to apply to the oldest of the Slow Movers, and throw myself upon his mercy, so to speak, to tell him of my longing to escape from the terrible fate threatening me, to return home to my beloved parents, who would go down in sorrow to their graves if I, their sole child, their pride and their hope, should never come again to gladden their old age.

But more than this, I determined if possible, to learn the history of the island and its mysterious folk, and to that end I resolved to beseech him to indicate to me where I might find some record of their past, some book or parchment, so that I might not go through life burdened with the brain-racking thought that I had been powerless to solve this mystery—a thought, which, if it did not shorten my days, would most surely embitter them.

As I have already explained, in attempting to converse with the Slow Movers I was confronted with a two-fold difficulty. In the first place, though I might burst with impatience, yet must I preserve a perfectly calm and placid exterior, and, in the second place, when, after the long and wearying delay, it came my turn to make reply, that reply must not exceed the snail's pace of the Slow Movers' speech, else their bright eyes clouded up and they seemed absolutely paralyzed by the rapidity of my utterance. Their eye-lids sank slowly down and they seemed to fall into a deep slumber, out of which it took hours to arouse them.

At the first streak of dawn I sought out the aged Slow Mover, whom I had often noted in his leafy temple, seated on a marble pediment his eyes fixed on the silent stream which bathed the very roots of the trees, whose wide-spreading branches helped to roof over his habitation.

All that day and the starry night which followed it, I sat at his feet.

Picture to yourself my utter despair at learning that not a word or a line, not a leaf or a parchment, was in existence, which, might end my fearful anxiety. I say fearful, for stronger and stronger, hour by hour, grew the impulse to put an end to this life of useless, senseless activity and join the throng of living statues into whose heart no vain regrets came to darken their placid dream-life.

On the morning of the second day a thought burst upon my mind. It was this:

Perchance there may dwell, somewhere on this isle, some one living creature, who, unlike his brothers, may possess the power of rapid speech, whose tongue, for some reason or other, may have stayed loosened.

I reasoned thus: In every land there were opposites, good and bad, beautiful and ugly, graceful and awkward, swift and slow. Surely on this isle must live such contrasts as these. True, it may be an exception; but it would be most wonderful if it did not exist.

All that day I spent in imparting unto the aged Slow Mover my train of thought.

It was deep in the twilight ere I had succeeded in putting the question to him: Whether there was not some living creature dwelling on this island whose powers of speech were more like mine, and to whom I might, in my ever increasing dread of transformation into a Slow Mover, flee for refuge from myself, for satisfaction of the irresistible longing pressing on my very soul.

But the shades of evening were not so deep that I could not note the darker shadow which began to gather on the face of the aged Slow Mover when I had completed my question.

I was startled.

So violent were the beatings of my heart that they sounded loud, though muffled, above the sighing of the zephyr, the rustle of the leaves, the plaintive warbling of the nightingale.

As this shadow went on growing, ever deeper and deeper, on the old man's visage, I felt that I had touched some ancient wound, which, though long-forgotten, now bled afresh.

His lips parted, his head sank slowly, slowly, a sigh came forth, so full of meaning, so like a tale-bearer of some long hidden sorrow, that I feared for the worst.

My limbs stiffened.

I could feel the blood lessen its pace in my veins and go groping along as if uncertain of its way.

I pressed the tips of my fingers to my cheeks. They were cold as polished marble.

I essayed to speak. The words would not come.

At last I made a violent effort—

"Bulger!" I whispered.

Poor dog, he slept at my feet.

I struggled to escape the spell for one brief moment, that I might stoop to give my faithful friend a farewell caress.

Hist!

The Slow Mover spoke.

"Son!"

I was saved!

He had aught to say to me.

The spell was broken.

My heart began to beat again; the warm blood ran tingling through my veins.

It was a narrow escape.

Already my finger tips had cooled.

Another moment and I would have joined the throng of Slow Movers, and become a brother to the marble dwellers on the Sculptors' Isle.

All that night the aged Slow Mover talked to me. And when the sun went up I knew all. I knew the secret which had so darkened his placid countenance. I knew the cave in which dwelt the hermit of the Sculptors' Isle—an outcast, a prisoner, shut in between the narrow walls of a cavern by the sea, for no fault of his, for no sin, for no wrong.

Nature had so willed it.

Why, the aged Slow Mover knew not.

Antonius was the name which the hermit bore.

When morning came I sought him out.

I found him seated by his cavern's portal, looking out upon the glory of the eastern sky.

This was the secret of his exile:

Some cruel fate had, in his youth, visited him with a dread disease, not unlike that which is known as St. Vitus' dance. When the fit was upon him, not only did he lose all control over his limbs, so that his feet bore him whither he willed not to go, and that, too, with extreme rapidity, but his arms likewise executed the most rapid and vigorous gestures, now in apparent anger, now entreaty, now wonder. You will readily understand why ill-fated Antonius came to be banished from the midst of the Slow Movers.

Although their brother, and deeply beloved of them, his lightning-like rapidity of motion, his violent gestures, his almost ceaseless change of attitude, not only offended the Slow Movers, it dazed them; it shocked them; it checked the sluggish flow of life blood within their veins, and threatened them all with slow but certain death.

He must go!

He did!

Antonius was banished to the cavern by the sea, where never came sound, save the ocean's roar when lashed by the demons of the gale, or its sad murmur and ceaseless break and splash in its moments of slumber and rest.

But, most terrible of all the manifestations of the unfortunate Antonius' fearful ailment was the utterly wild and ungovernable rapidity of his speech.

Like maddened steeds, tongue and lips rushed along!

To the eyes and ears of the Slow Movers, such a violently expressive face, such mad rapidity of utterance, were death itself!

Not one brief month would have found a living statue in that home of flinty hearts, had Antonius not gone!

Antonius was thankful for that dread decree, which housed him forever in the cavern by the sea!

He saw the sufferings of his people, and though his eyes in that brief time wept more tears than all his brethren ever had shed in their sluggish lives, yet were they but a poor proof of the awful grief he felt.

Antonius turned towards me as I approached the spot where he sat wrapped in deep meditation. A sad, but withal kindly smile flitted about his lips, like the quick but faint glimmer of the lightning in the distant sky.

He rose.

I paused to await his bidding to approach him.

He spake not a word, but stretched out his hand.

I bounded forward to clasp it and press it to my lips.

At that instant the fit fell on him.

I could see the look of pain which flashed across his face.

Away he glided, now backward, now forward, now sidewise, now obliquely, his hand outstretched in a desperate effort to reach me, who, with equal desperation, advanced and retreated in a mad endeavor to grasp what constantly eluded me.

Bulger utterly unable to comprehend this wild dance among the rocks of that cavernous shore, followed my heels barking furiously.

I could take no time to quiet him.

Away, away, sped Antonius with redoubled speed, his right hand extended toward me as if with a pitiful prayer to grasp it and thus end the fit which was shaking his limbs so furiously.

Pausing to catch my breath, I again pursued the flitting figure with a determination to overtake it or perish in the attempt.

At last it seemed to circle in smaller and ever smaller rings.

Now was my time!

I sprang upon that whirling form, with a sort of mad desperation, to seize and hold its outstretched hand.

At length I held it.

But no!

His body had come to a rest, but now high over my head, now at my feet, now flashing up one side, now down the other, now whizzing in front of my eyes, now encircling my head like a bird in swift flight that hand went on, ever on, in its wild and mysterious course!

My strength was failing me!

Shall I ever be able to grasp it!

Antonius, too, showed signs of yielding to the awful power of the dread disease which tormented him!

His face took on a strange pallor! His breast heaved convulsively. With one last despairing effort I succeeded in catching his hand in its flight around my head!

I clung to it with desperate vigor!

My touch dispelled the venom from his veins.

He seemed to awake as from some awful dream. He passed his hand across his eyes.

He smiled.

Still clinging to his hand, I gently forced him to be seated upon a rocky bench, over which the ocean had woven a velvety covering of sea-grass and weeds.

"Antonius!" I cried, "peace come upon thee! Forget thy suffering. Be as thou once wert! My touch can give thee rest at least for a brief respite!"

He pressed my hand. A deep sigh lifted his breast. It was the last gasp of the demon which oppressed him.

He was now at rest.

To me his utterance was rapid but not more so than that of many quick thinkers with whom I had conversed.

"What wouldst thou?" said he, in a low but strangely sweet, mild voice.

I unfolded to him the object of my coming.

I went back to the finding of the Roman newspaper and my departure from home.

All, all; I told him all; how I had come into the home of the Slow Movers, how I had mistaken them for marble like the rest of the figures about the island, how I longed to have the mystery cleared up.

All that day Antonius and I sat by the sea in most delightful converse.

Only once, at high noon, did he set a brief limit to his tale while we passed into his cavern to partake of food and drink.

With a high-bounding heart, I listened to his story of the landing of the Seven Sculptors upon the isle. Their first task had been to rear the glorious temple with its long flight of marble steps leading down to the sea. Then they, and, later, their sons, and their sons' sons, had set to work to people this beautiful island with almost countless figures of the rarest grace and finish.

In the forests, by the river's banks, through the valley, on the hillside, adown the terraces, to the very water's edge, rose the faultless statues in wondrous beauty and profusion.

Here, there and everywhere, forms of matchless grace gleamed, snow-white amid the leafy bowers or tangled underwood.

A mysterious ardor burned within the hearts of these exiled artists. It would seem that theirs was a wild sort of hope to rear on that far-distant isle another Rome—an infant daughter, but fairer and whiter in her marble magnificence than the glorious mother who sate upon her seven hills!

Times and times again, aye, thrice three score and ten, the wretched Paula arose out of the quarried blocks, ever fair and ever fairer, now bent in awful grief, now putting the very skies to shame with the entrancing beauty of her upturned, pleading, sweet and pitiful face.

Here and there, too, stood great Cæsar, never to be forgotten for his godlike clemency in snatching the sculptors from terrible death.

As the second century of the exile dawned upon the little Roman Kingdom, far away beneath the Southern skies, at the very moment when the colony was waxing strong and vigorous a strange and mysterious thing happened to the dwellers in this island home of sweet content.

No more male children were born!

The seven sculptors, now bent with age, and their faces hollowed by the sharp chisels of remorse, went, one after the other to the dark realm of Death.

Their sons, too, came into ripe manhood. And their sons grew up, happy in the possession of that glorious talent which had peopled the isle with such matchless forms of beauty.

But now the race had reached the end of its long reign in the world of art.

Decade after decade slipped away, and still there came not one male child to gladden a sculptor's home.

A sort of blank despair sank upon the colony.

The elder sculptors laid their chisels down in utter hopelessness.

Even the younger wrought less and less.

Still there came no boy to wake the old-time song and laughter of that once joyous island home.

Fingers cunning in art grew stiff with age.

Hearts full of glorious inspiration waxed dull and spiritless! One by one they all went the way which mortal feet must tread.

A terrible, a wonderful change came over the people.

Weighed down by this leaden grief, surrounded day and night by these speechless, motionless marble forms, which, although silent as the very clod itself, yet cried out unceasingly: "Give us more companions in these solitudes!" these unfortunate people almost turned to marble itself.

They became, in good sooth, brothers and sisters to the marble dwellers on this island.

At length the end came!

The last sculptor was laid upon the carved bier of the great white temple by the sea!

A silence so long, so deep, so dreadful, fell upon the people that it almost seemed their speech was lost forever.

Within the dark grottoes and bosky underwood, they crawled to hide away from the very light of day.

Their limbs, once so supple and elastic, ever ready to bear their owners over hill and across plain, delighting in the dance, inured to the race, now became heavy and slow.

They seemed almost about to turn to stone, and join the silent company around them.

In good sooth, such a fate was imminent, when the happening of a joyful event averted it.

A year had passed since the last sculptor had gone to join the shadowy caravan which moves forever across the desert of Eternal Silence, when his seven sad-faced daughters were fairly startled by an infant's cry.

But look!

Their widowed mother stands before them with a babe nestled in her arms.

It is a son!

The joyful tidings can only creep from family to family.

Alas! it was too late to call them back to old-time customs and habits, too late to start their blood again in old-time bounding, leaping course through their veins.

They were a changed people!

True, their happiness came again, but it was not the same. They could smile and laugh, but it was scarcely more than faces of marble moved by some mysterious power. They could talk, but so slowly fell the words that it almost seemed some statue spoke amid the leafy coverts of the island. They could move, but snail or tortoise outstripped them with ease.

Ay, they were changed indeed; fated henceforth to people their beautiful island home with living statues.

For years in long flight sped away, till one century followed another, and yet the wondrous talent came back no more.

It was lost forever!

Long, long ago, too, the people forgot the story of their fathers.

It is kept alive in the hearts of a few chosen ones, and they hand it down, each quarter century, to younger keepers selected for the purpose.

To Antonius the secret had been thus confided.

And such was the tale he told to me!

With a light heart, now that its weight of doubt and uncertainty had been lifted from it, I bade Antonius farewell, and, followed by Bulger wended my way back to the abodes of the Slow Movers.

As I passed through one of the groves peopled with marble forms, I paused, I hardly knew why, in front of an admirable bust of the great Cæsar.

Bulger joined me, and there we stood, children of this late day, with our eyes uplifted to the face of him whose smallest word was once copied down on waxen tablet as if it were the utterance of a god.

I had always liked Cæsar.

We resembled each other in many ways.

We were both men of action.

I felt sorry for him now, that he should be forced to live, even in the shape of marble, among such dull and inactive people as the Slow Movers.

I told him so.

"And yet, Julius," said I, "called of men the Great Cæsar, what a fortunate thing it is that thou art not living now, for thou wouldst be overcome with shame at finding everybody reading my adventures while the book which thou wrotest concerning Gaul lies mouldy and dust-covered on the shelves of the libraries!"

The following day, in passing that way again, and glancing up at great Cæsar's face, I noticed that a smile had just started in the right corner of his mouth. So stolid had he become through his long residence among the Slow Movers that he had just begun to be amused by the remark I had made on the previous day.

Thoughts of home now arose in my mind.

The fact is that shortly after my interview with Antonius in his cavern by the sea, Bulger had commenced to show unmistakable signs of home-sickness. So I dispatched him with a note to the officer of my vessel to begin preparations at once for the return voyage.

Bulger made haste to execute the commission.

He proceeded to the foot of the marble staircase, and then by loud barking attracted the attention of the officer whom I had left in command.

He sent a boat ashore and Bulger met it with my letter in his mouth.

To tell the truth, I would have fain lingered for a week or so longer among the Slow Movers, but it was plain to be seen that they were growing restive at my presence.

On the cheeks of many of them all signs of ruddy peach-bloom had disappeared.

Day by day they grew more and more like their marble brethren.

My quick movements so wearied their eyes that after a few hours' stay in their midst I found myself surrounded by a company of deep sleepers.

Nor dared I speak.

For no matter how I softened my voice, or how slowly I uttered my words, they jarred upon the delicate ears of the Slow Movers, and signs of suffering gradually passed over their faces.

My resolution was therefore quickly formed.

With a snail's pace I passed from group to group, from bower to bower, from grove to grove, saying in a soft and measured tone: "Fare———well! Fare———well!"

Then I directed my steps toward the white temple by the sea, for I knew my boat's crew were waiting for me at the foot of the marble staircase.

As I passed in front of Great Cæsar's statue I turned to wave a last adieu.

What saw I, think you?

Why, that same smile which had begun in the right corner of his mouth several days ago, had crossed over to the other side of his face and was just at the left corner of his mouth.

On the right side, whence it had come, all was as stern and calm as when he sat enthroned at Rome, and ruled the world.

Several hours later, as we were busy setting the sails of my good ship there fell upon my ear in a soft, echo-like tone, the word.

"Fare!"

The Slow Movers had begun to speak their adieu. The winds were favorable. The sails filled.

As the sun went down, pouring a flood of golden light upon the beautiful marble staircase, the great white temple and the many snowy statues which gleamed so bright and fair amid the dark foliage of the trees and vines upon the terraces of that mysterious island I threw myself upon the deck with intent to keep my eyes fixed upon the lovely scene as long as possible.

My good ship sailed away in deepest silence. For I had given orders that no one should speak above a whisper.

Now the Sculptors' Isle had faded to a mere speck in the horizon, and now, in the gathering shades of night, it was swallowed up, and lost forever!

My heart grew heavy.

Bulger nestled his head in my lap, with his loving eyes fixed full upon me.

Sleep overcame us both.

The sky was star-studded when we awoke.

The cool night wind had refreshed me.

I sprang up with the intention of going below. At that instant there came floating along on the evening breeze, like a mountain echo nearly spent, a soft mysterious sound.

My ear caught it! It was:

"W—e l—l!"

The Slow Movers had finished speaking their adieu.

CHAPTER VII.

Like all lovers of a roving life, I was not long in growing tired of the quiet ways and simple pursuits of the inmates of the old baronial hall.

At times, I felt like an intruder, when I caught myself sitting with eyes riveted upon the pages of some musty, old volume of strange adventure in far-away lands, while the elder baron, the gracious baroness, my loving mother, and several cousins from the neighboring estate, gave themselves up to the sweet pleasures of the fireside, feasting upon honey-cake, drinking hot spiced wine, playing at draughts, dominoes, or cards, now chatting in the most animated manner of the trivial things of every-day life, now bursting out into uproarious laughter at some unexpected victory won at cards or at some fireside game.

Silently closing my book, and still more silently stealing away, I sought the quiet of my apartments, where, with no other companions, save faithful Bulger, I gave myself up to unrestrained indulgence in waking dreams of life in a storm-rocked ship, landings on strange shores, parleyings with curious beings, battling with the wild-visaged typhoon, or hurrying with sails close-reefed and hatches battened down, to gain a safe port ere the storm king's ebon chargers could rattle their hoofs over our heads.

My dear mother, the gracious baroness, made extraordinary exertions to drive away my low spirits.

Knowing my fondness for coffee cake, she suffered no one to make it for me excepting herself. And at dinner she took care to place a professor or, some learned person beside me, so that I might not find myself condemned to silence for the want of a gifted mind to measure mental swords with.

But all to no purpose. I grew daily more taciturn, absent-minded, and plunged into meditation. With my eyes fixed upon vacancy, I sat like one with unbalanced mind amidst the lightest-hearted merry-makers. In vain the company besought me to relate past adventures, to tell them tales already thrice told. I only shook my head with a mournful smile, and made good my escape from scenes which were painful to me.

Bulger felt that his little master was suffering, and coaxed with plaintive whining to have me make known to him the cause of my grief.

His joy was wild and boisterous when he saw my body-servant enter my apartments, bearing an empty traveling chest upon his shoulders.

To tell the truth, life at the baronial hall pleased Bulger not a whit more than it did me.

The house dogs annoyed him with their attentions, and he was wont to retire from the dining hall with a look of utter disgust upon his face, when one of the family cats, in the most friendly spirit, drew near and tasted a bit of his dinner.

All caresses, too, from other hands than mine were distasteful to him; and, although for my sake he would permit the gracious baroness to stroke his silken ears, yet any familiarity on the part of the elder baron was firmly, but respectfully, declined.

The very moment I saw my chests placed here and there in my apartments, my spirits rose. I became like another being. The color returned to my cheeks, the gleam to my eye, the old-time ring to my voice.

From lip to lip, the word was passed: "The little baron is making ready for another journey!"

From early morn to deepening shadows of twilight, I busied myself with superintending the packing of my boxes. It was a labor of love with me.

I never was born for a calm life beneath the time-stained tiles of paternal halls! My heart was filled with redder, warmer blood than ordinary mortals. My brain never slept. Night and day, shadowy forms of men and things, strange and curious, swept along before me in never-ending files.

One morning, while at work with my boxes, a low knock at my chamber door fell upon my ear. Bulger, scenting an enemy, gave a low growl. I swung the door open. It was the elder baron.

"Honored father," I cried gayly, "act as if thou wert master here! Be sad, be gay; sit, stand, drink, eat, or fast!"

"Little baron," began my father in a solemn voice, "I beseech thee give over thy jesting. When thou hast heard the object of my visit, grief will chase every vestige of mirth from thy light heart."

"Speak baron!"

"Art thou a dutiful and loving son?" asked my father, fixing his dark, mournful eyes full upon me.

"I am!"

"'Tis well!" he replied, "then arrest this making ready to abandon thy parents in their hour of misfortune. Put an end to all this unseemly hurlyburly, and to thy longing to be gone from beneath the paternal roof."

The clouded face, trembling and tear-filled eyes of the elder baron shocked me.

I could feel the blood leaving my cheeks, where, till then, it had bloomed like the glow of ripening fruit.

But I checked myself; and, motioning the baron to be seated, said in a calm— though spite of me—trembling voice:

"Noble father, it is thine to command; mine to obey! Speak, I pray thee, and speak too, plainly—if need be, harshly. Bare thy most secret thoughts. What aileth thee? What sends these dark shadows to rest on that calm, smooth brow?"

"Thanks, little baron," was my father's reply, "for thy promise of obedience. This is the weight which presses on my heart: Since thou hast taken up this rambling, roving life, robbed of thy counsel and co-operation, I have seen our ancestral estate hastening to ruin. Last year our tenantry scarcely harvested enough to keep body and soul together. This year promises to turn out worse yet. Desolation sits upon the broad acres once the prize of our family! Crops fail, grass withers, trees turn yellow! The poor cattle moan for sustenance as they winder about in the dried-up pastures. I look upon all this wreck and ruin, but am helpless as a babe to stay it! Speak, my son; wilt thou, hast thou the heart, canst thou be so cruel as to turn thy back upon these pitiful scenes without raising thy hand to avert the impending doom?"

"Baron!" I interposed mildly, but firmly, "facts first! eloquence thereafter! Impart unto me, in plain, King's speech, the cause of all this ruin! What hath wrought it? What hath desolated our fair fields? What hath carried this rapine among our flocks and herds? Speak!"

"I will, little baron, give attentive ear!" rejoined my father with stately bend of the body:

"As ancient Egypt was visited with scourge and plague, so have been our ancestral acres! In pasture and grain fields, myriads of moles feed upon the tender rootlets; in grass lands, swarms of meadow-mice fatten on the herbage; in orchards and nurseries, countless numbers of ground-squirrels spread destruction far and near! Such are the terrible scourges now laying waste our once fair estates, your pride and mine, and the envy of all beholders!

"Little baron, I feel, I know that thou canst help me; that somewhere in the vast storehouse of thy mind, rest plans and devices potent enough to restore these broad lands to all their former beauty and productiveness."

"Baron!" was my reply, "when was there a time that thou foundst me wanting in my duty to thee or lacking in power to assist thee?"

"Never!" ejaculated the elder baron with great emphasis.

"Then, betake thee to my gentle mother—the baroness—thy consort, comfort her. Bid her take heart! Say I will not go abroad until these pests are driven from our ancestral domain!"

The elder baron rose. I accompanied him to the door, then, we saluted each other with dignity and he withdrew to bear the glad message of my promised assistance to my sorrowing mother.

Alone in my apartments, a terrible feeling of disappointment came over me. I felt that it would be useless to continue in my preparations to leave home in the face of these dire misfortunes now threatening my family. For, as I reasoned—and I think with great clearness—the name of our family would dwindle to a shadow, were we robbed of these broad acres of pasture and meadow-land, forest and orchard.

To me, a landless nobleman had something very ludicrous about him; and I fully made up my mind that I would either save my ancestral estate from ruin, or lay aside forever my title of baron, as a gem which had lost its radiance, even as a pearl, which the stolid rustic ruins for the sake of a meal of victuals!

That night I partook of no food, so that I might lie down with unclouded mind.

Bulger noticing this, concluded that his little master was ailing, and likewise refused to touch food, although I ordered his favorite dish—roasted cocks' combs—to be prepared.

Till midnight I lay awake in deepest thought over the arduous task which confronted me. At the stroke of twelve from the old clock on the stair, I determined to let my mind work out the problem itself, and turned over and went to sleep.

The baron and baroness entered the breakfast-room with unclouded brows the next morning. I greeted them very cordially. The conversation was enlivened by one or two of the elder baron's ancient anecdotes which he furbished up for the occasion with several new characters and an entirely new ending. I laughed heartily—as I was in duty bound to do.

Breakfast over Bulger and I sallied forth to begin work. I resolved to attack the moles first.

To get rid of pest number one was not at all a difficult matter for me, when once I set about thinking it over. In fact, I may say right here, that this task, set me by the elder baron, would have been an impossible one had it not been for my intimate acquaintance with the natures, habits and peculiarities of animal life. Always a close student of natural history there was little about the four-footed tenants of the fields which had escaped my observation.

Accompanied by Bulger; armed with a pair of short, wooden tongs; and carrying a basket, I set out for the grain fields.

Bulger was in high glee for he had already made up his mind that there was sport ahead for him.

In less than an hour, with him to point out their hiding places and to unearth them, I had captured a hundred moles. Returning to the overseer's lodge, with his help I cut off the nails of each mole's fore feet close to the flesh and then gave orders to have the lot carried back to the grain fields and released. Turning my attention now to the meadow-mice, I realized at once that to get rid of pest number two would be the most difficult task of all.

The unthinking reader has doubtless already cried out in thought: "Why not turn a troop of cats into the meadows, and let them make short work of the destructive little creatures?"

Ah how easy it is to plan, how difficult to execute! Know then, my clever friend, that the meadows were wet and that though often tried the cats absolutely refused to enter them.

The merest tyro in natural history is aware of a cat's aversion to wetting its fur; and, above all, of stepping into water. Even moisture is disagreeable to a cat's feet and she will willingly walk a mile rather than cross a plot of dew-moistened green sward. However, I determined to begin my operations at once.

Knowing the wonderful changes which the pangs of hunger will work in an animal's nature, forcing the meat-eaters to turn to the herbage of the field for sustenance—I hoped for favorable results.

Selecting half a dozen vigorous young cats from the cottages of our tenantry, and providing myself with a lot of India rubber caps used for drawing down over the necks of bottles, in order to make them air-tight, I proceeded to encase the legs of each cat in these coverings, cutting a hole in each one, however, so as to allow the paws to pass through. I wished to accustom them to these leggings before covering the feet entirely. My next step was to subject the cats to twenty-four hours fast. After which, I caused some of their favorite food—broiled fish to be placed at the other end of a long room, covering the intervening space with long-napped rugs, which I had first dipped into water.

In spite of their hunger, they absolutely refused to cross the dripping rugs.

Advancing to the edge, they tested the condition of the obstacles which blocked their advance upon the savory food feeling here and there for a dry spot; and then retreating with piteous mewing, as they shook the wet from their feet.

Drawing the rubber caps completely over the feet of one of the cats, I now placed her on the wet rug, encouraging her to remain there by feeding her a few dainty bits of the fish. Finding that her feet did not get wet, she consented to walk here and there over the wet surface, in order to secure toothsome bits of food. I made the same experiment with the other cats, and everything went as well as I could wish.

The next day I continued my instruction, and to my great joy, succeeded in schooling the whole lot, not only to make no objection to having their feet encased in the rubber boots, but even to wade through an inch or more of water, in order to secure a particularly dainty bit of food.

I was now ready to make a practical test of my trained hunters.

The day preceding the trial they were again subjected to a prolonged fast.

I must frankly confess that my heart beat rather nervously as I, with the overseer and two other assistants set out for the low lands, carrying the trained mousers—already shod in their rubber boots—in three baskets.

We advanced cautiously upon the meadow-land, but so far as the mice were concerned, our caution was useless, for they ran about under our very feet.

As I stood gazing over the long stretch of devastated meadow-land, once so famous for its thick, velvety grass, the tears gathered in my eyes and my voice choked. Now or never, thought I, must the attempt be made to save these fair fields from utter ruin. At a wave of my hand, my assistants stooped and released the somewhat startled cats. They were not long, however, in collecting their wits and getting ready for business.

Sharp hunger is an excellent sauce! As the six monsters leaped among those troops of tiny creatures—till that moment nibbling, playing or teasing one another, without a thought of harm or danger—the wildest consternation seized upon them.

Not only near by us, but as far as the eye could reach, panic and disorder spread among these, till then peaceful little beings. Those which sought safety in their holes were hurled back by others rushing frantically out into the open air.

The cats kept at their work like avenging furies. They killed for the mere pleasure of killing, passing like a death-dealing blast here and there over the meadows.

After the work of destruction had been kept up for half an hour, I directed that the trained six should be carried back to their quarters, for I was too good a general to let my troops get their fill of sack and plunder.

The next day another attack was made upon the enemy. The trained six, if anything, spread death right and left with greater fury than at first. The wet lands no longer had any terrors for them. They splashed through the puddles like mischievous boys through roadside brooks and ponds.

I now bethought me of turning my attention to the ground squirrels. My first step was to send to town for several bushels of the smallest marbles that could be purchased. Then, having, with the assistance of my ever-faithful and loving friend and helper—my dear, dumb brother Bulger—located the whereabouts of several hundred burrows of the ground-squirrels, I gave orders to have a half-dozen or more of the marbles rolled down into each one of those holes.

These labors completed, I withdrew to my apartments and set about amusing myself in several ways, while awaiting a report from the overseer.

Many of the tenants who had watched my operations against the moles, meadow-mice and ground-squirrels, even ventured openly to denounce them as "wild whims", "a dreamer's ideas" "silly workings of a diseased mind."

Poor creatures! They had lost their all. They had seen the labor of long weary months ruined by these pests. They were embittered and skeptical. I had not the heart to notice their rather impertinent utterances. While awaiting the developments, I plunged into the delights of some tales of a bold traveler written in the ancient Assyrian tongue in the wedge-shaped letter.

Three days went by and no news from the superintendent!

Two more, made five full days!

On the sixth came nothing.

At last, with the dawn of the seventh I was awakened by loud and long continued cheering beneath my windows. Springing from my bed and drawing aside the curtains, I was astonished to see long lines of our tenantry, men, women and children bearing banners, wreaths, garlands, etc.

One company of children carried long, thin rods from the end of which dangled dead moles, meadow-mice and ground-squirrels.

The moment I presented myself at the window, there was an outburst of cheering, so sturdy that the windows rattled before it. A tap at my door called me in another direction. It was the elder baron!

"Haste! little baron!" he cried eagerly "descend to the castle platform, the people are beside themselves with joy! Canst thou catch their cries? Not a mole, nor a mouse, nor a squirrel is alive on the broad acres of thy estate. I say "thy" because it is justly thine! Thou hast saved it from utter ruin. Henceforth for the few years which kind Providence may will that I should tarry with thee, let it be as thy guest."

"Nay, nay, baron!" I replied laughingly, "that may not be! Till thou sleepest with the noble dead of our long and honored line, thou art master here!"

I pressed his hand reverently to my lips and sent him to talk to the people until I should be ready to take my place at his side.

I can well fancy how impatient the reader is to hear something more about the manner in which I rid my ancestral estate of these noisome pests. With regard to the meadow-mice that needs no explanation, but, the disappearance of the moles and ground-squirrels seems somewhat mysterious.

Well and good. I'll make it clear! Gentle reader, if you had been as close a student of the natures and habits of these animals as I, you could have done the same thing yourself. You must know, then, that the mole's body bears about the same relation to his forefeet, as a boiler does to a steam engine, which is admirably adjusted in all its parts, working smoothly and noiselessly, like a thing of life—polished and beautiful in all its bearings and put together so skillfully that no human thought could better it. That is to say, the only wonderful thing about a mole is his hand.

That is a delight to a student of natural history.

I have sat for hours and studied the marvelous shape of this hand. And strange though it may seem to you, no one knows better than the mole himself, that therein lies his hold on life.

You'll bear in mind, that I caused the nails to be clipped off the forefeet of the hundred moles, close to the flesh, and then turned them loose. In other words, without absolutely destroying their marvellous hands, I completely destroyed their usefulness.

Now another thing you must be taught, that in the busy communities of these little animals, there are no sluggards. Every one must work. Only one thing stops him from using his hands.

That is death. When a mole sees his fellow stop work, he knows what has happened.

Upon the return of the hundred captives to their burrows, there was joy mingled with terror!

Whose turn might come next?

But, when the moment arrived to fall into line and set to work, there was consternation!

What! alive, and not able to dig?

Immediately, the wildest panic seizes upon the community. They abandon their homes! With frantic haste, they pierce new burrows in every direction, leaving their ill-fated companions behind them to die a lingering death—literally buried alive. Weeks, months will elapse ere they recover from this wild fear. Then they will be miles away.

And the ground-squirrels, you ask. The ground-squirrel is as conceited, inquisitive, persistent and hard-headed as he is hard-toothed. If he knew that the world was round he would claim that it was simply a huge nut and wish that he were big enough to get at its kernel.

When the marbles first came rolling down his burrow, he was pleased. They were so smooth, so round! He rolled them hither and thither, as content as a child with a new toy. Then he stored them away for another day's amusement. Pretty soon he began to tire of them. They were dreadfully in his way. They annoyed him greatly. And yet, he couldn't bear to think of parting with them. Finally the question arose in his mind: What are they, anyway? Surely they must have a kernel! And so he set to work gnawing upon them. They were terribly hard, but he was determined to get at the pit. Day after day, he kept at the thankless task, gnawing, gnawing, until, one fine morning, he awoke to make the awful discovery that his teeth were gone!

Now, a ground-squirrel may be said to consist of four teeth, and nothing else. These gone there is no way to keep the other part alive.

True, he may, after infinite labor struggle through a nutshell, but it is too slow work to keep up his strength. Every nut becomes a harder task.

And so it was with the vast colony in our orchards. The first few days quite a number made their appearance as usual. Then, fewer and fewer came out of their holes, and they looked thin and feeble and showed no inclination to gambol and chatter. At the end of the week, the work was done. They had wrought their own destruction. The entire colony had perished from starvation.

Thus it was, I restored the fair lands of our family to their old-time productiveness and removed all the obstacles which stood between me and my immediate departure from home.

In a few days all was ready.

The elder baron and the gracious baroness, my mother, parted from me with a gentle rain of tears, and a refreshing shower of blessings. Accompanied by my dumb brother—the ever faithful Bulger—and one trusty servant, I set out by extra post for Vienna.

Thence at break-neck speed, I journeyed to Buda-Pesth and reached the Black Sea via Bucharest.

Traversing that body of water in a swift vessel, commanded by an old sailing-master of mine, I skirted the foot hills of the Caucasus Mountains, and made my way to Teheran.

Here I tarried several days, long enough to purchase a few camels and horses and join a caravan, soon to leave that city on a trading expedition.

The proprietor of the trading company renewed his welcome in heartier terms when he was informed that I had brought a goodly collection of European trinkets with me.

To clinch his good will—so to speak—I gave him a pair of fine German pistols. We were now sworn friends.

I remained with the expedition until it reached Cabul. The proprietor was astounded to learn that I did not contemplate returning westward with him. After a whole day spent in eloquent pleadings, he gave in, fell upon my neck, wept, and wished me good speed.

I was glad to be rid of him, for I was in no humor to form friendships with men whose souls never rose above a sharp bargain. Attended only by my faithful Bulger and a single guide, I set out from Cabul; crossed northern Hindoostan, and entered Thibet to the north of the Himalayas.

This was the land of which I had long dreamed—a land absolutely unknown to the outside world.

I never had any inclination to pass over beaten tracks. By nature and education, a lover of the strange and marvellous, my soul expanded beneath the skies of this far-away and curious land, like a flower beneath the sunlight of a warm May morning.

Scarcely had I penetrated more than a dozen leagues into this wild untrodden territory than I made the astonishing discovery that the sun's light was obscured the entire day; while the sky, by night, was flooded with a soft, mysterious light, quite bright enough to enable me to read the finest print with perfect ease. In other words, the natural order of things was exactly reversed. So, I—always quick to accommodate myself to existing circumstances—made use of the dark days for rest and sleep, and pursued my journey by night.

One morning, however, the mystery was explained. The impenetrable clouds, which had been veiling the heavens like a pall, suddenly sank earthward; and, to my almost unspeakable astonishment, I discovered that this blanket of inky blackness was made up of living creatures—gigantic fire-flies, quite as large as our ordinary bat, and far blacker in both body and wing.

When night came, this living tissue was changed into a robe of sparkling, shimmering glow, mantling the heavens like a garment of burnished gold spangles, upon which a burst of soft light, as if from ten times ten thousand waxen tapers, fell in dazzling effulgence. It was something to see and die for. Bulger's poor startled mind made him look up, half in dread, half in wonder at this mysterious fire, which enveloped everything in its flame, and yet consumed nothing. I had but one thought. It was to capture several of these huge fire-flies. Night after night I watched patiently for an opportunity.

It came at last.

I was preparing some coffee, and my back was turned. Suddenly, I was startled by a piteous outburst, half whine, half bark, from poor Bulger. A cluster of these living stars had fallen at his very feet. Quicker than thought, I sprang forward and threw my blanket over them. Then, with the greatest care, I transferred them to one of my wicker hampers.

Bulger, upon seeing this basket on fire and yet feeling no heat, was most painfully nonplused. He walked round and round the improvised cage, keeping at a safe distance, however, now sniffing the air, now looking up to me with a most imploring glance—as if to say:

"Dear little master, do explain this thing to me! Why doesn't it burn up?"

To my great disappointment, the three captives died after a few days' imprisonment, not, however, until they had laid a number of eggs—about the size of robins' eggs—which I packed away most carefully in my boxes of specimens.

I may say, right here, that, upon my return home, I subjected these eggs to a gentle warmth and was charmed to see emerge from each one of them a larva about the size of a pipe-stem; but, to my delight—and to Bulger's absolute terror—this pipe-stem affair had, inside twenty-four hours, become as large round as a Frankfort sausage.

In due time, they passed into the chrysalis state. But this apparent death seemed to become a real one.

Weeks went by and there were no signs of a metamorphosis.

I was cruelly disappointed.

More important matters, however, arose to occupy my thoughts. The sleeping fire-flies of the Orient were quite forgotten, when, one evening, the women servants of the manor house, with blanched faces and piercing shrieks came literally tumbling headlong down the main stairway.

Fortunately I was sitting on the first terrace of the park. With a bound I gained the hall-way, and snatching down a brace of fire-arms from the wall, throw myself in front of the wildly shrieking troop of women, calling out in stentorian tones, for silence.

"Has murder been committed?" I cried, "Is there revolt among the tenantry? Has blood been shed?"

"No! no! little baron!" they exclaimed, with wild eyes and clasped hands, "but the castle is on fire! Your rooms are in flames! Your treasures will be consumed! Quick! little baron; save them! save us! save the gracious lady and venerable master!"

Quicker than it takes to tell it, I laid hold of the rope of the alarm bell and set it pealing.

The retainers answered with a will. A score of them burst into the hall-way ready for the word of command.

"Seize the fire-buckets, my lads!" I called out calmly, but in a tone of sufficient dignity to inspire perfect confidence.

"Man ladders to the windows of my apartments."

By this time another gang of the tenantry came rushing in upon the scene. I met them with an order to unhang the portraits in the baronial dining-hall, and store them in a place of safety. Then, having spoken a few words of comfort to the gracious baroness, my mother, I seized a fire-bucket and led the line up the stairway. Laying my shoulder against the door of my apartments, I burst it open; and, with head lowered before the blaze of light dashed in, followed by the bucket-bearers.

"Halt!" I cried.

It was too late! some of my finest hangings and rugs were spoiled by half a dozen buckets of water emptied upon them.

The mystery was solved! The blaze of light that fairly flooded my apartments proceeded from the huge fire-flies which had hatched out without being noticed by me. But I didn't begrudge my ruined hangings.

There was my recompense clinging to the walls.

I need hardly say, that the giant fire-flies were the wonder of their day, and brief as it was it sufficed to cover my name with a glory as resplendent, as their mysterious fire.

I caused a huge lamp of exquisite oriental pattern to be constructed, and having placed the light-bearers beneath its dome of polished glass, passed several nights in the most perfect happiness, seated in its soft, white light, poring over musty volumes of travel, written in tongues long-forgotten, save by a few of the most learned scholars. But, my delight was short-lived. The gigantic fire-flies absolutely refused to eat anything, although I tempted them with a hundred different kinds of food. Little by little, their mysterious flame lost its bright effulgence—burning lower and lower until it went out in death.

To resume the thread of my story:

I was growing impatient to reach the table-lands of the Himalayas, and taxed the powers of endurance of my guide to their uttermost.

In our bivouacs at times he would encircle my slender ankle-joints with his thumb and index finger and exclaim: "All the gods helped make thee, little baron!" meaning that there dwelt great will-power and strength in my small body.

The skies now cleared up. The living pall rolled backward, toward the horizon, and naught remained to tell of the mighty flood of light which so lately overran the heavens save a faint shimmering streak of fire in far distant Western sky.

Soon it went out altogether. Thus far, our journey had been through an open country, with here and there a clump of forest trees which, at last grew so frequent that I felt sure we must be approaching the confines of some extensive piece of woodland.

In this I was not mistaken.

As we reached the summit of a range of hills, I could see in the distance a long, dark line of forests. My guide, who had pushed on ahead, in search of water, came galloping wildly back.

I paid no particular attention to him, until I noticed that he had dismounted in great haste and was running towards me.

"Turn back! turn back! little master!" he exclaimed, throwing himself at my feet, and clasping my legs with his arms!

"Enter not in the Palin-mâ-Talin! (Home of Darkness.) A hundred pilgrims have laid their bones in the moss-grown depths of the Great Gloomy Forest! It is as pathless as the ocean! It is as silent as death. It is as limitless as the heavens! Nor man nor beast can breathe its cool, moist air, and live! Turn back! I beseech thee, little baron; tempt not the Palin-mâ-Talin!"

"Palin-mâ-Talin! Palin-mâ-Talin!" I repeated, as if awakening from a dream, "why, it must be—ay, there can be no doubt of it—the Great Aryan Forest, in which, countless centuries ago, the human race having abandoned their holes in the clay banks, first learned to hunt the wild beast, feed on his flesh and clothe themselves in his skins."

In my joy at this discovery I threw a handful of gold pieces into the lap of my astonished guide.

Bulger, always ready to share my happiness, came bounding to my side, barking loud and shrill. To my infinite surprise, the answering bark of a dog came floating on the morning breeze.

"Hark!" I exclaimed, in a whisper. This time it was unmistakable.

"'Tis one of Benè-agâ's dogs!" was my guide's reply. "Come, little master, let me lead thee to his cave. It is beneath the very shadow of the Great Gloomy Forest. He can tell thee of its dangers, for he hath crossed it!"

"And come safely back?" I asked.

"While life lasts he will sit in the gloom of Palin-mâ-Talin!" murmured the man.

"What meanest thou?" I cried.

"I mean, that the noonday sun cannot chase the shadows from his eyes."

"He is blind?"

"Ay, little master, blind!" was the guide's reply, "and yet save this blind hermit, there lives no human creature who can lead thee safely through the Great Gloomy Forest!"

"Have done with thy jesting!" I cried.

"Nay, little master!" was the man's answer. "I speak in all truth and reverence, for Benè-agâ is a holy man, and in him dwells such a radiant spirit, that his path is illumined and his footsteps are sure when other men would walk to their destruction!"

"O, lead me to him!" I exclaimed with ill-concealed joy. "A thousand pieces of gold are thine, if the blind hermit consents to be my guide."

"A thousand pieces of gold!" repeated the guide with a gleam in his dark eyes. "Ah, little baron, no one can earn that princely reward, excepting thee thyself! Who am I, poor, miserable, ignorant slave that I am, that I should attempt to move this saintly and learned man in thy behalf? He would heed the cry of one of his dogs far more quickly than he would my chatter!"

"Is he so unlike his kind," I asked, as we rode slowly along, "as not to love gold?"

"Ay, little baron! if every dried leaf in his forest path were a coin of burnished gold, he would not stoop to pick one up!"

"Are his ears closed to flattery?"

"As closed as his eyes are to the sun's rays."

"Loves he not some savory dish?"

"Fruits and berries content him!"

"Surely a draught of rare old wine, mellow with age, fragrant as crushed roses, purple within the beaker, would warm his heart to quicker beating, and incline him to serve me!"

"Nay, nay, little baron! a gourd full of water from the sparkling rill near his home in the rocks, is sweeter to him than any nectar ever distilled by the hands of man!"

"They say he is learned! Then shall my gift be a score of rare old books, priceless parchments filled with thoughts so noble, so deep, so subtle, that, to read therein, means to live a thousand years in one!"

"Ah, little master," replied my guide, with a mournful smile, "thou art still astray. This dweller 'mid the rocks, this lover of solitude, the measure of whose life, they say, is full three hundred years, knows no other books than the pages of his own soul! On these he has turned his thoughts so long and so diligently, that the foolish outpourings of so-called authors seem like the merest prattle of childhood."

"But look, little master, we are drawing near the home of the blind hermit."

I turned my eyes in the direction indicated.

A rocky ledge, wild, craggy, broken, seamed and twisted, crowned with a growth of pine trees having knotted, gnarled and fantastically-shaped trunks and boughs, shut in our view. As we drew near the entrance to Benè-agâ's cave, a troop of dogs, of various ages and species, came bounding forward with loud barkings.

Bulger advanced to meet them boldly, after first glancing at my face to see whether I objected or not.

It was a long while since he had met any of the members of his race, and then again, he doubtless wished to get a good look at these residents of such a distant land.

The feeling seemed to be mutual, for in an instant the barking ceased, and the hermit's dogs gathered about Bulger in silent wonderment.

After a series of salutations, which plainly ended in the best of fellowships, the hermit's dogs endeavored to lure Bulger away for a run in the forest and fields, but in this they were, I need scarcely say, entirely unsuccessful. Bulger gave them to understand in very decided terms that he would talk with them, and even romp with them, but that it must all be done under the eyes of his master.

We now halted and dismounted.

"This is the place," said my guide in a low tone. "Through that deep fissure in the rocks thou wilt find a path that leads to Benè-agâ's cave. Enter it boldly, little master. At the entrance to the cave thou wilt find a dried gourd hanging on the rocky wall. Seize it! When shaken, its seeds will give forth a loud, rattling sound. This done, move not, though the shadows of evening find thee still standing at the door of Benè-agâ's cave. Farewell, little master; Heaven make good to thee tenfold thy kindness to me! I will await thee three days. If by that time I do not hear thy voice calling me to serve thee again, I shall return to my kindred!"

Advancing to the cleft in the rocky wall, I found the gourd hanging by a leathern thong.

The loud rattling of the seeds, as it broke the deep silence of this wild and lonely place—fit vestibule to a temple devoted to silence, solitude and meditation—startled me painfully.

Restoring the gourd to its place, I leaned forward to catch the faintest sound of the hermit's voice which might reach my ear.

It came not.

The silence grew more oppressive than before.

The broken, twisted rocks, overhanging and surrounding me, took on fantastic forms.

In every dark cavity I saw some misshapen creature stirring about.

A dreadful feeling of loneliness crept over me.

No sound came, save the loud throbbing of my own heart.

A half hour went by!

Benè-agâ spake not a word.

"Perhaps he sleeps!" I whispered to myself.

My words awakened the echoes of the rocky recesses, and the word "sleeps" came back to my ears in a hundred different tones, now loud and hissing, now soft and sibilant.

At last a full hour had now gone by since I had rattled the seeds of the dried gourd, and yet the blind hermit spake no word.

Again the death-like stillness sank upon the place, and the gathering shadows grew deeper and deeper.

Could the guide have played me false? I asked myself.

Nay, that cannot be!

And yet why comes there no sound from Benè-agâ's cave?

Shall I summon him once more? May he not have gone forth to gather food?

Am I doomed to be turned back when I have reached the very threshold of my long-wished-for desire?

These and a hundred other questions flitted through my mind as I stood in the dark and gloomy corridor that led to Benè-agâ's cave.

By the shadows on the rocky wall I could see that I had now been standing at least two hours awaiting summons to draw nearer.

But hush!

He speaks at last!

My heart bounded joyfully, and yet as if with a leaden weight upon it.

"Who is it that disturbs my meditation?" were the hermit's words.

"A stranger! A brother! One who needs thy guidance!" I replied in a firm, yet humble tone.

"No human creature is stranger to me! Thou art too young to be my brother! The light that is left me shines only for my own feet!" came slowly from the hermit's cave in a full, deep, rich voice.

"True, great master," I replied, "but then, may I not be thy son, and follow thy footsteps?"

"Thou art very wise for thy years," spake Benè-agâ.

"Not so wise, great master," was my reply, "as I shall be when I have sat at thy feet."

"Come somewhat closer; thy child-voice sounds like an echo," continued the blind hermit. "And yet thou art not a child! Some great spirit plays in sportive mood behind thy face! I see that thou art blue-eyed and flaxen-haired. Thine eyes are set wide asunder, and above them towers a dome of thought. Thy home is in the land of the Norseman. At least thy fathers dwelt there. On thy cheek glows the crimson which, in the peach and apple-land, stains the autumn foliage!"

As I had not yet even stepped within Benè-agâ's cave, these words of the blind hermit caused a strange feeling, half of fear, half of dread fascination, to creep over me.

My heart throbbed violently.

His ear, far keener than birds' or beasts', caught the sound.

"Fear not, little one!" said he, in deep, rich tones, full and swelling like the voice of organ pipes, "if thou canst content thyself with a handful of berries when thou art hungry, with a draught from the neighboring rill when thou art thirsty; if thy young limbs are sturdy enough to wrest repose from a rocky couch, then art thou welcome! If not, go thy way! For twenty years I've been busy with a certain problem, and have no time to stop and spread a more bountiful repast!"

"But season thy frugal fare with thy wisdom, great master," I returned, "and it will be sweeter to my palate than stall-fed ox and mellow wine."

"Come somewhat nearer, little traveler, so that I may see thee better!" spake the blind hermit, kindly and gently.

I did not wait for further summons, but stepped boldly into Benè-agâ's cave.

It was, in truth, little more than a lofty cleft in the rocks, with several deeper recesses, in which the shadows lay undisturbed. Its roof of jagged, broken and blackened masses of stone, was arched and lofty. In and about it, flocks of small swallow-like birds nested, and at times broke out in musical twitterings. Barren, gloomy and utterly forlorn as the place was, without chair, mat, bed or blanket, every thought of its awful loneliness and abject surroundings vanished from my mind, as I fixed my eyes upon its occupant.

As I had stepped within the limit of Benè-agâ's cave, he had slowly risen from his bench of stone, and now stood erect before me. Of powerful build, tall and majestic, with long snow-white hair and snowy beard, he towered like a statue of

Parian marble in the dim twilight, to which now, however, my eyes had become accustomed.

I gazed upon him, half in fear, half in delight.

I could feel my breath coming fast and faster, as I riveted my gaze upon his wonderful face, so full of love, patience, courage and contentment.

Had he bent his eyes upon me, I would never have believed him blind, for they were unclouded, full and lustrous. And yet, on second look, I saw that their gleam was like the brightness of the polished gem, that lacks the softness of living, sensitive orbs.

Benè-agâ was clad in a rude garb of dried skins, from which the hair had been skilfully scraped. Tossed back from his broad and massive brow, his white locks hung in heavy ringlets on his broad shoulders, while his wonderful beard, as white and glistening as spun glass—around his body twice entwined—clung like a snow-wreath twisted about a sturdy oak by the circling gale.

So, like a mighty son of earth he towered, rude, yet noble; untaught yet learned, human yet godlike that I stood transfixed. My tongue forgot its tricks of speech. I felt that I should turn to stone, if he did not speak to me.

While standing thus speechless, robbed of power to move a limb, Bulger broke the spell!

At Benè-agâ's feet lay a sick dog, infirm thro' age and not ailment; blind like his master, his head pillowed on some soft dry leaves—the only semblance of bed within the hermit's cave.

Bulger's gaze fell upon this pitiful spectacle. With cautious step, outstretched neck, and wide-opened eyes, he approached his sick brother, sniffed him over, licked his face and ears, whined piteously and then fixed a pleading look upon me as if to ask: "Dear little master, canst thou do nothing to help my poor, sick brother? Canst thou not make him well again, so that I may coax him out into the warm sunshine to play with him?"

Benè-agâ spake: "I see that thou art not alone, little wanderer, thou bringest a companion with thee. He is welcome. His tenderness and sympathy will carry joy and gladness to the heart of my suffering friend, whose head I've pillowed upon some soft grass! I, too, love dogs! Thou seest they are my sole companions. Their love is less exacting than human love. They require no pledge or promise. They understand my silence, read my thoughts and are content!"

"But, come! little traveler, time presses. Speak! What brings thee to Benè-agâ's cave? If it be idle curiosity, depart! But, if thou seekest counsel; if thou comest with honest intent to ask my advice in some arduous matter, I am ready to serve thee!"

"I thank thee, great master!" I replied, humbly. "Know then that I would traverse the Great Gloomy Forest and that report hath reached mine ear that thou alone, of all human beings, canst guide me through its never-lifting shadows, shield me from its poisonous vapors and let me not follow my own foot-prints in ever-widening circles, until reason itself feels the dreaded spell of that vast, trackless, pathless wilderness!"

"'Tis true!" gave answer Benè-agâ in deep, sad tones. "I can perform the service thou askest! But, O, my son! thou must know that a most sacred vow holds me in its mysterious power, securely locked, that I should lead no fellow-creature through that pathless wood, save on certain conditions!"

"Name them, great master!" I cried.

"That he who asks this service," continued Benè-agâ, "shall tarry thirty days and nights with me in my rocky home, to inure him to the burden of awful gloom and silence; that he, in all that time, taste of no food save the berries, on which I feed; slake his thirst with no draught other than that which I bring him from the neighboring rill and sleep on the bare rock, even as I do! Reflect! the apprenticeship is severe. Deem it not dishonorable, nor weak, to shrink from so hard a task! Pause, reflect, ere thou answerest. I'll resume my meditations for an hour and then question thee again!"

"Be it so, great master!" I made answer; and, Benè-agâ's sightless eyes seem to turn to the shrunken form of the dying dog.

Silence filled the cave, and feeble twilight struggled against the gathering gloom. My thoughts turned homewards! I could hear the gentle voice of the baroness, my mother. The castle windows were lighted, and the tall lindens shook a rich perfume from their blossoming boughs. All seemed so sweet and peaceful. My mother's voice reached me—I caught its every word: "Set forth my son's repast!" said she in soft, mild tones. "See that his favorite dishes are kept warm. Choose none but the choicest wine for him; and, take good care that his bed be soft and even, and his pillow's smooth!" My breath came only with painful effort as these words rang in my ears.

I started up with a bound. In spite of myself, I took a step toward the portal of Benè-agâ's cave, where the last rays of the setting sun tipped the angry, jagged, broken rocks with gold.

"Well, my son!" spake the blind hermit. "Art thou still resolute?"

"Ay, great master!" I cried, turning back and drawing near to him.

"Fear naught! Though puny in body, yet was I born with the strength of steel in my limbs, and the will power of a score of common men."

"Lead thou on! I will follow thee."

A faint smile spread over the noble countenance of the blind hermit, as he replied:

"I have not told thee all, my son! Till we pass from these walls of stone, and stand in the open air, thou must not speak a word aloud. Nay, nor in a whisper, either. I will set thy food and drink before thee, and that," he continued, pointing to a projecting shelf of rock, "shall be thy bed! On its bare surface, rest thy limbs when nature bids thee sleep. Art thou still resolute?"

"Ay, great master!" I replied with loud and buoyant voice, "I will do thy bidding!"

"'Tis well!" said Benè-agâ. "I like thy brave and steadfast soul! But hold me not hard of heart in condemning thee to this gloom and silence! Temper the bitterness of thy fate by giving thyself over to deep and earnest meditation, during the few brief hours that it shall last. Forget the so-called world—a bubble that bursts when thou thinkest to grasp it; a shadow, which thou pursuest with eager pace, and yet canst never overtake; a mirage, rising before the weary traveler's gaze, with visions of delicious gardens, watered by limpid rills and cooled by sparkling fountains, only to melt away and leave him more weak and fainting than before. Look within thyself! Thou art the temple of an immortal soul! Enter its portals! Fix thine eyes on the mysterious writings there unrolled! Grow not weary and discouraged if thou canst not decipher their meaning as easily as thou wouldst the books of man! And O, my son, should the gloom and silence of Benè-agâ's cave weigh too heavily on thy young soul, raise thine eyes to some one of the many lines which I have carved upon these rocky walls, in my hours of recreation. They will guide thee back to sweet contentment; give thee strength to persevere unto the end! And now, my son, farewell! Though with thee, near thee, even by thy side, yet remember, I am far from thee. Ay, farther than earthly staff can measure! Be hopeful, be strong, and thou wilt conquer! Again, farewell!"

"Farewell, great master, farewell!" I exclaimed; and, as my words echoed through the vast, rocky chamber, the last ray of light fled before the thickening gloom, and all was inky blackness.

I had noticed, ere the darkness came, that I was standing near the projecting shelf of rock which was to serve me as a bed, when nature called me to rest.

Turning now softly, I groped my way toward it and stretched myself at full length on its bare surface. For a few moments all went well. Such a conflict of thought was raging in the chambers of my mind, that I took no note of the chill which this couch of stone sent creeping through my limbs. I closed my eyes, thinking to coax sleep to them, and thus forget the ever-increasing pang!

In vain! It seemed as if death itself had seized my feet between his icy palms!

Sharp pains leapt from one joint to another, and wherever my body came into contact with that couch of stone, it seemed as if a thousand needles pricked my flesh. Half-crazed by the ever-increasing agony, I tossed from side to side, like one in delirium. At times I sat up to escape from stupefying dizziness which caught me in its swift, encircling whirl! My heated pulse beat at the thin walls of my temple, until it seemed as if I should go mad! A rushing, soughing, gurgling sound of many waters roared in my ears, while strange, fantastic forms, in lines of fire on inky background, flitted to and fro before my eyes, until I began to fear I should soon be doomed to sit in eternal gloom like Benè-agâ himself.

And now heat and cold held alternate sway within my tired and broken frame. Vainly I strove to wet my parched lips with my tongue! The fever had dried it to a chip. For a few brief moments the torture ceased!

I breathed more freely!

My limbs, thought I, are getting used to their couch of stone! I shall full asleep and forget my sufferings!

But no! With redoubled fury they came back to their work.

I dared not cry out so soon to Benè-agâ, for mercy, for release from the cruel conditions he had imposed upon me! Rather death than yield so quickly; shrink so like a coward who stands motionless and trembling on the battle field, as a spent ball strikes his breast.

I slept at last!

But O, what a broken, fevered sleep it was! A sleep with unclosed eyes, full of dark and dismal sights. I could stand no more. I yielded and longed for death. In thought, I kissed my parents' hands and felt their soft caresses on my brow and face. And then, it seemed the gracious baroness, my mother, caught my hand in hers and pressed it fervently on her lips. The kiss was so warm, so tender, so life-like, that I started up like one awakening from a long delirium. It cannot be a dream, I murmured, I am awake!

Tossing my racked form over on its side, so that I could touch my right hand—the one on which I had felt the kiss, with my left the mystery was explained.

'T was Bulger!

He was beside my couch of stone. It was he who had licked my cold, numb hand and turned my thoughts homeward. I caressed his head and ears and sought to make him lie down lest the rustle might disturb the blind hermit. He refused to obey, altho' I thrice let him know my wishes. It was his first act of disobedience and for an instant drove all thoughts of pain from my mind. To all my suffering now came this new grief.

Aroused from my stupor at last, by his persistent refusal to obey I collected my thoughts sufficiently to realize that he was bent upon leaping on my couch. His forefeet were already resting upon its edge. I dared not resist lest he should break the solemn stillness of Benè-agâ's cave by giving vent to some sound of entreaty. No sooner had he sprung upon the rocky shelf than I felt him crouching on its edge, and reaching down as if in the act of seizing something in his teeth, something so heavy, too, that it called for violent exertion. Whatever it was, I was not slow in discovering that he was endeavoring to drag it upon my rocky couch. Half rising, I stretched out my hand to solve the mystery.

O beloved Bulger!

In an outburst of affection I pressed my lips repeatedly upon his body. He took no note of my caresses, but only tugged the harder at the thing he held within his teeth. It was my blanket!

Taught in his early years to fetch my slippers, my gloves, my cap to me, when he found them lying here or there, he had never forgotten to render me these petty services. And thus, noticing that my blanket had, apparently, been forgotten, he seized it, heavy as it was and dragged it to his little master's bed.

Regardless of Benè-agâ's ire; unmindful of the fact that to accept Bulger's gift was plainly an open breach of the compact between the blind hermit and me, I wrapped my bruised and aching body in the thick, warm covering and fell into a long refreshing sleep.

Such was my first night in Benè-agâ's cave. The next day was bright and clear and the rocky chamber seemed less dismal to me. My eyes were becoming accustomed to the gloom.

From morn till night, I shunned that bed of torture, passing my time studying out the hidden meaning of the words which Benè-agâ has carved on the rocky walls; watching the birds as they flitted in with food for their nestlings or standing near the blind hermit with my gaze riveted upon his noble features, thick, clustering hair and far-flowing beard!

From this time forth all went well. I soon forgot the long hours of that terrible night of silence and despair. Indeed, I was astounded to find how swiftly the time sped along when one gives himself up to deep and all-absorbing meditation.

Days and nights flitted by like alternate hours of light and darkness.

I was startled from a deep sleep by hearing the full round voice of Benè-agâ saying: "Up! up! little traveler, up! my son, the morn is breaking. The appointed hour has come! To-day we must enter Palin-mâ-Talin or all thy apprenticeship shall have been in vain!"

I sprang up; and, approaching Benè-agâ, related in tones of unfeigned grief, how I had disregarded the sacred compact between us; and, that, altho' it cut me to the heart, to be obliged to turn back, when I stood upon the very confines of the Great Gloomy Forest, yet I was not worthy to follow him, and was firmly resolved not to plead for mercy!

All! I told him all! how my frame had been so racked by pain that I was upon the very point of crying out for release from the terrible compact, when my beloved Bulger came to my relief, and saved me from that degradation. He heard me in silence, his noble countenance giving no sign or hint of what was going on within that lofty soul.

At last, a sad and almost imperceptible smile spread over his face and he spake as follows: "Take heart, my son. All is forgiven. Thou art but a child and I should have lightened the burden of this apprenticeship. Nor can I hold thee worthy of blame for yielding to such a touching proof of thy dog's love for thee! Hadst thou repulsed him he would have lain in wakeful sorrow by thy bedside all that night—dear, faithful soul! Would he belonged to me!"

So saying, Benè-agâ bent his towering form and caressed Bulger's head and ears.

Nor was Bulger slow in returning the hermit's caresses. They had become the best of friends. Bulger felt the fascination of Benè-agâ's mysterious power from the very first.

When the hour arrived for us to leave the rocky chamber of gloom and silence, and step out into the sunlight once more, my heart broke out into its old-time beat. Had I not been in the presence of the venerable Benè-agâ, I should have leapt and danced for joy, as we emerged from that dreary abode, and I felt the warm air fan my cheek once more. But, one thing struck me now most forcibly. It was the wonderful change which I noted in the blind hermit himself, when he stood in the sunlight and the morning breezes tossed the curls of his white, silken hair, like April winds making merry with a flock of snowflakes. First, his appearance was quite different from that to which I had become accustomed. A leathern cap crowned his massive head, and held his thick, rebellious hair somewhat in control. His wide-flowing beard had entirely disappeared beneath his rude garb, save where it clothed his face and neck. I saw at once that he was clad for work— for toilsome progress through Palin-mâ-Talin's thick growth. In his right hand he carried a curious rod or wand, long, slender, polished and extremely flexible. I soon learned to wonder at his extraordinary skill in using this staff to guide his steps or discover the nature of any object not within the reach of his hands. A rude pouch or leather bag was swung across his shoulder.

The change in Benè-agâ's manner was still more noticeable. To me, this change was as pleasing as it was unexpected. In a brief half hour he became another man. His deep, rich voice, soft and round as the sound of an organ-pipe took on a mellower tone! A faint smile wreathed his noble features, as the sunlight fell upon them. His step became quick and elastic, his movements brisk and agile. So wonderfully keen were his remaining senses that only the closest observer could have guessed that he was blind.

Turning in the direction of the spot where his dogs were at play, he startled me by breaking out into a joyous,—

"Yo ho! my children! Yo ho! my brothers! Here to me! Here to me!"

His dogs—Bulger among them—bounded forward with a loud chorus of barking. Benè-agâ caught the stranger's voice. "It pains me deeply," he cried, "to rob him of his playfellows, for I see him gamboling and sporting with my children!"

As the blind hermit stooped, his dogs, with loud cries of sorrow at parting, sprang up to lick his face and hands.

"Go, my children! Go, my brothers!" said Benè-agâ. "Content yourselves. I'll come again soon, very soon, with love warmed by absence!"

All was now ready for the start. Beneath the rising sun I could see a long, dark line, far away, where earth and sky came together. It was Palin-mâ-Talin. Home of Darkness! The Great Gloomy Forest!

Thither Benè-agâ now directed his footsteps with astonishing rapidity of gait, tapping the ground with his long, polished wand as he hurried along!

Awe-struck, I followed my blind guide!

In comparison with such miraculous powers of hearing, smelling and feeling, my eyes were worthless. Ever and anon he called out to me:

"Guard thee well, my son, a viper stirred in the grass to thy left! Guard thee well, my son, to touch the leaves of the flowering shrub through which we are passing now—they are poisonous."

"Guard thee well, my son, to taste the waters of the rivulet to which we are coming, until I have made trial of its purity."

"Guard thee well, my son, to pluck one of the flowers which now delight thy eye, and charm thee with their odor. 'Tis next to death to breath their perfume close to thy nostrils."

"Guard thee well, my son, to crush upon thy skin one of the little insects which now fill the air, lest thou spread a subtle poison o'er thy flesh!"

As we drew near to the outer edge of the Great Gloomy Forest, a strange joy lit up Benè-agâ's face. He beat the air with his polished wand in graceful curves and circles, as he poured forth, half singing, half reciting, a sort of chant, invocation, or mysterious greeting to Palin-mâ-Talin, Home of Darkness!

As if charmed by the rich music of his own voice, his spirits ran higher and higher. At times he halted to catch the soft echoes as they came floating back on the wings of the morning air.

As nearly as I can remember Benè-agâ's chant was something like this:

"O, la, la, la, la, l-a-a-a-a! Hail to thee, Palin-mâ-Talin. Shadowy Land! La, la! Lu, la, lo, li! Lu, la, lo, li! We are coming to thee, beloved Temple of Silence and Gloom! Let us into thy dark corridors, Palin-mâ-Talin Lo-il-la! Lo-il-la! Thou art victor! Palin-mâ-Talin, my beautiful! From thy buckler of darkness fall the Sun's arrows, splintered and broken! O, la, la, la, la, la, l-a-a-aa-a-a! We are coming King of Gloom and Stillness! Palin-mâ-Talin. O silent domain! Let us in from the roar and the glare! Let us in from the roofless world. We are near at hand, Palin-mâ-Talin! Swing open thy black portals! Lift thy veil of Gloom! Admit thy children into thy silent chambers. O, Palin-mâ-Talin, Lo-il-lo! Lo-il-lo! Lo-il-lo! Lo-il-l-a-a-a-a-a-a!"

At last we stood by the very edge of Palin-mâ-Talin.

Benè-agâ swept his polished wand against the foliage of one of the low-hanging, far-reaching branches; then, sprang forward and seizing a handful of the leaves, crushed them in his grasp and raised them to his nostrils. "This is not the gateway, my son" he cried, "we must turn farther northward!"

After about half an hour, he again halted and reaching out for a handful of the leaves inhaled their odor.

"Not yet! not yet!" he murmured. "Somewhat northward still! Be not troubled, my son. Thou see'st Palin-mâ-Talin with thine outward eye! Not so Benè-agâ! He must lay his hand upon the very walls of this Temple of Silence and Gloom ere he can see it!"

Suddenly the blind hermit paused. His thin nostrils quivered, his massive breast heaved convulsively. "We are almost there!" he spoke in measured tones. "I catch the perfume of the foliage which clothes the two ebon columns of the gateway." I looked and saw before me two towering trees, whose wide-reaching branches swept the very ground. Side by side they stood, alike in size and grandeur. Benè-agâ passed his hand caressingly over the first branch which brushed his cheek and pressed its leaves to his lips; then, broke out into his wild chant once more.

I stood looking at the blind hermit and listening to his song of greeting, hardly knowing what to expect next when, suddenly, he threw himself upon his knees and crept under the far-reaching branches of one of these gigantic sentinels of the Great Gloomy Forest.

Bulger and I followed him! Thus it was we entered the domain of Palin-mâ-Talin, Home of Darkness. I shall not try to describe to you the solemn stillness, the mysterious twilight of the Great Gloomy Forest, nor to paint for you the wonderful beauty of the deep green mosses which covered rocks and trees: trailed from the swaying branches, carpeted the floorway, or hung like heavy canopies, from tree to tree, above our heads, and increased the gloom caused by the thick, interlacing foliage.

I had followed Benè-agâ's noiseless footsteps about half a mile into the stilly depths of Palin-mâ-Talin when, I began to feel a strange chill creep over me; beginning at my very finger tips and pursuing its insidious way toward my very vitals. So rapidly did it run its benumbing course that I was upon the point of calling out to the Benè-agâ, when he halted; and having broken a twig from a tree with foliage of dark green and polished leaves, bade me eat them, saying:

"Palin-mâ-Talin does no harm to those that know him!"

I found the leaves pungent and agreeable to the taste. Their effect was magical. My limbs at once forgot their numbness and my step lost its heaviness.

We had now been several hours in the Great Gloomy Forest; and, thus far, Benè-agâ had advanced into its ever-increasing gloom—for night was falling, without a halt.

Had Benè-agâ had as many eyes as Argus and each of lynx's power, he could not have pursued his way thro' Palin-mâ-Talin's gloomy corridors more easily and more securely. His polished wand flashed like a thing of life in his miraculously trained hand, touching everything, vibrating, swinging, advancing, retreating, with a rapidity, that my eyes could not follow.

"O, great master!" I called out to him, "let me not be presumptuous enough to speak to thee of things which should be left unstirred in the chambers of thy mind, but if it be permitted to me to know, tell me how thy rayless eyes can pierce this gloom and find a path thro' this trackless forest, wrapt in the gloom and silence of ten thousand years!"

"It shall be as thou wishest, son;" replied the blind hermit "the little there is to know thou shall hear! But surely, thy young limbs must be weary. First let me make ready a bed for the night and spread some food and drink!"

So saying, he swung his leathern bag off his shoulder, took from it a roll of dried skin and spread it on the ground; then, wrenching four pine boughs from a tree near by, he thrust them in the earth one at each corner of a square, and striking a spark with his tinder-box, set fire to the pitch which trickled down the boughs.

The flickering flames cast a thousand weird shadows on the trailing mosses and black shrouded trees, and filled the air with a grateful warmth.

Benè-agâ now drew forth some dried fruit and berries.

We ate in silence.

Bulger sniffed at the food but nothing more.

Our frugal repast concluded, the blind hermit took from his leathern pouch a sharp-pointed piece of flint with which he pierced the bark of a tree near our bivouac. Into the hole he thrust a slender reed. I was astonished to see a limpid liquid flow from the end of the reed. He filled a gourd with it and placing the drinking vessel in my hand said in a low, caressing voice:

"Drink, my son! 'Twill refresh and strengthen thee!"

I raised the gourd to my lips. The liquid was cool and sweet, and very pleasing to the taste.

"Drink as deep as thou wilt, my son," cried Benè-agâ, "for Palin-mâ-Talin could slake the thirst of an army."

Again I placed the gourd to my lips. This time I drank long and deep. A gentle warmth now coursed thro' my limbs. My eye-lids sank downward, oppressed with a most delicious longing for sleep. Pillowing my head on Benè-agâ's pouch, with my hand resting on my faithful Bulger's head, I was soon wrapped in slumber.

When I awoke, it was still night. The pine knots had burned nearly out. There sat the blind hermit beside me. I could see that he was keeping watch. His head turned as I stirred.

"Thou hast asked me," he began, to tell thee how I am able to find my way thro' Palin-mâ-Talin's gloom. Here, in this trackless home of shadow no outward eyes would avail me aught. Thou hast seen how the floor of this vast Temple is everywhere alike. For it, nature has woven a carpet of thick, velvet moss which, in the flight of centuries, takes on no change of hue. 'Tis ever the same! Tear a pathway in it, in a few short days the rent will be made whole. Blaze the trees, the encircling mosses will, in a brief period hide the marks, and all thy labor will be in vain. Even supposing that thou couldst succeed in leaving a lasting trail behind thee, the deadly poison which lurks in this damp air would chill thy life blood ere thou couldst cross from outer wall to outer wall of this vast Temple, with its roof of interwoven moss and foliage, impenetrable to the noonday sun.

"Thou hast felt the first touch of that deadly chill, which curdles the warmest blood and sends a sleep of death upon the rash intruder! But to me, O, my son, Palin-mâ-Talin is all light and glow! I cannot see that gloom which strikes such terror to thy soul. And thou must know, my son, that Palin-mâ-Talin has no shadows deep enough to hide the north star from my sight. I always know which way it was the sun went down, and which way it will be that he will rise; for all the winds are known to me, and whence they blow. To thy cheek the air appears to sleep at times. To mine, never! 'Tis no more a task for me to catch the breath-like zephyr—unfelt by thee—than it is for thy faithful dog to take up the trail of his master's footsteps and follow it through the crowded mart. Then again, thou must bear in mind that for a hundred years and more I've been a shadowless figure in this, home of shadows; that the trees of Palin-mâ-Talin have taken me to their hearts, and I them to mine; that not only do I know how and where they grow, but it hath been revealed to me that these towering children of Palin-mâ-Talin are not scattered helter-skelter, here and there, in orderless manner; but, that in a certain measure, they are ranged in lines from the rising toward the setting sun, each species forming a belt to itself, not like a grove by man's hand planted, but in a wild, yet orderly confusion. To thee, this would be a useless guide, for thou hast seen how the trunks are swathed up in garbs of moss, and how the gloom gives all the foliage the same deep-dark hue of green. To thine eye, here, all these trees seem alike, the countless offspring of a single sire! And yet it is not so! For, when in my progress through these lofty corridors of gloom and silence I sway too far northward or southward, a single handful of leaves crushed in my grasp, gives up the secret of my whereabouts. But, even this sure guiding string has failed me at times, and I have gone astray in the home of my friend! And yet in such moments, Palin-mâ-Talin had no terrors for me! When thus, an aimless wanderer in this trackless wood, I learned to draw aside this garb of green which decks Palin-mâ-Talin's breast, and lay my hand upon his very heart!

"So has kind nature sharpened my sense of feeling that by the simple touch of the clay beneath our feet I can set my erring footsteps right and regain my lost path. Be thou, my son, in coming years, as steadfast in thy search for truth as I have been in my endeavors to change this gloom and silence into living light and speech, and thou wilt walk through life's devious paths as easily as I thread my way through the trackless chambers of Palin-mâ-Talin!"

As Benè-agâ ceased speaking, he lifted his song, making the trailing mosses sway with the vigor of his notes, now deep and solemn, now clear and far-reaching.

The echoes came back softened down to flute notes. He listened breathlessly.

"O wonderful man!" thought I, "even the sleeping echoes rouse themselves to guide thy footsteps aright."

"Come, my son!" he cried in tones of gladness, "our torches go to their end. Let us push on! Though the sun be not yet high enough to chase the inky darkness out of Palin-mâ-Talin's depths, still, with this guiding string thou canst follow me!"

Saying this, he placed the end of a leather thong in my hand, and we set out once more.

After we had been an hour or so under way, the sun's rays began so to temper the darkness of the Great Gloomy Forest, that my eyes were of some slight use to me!

Again Benè-agâ broke out in a wild chant, and paused to catch the echo.

"Ah," murmured the blind hermit, half in soliloquy "that was a greeting from the drowsy waters of Lool-pâ-Tool!"

Imagine the feeling of utter helplessness which came over me an hour or so later when, suddenly I found myself standing upon the banks of a broad streamlet, of hue blacker than the wings of night, apparently stagnant; or, at least so sluggish as to seem well deserving of the title "Drowsy Waters."

"This is Lool-pâ-Tool!" said Benè-agâ, as he rested his chin on his hand and seemed to be gazing down on its inky surface.

But how to cross it, for no bark was moored in sight—was now the bewildering thought which oppressed my mind! Surely it cannot be forded, for to the eye it seemed as deep as it was silent and mysterious. Nor yet, would it be otherwise than inviting death itself to plunge into its stagnant waters and swim to the other side.

While I stood thus wrapped in a cloud of anxious thought, Benè-agâ himself seemed scarcely less perplexed. His usual calmness had deserted him.

Drawing some pebbles from his leather pouch, he cast them one by one into the stream, bending forward to catch the sound they made with eager, listening air. Then turning to the right he followed the banks of Lool-pâ-Tool, keeping his staff in the water and beating it gently with the tip as if striving to draw some secret from it.

Again he paused and cast some pebbles into the dark and sluggish stream, and bent forward to get their answer. Again, he woke the echoes, and listened breathlessly to the reply that came, only to take up the march after a brief delay with what seemed to me a somewhat hesitating step. Evidently he was astray. His calm, noble face lost its look of serene confidence. Suddenly halting, he reached out for a handful of foliage, crushed the leaves in a quick and nervous grasp, inhaled their odor, and then resumed his march as before, with head dropped forward on his breast, and doubt and uncertainty visible in every movement.

For an instant the thought flashed thro' my mind that possibly Benè-agâ had gone so far astray as to make the discovery of the right course impossible. I could feel my lips draw apart, and my heart creep slowly upward into my throat!

The thought of a lingering death from starvation in the chill, dark corridors of Palin-mâ-Talin, set a knife in my heart.

I almost tottered as I followed the blind hermit's lead. My tongue was too dry to let me cry out to him in my sudden despair.

While these terrible thoughts were chasing each other thro' my mind, Benè-agâ halted; and, resting his staff upon the branches of the nearest tree, broke out into one of his wild invocations:

"O Palin-mâ-Talin, Benè-agâ calls unto thee! Hear him! He is astray! Set his feet in the right path! Let him not wander aimlessly about in thy gloom and silence. O, Palin-mâ-Talin! He is thy child; be kind and loving to him!"

With these words Benè-agâ threw himself upon his knees, tore away the thick covering of moss, until he had laid bare the forest floor; from this, he took up a handful of the soil and pressed it between his fingers as if to test some secret quality.

When he arose I knew that all was well. A radiant glow played about his features. He was himself again!

Catching up his wand, he broke away with mad strides, as if pursued by very demons. Only by running could I keep within sight of him.

On! on! we sped along the banks of Lool-pâ-Tool stream of the "Drowsy Watery," mile by mile, Benè-agâ carolling his wild chants of glad thanks, I panting as if bent upon escaping fleshless death himself. Another hundred paces and I would have fallen headlong to the ground.

My feet seemed shod with lead.

Bulger set up a most piteous whining as he saw the look of despair settling on my face.

Suddenly the blind hermit halted; and, turning towards me, cried out in a joyous tone:

"This is the place my son. It is all over now! Fear nothing! Mount on my shoulders! Thou wilt not add a feather's weight to the burdens which I carry there! Be not troubled about thy dog. Lool-pâ-Tool has no terrors for him." Such was my confidence in the blind hermit's power to bear me safety across the mysterious stream that I did not wait for a second bidding to mount upon his shoulders altho' as far as I could see, the waters of Lool-pâ-Tool looked just as black and deep as ever. Advancing to the edge of the stream Benè-agâ now began, with quick and nervous movement of his staff, to search for hidden stepping stones.

In vain I strained my eyes to catch some sign of resting place for his feet.

And yet, they were there: for with giant strides, steady, sure and rapid, Benè-agâ passed over the "Drowsy Waters" of Lool-pâ-Tool and set me safety down on the other bank. I made effort to speak my thanks. But, wonderment had robbed my tongue of power of utterance. I could only gaze in silence upon that noble face— now clad in all its former serenity—then turn and follow its owner's footsteps.

After a few miles further advance Benè-agâ halted, and, bending his gaze upon me, as if his eyes were as full of light as his look was of radiance, spoke as follows:

"My son, my task is done! Look, dost thou not see that gleam of light yonder? 'Tis the outer wall of Palin-mâ-Talin. Pass it and thou wilt enter the world of noise and glare once more! Thou hast no further need of me. Go straight on; and, in a brief half hour, the sun's rays will greet thee again! Once outside of this pathless wood, thou wilt find thyself upon a lofty parapet—a sheer height of two hundred feet above the plains below. Look about thee and thou wilt see a stairway of solid rock, leading downward to the plain—not such as built by hands of man, with steps of even height, hewn regular and smooth, but a rude, fantastic flight of stairs left standing there by nature when she cleared away the mass each side. Upon these narrow steps, smoothed by the beating storms of ten thousand years, the waters daily pour a treacherous slime, so that those who have rashly tried to pass to the fair land below, now lie among the jagged rocks. No foot is sure enough to tread on the slippery steps of Bōga-Drappa. To fall means certain death. I cannot counsel thee my son. Be wary! Be wise! Farewell."

As this last word fell from Benè-agâ's lips he flashed out of my sight like a spirit form.

The Palin-mâ-Talin covered him with her darkness.

He was gone.

The tears gathered in my eyes.

Fain would I have pressed its hand to my lips.

I knew it was useless for me to try and call him back or to follow him. So, with a heavy heart I turned and pressed forward in the direction he had indicated.

I was soon at the outer edge of Palin-mâ-Talin and to tell the truth I felt my heavy heart grow light again. Bulger too, showed his delight at being once more in the warm sunshine. Breaking out into the wildest barking he raced hither and thither with the joyous air of a boy set free from long and irksome task.

As Benè-agâ had described to me, I now found myself standing upon a lofty parapet, overlooking a delightful valley, thro' which I longed to wander, after my long stay in Benè-agâ's cave and the gloomy trail through Palin-mâ-Talin's depths.

Walking along the edge of the cliff I was not long in coming upon the Stair of the Evil Spirit or Bōga-Drappa as it was called.

It was jagged, irregular and tilted here and there; and yet, quite even and stair-like when one considered that it was of nature's building. As the blind hermit had warned me the treacherous slime covered Bōga-Drappa's entire length, forever renewed by the impure waters which trickled down its steps.

To attempt to descend would have been worse than madness.

No human foot was sure enough to tread those slippery stones and reach the bottom.

Although I was impelled by the strongest desire to hasten forward I saw that a single rash act might end my life.

Ordinary obstacles have no terror for me. But when nature sets a threatening barrier in my way I halt, but do not surrender.

And, therefore, I sat calmly down to ponder over the problem that faced me.

For three days I tarried on this parapet and each day I visited Bōga-Drappa and gazed long and fixedly upon its far-reaching flight of rocky steps.

On the third day I had solved the problem.

Hastily gathering up every fragment of lime-stone lying near, I piled it in a cone-shaped heap and around it and over it I laid a mass of dry leaves and billets and over all such logs as I could lift. Then, striking fire with my flint and tinder I set the pile in flames.

In the morning I was rejoiced to find a heap of the purest quick-lime beneath the ashes.

By means of an empty skull of some animal of the deer family, which I found lying near, I at once began to feed the waters trickling over Bōga-Drappa's steps with the lime.

All that day and up to the noon hour of the next, I kept the water which flowed down the stairway, milk white with the lime.

Now, however, came the greatest difficulty. From the size of the stream I realized that it would be impossible for me to stay its course by means of any dam that I could build, for a longer time than one brief half hour. But, I dared not wait too long, for the coating of lime, which, by this time I knew must have been deposited on the rocky steps, to harden in the sun.

The dam might break and undo all my work.

At high noon, when the sun was beating down the hottest, I put the last touch to my dam. I was startled to see with what rapidity the waters gathered in the basin I had built. With anxious eyes and throbbing heart, I stood at the head of Bōga-Drappa's stair of rock and gazed up and down.

I could see no signs of drying on the black and glistening steps. One moment after another glided by. At last a faint trace of whiteness began to show itself here and there. I turned an anxious glance at the gathering waters. The frail dam seemed about to yield to the ever-increasing pressure.

In one or two places, I caught glimpses of tiny rivulets trickling through.

Once more, with a terrible feeling of faintness I glanced down the long dark flight of steps. Half blinded by the noon day sun I nevertheless caught sight of a snow white crust on the stairway.

Now was my time or never!

Calling out to Bulger to precede me I sprang boldly down the stair which, till that moment had been black with treacherous slime. The waters broke away and came rushing on my very heels. Down, down, I went in headlong haste, bounding like a deer from step to step!

My heart sank within me as I felt the torrent, now mad and raging spatter its spray on my neck.

Another instant and I'm saved! My feet strike firm.

I see the fair country come nearer and nearer.

Another leap, and with my faithful Bulger I've cleared the dreaded stairway of Bōga-Drappa! Staggering forward, I reach the greensward of the valley and fall fainting, after my terrible race for life!

Bulger's mingled wailing and caresses roused me after a few moments of clouded brain and then all was well. And yet a shudder stole over me as I raised my eyes to take a last look at the rocky stairway of Bōga-Drappa, now clad once more in its black, glistening, treacherous slime.

Refreshed by a hearty meal upon the luscious fruit which grew in wonderful profusion on every side, followed by a deep draught of cool, clear spring water, and calling joyfully to my faithful Bulger to follow me, I set out for the distant summit of the ridge which shut in this peaceful little corner of the earth's surface, so well fitted for the home of human beings, and yet so utterly abandoned and tenantless, even by four footed creatures. While, I am a great admirer of nature in all her aspects from wildest grandeur to picture-like delicacy, yet no spot which is not inhabited by man or beast, can long hold me content.

I must have life, not the dull spiritless life of tree, shrub or plant, ever-chained to one spot, but the restive, bounding, throbbing life of man or animal to study, contemplate and reflect upon. Therefore, it was that I determined to pass at once out of this beautiful little valley.

I pushed on with eager step for I was desirous of gaining the high land before nightfall. In this I was successful, but the twilight had so deepened when I reached the crest of the ridge, that any survey of the country lying beyond was impossible.

Shortly after I had lighted a bivouac fire, Bulger came in with a bird—of the quail kind—and I proceeded to broil it on the live embers.

The faithful animal was delighted to be once more in a country in which he could serve me and while our supper was cooking, took occasion to go through a number of his old tricks, in order to see his little master's face brighten up.

Side by side, we lay down for the night in that far-away land, and were soon fast asleep.

The morning broke with rare splendor. I hastened to examine the country beneath me. It was dotted here and there by groves and bits of woodland and seemed unusually green and fruitful.

What attracted my attention more than anything else was the fact that, as far as my eye could reach, the region was watered by a perfect network of little rivers, which glistened in the morning sun like bands of burnished silver.

I had never seen the like. It occurred to me at once, that should these streams prove too deep and rapid to ford, it would force me to change my course entirely, and pass either to the north or south, until I reached a clear country. It was pretty well toward sundown when I stood upon the confines of this strange land which I named Polypotamo or "Many Rivers." The streams, which varied from ten to twenty feet in width, were deep, clear and swift.

As you may readily imagine such a country was very productive. Fruit and flower-bearing shrubs and trees, all of a most beautiful green grew in the wildest abundance. The air, cooled and purified as it was by the numerous streams of limpid water, was like a magic inhalation, carrying a strange feeling of dreamy delight to every part of the body.

Said I to myself:

"If this fair land be not inhabited then it is a monstrous pity, for here kind nature has spread her riches with a more than usually lavish hand."

Bulger and I stretched ourselves upon the bank of the first stream that we reached and were preparing for a nap after our long days tramp, when suddenly the strangest noises reached our ears. He started up with a look of mingled alarm and curiosity which, could I have seen my own face, I would undoubtedly have found pictured there in equally strong lines.

Louder and louder grew these curious sounds.

I listened with pricked-up ears, as I strained my eyes in the direction whence they came, eager to catch the first glimpse of the beings who uttered them.

I had not long to wait. About an eighth of a mile away, my eyes fell upon a sight, which, in spite of the possible dangers threatening my life, in case these creatures had proven to be vicious or savage, caused me to burst out into a fit of uncontrollable laughter.

There, in full view, was a troop of human creatures, dwarfish in stature—not being much over four feet in height—who seemed incapable of using their legs as we do; but moved about from one place to another by hopping, as some birds do, or as rabbits would do if they moved about standing upright on their hind legs.

In an instant they caught the sound of my voice; and, with the swiftness of

Ingersoll Lockwood

the wind, and with an ease that astounded me, leaped over the two intervening streams—each of which was at least fifteen feet in width—and came bounding toward us with the same gigantic leaps! The whole thing was done so quickly, and the mode of locomotion was so novel and altogether wonderful, that I was surrounded before I knew what happened to me.

It is needless to say that I couldn't understand their language, although I soon mastered it, consisting as it did of pure Aryan roots, no word being of more than three letters.

The Man-Hoppers—such was my translation of their name, Umi-Lobas—ranged themselves in a circle around Bulger and me, threw themselves on their faces, so to speak—for their arms were ridiculously out of all proportion to their bodies—and threatened with shrill outcries and menacing movements, to kick Bulger and me to death instantly unless we surrendered unconditionally.

It was a novel sight.

Bulger was inclined to advise resistance; but, when I had given a hurried glance at their feet, which were very large and attached to astonishingly vigorous legs, I deemed it only prudent to run up the white flag; in fact, I gave them to understand that we threw ourselves on their mercy.

But first, a word about these strange people:

They were, as I have said, small of stature, and let me add that, upon their narrow, sloping shoulders were set delicate, doll-like heads, animated by large, lustrous, black eyes of extreme softness in expression. Their arms looked like the arms of a boy on the body of a man. But, although so small, for they reached only to their waists and ended in tiny, shapely hands, yet they showed themselves possessed of extraordinary strength and dexterity. Their legs, however, were the most wonderful part of them.

In fact, I might almost say that the Umi-Lobas were all legs, so out of all proportion was the development of their limbs. The effect of this disproportion may be easily imagined. It so dwarfed their bodies that they appeared like cones set upon two legs.

"Miscreant!" cried the leader, as I learned three days later when I had mastered their language, "if thou dost not instantly admit that his majesty, Gâ-roo, King of the Umi-Lobas, is not the fastest, farthest and most graceful jumper in the world, thou shalt be kicked to death without the least ceremony!"

I made signs that I was quite willing to admit this, although I didn't understand exactly what it was!

Seeing that I was not disposed to attempt any harm, the Man-Hoppers sprang to their feet and seated themselves in a perfect ring around Bulger and me, like so many rabbits when standing on their hind feet to reach something, intent upon getting a good look at us, or at me rather, for Bulger was evidently no great novelty for them.

They kept up a perfect rattle of remarks in shrill piping tones upon my personal appearance. I, too, was by no means idle.

I kept even pace with their galloping curiosity, studying the expression of their faces and the movements of their bodies. After a few moments I was given to understand that I must start at once for the palace of their gracious monarch, Gâ-roo, the One Thousandth, for they were a very ancient people.

As I rose to my feet and took a few steps toward the water, intending to assure them that I could not leap across the stream, it became their turn to laugh.

And laugh they did too, with such spirit, such heartiness—I might almost say such violence—that I never realized till then that they laugh best who laugh last.

Again and again their piping, pygmy voices broke out in shrill chorus while their pretty doll faces were convulsed with merriment.

Bulger repeatedly showed his teeth, and gave vent to short, spiteful barks as the Umi-Lobas continued their, to him, unseemly behavior. But I knew it would only injure us in the end, if I showed any signs of anger, so I simply shrugged my shoulders and waited for them to recover from their fit of merriment. Finally, between the pauses of laughter I caught such words as:

"Pendulum-legs!"

"Man-scissors!"

"Man Tongs!"

"Flip-flop! Wiggle-waggle!"

"Here she goes, there she goes!"

Such were a few of the terms expressive of the impression which my poor unoffending legs made upon the minds of the Umi-Lobas.

They quieted down at last and again began to make signs that I should prepare to follow them.

When at last I succeeded in making them understand that I was not a jumper, and could no more leap across the stream in front of us than I could hop over the moon, their mirth now gave place to disgust. Such pleasant phrases as:—

"Lead legs!"

"Two-legged snail!"

"Little man stuck-in-the-ground!"

"Little man tied-to-his-head!" etc., etc., were fired at me.

After a consultation, it was determined to dispatch two of their number for a sort of porte-chaise in use among the Umi-Lobas in which to transport Bulger and me to the King's palace.

Away went the messengers like the wind, in leaps of twenty feet seeming scarcely to touch the ground, bounding along in the distance like pith balls. After a short delay they reappeared bearing, slung on a sort of yoke resting upon their shoulders, a stout wicker basket.

Bulger and I were invited to step into it; the cover was closed and securely fastened by a stout leathern thong. Then with a bumpety bump sort of motion away we went across land and water.

Bulger whined piteously and fixed his lustrous eyes upon me, as if to say:

"Little master, if they are transporting us to torture or death I'm glad I am with thee!"

I soon gave him to understand that there was no danger.

He returned my caresses and we both awaited further developments. It seems that the two Man-Hoppers who had been sent for the porte-chaise had spread the news of their strange capture, so the whole town was on the watch for our arrival.

At last we came to a full stop. The basket was set down on the ground and the leathern thong loosened. To tell the truth, I was as anxious to see as they were.

A terrible hubbub was in progress, those in authority having seemingly lost all control over the pushing, pulling, scrambling mass of Umi-Lobas. With such violent outcries and still more violent gestures did they gather about us, that I began to fear that they would overturn our carriage and do Bulger and me some real injury, in their mad curiosity.

Suddenly a voice, louder and shriller than all the rest, called out:

"Silence! His majesty, Gâ-roo, the Thousandth, King of the Umi-Lobas, is approaching. Down! Down! Silence! Fall back!"

One of the attendants now raised the lid of our basket and courteously invited me to step out.

Without stopping to give the thing a thought, I seized the leathern thong, sprang lightly up and threw one of my legs over the side of the basket.

Instantly there was an outburst of shrill, ear-piercing exclamations of wonder, fear, surprise, horror, delight and I don't know how many other emotions.

For a moment I was startled, and half inclined to make my way back into my basket again. Suddenly, however, it occurred to me what it all meant.

The Umi-Lobas being able to move their legs only backward and forward, and utterly incapable of moving one leg without the other, were about as much astonished at seeing one of my legs come flopping over the side of the basket, as I would be if you should throw one of your legs out sidewise and strike your foot against your shoulder.

As I sprang lightly to the ground and took a few steps towards King Gâ-roo, who stood surrounded by his court officials, a very lean Umi-Loba on one side of him and a very fat one on the other—a perfect whirlwind of such cries as: "Pendulum-legs" "Walking-Scissors!" "Measuring-Man!" "Little Man All Head!" etc., etc., burst forth.

King Gâ-roo received me very pleasantly; requesting me to walk, run, hop on one foot, cross my legs, he, standing with wide opened eyes as I went through my paces to please him.

He then asked me my name, my rank at home, my profession, my age, what I liked to eat and drink, how much heavier my head was than my body, etc., etc. I made such a good impression on the King of the Umi-Lobas that he turned and invited me to spend some time at his palace.

I was delighted, for I was very desirous of studying the manners and customs of these strange people, and of conversing with their learned men. Suddenly, there was a great change manifest in the King's manner toward me. He listened with knitted brows and compressed lips, first to his fat counsellor and then to his lean one.

His lean minister, so lean that he appeared to me to be an animated steel spring snapping apart, was named, Megâ-Zaltô or "Great Jumper," than the King himself no one being able to leap across a broader stream.

His fat minister, so fat that he was able to advance only by little hops of a few inches at a time, was named Migrô-Zaltô, or "Small Jumper," and as he had for many years been unable to race about the country like the other Umi-Lobas and had consequently had much time on his hands, which he had used to improve his mind reading and studying, until he had acquired great wisdom. Hence King Gâ-roo's choice of him as royal minister and court adviser.

I was again ordered to stand in front of his majesty, the ruler of all the Umi-Lobas.

"Sir Pendulum-legs!" said he, "upon reflection, I am persuaded that thy visit to my dominions bodes no good. Thou must know that I have two privy councillors, to whose advice I always listen and then do as I see fit. His excellency Megâ-Zaltô," continued King Gâ-roo, pointing to his lean minister, "counsels me to command that thou be stamped and kicked to death at once, saying that thou wilt work great injury among my people; thou being a foreigner from a far-away land, they will endeavor to imitate thy manner of walking. Our good old-fashioned ways of walking will be sneered at; and my people's legs will soon lose their wonderful strength and activity.

"My other councillor, who is a very learned man and loves to discuss questions of race, manners and customs with strangers, advises me to let thee live for several weeks, at least, until he has had an opportunity to get some valuable information from thee. Now, I am a quiet and peace-loving King, for nature by surrounding my dominions with such a network of rivers, and giving us the power to leap over them, makes it next to impossible for an enemy to follow us. Therefore, Little Man All Head, it is my royal will that for the present no harm come to thee!"

"Thanks, most powerful and graceful jumper in this or any other world!" said I, with a very low bow. "I accept my life at thy hands in order to use it to make known thy goodness and greatness in every land I shall pass through."

My delicate flattery touched King Gâ-roo very perceptibly. He smiled and nodded his little doll head in the friendliest manner. But Megâ-Zaltô's fierce, little face was screwed up in a thousand wrinkles. I felt within me that he was firmly resolved to do me injury.

Now, there was another interruption. A shrill, piping baby-voice suddenly rang out in a series of angry screams, while a score of other voices in soft, soothing tones could be heard as if endeavoring to comfort the screamer.

I turned my eyes in the direction of the voices. To my surprise and delight I saw coming towards me one of the female Umi-Lobas, advancing timidly with light and graceful hops, like a sparrow on the greensward. Her head and face looked for all the world like some of the wax dolls I had seen in Paris, only she was a trifle paler than they.

It was the beautiful princess, Hoppâ-Hoppâ. She seemed to be in a very fretful and petulant humor, and showed her peevishness in every movement.

Nothing pleased her. She pouted, hung her head, and threw her baby-arms about, upon the most trivial provocation.

As I learned afterwards, this all proceeded from her unwillingness to marry the lean, bony Megâ-Zaltô, who was violently in love with her, and to whom the King, in a moment of some great contentment, had rashly promised the princess in marriage, and as King Gâ-roo had in doing so taken the Umi-Lobas' vow: "May I never be able to jump farther than the length of my nose, if I break my vow," he dared not break his word, and, of course, the old, thin, bony, wrinkled Megâ-Zaltô insisted upon his sticking to the bargain.

The effect of all this was to throw the beautiful princess Hoppâ-Hoppâ into a deep melancholy. In fact, she refused absolutely to partake of any food for so long a while that everybody said sadly, "She will die!"

King Gâ-roo was beside himself with grief. But, as Megâ-Zaltô had no blood, he couldn't feel any pity for either father or daughter, and insisted that the King should stick to his bargain with him.

Led on at last by the rich reward offered by King Gâ-roo to any physician who could succeed in making princess Hoppâ-Hoppâ partake of food, one of the court physicians hit upon the following plan:

The attendants were directed to set a table in the princess' apartment, and load it down with her favorite dishes. Then the lady-in-waiting was instructed to bind a silk band around the princess Hoppâ-Hoppâ's body, when the latter retired for the night, so arranged that it should press gently, but continuously on the sympathetic nerve, and cause her to walk in her sleep.

The plan worked successfully. Every night about midnight princess Hoppâ-Hoppâ would rise from her bed, while in the deepest sleep, sit down at the table and partake of a hearty meal. After which she returned to bed, when one of the ladies of the bed-chamber immediately loosened the silken band, lest she might arise the second time and overeat herself.

Princess Hoppâ-Hoppâ advanced towards me, hopping along with a timid air, until she was close enough to get a good look at me.

I was then desired to go through my paces once more, which I did with a great deal of vigor, concluding the performance by sitting down and crossing my legs.

Hoppâ-Hoppâ smiled faintly at first; but, when it came to the leg-crossing feat, she clapped her little doll hands and broke out in a laugh about as loud as the low notes of a flute.

King Gâ-roo was crazed with joy. It was the first time Hoppâ-Hoppâ had laughed for a year. I could see that there was a hurried consultation going on between King Gâ-roo and his fat and lean ministers. I knew only too well what it all meant. But princess Hoppâ-Hoppâ interrupted the consultation, and solved the whole question herself by crying out like a spoilt child clamoring for a toy, "I want him!"

King Gâ-roo burst forth into a loud laugh, in which everyone joined, save the lean, rattle-jointed Megâ-Zaltô, who scowled fiercely at me, screwing his little face up like a dried apple.

"He is thine; take him, beloved daughter," exclaimed King Gâ-roo gayly, "and if he can cure thy melancholy and make thee once more the joy and sunshine of our Court, no one of the glorious gems which deck our royal diadem shall be too good for him."

Amid great rejoicing and loud huzzas, a silk cord was tied about my body and I was led away by the beautiful princess Hoppâ-Hoppâ. Bulger resented the indignity of tying a cord around my waist and came within an ace of setting his teeth in the thick leg of the attendant who performed that service for me. Growling and showing his teeth right and left, the poor, puzzled animal followed me to prison; I say to prison, for that was what it proved to be.

Night and day, a guard surrounded my apartments and kept within respectful distance when I was summoned to divert the gentle princess by running, hopping on one foot, walking with my toes turned out or in, or with my feet stretched far apart.

But the one thing which delighted the princess and chased the melancholy from the pretty doll face was my ability to cross my legs. This wonderful feat I was obliged to repeat and repeat until my limbs fairly ached; but no matter how often repeated to the gentle Hoppâ-Hoppâ it was ever new and wonderful, and she invariably rewarded me by smiling and clapping her baby-hands.

About this time it was that my beloved brother Bulger gave me another proof of his deep affection and most extraordinary intelligence. I had no sooner begun to prepare for bed than I noticed that something was the matter with him. He fixed his lustrous black eyes pleadingly upon me, bit my shoe playfully, tugged at my clothing, sprang upon me, then bounded off toward the bed, sniffed at it, growled in unfeigned anger, and then making his way back to me, began to tease and worry me once more. I was half inclined to get provoked. By turns I scolded and petted him. All to no purpose; he continued his strange actions, growing, if anything, more and more violent in his manner. At last I was ready for bed. Striving with all my power to quiet and console him, I made an effort to throw myself on my bed, so that he might leap up and lie down beside me.

But no, it was impossible. With grip of iron he laid hold of my night-robe and held me firmly fast, whining and crying most piteously, as if to say,

"O, loved little master, why is it that thou canst not understand me?"

Suddenly a strange thought flashed across my mind. I stooped and glanced under my couch.

Nothing seemed amiss.

Then, as if urged on by some unseen hand, I seized the bed-clothing and hurled it on the floor. Lo, the mystery was solved! There, hidden beneath the drapery, shone the tips of a dozen or more tiny blades, each sharper than a needle's point, and as I found upon examination, stained with a poison so subtle that the slightest prick would have robbed me of life. Need that I tell you how the tears burst forth, how I flung myself upon my knees and caught that beloved animal in my arms, covering him with kisses?

He was satisfied.

Again, had he added to that long list of debts due him from me—debts only to be discharged in coin fresh and bright from the heart's mint. As you have doubtless guessed, this cowardly and cruel attempt on my life was the work of that living coil of steel springs, Megâ-Zaltô, who had determined to put out of the way the hated foreigner, whose monstrous deformities were so pleasing to the being he loved.

King Gâ-roo was greatly incensed when, upon Bulger's recognition of the would-be murderer in the presence of the whole Court, the miserable wretch made a clean breast of it, and related how he had arranged the knives with his own hands.

"Out of my sight, thou unworthy servant! If I do not command that thy vile heart and viler head be parted by the executioner's axe, it is because thy father rendered mine priceless services. Go! Come not again until I summon thee!"

King Gâ-roo now took me into special favor.

In the first place, he was delighted to see how successful my efforts had been to amuse the princess Hoppâ-Hoppâ, on whose baby cheeks the roses glowed once more, and whose child-voice rang out again as of old, like a flute note or a tiny silver bell.

His majesty ordered that the Court painter should forthwith make a portrait of Bulger for the royal gallery, and that a plaster cast of my head should be taken for the royal museum.

I was much pleased with all this attention.

But I noticed that the very moment I hinted at the necessity of my speedy return home, King Gâ-roo skillfully turned the conversation to some other subject. The fact of the matter was, he feared to have me leave the palace lest his beloved Hoppâ-Hoppâ should miss my daily performances and fall back again into her melancholy.

The little princess herself was not slow in exerting her power over me. Snapping the ground with her feet, like a rabbit, when I failed to be quite as entertaining as usual, and even going so far as to threaten me with a dose of that living coil of steel-spring, called Megâ-Zaltô, when I refused to cross my legs and uncross them quickly enough to please her ladyship.

One day, being in a sort of brown study, over my position, and revolving in my mind several different ways of making my escape from King Gâ-roo's dominions, I unwittingly paid little attention to Hoppâ-Hoppâ's commands. In vain she stormed, snapping the ground with her little feet, shaking her baby hands at me, piping out in shrill and angry tones at my negligence.

I didn't quicken my pace one jot. A heavy load of thoughts oppressed my mind.

My heart was full of sorrow.

All that day I had been thinking of home, of the dear old baron and the gentle baroness, my mother, and wondering whether they missed me at the castle.

Suddenly came a messenger from King Gâ-roo summoning me at once to go to the audience chamber.

With a bound I came to myself.

The little princess Hoppâ-Hoppâ had gone to her apartments.

I started to call her back.

Every instant I expected to hear that little bundle of bones and malevolence jump out at me like a venomous toad.

With fear and trembling I betook me to the King's chamber.

To my unspeakable delight his majesty, the ruler of the Umi-Lobas, was in the rosiest of humors.

He met me with outstretched hands, poured out a beaker of wine for me, and bade me sit down at the very foot of the throne.

I strove in vain to stammer out my thanks.

He would not hear a word of them; said that "the stream should flow the other way," meaning that I was the one to be thanked.

"Now, little man all head," began the King, after I had finished my wine, "I have sent for thee to try and make thee happy, in the same measure as thou hast contributed to my happiness. This day I speak to thee from a father's heart. Thou hast restored my darling child to health and contentment, and remembering from my conversations with thee that thou art a great lover of rare and useful books, I have had copies made of every book on the shelves of the royal library, and I now beg thee to accept them as a very slight token of my gratitude."

I was speechless.

The blood rushed fast and hot to my cheeks.

I stammered out a few senseless words of protest, thanks, surprise, and what not.

The plan seemed to me only too plainly a scheme to tie me in King Gâ-roo's service, to load me with several thousand volumes which I would have no possible means of carrying with me, and which, to leave behind would be such an insult that arrest and imprisonment would most surely follow.

At last I succeeded in getting myself together in some shape, and spake as follows:

"O, most powerful, wonderful and graceful jumper of all the Umi-Lobas, Gâ-roo, thousandth of thy line, I implore thee do not load me down with such a vast and priceless treasure. Thou knowest I am but a sojourner for a brief term in thy kingdom; I have no caravan, when I go hence to transport this vast accumulation of wisdom, stored in so many thousands of thick and bulky volumes, steel-clasped and iron-hinged. Thy gift is far too princely for so humble a visitor as I. Therefore, most gracious King Gâ-roo, bestow it upon some wealthy noble of thy land, in whose spacious castle halls these books may find a safe resting-place, shelf rising on shelf, a very fortress of learning, impregnable to the cohorts of ignorance."

King Gâ-roo smiled.

Then, turning to an attendant, he said:

"Summon Poly-dotto to attend before me, and bid him bring the library with him."

I was more puzzled than ever by this command.

In a few moments the door swung open, and an aged Umi-Loba, well bent with years, with long tufts of white hair growing from his ears—for these people do not permit hair to grow upon their faces, plucking it out and destroying its roots in early life—and carrying a single volume of goodly size under his arm.

He advanced with feeble hops, steadying himself upon a staff.

His voice brought a smile to my face in spite of myself, for it whistled like a flute, unskilfully stopped, and ever and anon broke out into a funny squeak.

But although infirm of body, Poly-dotto was a perfect wonder of mind and memory.

I was fairly startled to find that Poly-dotto could understand my language with perfect ease, not a thing to startle one, either, when we stop to think that all our European tongues originated in this part of the world.

Poly-dotto hopped forward, made an attempt to bend his body more than it was, thrust the long, white tufts of hair growing from his ears into the bosom of his garb, and placed the book he had brought with him into King Gâ-roo's hands.

His majesty returned the salutation of the aged sage, and then, bending a look upon me, beckoned to me to draw near.

I obeyed.

"Receive, Sir Pendulum-legs," cried King Gâ-roo, "as a mark of my affection and a proof of my gratitude, this complete and perfect transcript of the entire royal library, for many centuries the pride of the Kings of the Umi-Lobas."

I glanced at King Gâ-roo, then at the back of the book thinking that it was merely the catalogue of the books contained in the royal library.

But, no; there was the title, "Complete Transcript," etc.

I opened the book.

Its pages were thinner than the finest tissue I had ever seen.

I turned to the last page.

Twenty thousand pages!

My astonishment was redoubled.

With some difficulty, on account of my unskilled fingers, I turned over some pages here and there. They were all closely filled with minute dots and strokes.

To my eye, one page seemed like another, a bewildering repetition of these same little dots and strokes.

I looked up at King Gâ-roo and Poly-dotto. They were both much amused over my confusion.

Like a flash the truth burst upon me. It seemed to me like waking from a dream.

Yes, there was no doubt of it. I was that moment in the land of the original short-hand writers. Here had arisen that mysterious system of recording language by means of dots and strokes, of which so many men, in so many different countries, in different centuries, had claimed to be the inventors.

In my readings of ancient peoples I had often seen it darkly hinted at, that far, far back in remote ages there existed a race of beings, with short arms and tiny hands, who had invented a written language to suit their wants, in which absolutely no letters at all were used, the words being represented by dots and strokes placed at different heights to denote different sounds.

With a sort of breathless delight I now sat down and began to examine the book anew, pausing every now and then to repeat a few words of thanks to the King of the Umi-Lobas.

"Inform little man all head, most learned Poly-dotto," cried the King, "how many volumes he holds in his hand."

Poly-dotto caressed the white tufts hanging from his ears, and spake as follows:

"The royal library which thou holdest in thy hand, contains eight thousand volumes all rare and valuable, and only to be found in the library of our royal master. These volumes treat of astrology, alchemy, divination, cheirosophy, medicine, mathematics, law, politics, philosophy, pastimes, warfare, fifty volumes of poetry, fifty of history, fifty of wonder-stories, besides several hundred treatises on theosophy, altruism, positivism, hypnotism, mind-reading, transmigration of souls, art of flying, embalming etc., etc.!"

"O, wonderful! Most wonderful!" was my ejaculation.

"But I beseech thee, O, learned Poly-dotto," I continued, "impart to me the secret of all this! Unfold to me the origin of this most wonderful system of writing whereby the wisdom of ages may be recorded in one small volume!"

Poly-dotto glanced at the king, who bowed his head in sign of his royal consent that the aged sage might speak.

"Where we now stand," began Poly-dotto, tossing back the long tufts of white hair which reached from his ears to his shoulders, "was once a rugged and mountainous country. In those days, now some thirty thousand years ago, our people were more like thine than at present. To climb the rocky sides of these mountains required long, sinewy arms and strong hands of great grasping power, and flexible legs, moving quite independently of each other, like mountaineers in all lands. But, all of a sudden, these rock-crested heights began to sink and the valleys to rise; true, very slowly and gradually, but yet uninterruptedly, so that in a few years, what had been a rough, broken country, ridged and wrinkled, began to take on the aspect of a perfectly level land. With these changes our people began to change.

"Having no longer any use for hands of iron grip and arms of tireless muscles, they were not long in finding out that this strength was leaving them, that their great breadth of shoulder and depth of chest were slowly but surely disappearing in their sons and grandsons. By a strange fatality, about this time, a terrible flood passed over our luckless land. Our panic-stricken people had just time enough to escape. For several months the regions once inhabited by a contented little nation were covered by water many fathoms deep. When, at last, the waters had subsided, and our ancestors were permitted to set foot again on their native soil, what a change met their eyes! This vast domain of our gracious master, King Gâ-roo—the Thousandth, had become as you now see it, a perfectly level plain, net-worked by the countless narrow but deep and swift-rolling streams. But the soil brought in the arms, so to speak, of these raging waters and cast upon our houses, burying them far beneath, was of most extraordinary fertility, just as you see it now. Every manner of plant, fruit, flower, vegetable and grain grows here without cultivation when once planted. Our people were not slow to take advantage of Nature's kindness and build up once more the happy homes destroyed by the flood. But now we were brought face to face with a most wonderful state of things. Here we were shut in, surrounded by a vast network of streams, and yet taught by our terrible experience so to dread water, that not even to escape from death itself could our people be induced to swim across one of these little rivers or pass over it in any sort of boat. Time went on. It was either a question of living on these long narrow necks of land, and walking scores of miles to pass around the bends and curves of the streams, or else jump over them. Our wise men issued instructions to our forefathers, telling them how from early childhood they must train their little ones to leap, encouraging them by rewards to keep up the practice until leaping became as easy to them as walking and running had been. The royal ancestors of our most gracious master enacted most stringent laws against walking and running. In a few generations great changes took place. It was not an unusual thing to see a child of eight or ten leap six or eight feet over rivulets while playing some game like your hide and seek. As these child-hoppers increased in years, their power of leaping soon led them to see that they could advance much more rapidly by jumping than by the ancient, toilsome way of setting first one and then the other foot forward.

"The streams now widened, putting the leaping powers of our people to severe tests. But we overcame every obstacle, and in a few generations it became a rare thing indeed to see a Umi-Loba moving about in the ancient manner. As you may easily imagine, Nature could not furnish vigor enough to enable our people to transform themselves in this manner, and at the same time preserve their length, strength and power of shoulders, arms and hands. A most astonishing result showed itself. What was gained below was lost above. Our people's arms began to grow flabby; their hands took on a delicate and nerveless appearance, as if a long illness had bleached and softened them. Then the wise men of our nation noticed another change. After a certain age, the arms of our children ceased growing entirely, and although our physicians made extraordinary efforts to overcome this sudden stoppage of growth, which usually occurred when our children reached their tenth year, yet all their exertions were of no avail.

"Our king, to his great dismay, saw growing up about him a race of young men whose arms were so short, and whose hands were so small and delicate, that they could no longer wield the spears and bows and arrows of our forefathers. Even the knives and forks and drinking cups had to be made smaller and smaller as these wonderful changes came about.

"And not long, too, was it before our wise men found it utterly impossible to hold and guide the long, heavy pens of their ancestors, or to lift the ponderous volumes in which our fathers had kept the records of our nation.

"With smaller pens came smaller books, and finer writing, until at last one of my ancestors, in a moment of happy inspiration, conceived the idea of giving up the ancient way of writing by means of two score or more of letters, so large that only a few of them could be written upon one line, and of which two or three were necessary in order to record one simple sound, and of using little dots and strokes as fine as hairs, to represent the sound of our words.

"Our children were delighted.

"Their short arms and tiny hands were well fitted for such work.

"In a few years the new system of writing was taught in all our schools, and by royal edict became the only lawful method of writing throughout the kingdom. Later, another of my ancestors greatly improved the system, so simplifying it that whole sentences could be recorded by a single tiny dot or hair-stroke.

"By means of this wonderful system is it that we are enabled to compress a whole library into one single book, as you have seen, and to make it possible for our royal master to carry about with him on his journeys the assorted wisdom of ages, in so compact a form that it may be placed under the royal pillow and yet not wrinkle it.

"Thou knowest full well," continued Poly-dotto, with a smile, as he raised one of his baby hands and pointed a tiny finger at the book I held in my hands, and upon whose pages my eyes were fixed in wide-opened astonishment, "that in thy country a story writer could not possibly squeeze a single one of his tales between those covers!"

King Gâ-roo laughed heartily at this speech.

After a few moments more of pleasant chat, I was dismissed by his majesty with promises of continued favor.

As I was backing out of the audience chamber, King Gâ-roo cried out gayly, as he shook a tiny finger at me:

"Look well after princess Hoppâ-Hoppâ, Little Man-All-Head!"

While seated in my apartment, the day following my reception at court and the presentation of the royal library to me, whiling away the time as best I could by dipping into the early history of the Umi-Lobas, I suddenly heard a great wheezing and whistling noise, as if some one suffering from the asthma were approaching.

Bulger gave a low growl.

I sprang up, and upon going to the door was not a little surprised to see Migrô-Zaltô, coming toward me with very short hops, every one of which drew forth a grunt.

However, he finally reached a seat in my apartment, and after half an hour's rest, addressed me as follows:

"I bring thee good news, Little Man-All-Head. His majesty, King Gâ-roo, has graciously resolved to appoint thee one of his Ministers of State. Poly-dotto has informed him that your head is exactly three times larger that the largest Umi-Lobas, and that, consequently, you must be at least three times as wise as any of his counsellors. He is, quite naturally, unwilling that any other monarch should have the use of the vast treasure of wisdom stored in thy head. His design is to treat thee like a son, to surround thee with everything that gold can buy or cunning hands fashion, for thy comfort and amusement; in a word, so to shower honors upon thee that thou shalt soon forget thy home and kinspeople."

The effect of Migrô-Zaltô's words upon me was indescribable.

I felt as if my heart were about to beat its last.

It was only by the greatest effort that I could pull myself together, stammer out my thanks to his majesty, King Gâ-roo, and save myself from betraying my utterly disconsolate condition.

Behold me now a prisoner for life! For in spite of all these honeyed words, King Gâ-roo now proceeded to double the number of guards set to watch my movements, and thus head off any attempt at escape.

I, of course, pretended not to notice this extra precaution.

In fact, I put a smiling face over my sad heart, and pretended to be perfectly contented; to have given up all thoughts of ever returning home.

I took good care to let Migrô-Zaltô know that I now intended to begin studying the ancient history of his people.

With the princess Hoppâ-Hoppâ, too, I was all kindness and sympathy. But while I was thus engaged in throwing my keepers off their guard, I was diving deep into the folk-lore of the Umi-Lobas.

The books of the royal library, so graciously bestowed upon me by King Gâ-roo, stood me in good service.

I determined to get at all the weaknesses of the Umi-Lobas, in order to see if I could not discover some way to elude their vigilance.

It was all dark to me for the first few days, but at length I caught a glimmer of hope.

It came about this way:

The Umi-Lobas dread water. My own observation, as well as Poly-dotto's words, had directed my attention to this strange fact.

Provided by nature with limbs of such extraordinary strength that they can leap over streams, even thirty feet in width, they have a superstition that nature intended them to avoid touching the surface of a stream.

For the first, I now observed that they had no boats of any kind, and that their children, unlike other children, never played upon the banks of the beautiful streamlets which flowed in every direction around their homes.

"A boat is the thing I need!" said I to myself, every pulse beating with suppressed excitement.

But, ah! where to get it!

It were idle to attempt to build a boat or even a raft without attracting the attention of my watchers and raising an outcry.

I must abandon that idea.

By a strange fatality my bitterest enemy now came to my assistance. You doubtless remember how that animated coil of steel spring, Megâ-Zaltô, tried to kill me by placing tiny poisoned knife-blades in my bed.

Well, after that I never laid down at night that I didn't first pull off the cushions, drapery and coverings of my couch in search of any more of the same kind.

I never found any, for Megâ-Zaltô was still in disgrace, and forbidden, under penalty of instant death, to approach the royal palace.

But I did find something else.

It was this:

I discovered that my bedstead emptied of its cushions and clothes, was exactly the shape of a yawl boat; in fact, of so fine a model as to give infinite pleasure to my sailor's eye, and, most astonishing discovery of all, that it was already fitted with a staunch and shapely mast, the staff which supported the hangings. All I needed was a couple of thin, straight sticks for booms, and I would be able to take one of my sheets and rig a square sail in a few moments.

Here again I found myself face to face with an appalling difficulty.

Even admitting that I could elude the vigilance of my keepers, how was I, all alone by myself, to transport the heavy bedstead to the water's edge, a quarter of a mile away!

I was upon the point of giving up the whole scheme.

The more I turned it over in my mind the more its dangers and difficulties increased.

I paced the floor with quick and anxious step, scarcely aware of Bulger's solicitude.

He was at my heels with vain coaxings, trying to quiet me down.

At last, in blank despair, I threw myself in a chair.

Bulger raised himself on his hind legs and gazed inquiringly into my face.

His tongue was out.

He was suffering from the heat.

For the first time I became aware of my condition.

The perspiration was streaming down my face. Suddenly a new idea flashed though my mind and helped out the old one.

Said I to myself:

"I'll complain to the King of the heat; I'll tell him how accustomed I am to outdoor life and sleeping in the open air with no covering, save the blue sky and twinkling stars; that I shall most surely pine away with inward wasting unless I be permitted to move my bed during the midsummer heat down by the river side, where the air is coolest and purest."

King Gâ-roo listened to my request without the slightest suspicion that any idea of escaping from his domain was flitting through my mind.

In fact, he would have as soon expected to see one of his royal beds spread its drapery for wings and fly away to the mountains as to see it go flashing down the river with one of the sheets set for a sail.

So my request was granted at once.

My bed was moved down to the river's edge, where one tent was raised to house me in case of a rain storm, and another to shelter the troop of guards which always kept at a respectable distance from me, and yet near enough to hop down upon me in about three seconds.

So far all had gone well. At first my plan was to launch my boat and make my escape in the night, but I was obliged to give this up, for I discovered that the guard was always doubled at night fall.

Escape, if I escape at all, then must be in the broad daylight.

Six of the Umi-Lobas soldiers stood sentry about my quarters from sun-rise to sun-set.

That they were armed it is needless to say.

But their tiny swords and pikes had no terror for me.

With a stout club I could have beaten them down in a few moments.

Their terrible legs and feet, however, were quite another thing.

One blow from the feet of a vigorous Umi-Loba would have laid me dead on the ground.

I have often seen these guards amuse themselves by striking deep holes in the ground or by breaking stone slabs an inch thick with a single blow of their heels.

I must choose a different mode of eluding such dangerous pursuers.

They must be drugged.

But how to accomplish it?

To offer them all food at the same moment would most surely arouse their suspicions.

Then again, they did not all eat together.

So too, it would be worse than folly to attempt to drug their drink.

What was to be done?

Again my heart grew sick and faint within me.

I sat down to collect my scattered thoughts.

At that moment the attendant began to serve my midday repast. I glanced at the tempting dishes and sparkling wines. It was a feast fit for a King.

"Sir Pendulum-legs," said the serving man, with a low bow, "this is the season for O-loo-loo eggs. The first find was made to-day. The nest held six. His majesty sends thee two and wishes thee a pleasant dream."

Now let me tell you what this strange speech all meant.

The O-loo-loo bird is about the size of a quail, and lays from six to a dozen eggs of a jet black hue. But as the bird, whose plumage is as black as a bat's wing, makes its nest in the wilderness, among the rank growth of a heather-like plant, of so dark green a foliage as to seem almost black, the eggs are invisible to the hunter's eye, and the nests can only be found by posting sentinels to mark the spots where the birds alight.

As you may imagine, O-loo-loo eggs are worth their weight in gold. Nay more, the people are forbidden to eat one.

Such is the King's command!

They all belong to him, and the finder must straightway bear his prize to the royal palace where a rich reward awaits him.

But the most mysterious thing about them is yet to be told! Not only are these eggs of most delicious flavor, but two of them are sufficient to throw the eater into a deep sleep, during which the most delightful dreams steal over him! Visions of exquisite loveliness flit before his eyes, and life seems so sweet and satisfactory that waking is really the keenest pain. The cause of this strange effect was for many centuries a mystery and the ancestors of the Umi-Lobas were wont to worship the O-loo-loo bird as a sort of sacred creature. But the mystery was solved at last. It was found that these birds fed upon the seed of the poppy plant, and hence the power of their eggs to cause sleep in those partaking of them.

I ate the two O-loo-loo eggs to test the matter, and in a few moments found myself sinking into a most delicious slumber.

When I awoke I saw light where darkness had lately reigned.

The way to escape from King Gâ-roo's guards was now clear to me. I at once proceeded to save up my O-loo-loo eggs.

In a few days, they became more plentiful, and it was not long before I had accumulated two dozen of them.

And now, thought I, if I offer them to my keepers as a feast, their suspicions will be aroused; they will refuse to partake of them, and the whole matter will be laid before the king and I shall be shorn of the little liberty I have. Therefore, I must use my knowledge of human nature.

As each man passed on his rounds I called him to me, and showing him four of the O-loo-loo eggs, said:

"I like thee; thou art my favorite, couldst thou be very close mouthed?"

The fellow's eyes sparkled with delight, and I could see that his mouth was watering at the sight of the dainty morsels.

Upon his assuring me that he would take good care that no one should know how kind I had been to him, I gave him four of the eggs, enough to make him sleep like a log for three hours.

He bolted them, shells and all.

I was much pleased with the working of my plan.

The next sentinel, who made his appearance a few moments after the first, was served in the same way. And so on with all the others. Each promised most solemnly never to reveal his good fortune to his comrades.

My plan thus far had worked splendidly.

In about a quarter of an hour I had the supreme satisfaction of seeing all six of them begin to rub their eyes, then yawn, then stretch their little arms up over their heads in the sleepiest manner possible. In less than half an hour they were all stretched out on the greensward, snoring like good fellows.

Now was my time to act!

I sprang toward my bed to empty it of its contents and launch it on the little river which flowed near by, when, to my horror, I heard the princess Hoppâ-Hoppâ calling, "Little Man All Head! Little Man All Head!"

A cold chill crept over me! There she came, hopping toward me like the wind, calling out for me to come and make her laugh!

What was I to do?

Strike her down?

Smother her?

Oh no; I could not have harmed that innocent little doll-faced being, had it been to save myself from life-long imprisonment.

Suddenly, like a flash of lightning, a bright thought flitted through my brain.

I have run, hopped, and stood on one foot, kicked one foot high in the air, crossed my legs, etc., to amuse the little princess, but I have never danced for her!

If she can find it amusing enough to laugh heartily at such plain old-fashioned antics, she will surely go into convulsions when she sees me dancing a quick time jig with heels flying in the air.

So, calling out to her in my gayest manner, I said:

"Come, little princess, come little Umi-Loba. Hop this way! Be quick; I've something very funny to show you."

She didn't wait for a second bidding.

With two bounds she was beside me.

Bidding her be seated I began to dance and she began to laugh. In half a moment I quickened my step and she broke out into the wildest merriment.

"O, do stop, Little Man All Head," she gasped. "O, do stop, or I shall die!" I didn't want her to die, but I did want her to fall down into a swoon.

So now I let myself out.

My legs flashed like sunbeams dancing on the water.

Bulger looked on in dignified astonishment.

He failed utterly to make out what his little master meant by these furious antics.

Indeed they were furious.

Faster and faster my nimble feet beat the ground. Wilder and more uncontrollable became the laughter of the little princess Hoppâ-Hoppâ. The tears coursed down her pretty face she rocked from side to side; she bent forward and back.

Adding still more speed to my movements, I kept my eyes fixed upon her.

Victory!

The end came at last!

She rolled over on the greensward in a swoon.

"Now or never!" I murmured to myself.

In quicker time than it takes to tell it, aided by my faithful Bulger, I emptied the bed of its contents, set my shoulder to one end of it, while Bulger fastened his teeth in some fringe that hung from the other, and then, he pulling with might and main, and I pushing with all the desperation of a battle for freedom, the wooden structure was slowly brought to the bank of the river.

It was a hard task for us!

But we did it.

Now down the slippery bank it glided with a rush, striking the water and floating like a duck.

In an instant Bulger and I sprang on board of the little craft.

To rig up one of the sheets as a square sail and set it on the pole which had held the curtains was only the work of a few seconds.

A stout long-handled fan served me for a rudder.

Away! Away! I was off at last!

The wind was fresh and strong, and my square sail worked to a charm.

At that moment a shrill, piping voice reached my ear.

"Little Man All Head! Little Man All Head! Where art thou? Come to me!"

The shrill, far-reaching tones of her voice attracted a hundred attendants. They seemed fairly to spring up out of the ground.

Pell-mell, with a wild rush, the stronger ones leaping over the heads of the less vigorous ones, they made for the river banks.

Alarm bells now sounded on every side.

Gongs and strangely-sounding horns and rattles called the people to the spot where the little princess had been found lying half unconscious on the greensward.

The sight of the half dozen sentinels stretched out here and there in the deepest sleep, the scattered drapery of my couch, the bed itself missing, all told too plainly the story of my escape.

All this time, my snug little craft was making good headway down the river, which grew wider at every hundred feet.

With one wild outburst of shrill, angry voices, the Umi-Lobas turned to pursue the fugitive.

Bulger whined piteously as he saw them swarming on the banks.

In another moment they began leaping from one bank to another, passing over our heads in perfect clouds.

I knew full well that they would not dare to leap into my boat but I feared that they might overwhelm us with showers of their little spears. However I determined to try the effect of one of my pistols on them if their spears annoyed me.

King Gâ-roo, beside himself with spiteful anger, now arrived upon the scene, and took command of his assembled troops and serving men.

First he tried entreaty upon me, offering me princely sums and royal honors if I would only turn back.

But I was deaf to his honeyed words. Whereupon he fell into a towering passion. He ordered his soldiers to recapture me dead or alive.

A shower of spears now whistled through the air.

Most of them fell far short of their mark, for the river had now widened so that I was at least thirty feet from the shore whereon they were standing.

But a few of these spearlets fell dangerously near me.

Fearing that their points might be poisoned, I determined to try the effect of a pistol shot in the air.

The loud report of the fire-arm, and the puff of smoke which followed it, filled the Umi-Lobas with the most abject fear.

They threw themselves on their faces and cried out that I was an evil spirit.

I could now see that King Gâ-roo had given orders to let me sail away in peace.

They made no further attempts to molest me, and yet it was very plain that they were loth to part with the "little man all head," for whom their King and the princess Hoppâ-Hoppâ had conceived so warm an affection.

I, too, felt a wrinkle in my heart as my little boat bore Bulger and me away on the rippling waters of the beautiful river now grown so wide that I was at least a hundred feet from the bank, and the palace of King Gâ-roo began to fade away in the distance.

For several miles they followed the banks of the stream, keeping opposite me, and ever and anon sending me a good bye in a soft and plaintive voice.

Straining my eyes, I could see little princess Hoppâ-Hoppâ, borne aloft on the shoulders of a group of serving-men, and waving me a last adieu.

Then, once more, I caught the sound of that shrill baby voice:

"Good bye! Good bye! Little Man-All-Head! Hoppâ-Hoppâ says good bye forever!"

And so I sailed away from the land of the Umi-Lobas, the land of the Man-Hoppers!

In a few days the river began to broaden out and the land of the Umi-Lobas was left far behind! The moment I caught sight of any signs of human beings on the river banks, I steered my staunch little boat into a broad cove, whose sloping shores led to lofty table lands. Here, with tear-moistened eyes, I moored the little craft which had snatched me from a life of keen, though silent, sorrow, and followed by faithful Bulger, struck out boldly for the interior. After a few weeks' journeying I entered a country which was now and then traversed by traders. They were astonished to find me traveling all alone by myself, but readily accepted my statement that I had become separated from a troop of traders, and that my horse had died.

I now made haste to re-cross India and gain the shores of the Mediterranean, whence I took passage for home, with a joyous heart and a memory well-stored with quaint facts and curious recollections.

CHAPTER VIII.

While sauntering through the streets of Constantinople, one day, loitering in front of the bazars, or listening to the tales of some story-teller on the street-corner, I fell in with an Armenian merchant.

He was a man of varied attainments, had read much, traveled much, seen much.

We ate sweetmeats and drank coffee together for several days.

He was so delighted with my keen intellect, sharp, nipping wit, and great powers of imagination, that he expressed himself as being more than paid for his journey to Constantinople, although he had not yet opened his packs.

When the time came for us to part, he proceeded to loosen the leather thongs which held down the lid of a strange looking chest, whose top and sides were covered over with curious figures in inlays of several colors.

From one corner of this receptacle he drew forth a volumen or roll-book of antiquity.

To one end of it was attached, by a strip of parchment, a waxen seal, stamped with what seemed to have been a monarch's signet ring. This ancient and venerable book exhaled a very musty smell.

The Armenian handled it carefully, saying:

"It is quite old; some 6,000 years." Seeing astonishment depicted on my countenance, he smiled and continued:

"Yes, 6,000 years! It has only been unrolled far enough for me to decipher the nature of its contents. It treats of the human soul, and pretends to have solved its mystery completely—a problem which has baffled the philosophers of all ages. It even goes so far as to claim that the essence which we call "soul" may be taken out of a body and put into a bottle; that one soul may be thrust into a man's body to keep his own company, and that in this manner the whole world may be reformed, made over; evil being entirely destroyed and good only remaining.

"You smile, little baron, but it seems to me quite feasible. For instance, this rare old book quite rightly assumes that if we could thrust a good soul into a body already inhabited by a bad one, that man or woman would henceforth cease to do evil, or, at least, the good soul would continually betray its bad companion, and, altho' the man might plan a murder, he would not fail to inform some one of his dread purpose, and thus defeat his own ends."

"Or," continued the merchant, "take the case of a miser; by thrusting the soul of a spendthrift into his body, his inclination to hoard money and starve his family would be forever and always opposed by an ardent desire to waste his earnings, and the result would be that these two vices would neutralize each other; and so with a drunkard or a thief: by placing the soul of a water-drinker in the one and of a moral man in the other, a perfect reformation could be brought about. This is a valuable book, little baron, but I give it to you, merely exacting a promise from you that in case I am right in my understanding of it, you will impart the secret to the fathers of the church."

I gave the merchant my promise, and not wishing to accept so valuable a present without making some return therefore, I drew from my finger a ring containing the petrified eye of a basilisk, which, in the dark, emitted light enough to read the hour on a watch dial.

He was almost tiresome in his expression of thanks.

We separated.

I laid the ancient volume away in my chest and gave no thought to it until some time after my return home, when, one fine day, Bulger, attracted by its very musty odor, seized it by the vellum strip holding the seal and drew it forth from its hiding-place, then looked up at my face as much as to say:

"What is it, any way, little master?"

I determined to unroll the book at once.

The merchant had warned me to be most careful in so doing, lest the whole thing fly into a thousand pieces.

I therefore proceeded to prepare a wooden tablet or panel, which I smeared with a strong glue, so that, as the parchment unwound, it should be caught by this sticky surface and held firmly fast.

The plan succeeded admirably.

After several hours' close application I was overjoyed to see the volume entirely unrolled and held firmly and evenly to the surface of the panel.

Fancy my delight, after the glue had dried sufficiently to make an examination of the writing, to find that this ancient volume was a palimpsest!

I felt instinctively that this dissertation upon the nature of the soul was the sick man's dream of some poor dweller in the double darkness of ignorance and superstition. So I made haste to wash away his fervid outpourings by a plentiful use of something still hotter—namely, hot water and soap; for my studies had told me that the ink used by the people of his time and generation contained no mordant, and was, in fact, only lamp-black and grease.

I now got at the real contents of this venerable book.

The writing was dim and shadowy. I did not let that trouble me, for, skilled as I am in the chemist's art, I lost no time in applying an acid which restored the writing to its old time blackness.

I had some difficulty in deciphering the language in which it was written—the ancient Phoenician—but, with the aid of several scores of dictionaries, I finally rendered it into a modern tongue, passing it through the Aramaic, thence into the Greek, and, finally, into my own tongue.

When at last I had gotten over all difficulties and could read the descriptions with that ease necessary to bring out their full sense, I was nearly beside myself with joy.

It was the story of a voyage made by a venturesome navigator, six thousand years ago, when the earth was still in its infancy; still hot in some places; in fact, only the highest mountains and table lands had cooled off enough to be habitable.

Pushing off from the shores of Arabia, this bold captain had pointed his ship towards the rising sun.

And, wonder of wonders! after many awful perils and terrible privations, he had entered waters which, to his almost unutterable amazement, grew warmer and warmer as he sailed over them.

At first his men refused to proceed any farther, but by dint of threats, persuasion and goodly presents, the bold sailor went his way, wondering and rejoicing. After many days he entered a body of water, which, from his descriptions, I at once recognized as the China Sea. But now all further advance was impossible.

In vain his oarsmen lent their aid to drive the little vessel forward.

Huge waves of heated water, always from the same direction drove his craft backward.

At last the truth of the matter dawned upon him.

He was on the outer edge of some vast boiling sea, which, rolling its hot waves ever outward, drove back his cockle shell of a bark. Making for a lofty promontory, he clambered to its highest point, wearing thick felt shoes and gloves to protect his feet and hands from the heated rocks.

A fearful and yet a sublimely beautiful sight met his gaze.

For hundreds and hundreds of miles the waters were in a state of most violent boiling, springing and leaping into the air as if a legion of giant demons were beneath forcing their hot breath upward from vast cavernous lurking places.

Upon reading of this boiling sea, I was seized with an uncontrollable desire to go in search of it.

True the waters might have cooled down in all these centuries, and yet I was confident I should find some trace of this once terrible caldron of seething waters.

The China Sea was only slightly known to navigators of my day and generation.

It had often been darkly hinted at that this vast body of water was studded with wonderful isles and filled with rare monsters.

I had no time to lose.

Hastily penning a letter of adieu to my father and mother, I joined my ship—accompanied by my ever faithful Bulger—and turned her prow towards the rising sun.

So well were the waters of the East known to me, from my long and close study of the most reliable charts, that I found I could almost steer my craft through them blindfolded.

It was not many days ere I entered this beautiful expanse of water, which, in the youth of the world, was filled with such marvelous creatures swimming on it and in it.

Onward, ever onward, through its dark blue waves, now mounting their foam-crested heights, now rocking like a thing of life upon this billowy highway, my trusty little vessel ploughed her way. Ten times a day, under plea of wishing to cool my brow in a basin of sea water, I called out to some one of my men to let down a bucket, but only to find, to my deep disappointment, that its temperature was no higher than is usual in those latitudes.

I began to grow low-spirited. My crew noticed my dejection, and at times my attentive ear caught murmurs of discontent.

To restore my men to their usual good spirits, I offered a reward of a thousand ducats to the one who should first discover that the water was growing warmer.

A thousand ducats!

It was a goodly sum, but I was growing desperate.

The large reward, however, had one good effect; it put new life into my men.

All day long buckets rattled against the ship's side.

Three of the more venturesome men hit upon a plan to earn the reward and divide it among them.

Lashing themselves together, they then lowered themselves down over the side of the vessel, until their feet just touched the water. Here they determined to stay, so that they might be the first to announce the increase of warmth in the water, and in this way make sure of the thousand ducats.

Suddenly a fearful outcry, accompanied by the most piteous whining on the part of Bulger, caused me to rush up on deck.

A sea-monster, a third as long as our ship, had risen directly under them.

Motionless with fright, they fell an easy prey to this terrible foe.

Opening his vast, cavernous jaws, he swallowed the whole three at a single gulp!

My men were wild with grief!

They heaped mad words of reproach upon me.

I had great difficulty in restoring anything like order or discipline.

My commands fell upon deaf ears.

At last I succeeded in quieting the raging, weeping crowd.

Knowing from my experience with such dread inhabitants of the deep, that this monster had only whetted his appetite by these morsels of human flesh, I directed my men to make haste and construct a straw man, using clothes of the same color as those worn by the three unfortunates.

Into the bosom of this effigy I stored away a quarter quintal of ipecacuanha, of prime quality, which, by good luck, I found in my stock of medicines.

The dummy was now lowered to the water's edge, at exactly the same spot where the monster had made his luncheon on my three excellent seamen.

We had not long to wait.

He rose to the bait in a few moments, and, opening his huge jaws, thrust out a tongue as large and as red as a roasted ox, and gulped down the savory morsel I had provided for him, with a rumbling gurgle which made my blood run cold.

Recovering myself, I sprang up into the shrouds and kept my eyes fixed upon this rare monster, who floated away lazily a ship's length and then came to a dead halt.

Ever and anon a quiver shot thro' the entire length of his body.

Evidently he was having no little difficulty in swallowing this last morsel.

Huge ridges formed about his neck and rolled backward till they were lost beneath the waters. A certain uneasiness now marked his movements.

He rolled from side to side, opening and shutting his jaws with a snap that sounded like the bang of two great oaken doors.

The dainty quarter quintal of ipecacuanha was manifestly beginning to distress him.

His rocking and rolling motion increased in violence.

At one moment his huge body turned upon its side, bent itself until head and tail met; at another it arched itself in the air until its black back spanned the waters like a bow.

I now felt that it was time to act.

"Stand by the starboard launch!" I called out to my men. "Avast that blubbering! All ready?"

"Ay! ay!" came back from the gang.

"Lower away, then!"

I was not a whit too quick with my orders.

The launch had no sooner struck the water than the sea-monster—after a series of terrible contortions, during which it almost seemed as if his huge body would be snapped in twain—began to disgorge the varied contents of his stomach.

First, shower after shower of many colored fishes, of all sizes, from a hand's length to three cubits, filled the air.

As they fell into the water, they calmly swam away, no doubt well pleased to find themselves in more agreeable surroundings.

Thousands of shell fish, all kinds, sizes and colors, then came flying forth, rattling their claws together as they fell into the water, as if in defiance at their huge foe that had been so unceremoniously called upon to give up the results of many a long hour's hunt.

The living was followed by the dead, for now came forth several wooden buckets, three old blankets, numerous bits of plank, rope ends, shreds of sail, paint pots, bundles of oakum, and wads of cotton, all of which he had picked up while following in the wake of our vessel. At last the man of straw was cast out high into the air with a deep grunt of satisfaction.

After him came number one of the lost seamen.

Numbers two and three were not slow in arriving.

The launch made haste to pick them up, leaving the sick monster to recover his health and spirits as well he might.

Bulger received the rescued men with the wildest manifestations of delight, and clapping on all sail, away we bounded before a rattling breeze.

To my infinite joy, the water now began to increase in warmth.

Hour by hour the rise in temperature, although slow, was steady.

"At length, my men!" cried I to my crew, "we are on the right track. Be patient! I promise you that before the sun has quenched his fire in the western seas we shall cast anchor in Neptune's Caldron!"

My predictions came true to the very letter.

Just as the last rays of sunlight were gilding the foam-crested waves of this mysterious sea, a long, low line of shore was sighted dead ahead, ending in a precipitous headland.

Bearing away we rounded this and found ourselves at the entrance of a large land-blocked bay or gulf, from different points in which huge columns of snow-white steam floated lazily skyward, twisting themselves in most fantastic shapes ere they vanished in the purple twilight.

My men sent up a loud, long, lusty cheer, as we sailed into Neptune's Caldron.

As we drew near shore, to my great bewilderment, for I had not dared to think that living creatures could exist in these heated waters, I caught sight of moving things in the Caldron. Nay, there could be no doubt, for these heated waters were as limpid as a mountain spring and the bottom plainly visible ten fathoms below.

Fish of all colors and sizes floated hither and thither, while myriads of crabs, lobsters and other queerly shaped crustaceans crawled about on the snow-white sands, following their leaders in long lines, like a procession of cardinals, over the white marble pavement of some great city in the western world.

I say "crimson lines," for the heat of the water had clothed them all in suits of richest red.

As I sat in the ship's launch on my way to the shore, gazing dreamily down into the waters, half-dazed by these marvellous sights, a shoal of fish rose near the boat and turned their beautiful tinted sides for an instant to the cool air.

To my amazement I saw that their eyes were sightless, that the extreme heat of the waters had clouded their limpid orbs milk white and shut out the light forever!

A cold chill crept over me, for, to me, the spectacle was as uncanny as if the carp had sprung from the elder baron's table and begun to swim about in their native element once more.

But the list of strange things was not yet exhausted, for as I drew nearer to the beach, you may imagine my mingled wonder and amusement at seeing scores of fish with their backs planted against the sand furrows, calmly fanning themselves with their broad, flat tails.

Upon setting foot upon the shore, I was astonished to find the land, for far as the eye could reach, covered deep with millions and millions of eggs of different sizes, varying from that of a pigeon to that of an albatross or wild goose.

In places these eggs lay in heaps far higher than my head; in others they were ranged in long lines, like white furrows turned by some gigantic plough!

Suddenly the truth dawned upon me. To these shores vast flocks of sea-birds came to lay their eggs year after year, attracted by the warmth of the atmosphere. There they build their rude nests and fill them with eggs and enter upon the task of hatching out their young, when suddenly the heated waters hurled by some gale or resistless current, rises upon their resting places and spreads death where life was just beginning, by cooking the countless thousands of eggs which fill their nests. And so on from year to year, until now I behold the work of a thousand floods, which have in turn added their contribution to this vast stock!

While standing on the shores of this wonderland, one morning, gazing out across the steaming surface of Neptune's Caldron, several of my crew came running toward me with startled mien and great outcry, all pointing skyward. I turned and looked in the direction indicated.

A vast cloud, black and threatening, hung in the heavens.

As I stood watching it, it broadened and widened until it fairly darkened the light of day.

My men were now on their knees, uttering the most piteous lamentations, for they imagined the end of the world was at hand.

I commanded them sternly to leave off their wailing and groaning, for I saw that the great black cloud was simply an enormous flock of birds, of what species I could not then tell.

Nearer and nearer they came, with the sound like the rushing of wild winds.

They covered the whole sky like an inky pall.

It was evident to me that they intended alighting upon the shore of the Caldron, and fearing lest their immense numbers, in settling down, might smother us, I called out to my men to stand by the ship's launch.

There was no time to lose.

For, as we pushed out from the shore, tens of thousands of these birds—a species of crow, but twice the size of those at home—began to settle down in long rows as far as the eye could reach.

For the first, now I noticed that every crow held something in its claws. I looked again, and saw that each of these birds carried an immense mollusk, fully as large as a watchman's club and something the same shape. Imagine my mingled surprise and amusement upon observing that those in the first row were now making for the water's edge. Approaching cautiously, each crow thrust his mollusk into the shoal waters of the Caldron and stood by, with eyes sparkling with joyful anticipation, to watch for results.

He had not long to wait.

Unaccustomed to the great heat of the water, the mollusk soon began to open its shell, first cautiously, but as the hot water poured in upon it, with great precipitation, fairly with a snap. Waiting for a moment or so until the hot water had curled the animal quite free from its shell, the fastidious birds then partook of the savory contents, gave a few caws of grateful acknowledgement, and withdrew to make room for the next row. This changing places, cooking of provisions and feasting lasted for half a day.

By that time the entire flock had exhausted its raw material. Then with deafening cries and loud flapping of pinions, these feathered epicures rose into the air and disappeared as they had come.

Fain would I have prolonged my stay upon the shores of Neptune's Caldron, but I observed that the steam from the waters was disagreeable to Bulger.

With speaking eyes, he implored me to hoist sail and seek some, to him pleasanter land.

I could not withstand that appeal.

So I made a farewell survey of the egg mounds, gazed my last at the red-shelled crustaceans and chalky-eyed fish of the Caldron and went aboard of my staunch vessel.

Heading now westward, I crowded sail, intending to hug the China Coast pretty closely on my homeward voyage. All went well for the first few days after leaving Neptune's Caldron.

Bulger ranged the deck, playing the maddest capers.

Thoughts of home now began to occupy my mind.

The elder baron was growing old. I felt that I ought not to prolong my voyage. He might be in need of my counsels.

Suddenly, one day, at high noon, the skies darkened, the winds sprang up.

I thought nothing of it.

It will only be a mad romp, which will serve right well to blow us along homeward.

But, oh, what a short-sighted creature is vain man, who thinks to read the signs of the skies, the winds and the waves!

The merry whistling of the wind soon gave place to the dismal howl of the blast.

The storm fiend was stalking abroad.

The startled waters now leaped wildly up from their beds, rolled tumultuously onward, whipped into foam and fury by ten thousand lashes of the blast, till, in their mad efforts to escape, they dashed themselves against the very clouds.

The scene was terrible. 'Twas useless to command, for not a throat of steel could have drowned the wild yells of the tempest.

To my horror, I discovered that we had sprung a leak.

The pitch and tar, softened by the heat of the water in Neptune's Caldron, had bulged from the ship's joints and allowed the calking to escape.

Like a sheet of card board, our rudder was now torn from its place and whirled away on the crest of a giant billow.

Behold us now at the very mercy of the storm, the plaything of wind and wave, a cockle shell fallen on the battle ground of nature's waning elements.

Bulger, lashed to the rigging by my side, uttered no plaint, no cry of fear, no sound of distrust.

I could see that his speaking eyes were following me about as much as to say:

"I am not afraid, little master, so long as you are by me."

I could feel my heart thump out a loud "thank thee, dear, faithful, little friend!"

From time to time I passed my hand caressingly over his head and neck.

His tail moved sadly, but I knew its meaning.

It meant:

"Little master, I am ready to die; ay, most willing to die, if I can die with you by my side."

It really seemed as if his love was about to be put to a final test for the dreadful cry of—"Breakers ahead!" was passed from man to man till it reached my ears.

It was only too true.

Their roar now broke upon my ears, faint, low but deep, terrible, half like distant thunder or the growl of some gigantic beast of prey.

In a few brief moments we were on the reef.

With a terrible crash our staunch little vessel leaped upon the rocks and wedged herself in, tight and fast, between two jagged ledges.

The relentless sea now broke over and over us.

"Oh! if the day would only break!" I murmured, "possibly we might find some means to reach the main land."

To stay here simply means destruction.

After hours of the severest suffering, for every sea which broke over us seemed as if bent upon the fell purpose of tearing our limbs from their lashings—day came at last.

I discovered now that we were about a quarter of a mile from the main land.

With my glass, I could distinguish great crowds of people running hither and thither on shore. But they made no effort to send us succor or to encourage us to cling to the wreck until the storm should abate.

What was to be done?

With a fearful crash, our masts now went by the board.

Our ship was showing signs of breaking up.

Neither threat nor reward could move any one of my men to attempt to swim ashore with a line.

The sun now burst forth in a blaze of golden light.

I could feel the tears gather in my eyes as I looked about and saw the sad ravages of wind and wave.

Although the storm had abated somewhat of its fury, there was no time to be lost.

Dread creakings of the ship's timbers warned me to leave the wreck ere I should be crushed against the rocks.

Only disorder and confusion seemed to characterize the movements of the crowds gathered on shore.

While apparently aware of the terrible import of our signals of distress, they showed no inclination to risk their lives in trying to save ours.

Turning to Bulger I cried out:

"O, dearest Bulger! thou tried and true friend, companion of my sorrows and sharer of my every joy, thou alone canst save us! Thou alone canst rescue thy loving master and these poor wretched creatures from impending death! I know thy courage; I know thy affection. In thy radiant eyes I read thy willingness to do or die!"

From his earliest youth I had trained Bulger to be a bold and skilful swimmer. No eddy, current, undertow or whirlpool was angry or wild enough to strike any fear to his stout heart.

With ease, at my commands, he would dive two fathoms deep and bring the smallest coin from the bottom.

Our vessel might go to pieces at any moment, for she had wrenched herself loose from the rocky ledge and was pounding on the jagged, flinty edges of the reef with a wild and ungovernable fury.

Every fleeting moment became more precious than its predecessor.

Making a superhuman effort, I caught the end of a reel of twine, and, having fastened it to Bulger's collar, bade him leap into the bubbling, boiling, seething, swirling, madly-rolling waters, storm-lashed, whipped into foam, till billow broke on billow and all seemed but one mingled mass of fury, rage and fright. With a rapid succession of anxious, whining cries followed by a series of quick, loud, sharp barks, Bulger gave me one last look; and, placing his paws on the taffrail, sprang lightly over and disappeared.

My heart stood still for a moment.

But look!

He rises!

He strikes out for the shore, now tossed like a bit of cork on the arched backs of a storm-affrighted billow, now sunken out of sight into the foam-flecked trough of the sea.

Look again!

Hark! I can catch the faint sound of that sharp, joyous bark sent back to cheer his little master's heart.

And now he is gone!

I see him not; but as the twine runs through my hands, I can almost feel every throb of that dear, stout heart!

Steadily he keeps at his work, for steadily and rapidly the reel spins round.

Crack!

There goes our keel in twain.

Quick, good Bulger; the end is near!

But look!

What means that commotion on shore?

See the crowd, how it presses down to the very breaker's edge!

Now they fall back!

Hark!

Did you not hear that shout?

Saved! Saved!

Bulger has landed!

The men on shore have hold of the twine.

The reel whirls swiftly around!

My men, ashamed of their cowardice, crawl from their hiding-places and set to work with a will.

Already they have fastened a line to the end of the twine and it is moving briskly over the rail.

There can be no doubt now.

Bulger has saved us!

Springing into the main-shrouds and shielding my mouth from the gale with my hands, I called out to my men:

"Stand by the hawser! Make fast the line! Now heave, O! Let go all!"

With an angry splash the hawser fell into the sea and was soon on its way shorewards.

And this was the way Bulger saved the life of master, mate and twelve seamen! I was the last man to leave the ship.

As I did so, she shook herself loose, drew back, ran hard on the rocks with such a terrific blow that she broke into pieces as if struck by lightening bolt or some gigantic hammer wielded by an unseen Thor.

With a wild cry of joy Bulger met me as I was drawn through the breakers.

I threw myself on my knees and covered him with kisses, while tears rolled hot and fast down my cheeks.

The people of the land gathered group-wise about us and watched our interchanging of caresses in deepest silence, agitating their thumbs and twitching the corners of their mouths.

"What land is this? Where are we, good people?" I inquired, after this first outpouring of love and gratitude had spent its fervor.

"Bold barbarians!" replied one of the nearest group, whose richer dress bespoke the man of rank and authority, "thou standest on the shores of the mighty dominion of Kublai, Child of the Sun, Lord of the Imperial Yellow Garb, Knight of all the Buttons, Man of the Sacred Countenance, Successor to all the Glories of his Ancestors now Guests of Heaven, Source of all Law and Equity, and Chevalier of all the Orders, and we are his wretched, miserable, unworthy, good-for-nothing slaves!"

Whereupon the entire multitude performed the kowtow.

"So then! I cried, most puissant, noble, and altogether delightful, Sir,"—at the same time performing the kowtow with that grace which only the genuine citizen of the world can command—"I stand upon the sacred soil of the mighty Chinese Empire."

"Aye, bold barbarian," answered the speaker, "in the province of Kwang Tung, in the district of Yang-chiang, of which I, So Too, Mandarin of the White Glass Button, am Imperial superintendent." Hearing this, I begged So Too to give me leave to speak, which granted, in a brief but eloquent speech, well larded with all those savory epithets so sweet to the ears of an official in that land, I told him of my illustrious family, my strange desire to scour the remotest seas and least-visited lands for marvellous things; how I had sailed in search of Neptune's Caldron, of the strange things seen there, of my setting out on my voyage homeward, my encounter with the storm-fiend, and last of all, my shipwreck on the shores of the boundless dominions of the Child of the Sun.

And now, all that I craved from the servants of the Man of the Sacred

Countenance was such aid and assistance as would enable me and my men to reach the nearest seaport where foreign ships cast anchor, so that we might go down to the sea once more and reach our loved ones. To all this So Too gave response with a most gracious smile, and then invited me to pass beneath his roof, lay off my wet clothes, drink some warm tea, and have his rubbers smooth the wrinkles out of my tired flesh.

My seamen were not forgotten. His retainers were ordered to look well after their wants.

Just as we were about to set out for So Too's residence, several of his body guards struck their gongs a furious blow.

The din was ear-splitting.

With a loud bark Bulger rushed towards me, and laying one ear against my leg closed his other with his paw.

So Too and his retainers, at seeing this to me laughable sight, looked grave, agitated their thumbs and twitched the corners of their mouths.

Just as I was about crossing So Too's threshold, to my inexpressible chagrin I discovered that I had lost my purse containing a large sum of money. In a desperate hope that I might have dropped it on the sea shore, I bounded away in that direction, but I had not gone a hundred paces ere I met Bulger carrying the purse in his mouth. I had in truth dropped it while kneeling on the beach and caressing my beloved rescuer.

Noting that in my eagerness to follow my gracious host, I had not missed the lost treasure, Bulger had driven away several of So Too's retainers, who manifested a desire to appropriate the pouch of gold to their own use, and picking it up in his teeth, had raced after me as fast as his burden would permit.

As we crossed So Too's threshold, several small, woolly dogs sprang out and gathered about Bulger. They were apparently delighted to meet with one of their race, so distinguished in appearance and dignified in carriage. Fain would they have exchanged the usual canine civilities with Bulger, but he absolutely declined to enter into any conversation with them or to express any surprise at these extraordinary looking cousins of his, which seemed like so many animated bundles of freshly-ginned cotton. Keeping close at my heels, he skillfully avoided their advances, and gave a low growl of relief when the door of the ante-chamber was closed upon them.

After a warm bath, my stiffened limbs were limbered up by the stroking, patting and rubbing of So Too's bath assistants.

I was then invited to encase my body in a rich suit of embroidered silk, and this done, was conducted into the presence of the amiable So Too, who received me with a smile that was as persistent as it was broad.

Several hours were now consumed in drinking tea, eating dainty little sugar cakes, and telling each other the most extravagant and shameless fibs in the shape of compliments,—compliments about everything, voice, eyes, ears, chin, mouth, hands, feet, etc. Although I only reached to So Too's shoulder, he regretted, in a piteous tone, his lack of stature and praised my tall, stately, noble, commanding height.

Overcome at last by sheer exhaustion, So Too closed his eyes and appeared to have dropped off in a little nap.

Seizing upon the opportunity, I raised my voice and began to urge upon him the necessity of immediate action with regard to me and my men.

Whereupon he arose, and after a series of kowtows, the same broad smile playing around his wide mouth and small kindly black eyes—withdrew to consult with his assistant, sub-assistant, and first and second sub-assistants.

It was quite dark when So Too re-entered the room.

Bulger and I, during his absence, had slept most soundly.

No wonder, for we were both tired to the bone.

Orders were now given to illuminate the halls and apartments.

In a few moments, thousands of the most brilliantly colored and quaintly decorated lanterns shed a delightfully soft glow over everybody and everything.

Again we took our places around the superbly decorated table which held the paraphernalia for brewing tea and the exquisitely painted cups and saucers of egg-shell thinness, and the tea drinking and cake-eating were resumed. Again I skillfully turned the conversation to the subject of my departure for the nearest seaport.

Again So Too arose and backed out of the room for the purpose of holding another consultation.

By this time my stock of patience had dwindled down considerable.

Every moment I could feel my blood grow warmer and warmer.

After a delay of half an hour or so, a retainer entered to inform me that So Too had fallen asleep in the council-room, and that no one save a Mandarin with an opaque blue, transparent blue, flowered red or plain red button could presume to awaken him, and that there was no Mandarin of so exalted a dignity within fifty miles of that spot.

At these words my blood fairly boiled over.

I sprang to my feet and began to pace the floor like a caged animal.

Coming to a halt in front of a tall lacquer cabinet loaded down with costly porcelain cups and vases, I raised my foot, and kicking out vigorously, toppled the thing over on the floor.

The crash was terrible.

I was really startled, for I was afraid I had knocked half the house down.

But I had the satisfaction of seeing the Mandarin come rushing into the room, followed by assistants, sub-assistants, gong-beaters, sword-bearers, head-shavers, ear-ticklers, tongue-scrapers, nail-polishers, and skin-rubbers, besides many others of his retainers, whose offices and callings were unknown to me.

"You have deliberated, now decide!" I exclaimed in a tone of voice that for depth and volume would have done credit to the hero of a blood curdling drama; and at the same moment I placed the sole of my foot against another cabinet, quite as lofty as the one I had just toppled over, and quite as richly laden with curios, vases and ivories.

So Too was now wide awake and not at all anxious to see this second cabinet share the fate of the first.

"Thy foot to its place!" he called out, waving me to a seat, and placing himself between me and the threatened cabinet. "Thy foot to its place, my gracious benefactor."

After he had seen me safely seated, he continued thus:

"Know, then, my gentle guest, that I, So Too, Imperial Mandarin of the white glass button, after mature deliberation with my most honorable Council, do order and decree that thou and thy servants shall be, as thou hast prayed, forthwith conducted to the city of Canton, and there be delivered into the keeping and custody of the officers of him of the Sacred Countenance, until opportunity shall present itself to procure means of sending thee and thy servants back to your native land!"

Here I bent my body in token of my profound gratitude.

The Mandarin likewise made a low obeisance, and then continued:

"I do further decree that the evil spirit which attends thee in the shape of a dog shall be at once bound with chains and cast into prison there to await, his trial for witchcraft!"

Had So Too plunged a two-edged knife into my vitals I could not have felt a more agonizing hurt.

"Bulger? My beloved—Arrested? Witchcraft? Chains; Prison?" I stammered out.

"I have so decreed!" calmly replied So Too. "Oh! no! no! no! I cried, it cannot—it must not be! He is no evil spirit—no evil dwells in him. He is but a simple, loving, intelligent dog! I crave suspension of this terrible decree! What hath he done? O beloved Bulger, is this thy reward for saving fourteen human lives? Is this the way in which thou art to be repaid for all thy courage, thy love, thy devotion? O, no! no! Kill me if you will, cruel stranger, thrust me into a prison cell, but spare Bulger, spare him———"

I could say no more.

It grew black before me. A fit of vertigo came upon me. I staggered, reeled, fell lifeless to the floor.

When I came to my senses, So Too's servants were busy rubbing and chafing my hands and feet and burning pungent wax beneath my nostrils. Bulger, uttering the most piteous and anxious cries, was hastening from one side to the other, pausing now and then for an instant to lick my hand or face. I sat upright to collect my senses; then clasping Bulger in my arms I patted, smoothed, kissed and caressed him amid a hundred sighs and groans, heart-rending enough to melt a breast of stone. Then throwing myself on my knees in front of So Too, I implored him to be merciful—to spare a faithful, loving being, whose heart was as free from guile as the flinty rock from tenderness; whose life had but one thought: to serve, guard, defend, save his master.

"Rise, unfortunate stranger!" was So Too's reply, in a tone of deep commiseration, taking me by the hand and gently compelling me to be seated by his side. "List! If thou shouldst slice my body into ten thousand pieces I could not revoke this decree. Know that in this land of the Child of the Sun, a magistrate may not unsay his words. Mercy belongs to him, who dwells in higher places. This creature which thou lovest so, hath been adjudged to be an evil spirit. It is a favorite form of theirs; for as the dog is man's close and trusted companion, malevolent spirits are most likely to assume that form, when desirous of obtaining admission to his house and heart in order to work his ruin. This wild and unreasoning affection for thy dog proves only too clearly that the evil spirit which dwells within him has already drawn the black lines of his mysterious art thrice around thy soul. Thrice three times will complete his dread purpose. Thou wilt then be lost forever! 'Tis well that some good spirit of the air or water hath delivered thee into the keeping of the Child of the Sun. For now, upon the trial in the Imperial Chamber of Perfect Justice, thine eyes will be opened; thou wilt be fully persuaded that an evil spirit of tremendous size and fearful power is squeezed into that small creature."

"Never!" I exclaimed with flashing eye and glowing cheek.

So Too smiled faintly and laying his hand upon my arm continued: "Soft, illustrious guest, thou forgettest that Perfect Justice dwells in the bosom of our gracious Monarch. His ministers and judges have tongues; but they are not their own; they only utter the thought of the Imperial mind; therefore, what they decree must be right!"

"And if the Court," I inquired, with bated breath, "should decree that some evil spirit hath taken up its abode, as thou claimest, in the body of my faithful Bulger—what—what—would be the—the—penalty?"

"Death!" whispered So Too.

"And is this thy boasted justice!" I cried, with tear-bedimmed eyes, "to condemn a dumb creature to death with no voice to plead for him?"

"Nay!" interposed So Too, "thou shalt speak for him, thou shalt be heard in his behalf—thou shalt be his advocate."

"For this mercy," said I, "my heart empties its thanks at thy feet; and, if my words, my pleading prove not powerful enough to avert the fearful penalty thou hast named, the executioner shall but whet his axe on that small neck, for I shall lay my head beside this dearer head than shoulders ever bore! Blow out the spark that illumines those loving eyes and all this great world could not light a fire bright enough to cast the gloom out of my life!"

So Too shook his head mournfully, but made no reply.

Calling my men to me I spoke as follows:

"Go, honest souls, I cannot be one of you. Return to your homes and firesides. An Imperial escort will conduct you to the port of Canton. There, beneath some friendly flag you will find means to reach your native land! Peace and good fortune go with you!"

Then, turning to my first mate, I added:

"Seek out my father, the elder baron, impart unto him the story of my shipwreck; the arrest of Bulger; and my firm determination to save him from the terrible fate now impending, or to die with him! The elder baron knows my love for Bulger. He would deem me a degenerate son of his illustrous house, were I to abandon this faithful companion of my dangers and sufferings to so unmerited a fate. Go! Place this signet ring on thy finger. Deliver it to my mother, with my most dutiful and humble greeting. Be wise; be brave; be honest!"

My men now formed in single file, and as they passed in front of me each one paused and pressed my hand to his lips.

Bulger, too, was ready for the leave taking. Mounted upon a chair at my side he extended his right paw to each seaman.

Tears streamed down their weather-beaten faces and, they invoked blessings on the head of their brave little companion who had saved them from a deep grave in the briny waters.

Scarcely were they out of my sight when a deafening beating of gongs announced the arrival of the guard. My heart slipped from its resting place. A cold sweat gathered in beads on my temples. It was only with the greatest effort that I could draw breath enough to keep me from sinking lifeless to the floor.

So Too murmured a word of sympathy.

At the sight of the gailors and sound of the chains, I uttered a piercing cry and threw myself on my knees with Bulger clasped tightly in my arms. Poor, innocent beast! he was utterly unable to comprehend the actions of those about him.

"He shall be well-treated!" murmured So Too. "Fear not for his safety or comfort!"

The gailors now advanced, and stooping down, clasped the delicate manacles—which were of polished silver, upon Bulger's feet.

He looked up at me with eyes so speaking, so full of love and so trusting that I could not bear their gaze. It meant: "I submit without a murmur, for I know that thou wouldst not let any harm come to me!"

Then one of the guards lifted him gently and placed him in a silk-lined hamper, slung upon two poles. The lid was quickly adjusted and fastened, and ere I could collect my senses to speak a last farewell they hurried away with their prisoner, for it was plain to be seen their hearts were deeply moved by my woful countenance and grief-shaken voice.

At So Too's solicitation I now went to rest.

Rest? Alas! how could sleep get into my tearful eyes? All night long I lay awake bemoaning the sad fate which had overtaken me. Had accusation and arrest fallen upon me, I could have borne it like a man; but that Bulger's loving heart should have been singled out to bear a blow so undeserved was almost death to me.

As the hours dragged wearily along I thought of reversing my order sending my men away, and of attempting a rescue. I thought of schemes to bribe the gailor. I thought of demands for the interference of my government. I thought of an appeal for mercy direct to the Emperor himself. When day dawned I was utterly exhausted and sank back upon my pillow with a groan. Anticipating my inability to get any rest for my throbbing brow and fever-heated limbs, So Too was early at my chamber door with his attendants. Under his directions they bathed me in cooling lotions, patted, rubbed, and chafed my limbs; fanned me, stroked my wrists and temples, gave me draughts of quieting powders and gently pressed my eye-lids down, until gradually I sank into a deep sleep, which lasted quite until high noon.

I awoke with a strong heart. Now I was myself again. My sorrow had not grown less; but, for the time being, I was master of it.

So Too met me with a broad smile. I kowtowed profoundly. He expressed the hope that, his "tall, graceful, broad-shouldered, handsome visaged guest of knightly bearing" had slept well. "As for me," he added, "my miserable, little, crooked frame was full of pangs and tortures all night long."

To look at him it was hard to see any effects of all these "pangs and tortures."

He seemed the very picture of good health and spirits. His broad face was as smooth as a baby's and his little eyes sparkled with suppressed humor and mischief. We grew quite merry over our morning meal.

I was playing a part. I determined to let him think that by degrees I was becoming cured of my extravagant affection for Bulger.

With every cup of tea he drank his cold exterior kept melting off. I felt that if I left him quite to himself, he would give me a clearer view of his inside nature than if I attempted to draw him out by leading questions. I called into use all my wit and imagination. I buried him beneath compliments and fine speeches. I told him some of my most diverting stories. At last, I was successful. The servants were directed to withdraw. So Too now assured me in the name of all his ancestors, that I was the most delightful guest that had ever sipped tea beneath his roof. He entreated me to honor him by rising and placing my tall, graceful, knightly form along side of his miserable, puny little rack of bones.

I made haste to accept the invitation, protesting, however, that I was quite overcome by the honors showered upon me.

He maintained, with equal pertinacity that he was utterly unfit to occupy a seat by my side.

So we continued our war of compliments. Suddenly So Too thrust his right hand under his richly embroidered tunic and drew forth a small case of tablets, which folded upon each other in a curious way. He gave it a slight jerk and it flew open and unfolded itself. "I have been thinking," he began, "of the approaching trial of thy dog on the charge of witchcraft."

A lump arose in my throat at these words, but I gulped it down and simply bowed my head as a sign of my attention.

"Thou art a stranger in our land," continued So Too, "perchance thou wilt be pleased to know the things which I am about to tell thee. Nowhere else in the great world can Perfect Justice be found save in the dominions of our gracious

Emperor, him of the Sacred Countenance. While thy nation and the rest of the Western world knew no other law than force or fraud, we had already received from our ancestors thousands of volumes filled with the rules of Perfect Justice. Happy indeed should be that criminal whose good fortune leads him to commit his crime in our favored land. His punishment will be exactly what he deserves. Thou, as the advocate of this fortunate prisoner, who is so dear to thee, art allowed to choose the yamun before whom he shall be tried. I, So Too, thy friend, do here set before thee the list of yamuns so thou mayst choose thine own arbiter."

Saying this, So Too placed the unfolded tablets in my hand, and then dropped off into a gentle doze.

I scanned the list with mingled awe and curiosity. It read as follows:

THE LIST ITSELF. ALL BY ITSELF.		
OF AND NOTHING ELSE.		
ONLY THE JUST JUDGES. ALL BY THEMSELVES.		
FOLLOWED BY NOTHING ELSE.		
I.	Ling Boss,	A Just Judge.
II.	Quong Chong,	A Just Judge.
III.	Poo Pooh,	A Just Judge.
IV.	Wah Sat,	A Just Judge.
V.	Lung Tung,	A Just Judge.
VI.	Keen Chop,	A Just Judge.
The List of Just Judges. And Nothing Else.		

Thinking that So Too was sleeping soundly, I half unconsciously murmured to myself, as I glanced at the first name on the list: "Ling Boss, a just judge!" When to my great surprise—which, however, I was careful not to show—So Too, without opening his eyes spoke as follows:

"Aye, a just judge; a very just judge; but a dangerous one; neck too short, too much blood—hence, brain too hot—never willing to hear both sides; a good judge for him who speaks first before the blood begins to press upon his brain, a bad judge for a long cause."

"Quong Chong?" I repeated inquiringly.

"A just judge," replied So Too, "an extremely just judge, but too tall and thin; not blood enough for his long body; brain too far away from heart; cold and merciless; does not eat enough, only a little fish; a good judge for a very bad man."

"Poo Pooh?" I suggested, in a low tone.

"A just judge, a thoroughly just judge," continued So Too, "but not to be trusted; laughs too easily; too much given to making puns; always ready to deal out death to a solemn-visaged man; only too happy to sentence a man to death if he can make a pun with his name and the axe or block or something belonging to the executioner."

"Wah Sat?" I asked timorously.

"A just judge, an entirely just judge," said So Too, apparently half overcome with sleep, "but a judge to be avoided; too much given to asking questions; never weary of turning round and round like an auger, until he strikes bottom; a good judge for a hard and knotty cause—slow, but sure, eating away falsehood bit by bit; not a good judge for a plain case."

"Lung Tung?" I questioned, half in despair, glancing at number five.

"A just judge, an undoubtedly just judge," So Too gave answer, in the same sleepy tone, "but a dangerous judge; too fond of hearing himself talk; too liable to use up the criminal's time and then condemn him to death for not having defended himself within the hour allotted to him!"

Here my heart sank within me; but I drew myself together. There was still one name left. I glanced at it despairingly. "Keen Chop?" I murmured.

"A just judge, a perfectly just judge;" remarked So Too with a slight increase of animation, "a flower, a pearl of a judge; eats well, drinks well, digests well; fond of the good things of life, a great lover of beautiful vases and statues and screens and embroideries—always willing to hear both sides and—"

Here So Too came to a halt and fell into such a sound slumber that he snored loudly. I waited patiently for him to finish his nap. He resumed exactly at the point where he had left off.

"Very anxious to build a larger and finer house and to fill it with rich and rare ornaments."

Again So Too dropped off. Not to be outdone by him in apparent indifference at the matters under discussion, I likewise gave way to a feeling of drowsiness and was soon fast asleep.

How long we slept I know not; but, when we awoke my mind was perfectly clear on one point. I turned to So Too and said:

"I am resolved! Keen Chop is a just judge! Let him decide Bulger's fate!"

Three days, long and anxious ones for me, went by before I was accorded a hearing in the Hall of Justice. So Too made great efforts to amuse me and turn my thoughts away from the poor innocent captive. But all in vain. Those dark, lustrous eyes were always fixed upon me. Day and night, they kept repeating the same question: "Dear little master what does it all mean? I know you will not desert me, but why must I be so long separated from you?"

At last the long-wished for hour arrived. I was escorted to the Hall of Justice by a band of So Too's retainers. A seat was assigned me in front of the platform, which the judge and his suite were to occupy. The vast chamber was crowded with clerks, officers, gong-beaters, accused and accusers; but a deep silence rested upon them all. As I walked to my seat a subdued murmur ran over the multitude, for Bulger's case was in every one's mouth; and I could see that my youthful appearance excited great surprise.

Suddenly a beating of gongs announced the arrival of the judge.

Keen Chop entered the Hall of Justice with a majestic tread and solemn air, partly the effect of a pair of huge spectacles which were held astride his nose by heavy silken cords and tassels passed over his ears. He was followed by a vast array of clerks, servants and attendants. There were ink-bearers and pen-bearers;

there were fan-bearers and book-bearers; there were foot-rubbers to chafe his feet in case they got asleep from long sitting; there were nose-ticklers armed with long feathers, whose office it was to arouse Keen Chop should he drop off into too long a nap; there were eraser-bearers whose duty it was to blot out from the tablets all the judge had said when he resolved to change his mind. "Let the vile, miserable, wretched accused be brought into the august presence of Keen Chop, the just judge!" cried one of the Court officers, in a loud voice.

After a few moments' delay, the wicker hamper which contained my faithful Bulger, was carried into the chamber through a side entrance, set down in front of the judge and Bulger lifted gently therefrom and placed on a table at my side. The silver manacles were still attached to his feet. My heart stood motionless as I heard the rattling of the chains which ran from leg to leg. I had steeled myself to appear calm; but in spite of my efforts, the tears trickled down my cheeks. Bulger gave a start as his dark, lustrous eyes fell upon me and he uttered a long, low whine as if to ask: "What does all this mean, dear, little master?" And then he raised his right paw as high as the chain would permit, and held it out for me to shake—as was his custom when craving forgiveness for some mischievous act which had displeased me.

I pressed the outstretched paw long and tenderly.

"Doth the prisoner confess his guilt and humbly beg for mercy at our hands" inquired Keen Chop turning his huge eye glasses full upon Bulger. Whether it was the disagreeably shrill and creaking tone of the judge's voice or the glitter of the large glass discs set in front of his eyes, which displeased Bulger, I know not; certain it is he made answer for himself with a single loud and angry bark. Keen Chop was so startled that he dropped his smelling salts and motioned to his fan-bearers to cool his heated face.

"Silence!" roared one of the gong-beaters, giving a deafening thump upon his gong to inspire respect; and, at the same time fiercely agitating his bristling eye-brows and mustachios.

"My lord judge," said I performing the kowtow, "I crave consent to speak for the prisoner. He is not guilty of witchcraft. Nor doth any manner or kind of evil spirit dwell within his body. He is a true and faithful servant and companion of mine; perchance, with somewhat more than the usual intelligence of his kind. As his defender I call for the proofs of this most unmerited accusation!"

Keen Chop now fell asleep. But, after a few moments, his nose-tickler succeeded in arousing him.

"Let the proofs be read!" spake Keen Chop in slow and measured tones. One of the clerks arose; and unfolding a huge sheet of paper, with wooden rollers fastened at the top and bottom like a window shade, began to read in a drawling, singsong voice as follows:

Proof First: That the prisoner did, without any command, upon reaching the shore from the wreck, proceed to bite the twine attached to his collar in twain; and, taking up the end in his mouth, pass by a group of imperial officers, and a group of merchants, and a group of artisans, and a group of idlers, and make for a group of sailors, at whose feet he laid down the end of the twine.

Proof Second: That the prisoner did, at the sound of the official gong, unlike the animals of his race dwelling among us, manifest great displeasure and ill-humor, rush towards his master, lay one ear against his master's body and close the other with his paw.

Proof Third: That the prisoner did, on the same day, in the presence of imperial officers, without any command, pick up a purse of gold dropped by his master and restore it to him.

Proof Fourth: That the prisoner did, on the same day, in the presence of imperial officers, upon crossing the threshold of the Lord High Mandarin So Too, unlike animals of his kind, contemptuously and disdainfully reject the kindly welcome and friendly greetings given him by his Excellency's dogs.

I confess that, as the clerk of the Court finished reading these proofs, my heart rose slowly into my throat. They were, in good earnest, proofs of far more than the usual intelligence of animals of his race. I was staggered by the amount of proof they had collected. While I felt that I should have difficulty in persuading Keen Chop that all this was only the result of careful training, aided by a special aptitude on Bulger's part, I was very careful not to betray any nervousness or lack of confidence.

I called for some tea, on a plea of needing refreshment; but really to gain time to collect my thoughts and get myself together, after such a staggering blow.

Meanwhile, Keen Chop dropped off into a calm doze.

I finished my tea and sat waiting patiently for the nose-tickler to arouse him.

When I saw that Keen Chop was wide awake again, I arose with great dignity; and, placing myself beside Bulger, who was watching my every movement and listening to my words with an almost painfully anxious expression, which meant only too plainly: "What does it all mean, dear little master?" I began as follows:

"My Lord Judge! Most ancient, antique and venerable Patriarch, stricken in full five score of honorable years, thy snow-white locks bespeak thy wisdom!" The fact of the matter is, Keen Chop was quite a young man, and so far as I could see had no hair at all on his face or head save a scanty pig-tail; but I knew how flattering it was to a magistrate to be called "old and venerable" and hence my desire to make a good impression at the very outset. "My mother's breast knows no other child than me and I no other brother than this faithful creature whom heaven, for its own good reasons, hath set upon four feet; but who, if the strength of love could lift him up, would walk beside me, our two hearts on the same level. O, venerable judge—whose wisdom, like fair fruit red-ripened in the Autumn season, is now so ennobled by the flight of time, thou knowest what love can do! Thou knowest full well how it can so steel the thin beak of the mother bird, that the merciless talons of the hawk have no terror for her! Thou knowest, better than this poor bit of humanity which now pleads before thee, that man's spear hath not point sharp enough to drive the bear from her cub! Thou knowest how the timorous sparrow, to shield her nestlings, will face the viper's horrid crest, forked tongue and stony eye! And what shall I say of this faithful creature's race? When lived there one of his kind that was known to desert a poor and humble master, for a richer one; or to refuse forgiveness for a rash and undeserved blow? Where else can human hearts invest their love and draw such usurer's rates as here? We were babes together! The same sunbeams that danced a welcome on my awakening into life, found him, too, just arrived. Of quicker growth, he was his brother's keeper. I gave him all my love, for no other playmate was there to share it. I planted better than I knew, for on the thankful soil of his true heart, that love of mine struck such deep and vigorous root that it gave of its strength and power to his brain! Love hath so sharpened thought, that it hath grown wondrous strong! The spirit, thou callest 'evil,' is, as the learned know, a reasoning being; and, although it may go upon four feet and whine, and yelp, and growl, and bark, this is but the mask it wears.

"O aged judge, in the vast storehouse of whose mind experience hath piled wisdom many stories high, thou wilt ere long believe me, for I shall make it most plain to thee—that this faithful, loving animal, is not gifted with the mysterious power of reason! True, most true, nature hath widened his vision; but not removed its boundaries.

"Mark now, O learned patriarch, how easy a thing it is for truth to pierce the armor falsehood wears, for gird she ne'er so tightly, there are always some joints that will not come together!

"If my poor, weak mind be not strong enough to brush away the so-called proofs of this evil spirit, then let me be withered by the flame of thy just indignation! This creature loves me! Not the vigor of ten-thousand human hearts blent in one could yield a warmer love than his for me! And yet behold how short its vision is!

"This curious fire-arm was given me by a Turkish merchant whose life I saved in a brawl. I have so set it that a feather's weight will discharge it; but, first I smeared some sugar paste upon its trigger. Lo! I turn it toward my breast! If this creature now hath but the faintest glimmer of impending harm to his beloved master, he will refuse to lick away the sugar paste!"

A death-like silence fell upon the assembly. I held the fire-arm out towards Bulger. In an instant he scented the sweet odor of the paste and thrust his tongue out in several unsuccessful efforts to reach it. A sharp explosion rang through the great hall.

I stooped and picked up the ball—which had flattened itself upon a steel plate hidden beneath my robe.

Bulger's amazement was not so great as Keen Chop's. He made signs for refreshment. Tea was hurriedly served. A hundred fans wafted the sulphurous vapor away from his nostrils.

"Once more, O wiser judge than ever in Western Lands, shed the radiance of human wisdom on things dark and obscure, behold how I tear away the weft of falsehood which some ingenious mind would have this august tribunal adjudge to be pure truth! Here, on this salver, I hold some toasted bits of cocks' combs—to this creature's taste, the daintiest morsel which nature and art can unite in producing!" Catching a sniff of his favorite dish, my good Bulger began to bark and whine and strain his manacles to their utmost in wild endeavors to reach it. I held the salver out so as to permit him to reach a few pieces of the toothsome food. He was now beside himself; one moment begging, coaxing, pleading; the next, scolding, threatening, expostulating. No doubt he was very hungry, for it was hardly to be expected that the prison messes would suit his dainty palate.

"Most venerable judge!" I resumed, "as thou well knowest, evil spirits hold in great repugnance and dread all subtle and mysterious brews and poisonous compounds with which man strives to display or destroy them. Look now! I sprinkle this coveted dish, before his very eyes, with a powder so deadly and direful in its effect on life that this weak hand of mine holds power enough to change this mighty hall filled with light and life, into one vast charnel house. And again I bring the food within his reach, covering it with a sheet of glass lest his ardor out-wit my vigilance!"

Bulger now fell upon the plate of glass which covered the food, with renewed impetuosity, giving vent to sharp cries of disappointment as he vainly endeavored to lick up the tid-bits, rattling his chains as he strove to scratch away the glass which kept him from his expected feast.

Commanding him to be silent, I uncovered the dish and set it within reach of several dogs which I had caused to be tied near at hand.

At the first touch of the poisoned food they fell to the ground as if stricken by a thunderbolt.

"Again, most sapient and venerable judge, let me add proof to proof that naught of reason dwells within the mind of this faithful creature!"

"I was wounded once in his sight by a treacherous slave. His dagger point pierced my breast; but I smote him dead ere he could find my heart. Yet the danger of that moment seared the image of that poniard forever on this creature's memory.

"Bid now a retainer turn a dagger towards my breast!"

It was done!

With frantic cries and wild-starting eyes Bulger strove to leap upon my supposed assailant.

"Cover now the blade with its sheath!"

It was done!

Again my good Bulger made desperate efforts to reach the man, filling the room with cries of rage and fear.

"Cast away both sheath and blade!"

'T was done!

But still my loved Bulger made maddest effort to protect his master.

"Cast away the heft and blade and raise the empty sheath against my breast!"

'Twas done!

Still it was all the same! No matter whether covered or uncovered point; whether harmless heft, or still more harmless sheath, was turned towards my breast, Bulger's cries of mingled rage and fear, his mad attempts to break away from the shackles which bound foot to foot were first and last, exactly as fierce.

Keen Chop now did several things. He drank some tea. He ordered one of his menials to tickle his ear. He removed his huge spectacles and handed them to an attendant who proceeded to polish them. He then attempted to fall asleep. But, at a sign from me, Bulger began to bark so furiously that he gave a sudden start as if he thought the animal was about to lay hold of his calves. Taking advantage of this, I strode up in front of Keen Chop; and fixing my gaze upon him, spake as follows:

"Most ancient Magistrate, I crave your gracious consent to add another plea to my defense of this dumb creature. I would be the veriest ingrate, whom any wretched outcast might, with justice, spurn and revile, were I not to defend this devoted being with all my mind's cunning and heart's love!"

With these words, I sprang lightly up the steps which led to Keen Chop's chair, and ere he could say nay, caught up his fan which he had just laid down on the table beside him.

"Now, venerable judge, for a last,—and I trust overwhelming—proof that no evil spirit dwells within that creature's body.

"Here are two fans: Thine! Mine! Thine, made sacred by the touch of thy age-palsied and time-stricken hand! Mine, a worthless trifle; if it were possible, made still more worthless by the touch of my worthless hand. If, as this Court hath charged, an evil spirit dwells in this animal's body, it knows full well that power of life or death hangs on thy lips; that thou canst pardon with a smile or slay with a frown; that thou canst condemn to lingering torture or strike his shackles off with a nod!

"Ay, more! that if it should, to thine eyes seem meet and wise, thou canst adjudge both master and dog worthy of death and grant them no greater boon than that their blood shall flow together after life is over, as their love was one when living!

"Behold, I cast these two fans at his feet!"

Loud murmurs broke out all over the vast assembly. Many rose in their seats and craned their necks to watch the result.

Bulger looked up at me with a puzzled air at first; but his mind was soon made up. He picked up my fan tenderly and carefully, and with wide-opened, love-lit eyes, raised himself on his hind feet and laid it in my lap, wagging his tail the while, as much as to say: "Never fear, little master, I know what belongs to thee!"

Then, with an outburst of snarling, barking and growling, threw himself upon Keen Chop's fan, shook it savagely until the richly painted covering was torn in shreds and lay scattered about; tossed it up in the air, only to leap upon it with all fours as it touched the floor; and then, setting his stout claws in its joints wrenched them asunder as if they were made of paper.

But this was not all!

To complete the list of indignities which he had visited upon Keen Chop's property, he now turned his back toward that grave magistrate; and by several sudden and vigorous kicks with his hind feet, sent the sticks in a shower flying so close to his head that one actually struck against the huge disc of glass placed in front of Keen Chop's right eye. But a court officer, who had fallen sound asleep, and let his head fall backward, did not escape so luckily. Two of the largest sticks entered his nostrils and remained sticking there like arrows in a target. The man awoke with an ear-piercing shriek. In spite of the commands of the court officers, that every one who laughed should be bastinadoed, there was suppressed giggling here and there. Keen Chop himself twisted his face into the most comical grimaces in order to keep from bursting out into a fit of laughter. As for Bulger, he was beside himself with pleasure. In fact, he fairly howled with joy. Keen Chop now moved his thumb as a sign that he was about to speak, and a deep silence fell upon the multitude.

I was summoned to approach the steps of the judge's chair. He spake as follows:

"When thou art taller, thou wilt be stronger! When thou art older, thou wilt be wiser!

"Know then, that, as the abject slave of the Child of the Sun, him of the Sacred Countenance, Lord of all the Orders, I had intended to dismiss this charge against thy dog, cast off his manacles and set him free. But it may not now be done!

"Thy pleading hath convinced me that he doth deserve to die! A just cause needeth no other defence than words. But thou hast pleaded with hands and legs and feet! Thou hast been over-earnest! 'Tis proof, thou knewest the weakness of thy cause. Hadst thou not spoken at all and had thy dog himself but oped his mouth at the very outset, what had fallen therefrom would have freed him from his shackles.

"Now he must die!

"Let him be delivered to the public executioner!" And then, with a motion of his hand, he ordered the gongs to beat, so that it was impossible for me to make reply. The great chamber was now the scene of the wildest hubbub. The guards crowded around me as if they feared I might, in my desperation, sacrifice my life in attempting to rescue Bulger.

Poor Bulger! He had been quickly lifted into his wicker cage and borne out of the court-room.

Although I could feel my heart hammering on my ribs I gave no sign of the storm of emotion that was sweeping over my inward being. I could hear those terrible words "public executioner" ringing in my ears; but my infallible second sight caught no glimpse of that dreadful officer, and hence I felt that there was still hope. But, I moved neither hand nor foot.

The gongs ceased beating.

The throng departed from the hall of justice.

The guards, kowtowing, backed out of my presence. I stood there alone in that vast, silent chamber.

I was aroused at last from my deep reverie by the approach of a messenger from Keen Chop. He thus addressed me:

"The wretched, little, misshapen Keen Chop humbly begs the tall and stately stranger to drink tea with him in his private apartment."

Mechanically I followed the judge's servant, who lead me through long and winding corridors. Keen Chop had laid off his huge spectacles and received me most graciously.

All the servants were dismissed. We sipped our tea in silence for a while. At length, rising and stepping behind a screen, he returned, bearing a huge volume.

It was the record of Bulger's trial. He desired me to examine it while he refreshed himself after his long sitting on the judge's bench with a short nap.

I turned the leaves of the record over slowly. Not only were my words set down with the most perfect accuracy, but correct drawings of the various scenes filled the broad margins of the record.

On the last page I noticed that a blank space had been left between the words "must" and "die" and "him" and "be delivered."

"'Tis miraculous!" exclaimed Keen Chop, starting up and rubbing his eyes. "What a wonderful creature is thy dog! As I slept I dreamt that he oped his mouth and what fell therefrom convinced me of his innocence."

"Let him be brought into your august presence, O just judge!" I replied.

In a few moments Bulger's wicker house was deposited on the floor and he was lifted gently out of it. I could only with the greatest exertion keep back the tears as his large, speaking eyes were turned full upon me as if to ask: "When will all this mystery come to an end, little master?" I stroked his head with a loving hand to assure him that all was right.

No sooner were the attendants out of the apartment than, taking the purse of gold which Bulger had picked up on the beach and restored to me, I placed it in his mouth and made a sign for him to carry it to Keen Chop, who had now resumed his huge spectacles, and sat poring over the pages of the record of Bulger's trial.

Bulger did not wait for a second bidding.

Making straight for Keen Chop, he raised himself on his hind feet and dropped the purse in that dignitary's lap.

"'Tis wonderful! 'Tis very wonderful!" cried Keen Chop, testing the weight of the purse, with a pleased expression of countenance, first in one hand and then in the other. "Thy speech was silvern, but his silence is golden! 'Twere a crime to part two such faithful hearts. Go in peace!"

"But the record of the trial?" I asked. Keen Chop spoke not, but turning to the last page, he laid his finger on the place where the blank spaces had been left.

They were now both filled.

The word "not" had been written in each of them.

The guards were now summoned, and in a few moments the shackles were loosened from Bulger's feet. Upon finding himself free once more, he leapt into my lap with a wild cry of joy, and covered my hands and face with caresses.

I could not keep the tears back. Clasping the faithful animal convulsively in my arms, I wept like a child.

But a cloud came over our joy; for Keen Chop, upon my request for a safe conduct to the nearest seaport, informed me that he was powerless to grant my request; that I must apply to Slim Lim, the Taou-tai, or Imperial Governor of the province, Lord of the Peacock Feather, Knight of the Plain Red Button, etc., etc.

"'Tis well!" I exclaimed. "Deign to send one of thy servants to conduct me into the presence of his honor the Taou-tai! I pine to set foot once more on my native strand. I long to put an end to the sorrowful anxiety of my parents."

Keen Chop shook his head and smiled sadly.

"Know, O honored guest," said he, "that no one may approach the Taou-tai, Lord of the Peacock Feather, unless in answer to most humble petition of twenty pages length, his high and mighty Lordship deign to accord an audience! To attempt to do otherwise might mean death at the hands of the guards; but would most surely mean imprisonment in the deepest dungeon of the imperial fortress."

"So be it!" I replied. "Come death, come imprisonment, I stand this day in the presence of Slim Lim the Taou-tai, Knight of the Plain Red Button, and Lord of the Peacock Feather!"

Keen Chop groaned loud and deep. But seeing that I was resolved to set out at once for the governor's palace, he sent one of his attendants to conduct me to the gate, instructing him, in case the guards raised their swords to slay me, to cry out in a loud voice that I was a harmless lunatic and had escaped from my keepers.

To end all opposition I consented to this.

Whereupon Keen Chop bade me an affectionate adieu, and, followed by my faithful Bulger, I turned my steps toward the palace of the Taou-tai.

To tell the truth, chaos reigned within my mind.

In as many seconds, twenty different plans of action occupied my thoughts. How shall Bulger and I overcome the opposition of armed guards? It will be madness to provoke them to use their weapons upon us!

If I am fated to stand in the presence of the Lord Taou-tai, it must be accomplished by ruse and stratagem.

Luckily for me, the shades of night now began to fall, for, although the gateway and corridors of the governor's palace might be illumined by ten thousand lanterns—as in truth I found them to be, when I reached them—yet the light they shed was soft and uncertain.

Counting upon the almost lightning celerity of my movements and the utterly noiselessness of my footsteps, I succeeded quite easily in flitting by the group of sentries who were stationed at the outer gate.

Delighted with my good fortune, I sprang lightly up the steps of the portico, and, closely followed by Bulger, strode into the main corridor with dignified mien and stately air.

Eight towering fellows, armed with savage-looking pikes—for one of whom it would have been no more trouble to spit me and toss me out of the window, than for a boy to impale a frog on the end of his pointed stick and toss it on dry land—now blocked my advance.

So noiseless had been my step that I had approached within a few feet of them before they became aware of my presence. Had I dropped from the clouds, their astonishment could not have been greater and more ludicrous to behold.

They clutched each other by the arm, leveled their index fingers at me, and whispered in a hoarse voice, as one man:

"A little devil!"

"Nay, my good men," I replied, with a most gracious smile, "not a little devil, but a soldier like yourselves; one who has fought 'neath many skies, knows what a good sword is, what good wine is, would rather fight than run, can tell a good story, and loves war as a hunter loves the chase!"

The eight men looked at each other, tapped their foreheads significantly, and then fixed their gaze upon me as if they were in doubt whether my next move would be to jump down their throats, vanish into thin air, or expand into an awful ogre, and gulp them all down without pepper or salt.

"Come, comrades," I called out in a careless tone, "lay aside your pikes, and I'll show you something that I picked up on a battle-field in the war against the Algerines, something so curious, that if you had not slept a wink for three months and a day you would still be willing to keep awake and examine it."

Saying this, I drew my musical snuff box out of my pocket, and tapping its lid mysteriously, tiptoed my way towards the outside entrance of the corridor, and beckoned them to follow me.

They did so, with the most comical expression of half-wonder and half curiosity depicted on their faces. But first they quietly set their grim-looking pikes in the rack against the wall.

Motioning them to lay their heads together and bend down so that they could see and hear—for I reached about up to their girdles. I touched the spring of the snuff box and it began to play.

It is impossible for me to give you any idea of the delight which shone upon their great, round smooth faces.

Their mouths fell open.

Their fingers twitched nervously, as if they longed to touch the little wonder, and yet dared not. I felt now that the moment had arrived for me to act.

Winding up the snuff box to its utmost limit, I thrust it into the hands of one of the guards, who seemed beside himself with joy, and showed him how to touch the secret spring.

As the music began again, they closed up their group so tightly that even if I had wished to remain one of the circle it would have been an impossibility. To my infinite satisfaction they now seemed to dismiss me most unceremoniously from their society.

More quickly than it takes to tell it, I drew a ball of strong twine from my pocket, and fastening the ends of their cues securely together, I retreated to the outside entrance of the palace and placed the other end of the string between Bulger's teeth, with a motion that meant:

"Stand fast and pull hard!"

In another instant I had passed the group of guards and was making for the door of the audience chamber.

Suddenly the enormity of their negligence dawns upon them.

They look up.

They see me already at the end of the corridor!

They drop the enchanted box which has decoyed them from the path of duty!

They start towards their pikes!

Some mysterious force holds them chained to the floor!

Bulger is doing splendid work!

My hand is on the door of the audience chamber!

Smitten with a superstitious dread of some unseen power, the guards stand rooted to the spot.

A low whistle tells Bulger that his task is complete.

He flashes through the corridor like a spirit.

We enter the vestibule of the audience chamber, we pass through an outer apartment, we stand in the presence of Slim Lim, Lord of the Peacock Feather!

Slim Lim was at home.

He was seated in the centre of the spacious apartment, sipping a cup of very fragrant tea, the aroma of which was so fascinating that I paused and inhaled it with all the gusto of a fine taster.

Two ladies, clad in robes of great beauty and richness, were busy brewing tea and spreading before the Lord Taou-tai an infinite number of delicate viands and toothsome tid-bits.

But he ate nothing.

He was evidently somewhat disturbed by my sudden appearance, and I could see that one thought, to the exclusion of all others, was occupying his mind. It was: "How did this stranger pass the guards? True he is small; but if he can calmly walk into my apartment why may not an evil-disposed person do likewise?"

Determined to convince Slim Lim and the ladies of his household of my noble lineage and refined manners, I kowtowed with all the grace of a veteran courtier, and began the enumeration of their various virtues, excellencies, and charms of body and mind. When I had reached number one hundred and seventeen, the victory was complete.

They smiled.

But Slim Lim remained obdurate. He gazed into vacancy for several moments and then pretended to fall asleep.

I recited the purpose of my visit and waited patiently for the Lord of the

Peacock Feather to deign to reply.

He did so at last; but without opening his eyes, speaking as if half in a dream:

"Barbarian, son of a barbarian, grandson of a barbarian, great-grandson of a barbarian, great-great-grandson of a barbarian, great-great-great-grandson of a barbarian——"

Well knowing that this was a mere ruse to waste the night in words, I resolved to put an end to it at once.

I sat down and interrupted Slim Lim's long and dreary list by pretending to snore with that regularity which proves the accomplished sleeper.

He came to a sudden halt.

A deep silence now settled upon the scene, only broken by the nervous rattle of the ladies' fans.

Slim Lim now began to realize that he had no ordinary mortal before him.

For the first time he looked me squarely in the face.

The ladies grew alarmed at the dark cloud gathering on the brow of their liege lord, and withdrew to the other end of the room.

The Taou-tai was now wide awake.

So was I!

"Bold, thoughtless, and ill-counselled stranger," he cried out, "by the decree of the Child of the Sun, him of the Sacred Countenance, it is not lawful to punish a rash petitioner like thee, provided his prayer be one that may be granted. But what thou askest is impossible, for at this hour there is neither paper, ink nor brush within the palace! Thou must suffer for thy rash conduct. Thou hast been cunning enough to pass the guards in coming hither: but already a score of pikes are leveled at thy breast. Escape is impossible. Prepare for death or imprisonment in dungeon cell which knows neither light nor warmth!"

To speak the truth, my legs bent beneath the weight of my body as these cruel words made clear to me the danger I was in.

I could see that tears had gathered in the eyes of the two gracious ladies, standing near me.

"Paper—ink—brush!" I murmured, half dazed, "brush—paper—ink—or death!"

"It must not be!" I glanced about me. I closed my eyes. I fixed my gaze on Bulger, but all in vain—no help came to me.

A cold perspiration stood on my brow.

Suddenly, a huge parrot which was perched on a bamboo cage at one end of the room, uttered a harsh cry.

Quicker than it takes to tell it, I called Bulger to my side and set him teasing the bird.

He was not averse to enter upon the sport.

When it was well under way, I approached the bird from the rear, and as he bent forward to repel Bulger's familiarity, I deftly laid hold of one of his longest tail-feathers and pulled it out. An ear-splitting yell went up, and the two ladies threw themselves towards their pet with a thousand tearful expressions of pity and endearment.

I now turned my attentions to Slim Lim.

Drawing a pair of tiny shears from my pocket, I caught at the end of his cue and snipped off an inch of it.

My audacity struck him dumb. He could only stare at me with wide opened mouth.

I set to work now in good earnest.

Drawing some silk threads from my sleeve, I fitted the hair into the quill with such nimble, cunning fingers that Slim Lim looked on quite awe-struck.

"The brush is ready, Lord of the Peacock Feather!" I cried, laying it down in front of him. "And the paper too!" I continued, drawing out a paper mat from under a curio and turning up the white underside.

He followed my movements as a child would those of a necromancer.

Ink now was only lacking!

With one of my most winning smiles I drew near the ladies, and thus addressed them:

"Fasten forever the images of your beautiful faces upon the pages of my memory by lending me the jar of ebon pigment with which you add lustre to those matchless arches that shade your eyes!"

They returned my smile with entrancing grace and sweetness. But what was more pleasing still, they granted my request.

Halting for a moment at the cage of my friend, the parrot, who ruffled his feathers and eyed me most suspiciously, to moisten the pigment from his drinking vessel, I then strode with an air of triumph back to the table where Slim Lim sat nervously fanning himself, and said:

"Most noble Lord of the Peacock Feather, thy dull-witted, misshapen and worthless slave hath prepared brush, ink and paper; deign to set thy most honorable sign-manual to this paper so that he may withdraw his poor, miserable body and limbs from beneath thy sacred roof!"

So saying, I held out the brush to Slim Lim.

With trembling hand he took hold of it and rapidly traced the mysterious characters which were destined to open every gate and unbar every door until I stood once more on shipboard bound for my native land.

Folding up the precious document, I thrust it into my sailor's pouch. But while I was flushed with victory, Slim Lim showed only too plainly that he was nearly beside himself with chagrin and vexation.

The ladies of his household approached him with most profound obeisances and with loud and deep-drawn sighs at every step. But Slim Lim repulsed them in the rudest manner. He would have none of their sympathy, none of their pity or tender offices.

They redoubled their efforts; their sighs became more tender and louder.

It was all in vain.

Slim Lim was determined not to be propitiated.

Turning to me, he cried out:

"Let the barbarian, the son of a barbarian, the grandson of a barbarian, the great-grandson of a barbarian, the great-great-grandson of a barbarian, the great-great-great-grandson of a barbarian, the great-great-great-great-grandson of a barbarian inscribe his wretched, worthless, mean, common, ordinary, insignificant and despicable name upon a sheet of paper ere he goes forth, so that I and my children, and my children's children, and my children's children's children, and my children's children's children's children may speak it with contempt!"

And then, in order to prove to me that he considered himself disgraced to sit in my presence, he threw himself full length upon the floor.

Bulger got it into his head that this strange proceeding was in some way a menace to me, for he walked cautiously around Slim Lim, sniffing at him and growling in a threatening way, as if to say: "Don't play any tricks on my little master, or it will go hard with you!"

The ladies of Slim Lim's household were nearly crazed with grief and anxiety.

I assured them of my protection, but this only seemed to increase their solicitation.

To tell the truth, however, I was not half so calm as I appeared to be.

Cruel fate seemed to have woven her meshes about me once again.

Slim Lim, with deep cunning, had set another task for me which seemed so impossible of performance that he doubtless was already congratulating himself and applauding his own skilfully devised plan for holding me prisoner.

He had demanded that I should "write my name" before going forth; he had been most careful to use the word "write" so that I should not be permitted to use a brush after the manner of his people; but must have recourse to a pen after the manner of my own.

Feeling pretty confident in his mind that I would not have a pen in my possession, he had ground for flattering himself that I was still in his power.

Bulger caught a glimpse of the shadow that had settled upon my face, and whined nervously.

A thought struck me!

A quill will save me!

I looked towards the parrot.

Ah! deep-laid plan to rob me of my liberty!

The bird had been removed from the room.

The brush I had fashioned—the pigment, too, were gone!

I could feel my knees grow weak.

My breath came short and quick.

A cold chill crept over me.

There lay the Lord of the Peacock Feather flat on his back, but as I turned my glance quickly upon him, I was sure that one of his eyes was half open and fixed upon me, while a faint ripple of a smile played in the corners of his mouth most maliciously.

"Ah! man of guile!" thought I, "thou shalt not triumph, for I am about to shatter this last one of thy fetters, which thou dost think is already so firmly riveted upon my wrists. Thou art wise and thou art subtle, but not so wise and not so subtle as the little baron who stands beside thee!"

"To me, Bulger!" I cried.

With a single bound he reached my side.

"Take thy place there!" I continued, pointing to Slim Lim's breast, "and if my enemy moves but the poor space of a narrow inch, do thy duty!"

Bulger sprang lightly upon Slim Lim's breast, and with a low growl gave him to understand that there must be no trifling.

Then my turn came to act.

Whipping my pocket-knife out, I laid hold of Slim Lim's hand, and in less than a minute's time I cut a fine pen, with an excellent nib, on the end of the long nail of his little finger.

Bulger looked on very much interested, giving a low growl every time Slim Lim showed the slightest indication of resenting the treatment to which I was subjecting him.

My ink?

That was a simple matter. Pricking my thumb with the point of my knife, I let a few drops of the crimson fluid collect on the palm of my hand. Then, reaching out for one of the paper mats, I dipped the pen which now graced the little finger of the Lord of the Peacock Feather, and set my signature on the uncolored side of the mat in a neat, round hand.

Bidding Bulger descend from his post of honor, I now held out my hand to his excellency, the Taou-tai, with these words:

"Rise, Sir Knight of the Plain Red Button; be generous as thou art noble; I have triumphed! Forgive my audacity. In my place, thou wouldst have done likewise. Let thy enemy become thy friend. In birth, noble; in letters, learned; in arts, skilled; he is more worthy of thy friendship than deserving of thy enmity!"

Slim Lim seized my hand, and sprang to his feet with a good-humored smile on his broad face.

"By the sacred countenance of the Child of the Sun, Lord of all the Orders, thou art very clever for thy size!" he exclaimed, as he conducted me to a seat.

The ladies of the Taou-tai's household, who had retreated horror-stricken to their apartments, were now summoned to appear.

Tea was brewed and the Lord of the Peacock Feather insisted upon serving me with his own hands.

I was almost crazed with joy at thought of setting out for home under such happy auspices.

Bulger made friends with Slim Lim, and everybody forgave everybody.

His excellency, the Taou-tai, prevailed upon me to pass the night under his roof, assuring me that in the morning I should have a special escort, his own porte-chaise, and hampers packed in his own kitchen for my refreshment while on my journey to the seaport.

Until a late hour Slim Lim, the ladies of his household, Bulger and I gave ourselves up to feasting and merrymaking. In the morning I took my leave of the Taou-tai and his household in the happiest frame of mind.

A short week found me on board of a good staunch vessel bound for home again.

As the sails filled and we sped out of the harbor, I drew Bulger to my breast and the tears fell thick and fast. He licked my hands and face, and fixed his large, lustrous eyes full upon me.

He could not, and I would not, speak.

CHAPTER IX.

At this period of my life I had firmly resolved to settle down and enjoy a good, long rest.

Bulger and I both needed it. We were tired of strange sights, strange lands and strange people.

"Why should we not," thought I, "enjoy our world-wide fame?"

From the very ends of the earth, visitors flocked in thousands to my House Wonderful to see my treasures, my extraordinary curiosities, and above all, my remarkable dog, Bulger, the sole companion of my strange and eventful life, my guide, my friend, my counsellor, my all. Scarcely, however, were the valleys green again after a long and bitterly cold winter—so cold in fact that I drank nothing but iced tea for full three months, as it was utterly impossible to carry the pot from the stove to the table quickly enough to prevent its freezing,—than my thoughts turned to the pleasures and dangers of a roving life, and I longed to be up and off again in quest of new adventures.

As I roused myself from my reverie I found Bulger sitting at my feet with his kind, lustrous eyes fixed full upon my face. He had read my thoughts as correctly and easily as I might the words of a child's primer, and as he saw that I was wide awake and in full possession of my faculties, he seized hold of my sleeve and whined most piteously.

Dear, faithful animal! Oh, that I had heeded thy remonstrance!

But no, it was not to be.

Unwilling to fret and worry good Bulger, I now resolved to make use of a faculty which had no place in his nature—namely hypocrisy.

When he was in my presence I pretended to be perfectly happy and contented, going about laughing, singing and dancing; but the very moment he had quitted the room I set to work making ready for another journey.

At last all was ready.

When Bulger entered the house and set eyes upon boxes and packages, he lifted his head and gave one long, dismal howl of entreaty; but seeing that my purpose was fixed, like a true and faithful servitor, he bounded to my side and licked my outstretched hand, as much as to say: "Thy road is my road, thy fate is my fate!"

In a few hours we were on our way to the sea-board.

My heart was light, my spirits buoyant and gay.

"What is life?" I cried. "Am I a worm to vegetate in mold and darkness? Nay! I am a creature of intelligence, of mind, of soul; the air, the sunlight, the boundless universe, are mine; I will enjoy them."

Luckily I had not long to wait in the seaport, for a good, staunch vessel was nearly loaded.

Learning that she was bound for the Southern ocean, I at once ordered my effects to be set on board, and before the new moon had lost its crescent I was on the high seas with my faithful Bulger by my side and a bounding heart beating joyful music in my breast.

For a while all went well.

Bulger seemed to have gotten over his strange presentiment of evil and romped about the deck with all his old-time love of mirth and jollity. But upon me, however, after our good vessel was a few days out, there came a strange feeling never experienced before.

In my dreams, light and darkness alternately oppressed me; the one more dazzling than the electric flash, the other deeper than earthly night.

Our seventh day out, at high noon, suddenly it seemed as if some mighty hand had drawn a vast and impenetrable curtain of inky blackness over the entire sky. It almost appeared as if some terrible demon of the skies had suddenly blown out the very sun itself.

Bulger, with one bound, gained my side, and, fastening his teeth in my sash, moaned piteously, as was his custom when he thought my life in danger. I stooped and stroked his head. The palm of my hand felt the hot tears that were streaming from his eyes. Just then the vessel gave a lurch, and Bulger's weight tore his teeth from their hold in my sash, and in an instant he was separated from me. I heard his supplicating bark in a distant part of the ship.

"Bulger! Bulger!" I cried, "here! here! this way, to me, to me!" and in my desperation at thought of losing my loved companion, I darted in the direction of the barking, regardless of the black night which enveloped us, and stumbling over some object fell headlong on the deck.

My fall stunned me.

I rose upon my elbow and passed my hand over my eyes like a person just waking from a deep sleep.

Sulphurous flames now darted from the four quarters of the heavens, and crash upon crash of deafening thunder rattled and pealed over our heads.

A terrific blast of wind caught up our ship like a cockle shell and hurled it along through the seething, bubbling, maddened waters at such a fearful rate that every instant it seemed as if she must go to the bottom.

I know not how long we were driven along at this furious speed, for I was half dazed by the roar of the warring elements and blinded by the continuous flashing of the lightning. To my horror, the sound of terrible blows, dull but awful in their energy, now fell upon my ears.

We had struck upon the rocks, and our ship was pounding out her own life beneath my very feet.

Instinctively I called upon my faithful Bulger.

But not the voice of brazen throat and lungs could overcome the din of that tempest.

The intense darkness was now dissipated by showers of meteoric fire, which fell like ten times ten thousand bursting rockets as far as the eye could reach. And then deep rifts broke in the inky mantle of the heavens and showers of hail stones, each as large as a goose egg, rattled with the fury of musketry upon the deck.

At that moment a lurch of the vessel had rolled me under a huge copper kettle or my life would have been beaten out of me.

"Farewell, dear Bulger!" I cried, in a tear-strangled voice, "this terrible discharge from heaven's frozen artillery will surely end thy life! Farewell, faithful dog; a long farewell!"

Gradually this terrifying shower of huge hail-stones lessened its fury, and strange to say, in doing so the falling stones drew most wonderful music from the great copper kettle which covered me like a huge buckler.

The wind moaned a deep bass and the pounding of the vessel kept time like some gigantic drum.

Although half-dead with fear, I listened with ecstatic pleasure to this awful concert played by the warring forces of nature. When it had ceased, I looked out from my hiding-place.

Not a living soul was in sight. Every seaman and officer had perished beneath the strokes of the lightning, been crushed by the fall of hail, or swept by the resistless gale into the seething ocean.

So calm did it grow that I was beginning to take heart, when with a terrific swish and whirr, as if slit by some gigantic knife, the clouds parted and from the rent rushed blinding drifts of snow with such a wild and startling sweep and whirl that my knees swote together and I fell upon my face in utter despair.

But look! Had heaven slain the monster of the storm?

The snow was blood-red.

The sight froze the very marrow of my bones.

I rolled over upon my back; my senses fled; death seemed to have overtaken me.

How long I lay in this stupor I know not, but when I awoke the storm had spent its fury, the sun was sending down its brightest rays, the air was pleasantly cool and bracing.

Slowly my strength came back to me, and I emerged from my hiding-place, crawling on my hands and feet, for I was too weak to stand upright at first. Little by little, however, I took heart, and, as I felt my blood go tingling thro' my veins, I made an effort and rose to my feet.

Yes, my worst fears had been realized.

Not a living being had survived the storm.

As I walked upon the blood-red snow, every foot-fall brought forth most piteous sighs and groans.

"What dread warning," thought I, "does this mysterious murmuring give me? What is the meaning of these sobs and moans which issue from these crimson crystals beneath the pressure of my feet? Am I walking upon the blood of my ancestors?"

Clinging to the frozen sheets, I crept slowly along the red-encrusted deck.

But stay!

Hark!

Are my ears playing me still more fantastic tricks?

No! I'm wholly and entirely myself now, and as sure as the blood of the Trumps' courses through my veins, that bark came from my faithful dog!

"Bulger lives! Bulger lives!" I cried out in accents of the wildest joy; and breaking away from the hold of fear and trepidation, I rushed boldly forward, calling out "I'm coming, Bulger, I'm coming!" With reckless courage I sprang from one frozen plank to another, until I stood upon the quarter-deck. There, upon the hatch, sat, or rather lay, Bulger, for his life was almost extinct. His teeth were locked upon the straps of a life-preserver which he, ever thoughtful of my safety, was about to bring to me at the first outbreak of the storm, when its fury forced him to seek refuge under a water-cask, as his tracks on the snow indicated.

As quickly as my stiffened limbs would permit, I bounded forward, and throwing myself on my knees, in the crimson snow,—which sent forth most heart-rending groans and sighs at the pressure of my body upon its blood-red surface—I clasped Bulger in my arms and our cries of joy mingled,—our tears ran together.

All my suffering was forgotten in that moment, for Bulger was alive, his head was clasped to my breast.

The winds had now fallen, the sea had grown calm again, and I determined at once to quit the wreck if possible, for the setting sun revealed to me the shores of a beautiful land at the mouth of a small but extremely picturesque river, whose banks were rich in palm-trees, fruit-trees and flowering shrubs.

I lost no time in lowering one of the boats which had happily escaped with slight injuries, and being an expert seaman, I found no difficulty in rigging a tackle and lowering first, Bulger, and then myself into the boat, and paddling leisurely towards the shore.

Here I drew the boat high and dry on the beach, and calling out gayly to faithful Bulger to follow me, I clambered up the bank and pushed boldly forward to survey the fair land upon which a strange fate had set our feet.

Now, for the first, I became conscious of the terrible hunger that was gnawing at my vitals—a fact which proved to me that I must have lain in an unconscious state beneath the huge kettle for at least two days if not more.

Bulger raised his kind eyes to me, and then bounding off to one of the fruit trees, ran around it, barking joyfully.

I shook one of the branches and the ripe fruit fell in abundance to the ground.

Its odor was so delicious that although it was unknown to me, I had no hesitation in partaking of it most freely, Bulger following my example, a fact which convinced me that it could not be otherwise than wholesome. A long, deep draught from a limpid spring refreshed us both greatly; but as the sun was sinking rapidly, and as I now began to feel the effects of the rack, strain and weariness resulting from the terrible experience of the past day or so, I called out to Bulger:

"Come, dear, faithful fellow, let us seek out a fit place to pass the night; some nook shielded by wide-spreading branches, where there is plenty of soft boughs to make a bed with."

As the country was quite level, I sighted a grove at some distance, and thither we directed our steps.

It had now grown quite dark. We quickened our pace, for I was too prudent a traveler to care to expose myself to the night dew.

As we drew near the grove there appeared to be a low wall on one side of it.

"This way, Bulger," said I, "this long line of boulders will protect us from the night winds, if any should rise. Let us creep under its edge and lay our tired limbs down on the soft grass." He looked up with softened gaze and gave one or two consenting wags to his tail.

Nestling close under the edges of several of the largest of the boulders, at a point where they formed a sort of sheltered nook, we soon fell into a deep sleep, I sitting half upright and Bulger pillowing his head upon my lap.

Once or twice in the course of the night I awoke to find my brow beaded with perspiration. I put my hand on Bulger; he too was awake, and his tongue was lolling from his mouth. Both of us seemed to have been seized with a strange fever. The direst forebodings took possession of me. Had we landed upon a shore along which lurked some deadly miasm? Possibly we might not live to see the light of another day. It required all my self-control to banish such terrible thoughts from my mind. But so tired was I to the very bone that I soon fell asleep again, reassured as I was by the example set me by Bulger. It was, however, a fitful slumber, for the heat of our bodies had now become so great that the very ground upon which we were lying felt warm to my touch. At length, to my joy, I caught the first, faint glimpse of the dawn. I was now in a perfect glow from head to foot. And so was Bulger. Suddenly it burst upon my mind that possibly we might have lain down in a volcanic region; that, mayhap, fierce, subterranean fires were raging beneath our very heads. I rose to my knees with a bound, and placed both of my hands upon the nearest boulder. Fancy my horror upon feeling that its surface was not only hot, but that it yielded to the pressure of my hands, and gave forth groans, hissings and rumblings. In an instant I was on my feet. Bulger did not wait to be called. Determined to verify my suspicions,—for discretion was always a reasonable part of my valor, I hastened from one boulder to another within the circle where we had been lying, and pressed my hands upon them with all my strength. Deep, rumbling and hissing sounds came forth from the ground everywhere about me, and seemed to awaken responsive cries far and near, as if one giant tossing in his sleep disturbed the slumbers of his fellows.

"Bulger!" I cried, "we stand upon the ground of death; this is but the outer wall of a crater, it is aglow with subterranean heat; only the merest shell—so thin that it yields to my pressure—is between us and destruction. Fly, fly, faithful dog!"

The morning sun now burst forth with a flood of golden light.

As far as my eye could reach, extended this same boulder-like parapet, shutting out my gaze from the abyss through which the volcano was now about to spout its liquid fire; for all at once the boulders began to rock from side to side, giving forth such dreadful rumblings that I knew the eruption was to be preceded by an earthquake.

A sickening fear seized hold of me; my legs bent like pipe stems, beneath the weight of my body.

Bulger saw that his loved master was chained to the ground.

He refused to abandon me.

The whole wall, as far as my eye could reach, now trembled and rocked, threatening to engulf us every instant.

With a mighty effort I pulled myself together, and, followed by Bulger, darted away.

The measure of my horror was not complete.

With terrific rumblings, gurglings, hissing and groaning, the whole row of rocks now danced in violent agitation, and then, like so many gigantic balls, rolled by huge monsters at play, these boulders, propelled with fearful violence by the outburst of the volcano—as I supposed—came thundering down after our retreating forms, threatening us with a terrible death.

Bulger, running at my side, ever and anon sent out a mournful whine, as if to bid me an eternal farewell.

"Fly, Bulger! Faster, faster, good Bulger!" I called to him, as the roar and rumble of the advancing wall increased.

Now each and every boulder seemed urged on its course by some mysterious force of its own.

As I glanced over my shoulder, I could see that they were gaining in velocity, bounding, springing, now in single file, now three abreast, while the frightful and unearthly din and rumble went ever on increasing.

They were gaining upon us.

My legs again threatened to bend under the weight of my body and topple it over to certain and awful death, when a last glance revealed to me the terrible truth.

"Bulger! they are alive!"

A sharp, despairing yelp came from my poor dog.

"They're alive, I tell you! Some legion of monsters, devils, for aught I know, escaped from the depths of Tartarus, intent to roll over us and crush the life from our puny bodies!"

Again we redoubled our efforts.

"For your life, Bulger!" I gasped, "for your life! Look! the wood, the wood!"

He caught my meaning, and gave a sharp, encouraging bark.

But no, it was useless.

My strength had been used to its last poor throb.

It grew dark before my eyes.

A palsying fear laid hold of my heart.

My limbs stiffened.

I threw one last glance upon Bulger.

He answered me with a look of most tender affection, and then we both tripped, staggered, stumbled, fell headlong, side by side, while seemingly ten thousand living boulders, with awful shrieks, groans, and gurgling sounds, hung like a shadow over us for an instant, and all was black as night.

I felt my protuberant brow ground into the earth and the last bit of life crushed out of me.

My last though was:

"Bulger! O, Bulger! What a terrible death! But O, what a kind Providence to let us die together!"

"Rise! stunted, misshapen thing! Rise! thou wafer man, thou slice of humanity with cleft edges!"

It was not so much the thundering tones of this strange, human monster which caused me to sit bolt upright, rub my eyes and make a superhuman effort to collect my sadly scattered senses, as it was the caresses of my faithful Bulger, who was running from one side of me to the other, showering kisses upon my face and hands and whining piteously.

After a hard struggle the shadows were lifted from my eyes. My heart sank within me at sight of that wall of living boulders encircling us, with their fierce visages turned, half in wonder, half in rage, upon the, to them, two funny beings as utterly unlike themselves as each other.

But love is always stronger than fear.

Stretching out my arms and drawing Bulger close to my breast, I cried out:

"O, Bulger! do I really live? Am I not still the object of some demon's sportive malice?"

At sound of my voice the round-bodied monsters broke out into a hideous chorus of deep, rumbling laughter, during which their bodies rolled from side to side.

Then, as they pressed wildly forward, with fierce ejaculations of anger or impatience, it seemed as if Bulger and I had been only saved from one death to be set face to face with another.

"Alas! is there no power," thought I, "to save us from the furious impatience of these reckless monsters?"

Suddenly a terrible voice sounded loud above the din:

"Roll backward, Round bodies! What meaneth this unseemly impatience in the presence of your King?"

In an instant, the round-bodied monsters rolled silently backwards.

All was calm again.

Turning to his neighbor, the King exclaimed, with a gurgling laugh:

"Why, by my royal girth, its voice is all the world like one of the toy pipes of our baby prince!"

"'Its? Its?'" I repeated, with fire flashing from my upturned eyes. "Know, Sir Monster, that I am not a 'thing,' but a perfect man; a baron by birth, a scholar by profession, a traveler by choice."

At this outburst on my part, the crowd of living balls again sent up a deep, rumbling peel of laughter.

"Silence!" commanded the King, and then he continued: "Well, well, then, baron,—whatever that may be—but I think I ought to say 'little baron,' for by my royal roundness, thou art a wee, puny being! Let it be as thou sayest, but tell me, I implore thee, what is this walking box on four legs, which nature seems to have left unfinished?"

And so saying, he raised his terrible hand with fingers strong enough to crush me as I might a puff-ball, and waved it toward Bulger.

This contemptuous sneer did not escape Bulger.

He broke out into a volume of sharp, angry barks, and showed his white teeth in the most threatening manner.

Upon which the monsters rolled back in mock terror and consternation, crying out:

"The King! The King! Save the King! The walking box is filled with explosives; it may fly into pieces!"

When the hubbub was over, and the King had commanded silence, I stepped boldly forward and exclaimed:

"Unfinished! What meanest thou, thou globe-shaped monster?"

The term "globe" seemed to please his majesty very much.

A great, wrinkled smile overran his huge countenance.

"Mean?" he ejaculated, with a deep, gurgling, chuckling laugh. "Mean? why, little baron—whatever that may be—see for thyself. Has not Nature left useless flaps at one end of the box, and a still more useless bit of rope hanging down from the other?"

This insulting allusion to Bulger's ears and tail seemed to be perfectly understood by him, for he fairly bristled with rage, and advanced upon the round-bodied monster, snapping, snarling, and showing his teeth.

Whereupon the deep, rumbling laughter again broke forth, and the cry, "Save the King! Save the King!" went up in mock earnestness.

Having succeeded in appeasing Bulger's anger by means of a few affectionate words and tender caresses, I determined to make inquiry as to our whereabouts, and to ascertain who the strange beings were among whom capricious fate had so unceremoniously cast Bulger and me.

"Where are we, ball-shaped giant?" I inquired in my strongest voice, "and who are you?"

Again the monster screwed his leathery face up in a deep, wrinkled smile. The reason of his good will, as I afterwards learned, arose from the fact that I had bestowed the terms "globe," "round," "ball-shaped," etc., upon him, for it seemed that these wonderfully formed beings were extremely vain of their roundness, and that nothing could be uttered more pleasing and complimentary to them than to make use of such words and expressions as "ball," "orb," "sphere," "round-bodied," "bullet-shaped," etc.; that in their land, the greatest dignities honors and titles of nobility were awarded those whose bodies showed most perfect roundness; that in proportion as one's body deviated from the shape of a true sphere, he became degraded and excluded from society.

To such wretched subjects the King assigned the performance of all mean labor. They were the "squares," or outcasts, whom anybody might insult or even enslave with impunity. The richer ones were sometimes able to hide their deformity by means of padding, and in this manner conceal their uneven motion in rolling from the keen eyes of the King; but the poor ones, by their inability to correct their physical defects, at once attracted the King's attention, when he caused his people to roll up and down before him, while he kept up a searching lookout for "wabblers" or uneven rollers.

"Well, little baron—whatever that may be," replied the King, "or shall I call thee Wafer-man with cleft edges? Know, then, that I am King Bô-gôô-gôô, Monarch of the Roundbodies; that these, are some of my subjects.

"Know, furthermore, little baron—whatever that may be—that this island is my kingdom, in which no one rules saving me, and that unless it may please my royal daughter Rōlâ-Bōlâ to keep thee and thy attendant, the walking box with cord and flaps, as curiosities to amuse her, thou and thy companion perish at sundown, for, little baron—whatever that may be—it is my royal will, and so it was my father's, and his father's, and so back a thousand years, that no living creature shall set foot upon the shores of my domain and not pay for his temerity by being crushed to death, literally ground into the soil, until he become a very part of it!"

Bulger appeared to grasp the meaning of this fierce speech, which was delivered in thundering tones, and accompanied by hideous contortions of the speaker's great, round visage, flaming as the crimson disc of a tropical sun in the western sky, and followed by an outburst of grunts, groans and gurglings from the assembled Roundbodies; and, in spite of his inborn courage, his tail fell between his legs and he slunk nearer to me with a low, anxious whine.

But when good Bulger saw the calm expression of my countenance, he quickly recovered himself; his tail resumed its graceful curl, and as I faced King Bô-gôô-gôô with an unruffled exterior, to make reply to the latter's horrible threat, Bulger, too, placed himself at my side with a defiant air.

"Most gracious Sphere! Most royal Globe! Roundest monarch of the great, round world! true, I have set foot on the shores of thy domain, but it was not, most majestic Sphericity, through choice. A fearful storm, in which the warring elements seemed bent upon the destruction of the universe, during which the great ocean hurled itself against the walls of heaven as if to beat out the very stars, while the wide-mouthed gale swooped down upon this petty earth with seeming intent to swallow it and all it contained—?"

I could speak no further.

The Roundbodies broke in upon me with such dismal groans and cries that I stood as if rooted to the earth.

"Ah!" thought I, "they, too, felt the terrible blows of that storm-demon which so nearly beat out the life from mine and from Bulger's bodies!"

Waving my hand as a signal for silence, I proceeded:

"I bow before the will of thy spherical Majesty, whatever it may be! At the same time, I would beg to call the attention of your Imperial Roundness to the fact that, in the systems of law of all the nations of the globe, a man may not be held responsible for an act which he is made to commit by a force or strength greater than his own."

I saw that my flattery was telling upon King Bô-gôô-gôô, so I proceeded to make a still further application of the same remedy:

"However, most Royal Globe and perfect Sphere of Strength and Beauty, if, in thy great wisdom, thou dost decide that we must die, crushed beneath the weight of thy people's bodies, so be it! Great ball-shaped monarch, I am but a bit and shred of humanity, and how may I dare to oppose the will of your right royal Sphericity?"

King Bô-gôô-gôô smiled till his huge double teeth could be seen glittering in his cavernous mouth, like white rocks in a half-lighted pit, and his body swayed from one side to another in his gigantic glee.

"Send for the royal princess!" he roared.

In a few seconds, in answer to his command, a Roundbody came rolling across the plain with the swiftness of the wind.

The crowd of retainers fell back, and the new-comer arrested her flight by the side of King Bô-gôô-gôô.

I could not see that she was a bit more beautiful than those about her, although she was a royal princess.

True, she was a globe of smaller girth, her face was somewhat less repellent and beneath a long and heavy fringe of lashes, I caught glimpses of a pair of good-natured, roguish eyes, and my perfect knowledge of human and brute nature told me at a glance that if I could but gain the good will of that strange being, Bulger and I would be safe!

"My dear, little round papa," cried Rōlâ-Bōlâ—for such proved to be her name, "Where did those funny things come from? Are they really alive? Wont they bite or sting? What do they eat? What shall I keep them in? Will you make me a cage for them? Oh, I am so, so, so, so, so, so, so, so, so glad!" and she bounded about, now this way, now that, now into the air like an animated rubber ball, drumming like a partridge all the while.

Behold us, then, Bulger and me, prisoners in the land of the Roundbodies, with the Princess Rōlâ-Bōlâ as our keeper!

Hope sank low within our poor hearts.

I dared not breathe a word in opposition to the will of King Bô-gôô-gôô or the caprice of Rōlâ-Bōlâ lest the order should be revoked.

At least, in the keeping of the Princess Rōlâ-Bōlâ, we would be more likely to receive gentle treatment, and, what was almost a matter of life and death, we should have great chances of making our escape from the island of King Bô-gôô-gôô.

We were commanded to follow the Princess.

As Bulger and I started after Rōlâ-Bōlâ, with a brisk gait, the very clouds fairly snapt asunder, so great was the shout of laughter which the Roundbodies sent up.

Seemingly, it had not occurred to them until that moment how ridiculously different our mode of locomotion was from theirs.

"Look! look! O, King!" they cried, "he can neither roll nor hop! See how he edges along, leaning first on one foot and then on the other! He walks on his toe nails! Mark his companion, too! What monsters of clumsiness! How they rock and wabble! Why doth he not spring? Why doth he pound the earth as if he were beating flax?"

To all this mocking and jeering, Bulger and I turned a deaf ear, following our mistress, who ever and anon, turned her soft, black, mischievous eyes encouragingly upon us, as her head came uppermost.

Imagine our surprise when Rōlâ-Bōlâ halted at the beginning of a path having a gentle descent, and said:

"This is the entrance to the royal habitation. Follow me and fear nothing."

In a few moments we found ourselves in the outer room of a vast underground dwelling, consisting of corridors, chambers, dormitories, banquet-halls and arenas.

All the habitations of the Roundbodies are subterranean.

Why?

This you shall know anon.

Bulger and I were conducted to very pleasant quarters—well-lighted, as were all the rooms of the palace, by means of vast slabs of rock crystal, of which the roof was made, by a "square" or "lôb-bô" as he is called in the language of the Roundbodies, that is, one not perfectly round in form, and hence degraded to the position of serving man. Doubtless, long before this, the reader has grown impatient at my silence concerning the strange beings among whom Bulger and I now found ourselves prisoners.

Who were the Roundbodies?

Know then, gentle reader, that they were—mark well my words—the sole living creatures on the island of Gô-gû-lâh, upon which a strange fate had cast us. Whether or not any other beings had ever inhabited the island was unknown to them.

I found, upon conversing with their learned men, that there was a legend in existence among them—dim and shadowy in its details, from the long flight of centuries that it had come down through—that many thousands of years ago they had been quite like human beings, who walk upright, with bodies almost, if not quite, as long as mine; but that owing to the unvarying recurrence of terrible storms, of wind, rain, hail and snow, accompanied by the bursting of deafening thunderbolts, in fact, such as I had experienced, which swept over the island twelve times in the year, coming and going with a regularity as astonishing as their force is terrific, everything upright had long ago been swept from the land; that their ancestors, yielding to the irresistible forces of Nature, had gradually bent their bodies before these resistless winds, until even the time when they walked upright had been forgotten.

This was but the first change wrought by the forces which surrounded them. When overtaken by these wild winds, they soon learned that their only safety lay in rolling themselves up as much into the shape of balls as possible, so that the tornado would be powerless to pick them up and hurl them to destruction.

Another transformation now began to make itself apparent.

Their bodies, as centuries came and went, little by little, took on the rounded form they then had.

Still clinging to the desperate chance for life on these storm-swept plains, they drew down their heads and pressed in their limbs until these had made recesses for them, as some tortoises draw their legs so closely to their bodies that the eye fails to distinguish even the outline of the limb.

The last change that came upon these globe-shaped people was a very natural one: their arms took on a greater development of superhuman strength, while their legs grew shorter and shorter, until they consisted of little more than two broad, flexible feet, which they made use of mainly to propel their round bodies like huge balls across the vast plains of their island home.

Now, while they still dread the terrible blasts, yet is it rather an inherited fear, for at last they have become the true children of the gale.

If it should happen to blow in the direction of their homes, they simply allow it to help them on their way by rolling them across the plain. While, now and then, a lôb-bô, or "square" Roundbody, so to speak, would be blown into the ocean, yet for nearly a century not a single, genuine Roundbody had been caught up in the pitiless blast. As well might the wind attempt to pick up the round stones of the ocean strand.

One of the things which early attracted my attention in King Bô-gôô-gôô's palace, was the hangings, apparently of the softest leather, worked in mosaic patterns of transcendent beauty.

Imagine my surprise when told by the gentle princess Rōlâ-Bōlâ that they were simply the natural leaves from the various trees growing on the island, untouched by dye or stain of any kind.

They were so tough that my strength sufficed not to tear one in two.

Noticing my wide-opened eyes turned inquiringly upon her, the gentle Rōlâ-Bōlâ cried out with a soft, low gurgle:

"Go into the royal garden, Tôô-tôô-lō; that is, little 'flute-man,' and see for thyself."

Now, for the first, I learned the secret of the presence of such beautiful trees and shrubs upon this storm-swept land. Every leaf was as thick and as strong as leather, and the trunks and boughs were exactly of the nature of India rubber, so that, with a small bit which I brought home with me in one of my pockets, I could erase pencil-marks with the greatest ease.

To such foliage as this a tornado had no terrors.

When the storm struck these trees they went to the ground, until it had spent its fury. In a few hours the tropical sun lifted them again, and the beauty of their foliage was quite unharmed.

To return to the poor princess Rōlâ-Bōlâ:

Bulger began to fret and worry beneath the strain of our captivity.

I was constantly on the alert for a chance to escape, but none offered. In fact, we were, I began to fear, prisoners for life.

True, it was a pleasant captivity, for the gentle Rōlâ-Bōlâ almost killed us with dainty feeding, and our only toil was dancing, singing and capering for her amusement.

Night and day, the sole gateway of the royal habitation was guarded by a triple row of round-bodied sentinels, so fierce-visaged, so mighty-handed, that my heart grew sick as I gazed upon them.

To add to my despair, I now made a discovery which seemed to seal my fate forever—the princess Rōlâ-Bōlâ had become enamored of me!

What to me, at first, had seemed but a playful trick, to wit, her pinching my little toe ever and anon, had, as I was casually informed by one of the learned Roundbodies, in the course of a discussion with him, a terrible significance.

It was a solemn declaration of love!

Oh! miserable me!

And a declaration, too, which, coming from a woman to a man, it was certain, sure, inevitable death to ignore!

And yet I might be saved!

For the custom—made sacred by the observance of long ages—required the man to pursue the woman, who pretended to be frightened and extremely solicitous of escaping him, and while revolving with the same velocity as she, to pinch her little toe in return.

This ended the matter.

The couple was now betrothed.

It was not in the power of man to publish bans of greater strength.

If the man gave one pinch, the marriage was solemnized the following day; if two, the second day after, and so on.

But I was not a Roundbody!

How could I possibly comply with the ancient custom of the land?

Ah! Woman! Woman! it matters not whether thou belongest to the Roundbodies or to the Longbodies, in affairs of the heart thy ingenuity and subtlety overmatch the philosophy of man!

When it was made known to the princess Rōlâ-Bōlâ that the royal counselors had, after mature deliberation, reached the conclusion that the laws of the land— made sacred by the observance of ages—forbade any such union contemplated by her, she flew into a towering or, rather, I should call it, a bounding passion, for, from one end of her spacious salon to the other, sidewise and lengthwise, she bounded about like a great ball bouncing under the play of an invisible bat.

Alternately she wept, laughed, scolded and threatened.

But it made little difference how she began her tirades, they all had the same ending:

"I say, I shall marry Tôô-tôô-lō!"

King Bô-gôô-gôô, thinking to pacify his daughter, sent her messengers bearing the most beautiful presents; but she received them with disdain, scattering them on the floor.

Things went on this way for several days.

King Bô-gôô-gôô was horrified to find that the princess had eaten nothing for forty-eight hours, and that she was actually losing her beautifully round shape, for which she had so justly been famous.

Bulger saw plainly that something awful was going on, and he, too, became so worked up that he refused to eat or drink.

I passed most of my time going from his room to the princess Rōlâ-Bōlâ's, endeavoring to persuade them to take food.

But all in vain.

One morning the King's daughter met me with demonstrations of the wildest delight, laughing, singing, bounding and rolling about like mad. So beside herself was she that, forgetting her great weight and my puny build, she rolled against me and sent me flying like a little ten-pin struck by a monstrous ball.

By actual measurement I was thrown thirty feet, but, fortunately, struck against a heavy hanging which broke my fall.

Bulger gave a piteous howl.

He seemed to get an idea that Rōlâ-Bōlâ had struck me purposely.

Well, in a word, the cause of this frantic joy was simply this: The princess had finally thought out a solution to the terrible problem which had been for weeks

204 -   Ingersoll Lockwood

torturing her mind.

Briefly stated, it was as follows:

I should be placed in the boughs of a tree just high enough to clear her body. She then was to roll under me, and at the right moment, I was to lean downward and pinch her little toe when it came uppermost.

In vain I assured her that I should grow dizzy and fall headlong to the ground, breaking my neck, or, at very least, dislocating it.

But no, I need have no fear.

She would watch over me.

She would turn and catch me in time.

The royal counsellors were at once called together.

The plan of the princess Rōlâ-Bōlâ was laid before them.

At first they sent up a deep and ominous rumble of disagreement.

But Rōlâ-Bōlâ's messengers were at hand with most costly presents, and it all ended in their finding an almost similar case in their books, where a wounded prince, who was quite unable to roll an inch, had been placed upon an elevated platform in order that his round-bodied sweetheart might pass beneath and he be enabled to pinch her little toe while it was in the air at the highest point from the ground.

Seeing that it would be useless to make further opposition, I now submitted with a good grace, for it was plain to me that once the husband of the princess Rōlâ-Bōlâ I should become, to a certain extent, one of the family and be accorded greater liberty, by means of which I confidently hoped to make my escape from the land of the Roundbodies.

Preparations for the marriage were now begun with extraordinary haste, in order to have all things ready for the first feast-day in the calendar.

As the time drew near, however, I somewhat lost my courage.

"Was I not," I asked myself, "simply lending my aid in forging my own fetters, in laying chains upon my neck, which would render it impossible for Bulger and me ever to set eyes again upon our beloved home?"

I became very nervous, and found it impossible to catch a wink of sleep.

At last I resolved to postpone my fate, at least for several days.

And this was my scheme:—

I should explain to the fair Rōlâ-Bōlâ how utterly impossible it would be for me, in my fright and anxiety, to get my thumb and finger upon her little toe at all, as she revolved swiftly beneath me.

I therefore would implore her to roll very slowly.

And then my scheme would be to seize her foot, hold it fast, and pinch the little toe a score of times at least!

Each pinch would be a clear gain of a day!

Our wedding-day dawned at last.

The King's wine was dealt out to the people with liberal hand.

Mirth and gayety resounded on all sides.

The skies were one vast expanse of cloudless blue.

The flowering shrubs breathed out the most delightful odors.

The air was deliciously balmy.

The painted foliage hung in graceful festoons, unmoved by even a breath of air.

To his evident disgust, Bulger was decorated with a necklace of leaf mosaic of most delicate workmanship.

Had I not reproved him with a shake of the head, he would quickly have shaken off this useless adornment.

Vast crowds of the Roundbodies covered the plain as far as the eye could reach.

Children rolled in troops after their parents, like marbles chasing up a cannon ball.

At times I observed that the mothers, in order to amuse their little ones, or to quell some discussion which had broken out among them, halted by the wayside, and catching up three or four of them, tossed them into the air as a juggler does his balls, sometimes keeping three or more of them on the fly and one in each hand.

It was a strange sight, and amused me so much that I quite insisted upon halting the wedding procession in order that I might observe it more closely.

But the fair Rōlâ-Bōlâ was very impatient, and chided me in unmeasured terms for my lack of dignity.

In fact, I now began to notice a very evident desire on the part of the managers of the wedding arrangements to hurry things up.

King Bô-gôô-gôô ever and anon turned an anxious eye toward the horizon.

And then there would follow a whispered consultation with the soothsayers and magicians.

Behold me at last mounted upon my—scaffold, I had almost said—for such it seemed to be.

A terrible, tightening sensation took hold of my heart.

The air seemed too heavy to breathe.

I gasped like a fish thrown up on dry land.

"Let the marriage ceremony begin this instant, and move apace!" roared Bô-gôô-gôô.

"Make ready, Tôô-tôô-lō!" cried one of the royal councillors.

I turned to survey the multitude, and then prostrated myself upon the platform under which the princess Rōlâ-Bōlâ was to pass.

"She has started! She comes like the wind! She is here!" Such were the cries which arose from the vast multitude.

With head and shoulders thrust through the opening in the platform, I awaited my bride with bated breath and thumping heart.

Imagine my amazement when I saw her flash beneath me and disappear in the crowd of Roundbodies, almost like a ball from a cannon.

I had scarcely felt her body as it had rolled beneath me.

As for pinching her toe, that was certainly out of the question, seeing that I had only caught a hurried glimpse of her white feet, and then all was gone!

In an instant I was on my legs, and, advancing to the edge of the platform, I raised my hand to signify to King Bô-gôô-gôô that I desired to be heard:

"O, King with the globe-shaped body, hearken unto me! I have been wronged! There is vile treachery here! The judges of the land of Gô-gû-lâh have been corrupted! I demand their blood! Not only have I not pinched the little toe of the royal princess Rōlâ-Bōlâ, but I—"

At this instant, a deep, rumbling noise like a burst of distant artillery, cut short my harangue, by setting the air into such violent vibration that my lips moved without making the slightest sound.

The effect of this terrific "boom" upon the Roundbodies was astounding.

The wildest confusion came upon them.

In vain did King Bô-gôô-gôô command silence.

They rocked like the waves of the sea when struck by a sudden blast.

The most deafening groans and sighs rolled over the plains in a sort of half tuneful unison. Their faces blanched and they pressed together in the most abject fear.

At last King Bô-gôô-gôô was himself again, and, with a terrific voice, awed his people into silence, crying out:

"Ughgō! Raûlag pad Oüistimgâr!" (My people, the storm is upon us! Protect yourselves!)

More quickly than it takes me to tell it, the dreaded roar broke in upon the stilly air.

The Roundbodies gathered their children and aged people into a group, and then formed double and triple walls about them.

"Tôô-tôô-lō! Tôô-tôô-lō!"

It was Rōlâ-Bōlâ's voice.

But other thoughts were in my mind at this dread moment.

Again it sounded forth in most piteous accents:

"Tôô-tôô-lō! Tôô-tôô-lō!"

To that voice, now, the ears of the dead would have given more heed than mine! The storm-fiend was galloping amain.

Quicker than thought I swung myself down from the platform, and, encircling Bulger with my left arm, made my way back again.

The good dog was delighted to be with me again, although he was trembling like an aspen leaf at the distant sound of the winds.

He well knew what was coming.

But look! The sunlight is gone!

The very air seems affrighted.

A terrifying tremor of the ground beneath us causes the soles of our feet to tingle and prickle.

"Tôô-tôô-lō! Tôô-tôô-lō!"

It was Rōlâ-Bōlâ calling her lover away from the impending death with which the storm-cloud was fraught.

He was busy with one dearer to him than the weeping princess of the Roundbodies.

Happily the platform had been constructed by lashing together the uprights and flooring by means of hempen cords. To loosen one of these and bind Bulger and myself securely to the wooden structure was the work of a moment.

The Roundbodies had followed my movements in silence, fairly stricken dumb with amazement at what seemed to them the work of a madman.

When they could find their tongues, they motioned to me fiercely to leave the platform, crying:

"Pôô-döeg! Pôô-döeg!" (What madness! What madness!)

But I was not mad!

What is death but a thought?

One may live and yet be dead!

Look! the terrible storm-king is coming! He is a greater monarch than thou, O mighty Bô-gôô-gôô!

"Tôô-tôô-lō! Tôô-tôô-lō!"

It was the kind, good Rōlâ-Bōlâ's last farewell!

From that moment the roar of the coming gale drowned every sound of earth or its puny creatures.

Look again! See the black monster, how he draws nearer and nearer, his huge, shapeless, terrible body rolling and swaying as he rides along on his black wings, while, like a gigantic serpent, his tail drags over the fair earth, hissing, writhing and curling, now on this side, now on that, now coiling upward to gather strength, now beating and threshing the plain with a roar mighty enough to plunge the stoutest heart into despair.

Ah, Bulger! It comes! 'Tis here! We move! It lifts us! Away! Away! We ride on the bosom of the gale! What a roar! How dark! How black! The storm-king strangles me! Bulger, I die—

"Where am I? Ah, Bulger, good dog! Has the princess called us yet?

"King Bô-gôô-gôô comes to-day.

"We must amuse him!"

I made an effort to rise.

The cords held me down.

By degrees the shadows lifted from my mind, and thoughts of the storm-king's coming flashed through my brain, and how he had lifted the platform upon which we were bound, and borne it away, away, as if it were a feather caught up by the wind in play!

Something tickled my cheek.

I raised my head.

Oh! joy unutterable! It was grain! Ay, golden grain!

Wheat, ready for the sickle!

We are saved! We must be near the habitations of man!

And so we were.

Nay, more; we were not a thousand miles away from home.

Thus it was a mightier king than Bô-gôô-gôô, one to whom in my despair, I had appealed for aid, caught up my loved Bulger and me and bore us away from Gô-gû-lâh, the Land of the Roundbodies.

And here I end my story.

BARON TRUMP'S MARVELLOUS UNDERGROUND JOURNEY

CHAPTER I

Bulger was not himself at all, dear friends. There was a lack-lustre look in his eyes, and his tail responded with only a half-hearted wag when I spoke to him. I say half-hearted, for I always had a notion that the other end of Bulger's tail was fastened to his heart. His appetite, too, had gone down with his spirits; and he rarely did anything more than sniff at the dainty food which I set before him, although I tried to tempt him with fried chickens' livers and toasted cocks' combs—two of his favorite dishes.

There was evidently something on his mind, and yet it never occurred to me what that something was; for to be honest about it, it was something which of all things I never should have dreamed of finding there.

Possibly I might have discovered at an earlier day what it was all about, had it not been that just at this time I was very busy, too busy, in fact, to pay much attention to any one, even to my dear four-footed foster brother. As you may remember, dear friends, my brain is a very active one; and when once I become interested in a subject, Castle Trump itself might take fire and burn until the legs of my chair had become charred before I would hear the noise and confusion, or even smell the smoke.

It so happened at the time of Bulger's low spirits that the elder baron had, through the kindness of an old school friend, come into possession of a fifteenth-century manuscript from the pen of a no less celebrated thinker and philosopher than the learned Spaniard, Don Constantino Bartolomeo Strepholofidgeguaneriusfum, commonly known among scholars as Don Fum, entitled "A World within a World." In this work Don Fum advanced the wonderful theory that there is every reason to believe that the interior of our world is inhabited; that, as is well known, this vast earth ball is not solid, on the contrary, being in many places quite hollow; that ages and ages ago terrible disturbances had taken place on its surface and had driven the inhabitants to seek refuge in these vast underground chambers, so vast, in fact, as well to merit the name of "World within a World."

This book, with its crumpled, torn, and time-stained leaves exhaling the odors of vaulted crypt and worm-eaten chest, exercised a peculiar fascination upon me. All day long, and often far into the night, I sat poring over its musty and mildewed pages, quite forgetful of this surface world, and with the plummet of thought sounding these subterranean depths, and with the eye and ear of fancy visiting them, and gazing upon and listening to the dwellers therein.

While I would be thus engaged, Bulger's favorite position was on a quaintly embroidered leather cushion brought from the Orient by me on one of my journeys, and now placed on the end of my work-table nearest the window. From this point of vantage Bulger commanded a full view of the park and the terrace and of the drive leading up to the porte-cochère. Nothing escaped his watchful eye. Here he sat hour by hour, amusing himself by noting the comings and goings of all sorts of folk, from the hawkers of gewgaws to the noblest people in the shire. One day my attention was attracted by his suddenly leaping down from his cushion and giving a low growl of displeasure. I paid little heed to it, but to my surprise the next day about the same hour it occurred again.

My curiosity was now thoroughly aroused; and laying down Don Fum's musty manuscript, I hastened to the window to learn the cause of Bulger's irritation.

Lo, the secret was out! There stood half a dozen mongrel curs belonging to the tenantry of the baronial lands, looking up to the window, and by their barking and antics endeavoring to entice Bulger out for a romp. Dear friends, need I assure you that such familiarity was extremely distasteful to Bulger? Their impudence was just a little more than he could stand. Ringing my bell, I directed my servant to hunt them away. Whereupon Bulger consented to resume his seat by the window.

The next morning, just as I had settled myself down for a good long read, I was almost startled by Bulger bounding into the room with eyes flashing fire and teeth laid bare in anger. Laying hold of the skirt of my dressing-gown, he gave it quite a savage tug, which meant, "Put thy book aside, little master, and follow me."

I did so. He led me down-stairs across the hallway and into the dining-room, and then this new cause of discontent on his part became very apparent to me. There grouped around his silver breakfast plate sat an ancient tabby cat and four kittens, all calmly licking or lapping away at his breakfast. Looking up into my face, he uttered a sharp, complaining howl, as much as to say, "There, little master, look at that. Isn't that enough to roil the patience of a saint? Canst thou wonder that I am not happy with all these disagreeable things happening to me? I tell thee, little master, it is too much for flesh and blood to put up with."

And I thought so too, and did all in my power to comfort my unhappy little friend; but judge of my surprise upon reaching my room and directing him to take his place on his cushion, to see him refuse to obey.

It was something extraordinary, and set me to thinking. He noticed this and gave a joyful bark, then dashed into my sleeping apartment. He was gone for several moments, and then returned bearing in his mouth a pair of Oriental shoes which he laid at my feet. Again and again he disappeared, coming back each time with some article of clothing in his mouth. In a few moments he had laid a complete Oriental costume on the floor before my eyes; and would you believe me, dear friends, it was the identical suit which I had worn on my last travels in far-away lands, when he and I had been wrecked on the Island of Gogulah, the land of the Round Bodies. What did it all mean? Why, this, to be sure:—

"Little master, canst thou not understand thy dear Bulger? He is weary of this dull and spiritless existence. He is tired of this increasing familiarity on the part of these mongrel curs of the neighborhood and of the audacity of these kitchen tabbies and their families. He implores thee to break away from this life of revery and inaction, and for the honor of the Trumps to be up and away again." Stooping down and winding my arms around my dear Bulger, I cried out,—

"Yes, I understand thee now, faithful companion; and I promise thee that before this moon has filled her horns we shall once more turn our backs on Castle Trump, up and away in search of the portals to Don Fum's World within a World." Upon hearing these words, Bulger broke out into the wildest, maddest barking, bounding hither and thither as if the very spirit of mischief had suddenly nestled in his heart. In the midst of these mad gambols a low rap on my chamber door caused me to call out,—

"Peace, peace, good Bulger, some one knocks. Peace, I say."

It was the elder baron. With sombre mien and stately tread he advanced and took a seat beside me on the canopy.

"Welcome, honored father!" I exclaimed as I took his hand and raised it to my lips. "I was upon the very point of seeking thee out."

He smiled and then said,—

"Well, little baron, what thinkest thou of Don Fum's World within a World?"

"I think, my lord," was my reply, "that Don Fum is right: that such a world must exist; and with thy consent it is my intention to set out in search of its portals with all safe haste and as soon as my dear mother, the gracious baroness, may be able to bring her heart to part with me."

The elder baron was silent for a moment, and then added: "Little baron, much as thy mother and I shall dread to think of thy being again out from under the safe protection of this venerable roof, the moss-grown tiles of which have sheltered so many generations of the Trumps, yet must we not be selfish in this matter. Heaven forbid that such a thought should move our souls to stay thee! The honor of our family, thy fame as an explorer of strange lands in far-away corners of the globe, call unto us to be strong hearted. Therefore, my dear boy, make ready and go forth once more in search of new marvels. The learned Don Fum's chart will stand thee by like a safe and trusty counsellor. Remember, little baron, the motto of the Trumps, Per Ardua ad Astra—the pathway to glory is strewn with pitfalls and dangers—but the comforting thought shall ever be mine, that when thy keen intelligence fails, Bulger's unerring instinct will be there to guide thee."

As I stooped to kiss the elder baron's hand, the gracious baroness entered the room.

Bulger hastened to raise himself upon his hind legs and lick her hand in token of respectful greeting. The tears were pressing hard against her eyelids, but she kept them back, and encircling my neck with her loving arms, she pressed many and many a kiss upon my cheeks and brow.

"I know what it all means, my dear son," she murmured with the saddest of smiles; "but it never shall be said that Gertrude Baroness von Trump stood in the way of her son adding new glories to the family 'scutcheon. Go, go, little baron, and Heaven bring thee safely back to our arms and to our hearts in its own good time."

At these words Bulger, who had been listening to the conversation with pricked-up ears and glistening eyes, gave one long howl of joy, and then springing into my lap, covered my face with kisses. This done, he vented his happiness in a string of earsplitting barks and a series of the maddest gambols. It was one of the happiest and proudest days of his life, for he felt that he had exerted considerable influence in screwing to the sticking-point my resolution to set out on my travels once again.

And now the patter of hurrying feet and the loud murmur of anxious voices resounded through the castle corridors, while inside and out ever and anon I could hear the cry now whispered and now outspoken,—

"The little baron is making ready to leave home again."

Bulger ran hither and thither, surveying everything, taking note of all the preparations, and I could hear his joyous bark ring out as some familiar article used by me on my former journeys was dragged from its hiding-place.

Twenty times a day my gentle mother came to my room to repeat some good counsel or reiterate some valuable caution. It seemed to me that I had never seen her so calm, so stately, so lovable.

She was very proud of my great name and so, in fact, were every man, woman, and child in the castle. Had I not gotten off as I did, I should have been literally killed with kindness and Bulger slain with sweet-cake.

CHAPTER II

According to the learned Don Fum's manuscript, the portals to the World within a World were situated somewhere in Northern Russia, possibly, so he thought, from all indications, somewhere on the westerly slope of the upper Urals. But the great thinker could not locate them with any accuracy. "The people will tell thee" was the mysterious phrase that occurred again and again on the mildewed pages of this wonderful writing. "The people will tell thee." Ah, but what people will be learned enough to tell me that? was the brain-racking question which I asked myself, sleeping and waking, at sunrise, at high noon, and at sunset; at the crowing of the cock, and in the silent hours of the night.

"The people will tell thee," said learned Don Fum.

"Ah, but what people will tell me where to find the portals to the World within a World?"

Hitherto on my travels I had made choice of a semi-Oriental garb, both on account of its picturesqueness and its lightness and warmth, but now as I was about to pass quite across Russia for a number of months, I resolved to don the Russian national costume; for speaking Russian fluently, as I did a score or more of languages living and dead, I would thus be enabled to come and go without everlastingly displaying my passport, or having my trains of thought constantly disturbed by inquisitive travelling companions—a very important thing to me, for my mind possessed the extraordinary power of working out automatically any task assigned to it by me, provided it was not suddenly thrown off its track by some ridiculous interruption. For instance, I was upon the very point one day of discovering perpetual motion, when the gracious baroness suddenly opened the door and asked me whether I had pared the nails of my great toes lately, as she had observed that I had worn holes in several pairs of my best stockings.

It was about the middle of February when I set out from the Castle Trump, and I journeyed night and day in order to reach Petersburg by the first of March, for I knew that the government trains would leave that city for the White Sea during the first week of that month. Bulger and I were both in the best of health and spirits, and the fatigue of the journey didn't tell upon us in the least. The moment I arrived at the Russian capital I applied to the emperor for permission to join one of the government trains, which was most graciously accorded. Our route lay almost directly to the northward for several days, at the end of which time we reached the shores of Lake Ladoga. This we crossed on the ice with our sledges, as a few days later we did Lake Onega. Thence by land again, we kept on our way until Onega Bay had been reached, crossing it, too, on the ice, and so reaching the station of the same name, where we halted for a day to give our horses a well-deserved rest. From this point we proceeded in a straight line over the snow fields to Archangel, an important trading-post on the White Sea.

As this was the destination of the government train, I parted with its commandant after a few days' pleasant sojourn at the government house, and set out, attended only by my faithful Bulger and two servants, who had been assigned to me by the imperial commissioner.

My course now carried me up the River Dwina as far as Solvitchegodsk; thence I proceeded on my way over the frozen waters of the Witchegda River until we had reached the government post of Yarensk, and from here on we headed due East until our hardy little horses had dragged us into the picturesque village of Ilitch on the Ilitch. Here we were obliged to abandon our sledges, for the snows had disappeared like magic, uncovering long vistas of green fields, which in a few days the May sun dotted with flowers and sweet shrubs. At Ilitch I was obliged to relinquish from my service the two faithful government retainers who had accompanied me from Archangel, for they had now reached the most westerly point which they had been commissioned to visit. I had become very much attached to them, and so had Bulger, and after their departure we both felt as if we were now, for the first time, among strangers in a strange land; but I succeeded in engaging, as I thought, a trustworthy teamster, Ivan by name, who made a contract with me for a goodly wage to carry me a hundred miles farther north.

"But not another step farther, little baron!" said the fellow doggedly. I was now really at the foot hills of the Northern Urals, for the rocky crests and snow-clad peaks were in full sight.

I turned many a wistful look up toward the wild regions shut in by their sheer walls and parapets, shaggy and bristling with black pines, for a low, mysterious voice came a-whispering in my inward ear that somewhere, ah, somewhere in that awful wilderness, I should one day come upon the portals of the World within a World! In spite of all I could do Bulger took a violent dislike to Ivan and Ivan to him; and if the bargain had not been made and the money paid over, I should have looked about me for another teamster. And yet it would have been a foolish thing to do, for Ivan had two excellent horses, as I saw at a glance, and, what's more, he took the best of care of them, at every post rubbing them until they were quite dry, and never thinking of his own supper until they had been watered and fed.

His tarantass, too, was quite new and solidly built and well furnished with soft blankets, all in all as comfortable as you can make a wagon which has no other springs than the two long wooden supports that reach from axle to axle. True, they were somewhat elastic; but I could notice that Bulger was not overfond of riding in this curious vehicle with its rattlety-bang gait up and down these mountain roads, and often asked permission to leap out and follow on foot.

At length Ivan reported everything in readiness for the start; and although I would have fain taken my departure from Ilitch on the Ilitch in as quiet a manner as possible, yet the whole village turned out to see us off—Ivan's family, father, mother, sisters, and brothers, wife and children, uncles and aunts and cousins by dozens alone making up people enough to stock a small town. They cheered and waved their kerchiefs, Bulger barked, and I smiled and raised my cap with all the dignity of a Trump. And so we got away at last from Ilitch on the Ilitch, Ivan on the box, and Bulger and I at the back, sitting close together like two brothers that we were—two breasts with but a single heart-beat and two brains busy with the same thought—that come perils or come sudden attacks, come covert danger or bold and open-faced onslaught, we should stand together and fall together! Many and many a time as Ivan's horses went crawling up the long stretches of mountain road and I lay stretched upon the broad-cushioned seat of the tarantass with a blanket rolled up for a pillow, I would find myself unconsciously repeating those mysterious words of Don Fum:—

"The people will tell thee! The people will tell thee!"

So steep were the roads that some days we would not make more than five miles, and on others a halt of several hours would have to be made to enable Ivan to tighten his horses' shoes, grease the axles, or do some needful thing in or about his wagon. It was slow work, ay, it was very slow and tedious, but what matters it how many or great the difficulties, to a man who has made up his mind to accomplish a certain task? Do the storks or the wild geese stop to count the thousands of miles between them and their far-away homes when the time comes to turn their heads southward? Do the brown ants pause to count the hundreds of thousands of grains of sand which they must carry through their long corridors and winding passages before they have burrowed deep enough to escape the frost of midwinter?

There had been many Trumps, but never one that had thrown up his arms and cried, "I surrender!" and should I be the first to do it? "Never! Not even if it meant never to see dear old Castle Trump again!"

One morning as we went zigzagging up a particularly nasty bit of mountain road, Ivan suddenly wheeled about and without even taking off his hat, cried out,—

"Little baron, I cover the last mile of the hundred to-day. If thou wouldst go any farther north thou must hire thee another teamster; dost hear?"

"Silence!" said I sternly, for the fellow had broken in upon a very important train of thought.

Bulger, too, resented the man's insolence, and growled and showed his teeth.

"But, little baron, listen to reason," he continued in a more respectful tone, removing his cap: "my people will expect me back. I promised my father—I'm a dutiful son—I—"

"Nay, nay, Ivan," I interrupted sharply, "curb that tongue of thine lest it harm thy soul. Know, then, that I spoke with thy father, and he promised me that thou shouldst go a second hundred miles with me if need were, but on condition that I give thee double pay. It shall be done, and on top of that a goodly present for your golubtchika (darling)."

"Little baron, thou art a hard master," whimpered the man. "If the whim took thee thou wouldst bid me leap into the Giants' Well just to see whether it has a bottom or not. St. Nicholas, save me!"

"Nay, Ivan," said I kindly, "I know no such word as cruelty although I do confess that right seems harsh at times, but thou wert born to serve and I to command. Providence hath made thee poor and me rich. We need each other. Do thou thy duty, and thou wilt find me just and considerate. Disobey me, and thou wilt find that this short arm may be stretched from Ilitch to Petersburg."

Ivan turned pale at this hidden threat of mine; but I deemed it necessary to make it, for I as well as Bulger had scented treachery and rebellion about this boorish fellow, whose good trait was his love of his horses, and it has always been my rule in life to open my eyes wide to the good that there is in a man, and close them to his faults. But, in spite of kind words and kind treatment, Ivan grew surlier and moodier the moment we had passed the hundredth milestone.

Bulger watched him with a gaze so steady and thoughtful that the man fairly quailed before it. Hour by hour he became more and more restive, and upon leaving a roadside tavern, for the very first time since we had left Ilitch on the Ilitch, I noticed that the fellow had been drinking too much kwass. He let loose his tongue, and raised his hand against his horses, which until that moment he had been wont to load down with caresses and pet names.

"Look out for that driver of thine, little baron," whispered the tavern-keeper. "He's in a reckless mood. He'd not pull up if the Giants' Well were gaping in front of him. St. Nicholas have thee in his safe keeping!"

CHAPTER III

When we halted for the night it was only by threatening the man with severe punishment upon my return to Ilitch that I could bring him to rub his horses dry and feed and water them properly; but I stood over him until he had done his work thoroughly, for I knew that no such horses could be had for love or money in that country, and if they should go lame from standing with wet coats in the chill night air, it might mean a week's delay.

Scarcely had I thrown myself on the hard mattress which the tavern-keeper called the best bed in the house, when I was aroused by loud and boisterous talking in the next room. Ivan was drinking and quarrelling with the villagers. I strode into the room with the arrows of indignation shooting from my eyes, and the faithful Bulger close at my heels.

The moment Ivan set eyes upon us he shrank away, half in earnest and half in jest, and called out,—

"Hey, look at the mazuntchick! [Little Dandy!] How smart he looks! He frightens me! See his eyes, how they shine in the dark! Look at the little demon on four legs beside him! Save me, brothers! Save me—he will throw me down into the Giants' Well! Marianka will never see me again! Never! Save me, brothers!"

"Peace, fellow," I called out sternly. "How darest thou exercise thy dull wit on thy master? Get thee to bed at once, or I'll have thee whipped by the village constable for thy drunkenness."

Ivan clambered up upon the top of the bake oven, and stretched himself out on a sheepskin; then turning to the tavern-keeper, I forbade him under any pretext whatever to give my servant any more liquor to drink. "Akh, Vasha prevoskhoditelstvo [Ah, your Excellency!]" exclaimed the tavern-keeper with a gesture of disgust, "the fools never know when they have had enough. It matters not what the tavern-keeper may say to them. They tell us not to spoil our own trade. Akh! [Ah!] they don't know when to stop. They have throats as deep as the 'Giants' Well!'"

"The Giants' Well! The Giants' Well!" I murmured to myself, as I again threw myself down upon the bag of hay which did service as a mattress for those who could afford to pay for it. It's strange how those words seem to be in every peasant's mouth, but I thought no more about it at that time. Sleep got the better of me, and with my usual good-night to the elder baron and the gracious baroness, my mother, I dropped off into sweet forgetfulness.

It is a good thing that I had the power of falling asleep almost at will, for with my restless brain ever throbbing and pulsating with its own over-abundance of strength, ever tapping at the thin panels of bone which covered it, like an imprisoned inventor pounding on his cell door and pleading to be let out into the daylight with his plans and schemes, I should simply have become a lunatic.

As it was, with the mere power of thought I ordered sweet slumber to come to my rescue, and so obedient was this good angel of mine, that all I had to do was simply to set the time when I wished to awaken, and the thing was done to the very minute.

As for Bulger, I never pretended to lay down any rules for him. He made it a practice of catching forty winks when he was persuaded that no danger of any kind threatened me, and even then, I am half inclined to believe that, like an anxious mother over her babe, he never quite closed both eyes at once.

Though entirely sobered by daybreak, yet Ivan went about the task of harnessing up with such an ill grace that I was obliged to reprove him several times before we had left the tavern yard. He was like a vicious but cowardly animal that quails before a strong and steady eye, but watches its opportunity to spring upon you when your back is turned.

I not only called Bulger's attention to the fellow's actions, and warned him to be very watchful, but I also took the precaution to examine the priming of the brace of Spanish pistols which I carried thrust into my belt.

We had scarcely pulled out into the highway when a low growl from Bulger aroused me from a fit of meditation; and this growl was followed by such an anxious whine from my four-footed brother, as he raised his speaking eyes to me, that I glanced hastily from one side of the road to the other.

Lo and behold! the treacherous Ivan was deliberately engaged in an attempt to overturn the tarantass and to get rid of his enforced task of transporting us any farther on our journey.

"Wretch!" I cried, springing up and laying my hand on his shoulder. "I perceive very plainly what thou hast in mind, but I warn thee most solemnly that if thou makest another attempt to overturn thy wagon, I'll slay thee where thou sittest."

For only answer and with a lightning-like quickness he struck a back-hand blow at me with the loaded end of his whipstock.

It took me full in the right temple, and sent me to the bottom of the tarantass like a piece of lead.

For an instant the terrible blow robbed me of my senses, but then I saw that the cowardly villain had turned in his seat and had swung the heavy handled whip aloft with intent to despatch me with a second and a surer blow.

Poor fool! he reckoned without his host; for with a shriek of rage, Bulger leaped at his throat like a stone from a catapult, and struck his teeth deep into the fellow's flesh.

He roared with agony and attempted to shake off this unexpected foe, but in vain.

By this time I had come to a full realizing sense of the terrible danger Bulger and I were both in, for Ivan had dropped his whip and was reaching for his sheath-knife.

But he never gripped it, for a well-aimed shot from one of my pistols struck him in the forearm, for I had no wish to take the man's life, and broke it.

The shock and the pain so paralyzed him that he fell over against the dashboard half in a faint, and then rolled completely out of the wagon, dragging Bulger with him. The horses now began to rear and plunge. I saw no more. There was a noise as of the roar of angry waters in my ears, and then the light of life went out of my eyes entirely. I had swooned dead away.

It seemed to me hours that I lay there on my back in the bottom of the tarantass with my head hanging over the side, but of course it was only minutes. I was aroused by a prickling sensation in my left cheek, and as I slowly came to myself I discovered that it proceeded from the gravel thrown up against it by one of the front wheels of the tarantass, for the horses were galloping along at the top of their speed, and there on the driver's seat sat my faithful Bulger, the reins in his teeth, bracing himself so as to keep them taut over the horses' backs; and as I sat up and pressed my hand against my poor hurt head, the whole truth broke upon me:——

The moment Ivan had struck the ground Bulger had released his hold upon the fellow's throat, and ere he had had a chance to revive had leaped up into the driver's seat, and, catching up the reins in his teeth, had drawn them taut and thus put an end to the rearing and plunging of the frightened beasts and started them on their way, leaving the enraged Ivan brandishing his knife and uttering imprecations upon mine and Bulger's heads as he saw his horses and wagon disappear in the distance. Now was it that a mad shouting assailed my ears and I caught a glimpse of half a dozen peasants who, seeing this, as they thought, empty tarantass come nearer and nearer with its galloping horses, had abandoned their work and rushed out to intercept it.

Judge of their amazement, dear friends, as their eyes fell upon the calm and skilful driver bracing himself on the front seat, and with oft repeated backward tosses of his head urging those horses to bear his beloved master farther and farther away from the treacherous Ivan's sheath-knife.

As the peasants seized the animals by the heads and brought them to a standstill, I staggered to my feet, and threw my arms around my dear Bulger. He was more than pleased with what he had done, and licked my bruised brow with many a piteous moan.

"St. Nicholas, save us!" cried one of the peasants, devoutly making the sign of the cross; "but if I should live long enough to fill the Giants' Well with pebbles, I never would expect to see the like of this again."

"The Giants' Well, the Giants' Well!" I murmured to myself as I followed one of the peasants to his cot, standing a little back from the highway, for I stood sore in need of rest after the terrible experience I had just had. The blow of Ivan's whip-handle had jarred my brain, and I was skilled enough in surgery to know that the hurt called for immediate attention. As good luck would have it, I found beneath the peasant's roof one of those old women, half witches perhaps, who have recipes for everything and who know an herb for every ailment. After she had examined the cut made by the loaded whip-handle, she muttered out,——

"It is not as broad as the mountain, nor as deep as the Giants' Well, but it's bad enough, little master."

"The Giants' Well again," thought I, as I laid me down on the best bed they could make up for me. "I wonder where it may be, that Giants' Well, and how deep it is, and who drinks the water that is drawn from it?"

CHAPTER IV

It was a day or so before I could walk steadily, and meantime I made unusual efforts to keep my brain quiet, but in spite of all I could do every mention of the Giants' Well by one of the peasants sent a strange thrill through me, and I would find myself suddenly pacing up and down the floor, and repeating over and over again the words, "Giants' Well! Giants' Well!"

Bulger was greatly troubled in his mind, and sat watching me with a most bewildered look in his loving eyes. He had half a suspicion, I think, that that cruel blow from Ivan's whip-handle had injured my reasoning powers, for at times he uttered a low, plaintive whine. The moment I took notice of him, however, and acted more like myself, he gamboled about me in the wildest delight. As I had directed the peasants to drive Ivan's horses back towards Ilitch on the Ilitch, until they should meet that miscreant and deliver them to him, I was now without any means of continuing my journey northward, unless I set out, like many of my famous predecessors, on foot. They had longer legs than I, however, and were not loaded with so heavy a brain in proportion to their size, and a brain, too, that scarcely ever slept, at least not soundly. I was too impatient to reach the portals to the World within a World to go trudging along a dusty highway. I must have horses and another tarantass, or at least a peasant's cart. I must push on. My head was quite healed now, and my fever gone.

"Hearken, little master," whispered Yuliana; such was the name of the old woman who had taken care of me, "thou art not what thou seemst. I never saw the like of thee before. If thou wouldst, I believe thou couldst tell me how high the sky is, how thick through the mountains are, and how deep the Giants' Well is."

I smiled, and then I said,—

"Didst ever drink from the Giants' Well, Yuliana?"

At which she wagged her head and sent forth a low chuckle.

"Hearken, little master," she then whispered, coming close to me, and holding up one of her long, bony fingers, "thou canst not trick me—thou knowest that the Giants' Well hath no bottom."

"No bottom?" I repeated breathlessly, as Don Fum's mysterious words, "The people will tell thee!" flashed through my mind. "No bottom, Yuliana?"

"Not unless thine eyes are better than mine, little master," she murmured, nodding her head slowly.

"Listen, Yuliana," I burst out impetuously, "where is this bottomless well?

Thou shalt lead me to it; I must see it. Come, let's start at once. Thou shalt be well paid for thy pains."

"Nay, nay, little master, not so fast," she replied. "It's far up the mountains. The way is steep and rugged, the paths are narrow and winding, a false step might mean instant death, were there not some strong hand to save thee. Give up such a mad thought as ever getting there, except it be on the stout shoulders of some mountaineer."

"Ah, good woman," was my reply, "thou hast just said that I am not what I seem, and thou saidst truly. Know, then, thou seest before thee the world-renowned traveller, Wilhelm Heinrich Sebastian von Troomp, commonly called 'Little Baron Trump,' that though short of stature and frail of limb, yet what there is of me is of iron. There, Yuliana, there's gold for thee; now lead the way to the Giants' Well."

"Gently, gently, little baron," almost whispered the old peasant woman, as her shrivelled hand closed upon the gold piece. "I have not told thee all. For leagues about, I ween, no living being excepting me knows where the Giants' Well is. Ask them and they'll say, "It's up yonder in the mountains, away up under the eaves of the sky." That's all. That's all they can tell thee. But, little master, I know where it is, and the very herb that cured thy hurt head and saved thee from certain death by cooling thy blood, was plucked by me from the brink of the well!" These words sent a thrill of joy through me, for now I felt that I was on the right road, that the words of the great master of all masters, Don Fum, had come true.

"The people will tell thee!"

Ay, the people had told me, for now there was not the faintest shadow of doubt in my mind that I had found the portals to the World within a World! Yuliana should be my guide. She knew how to thread her way up the narrow pass, to turn aside from overhanging rocks which a mere touch might topple over, to find the steps which nature had hewn in the sides of the rocky parapets, and to pursue her way safely through clefts and gorges, even the entrance to which might be invisible to ordinary eyes. However, in order that the superstitious peasants might be kept friendly to me, I gave it out that I was about to betake myself to the mountains in search of curiosities for my cabinet, and begged them to furnish me with ropes and tackle, with two good stout fellows to carry it for me, promising generous payment for the services.

They made haste to provide me with all I asked for, and we set out for the mountain path at daybreak. Yuliana, in order not to seem to be of the party, had gone on ahead by the light of the moon, telling her people that she wished to gather certain herbs before the sun's rays struck them and dried the healing dew that beaded their leaves.

All went well until the sun was well up over our heads, when suddenly I heard a woman, who proved to be Yuliana, utter a piercing scream. In a moment or so the mystery was solved. The old beldam came rushing down the mountain, her thin wisp of gray hair fluttering in the wind. Her hands were tied behind her, and two young peasants with birchen rods were beating her every chance they got.

"Turn back, turn back, brothers," they cried to my two men. "The little wizard there has struck hands with this old witch. They're on their way to the Giants' Well. They'll loosen a band of black spirits about our ears. We shall all be bewitched. Quick! Quick! Cast off the loads ye're bearing and follow us."

The two men didn't wait for a second bidding, and throwing the tackle on the ground, they all disappeared like a flash, but for several moments I could hear the screams of poor Yuliana as these young wretches beat the old woman with their birchen rods.

Well, dear readers, what say ye to this? Was I not in a pleasant position truly? Alone with Bulger in that wild and gloomy mountain region, the black rocks hanging like frowning giants and ogres over our heads, with the dwarf pines for hair, clumps of white moss for eyes, vast, gaping cracks for mouths, and gnarled and twisted roots for terrible fingers, ready to reach down for my poor little weazen frame.

Did I fall a-trembling? Did I make haste to follow those craven spirits down the mountain side? Did I shift the peg of my courage a single hole lower?

Not I. If I had I wouldn't have been worthy of the name I bore. What I did do was to throw myself at full length on a bed of moss, call Bulger to my side, and close my eyes to the outer world.

I have heard of great men going to bed at high noon to give themselves up to thought, and I had often done it myself before I had heard of their doing it.

In fifteen minutes, by nature's watch—the sun on the face of the mountain—I had solved the problem. Now, there were two difficulties staring me in the face; namely, to find somebody to show me the way up the mountain, and if that body couldn't carry my tackle, then to find somebody else who could.

It suddenly occurred to me that I had noticed some cattle grazing at the foot of the mountain, and, what's more, that these cattle wore very peculiar yokes.

"What are those yokes for?" I asked myself, for they were of a make quite different from any that I remembered ever having seen, and consisted of a stout wooden collar from the bottom of which there projected backward between the beast's forelegs a straight piece of wood armed with an iron spike pointing toward the ground. At the top the yoke was bound by a leather thong to the animal's horns. So long, therefore, as the beast held his head naturally or even lowered it to graze, the yoke was drawn forward and the hook was kept free from the ground, but the very moment the animal raised his head in the air, at once the hook was thrown into the ground and he was prevented from taking another step forward. Now, dear readers, you may or may not know that when a cleft-hoofed animal starts to ascend a steep bank, unlike a solid-hoofed beast, he throws his head into the air instead of lowering it, and therefore it struck me at once that the purpose of this yoke was to keep the cattle from making their way up the sides of the mountain and getting lost.

But why should they want to clamber up the mountain sides? Simply because there was some kind of grass or herbage growing up there which was a delicacy to them, and knowing, as I well did, what risks animals will take and what fatigue they will undergo to reach a favorite grazing-ground, it struck me at once that if I would make it possible for them to reach this favorite food of theirs, they would be very glad to give me a lift on my way.

No sooner said than done. I forthwith retraced my steps until I fell in with a group of these cattle; and it did not take me many minutes to loosen their yokes from their horns and tie the hooks up under their bodies so that their progress up hill would not be interfered with.

They were delighted to find themselves so unexpectedly freed from the hateful drawback which permitted them merely to view the coveted grazing-grounds from afar, and then having cut me a suitable goad, I again started up the mountain, driving my new friends leisurely on ahead of me.

Upon reaching the spot where the superstitious peasants had thrown the tackle to the ground, I proceeded to load it upon the back of the gentlest beast of the lot, and was soon on my way again.

CHAPTER V

Generally speaking, people with very large heads are fitted out by nature with a pair of rather pipe-stemmy legs, but such was not my case. I was blest with legs of the sturdiest sort, and found no difficulty in keeping pace with my new four-footed friends who, to my delight, were not long in convincing me that they had been there before. Not for an instant did they halt at any fork in the path, but kept continually on the move, often passing over stretches of ground where there was no trail visible, but coming upon it again with unfailing accuracy. Once only they halted, and that was to slake their thirst at a mountain rill, Bulger and I following their example.

It was only too evident to me that they had in mind a certain grazing-ground, and were resolved to be satisfied with no other; so I let them have their own way, for, as it was still up, up, up, I felt that it was perfectly safe to follow their lead.

At last the mountain side began to take on quite another character. The gorges grew narrower, and at times overhanging rocks shut out the sunlight almost entirely. We were entering a region of peculiar wildness, of fantastic grandeur.

I had often read of what travellers termed the "Quarries of the Demons" in the Northern Urals, but never till now had I the faintest notion of what the expression meant.

Imagine to yourself the usual look of ruin and devastation around and about a quarry worked by human hands, then in your thoughts conceive every chip to be a block, and every block a mass; add four times its size to every slab and post and pediment, and then turn a mighty torrent through the place and roll and twist and lift them up in wild confusion, end on end and on each other piled, till these wild waters have builded fantastic portals to temples more fantastic, and arched wild gorges with roofs of rock which seem to hang so lightly that a breath or footfall might bring them down with terrible crash, and then, dear friends, you may succeed in getting a faint idea of the wild and awful grandeur of the scene which now lay spread out before me.

Would the cattle that had now led Bulger and me so safely up the mountain side know where to find an entrance to this wilderness of broken rock, and what was more important still, would they, when once engaged within its winding courts and corridors, its darkened maze of wall and parapet, its streets and plazas roughly paved as if by demon hands impatient of the task, know how to find their way out again?

Dear friends, man has always been too distrustful of his four-footed companions. They have much that they might tell us had they but speech to tell it with. I have often trusted them when it would have seemed foolhardy to you, and never once have I had cause to repent of doing so.

So Bulger and I, with stout hearts, followed straight after these silent guides, although I must confess my legs were beginning to feel the terrible strain I had put them to; but I resolved to push on ahead, at least until we had cleared the Demons' Quarry, and then to bring my little herd to a halt and pass the rest of the day and the night season in well-earned repose.

Once within the quarry, however, all sense of fatigue vanished, and my thankful mind, entranced and fascinated by the deep silence, the awful grandeur, the mysterious lights and shadows of the place, lent me new strength. At length we had traversed this city of silence and gloom, and once again we emerged into the full glory of the afternoon sun.

Suddenly my little drove of cattle, with playful tossing of their heads, broke into a run, Bulger and I at their heels, however. It was a mad race; but, dear friends, when it ended I took off my fur cap and tossed it high into the air with a wild cry of joy, and Bulger broke out in a string of yelps and barks, for, look ye, the cattle were grazing away for dear life there in front of me, and as their breath reached me my keen nostrils recognized the odor of Yuliana's herbs which she had bound on my hurt head.

Yes, we stood almost upon the brink of the Giants' Well, but I was too tired to take another step farther, too tired, in fact, to eat, although I had a stock of dried fruit in my pockets, and noticed that the nests of the wild fowl were well supplied with eggs. Having unloosened the tackle from the back of the good beast that had carried it up the mountain for me, I threw myself on the ground and was soon fast asleep, with my faithful Bulger coiled up close against my breast.

In the morning the cattle were nowhere to be seen, but I didn't trouble myself about them, for I knew that old Yuliana would be sent up after them the moment they were missed. After a hearty breakfast on half a dozen roasted eggs of the wild fowl, with some dried fruit and wintergreen berries, Bulger and I advanced to the edge of the Giants' Well, or, rather, to the edge of the vast terraces of rock leading down to it, each of which was from thirty to fifty feet in sheer height.

Before I go any farther, dear friends, I must beg you to remember that I am an expert in the use of tackle, there being no knot, noose, or splice known to a sailor which I didn't have at my fingers' ends, a fact not to be wondered at when you take into consideration the thousands of miles which I have travelled on water.

Nor would I have you shake your heads and look only half persuaded when I go on describing our descent into the Giants' Well, for of course you'll be asking yourselves how I succeeded in getting the tackle down when there was no one left at the other end to untie it!

Know, then, that that was the smallest of my troubles; for, as any sailor will tell you, you only need to tie your line in what is known as a "fool's knot," to one end of which you make fast a mere cord. The moment you have reached the bottom, a sharp tug at the cord unties the fool's knot, and your tackle falls down after you. My method was to lower Bulger down first, and then let myself down after him. In this way we proceeded from parapet to parapet, until at last we stood upon the very edge of the vast well, the existence of which had been so mysteriously hinted at in Don Fum's manuscript. Its mouth was probably fifty feet in width, and by straining my eyes I satisfied myself of the existence of a shelf of rock on one side, as nearly as I could judge about seventy-five feet down. It was a goodly stretch, and would require every foot of my rope. You will not smile, I'm sure, when I tell you that I pressed Bulger to my breast, and kissed him fondly before lowering away. He returned my caresses, and by his joyous yelp gave me to understand that he had perfect faith in his little master.

In a few moments I had joined him on this narrow shelf of rock. Below us now was darkness, but think you I hesitated? I knew that my eyes would soon become accustomed to the gloom, and I also knew that when my eyes failed Bulger's keener ones were there to help me out.

I rigged my tackle now with extra care, for I was really lowering my little brother on a sort of trip of discovery.

He was soon out of sight, and then, in spite of my calmness, I drew a quick breath, and my heart started upward a barleycorn or so. But hark! his quick, sharp bark comes plainly up to me. It means that he has landed upon a safe shelf or ledge, and the next moment my legs encircled the rope, and I began to glide noiselessly down into the stilly depths, his glad voice ringing in my ears.

Again and again did I send my wise and watchful little brother down ahead of me, until at last, standing there and looking up, naught remained to me of the mighty outside world but a bright silver speck, like a tiny ray of light streaming through a pin-hole in the curtains of your chamber.

But stop, have we reached the bottom of the Giants' Well? for with a trial plummet I find that the walls are no longer sheer; they slope inward, and gently too, almost so much so that I hardly need a line to continue my descent. Lighting one of my little tapers, I make my way cautiously around the edge. In half an hour I find myself back at the starting-place. The curve to the path has been always the same, while my trial plummet at all times has indicated the same slope to the rocky basin. And then for the first time, two certain words made use of by that learned Master of Masters, Don Fum, till then a mystery to me, stood out before my eyes as if written with a pen of fire upon those black walls thousands of feet below the great world of light which I had quitted a few hours before. Those words were Polyphemus' Funnel! Yes, there could be no doubt of it: I had reached the bottom of the Giants' Well. I stood upon the edge of Polyphemus' Funnel!

CHAPTER VI

The rocky sides of Polyphemus' Funnel were apparently as well polished as those of any tin funnel that I had ever seen hanging in the kitchen of Castle Trump, so making fast my tackle and taking Bulger in my arms, away we went sliding down the side with the line passed under my arm for safety's sake.

It was nearly a hundred feet to the bottom, for I had measured off the full length of my line before I had come to the apex of this gigantic cone, and not caring to tumble headlong down its pipe, I proceeded to light a taper and look about me.

Ah, dear friends, I can feel that shudder now, so terrible was it, and what wonder, too, for a glance at the pipe of the funnel told me that it was too small to let my body pass through. The agonizing thought flashed through my mind that I had committed a terrible error—that I had mistaken some vast pit for the Giants' Well, that I had thrown Bulger's and my own life away in mad and unreasoning haste, that I should never reach the wonderful World within a World, that there in that thick gloom must we lay our bodies and bones.

Or, thought I, may not the learned Master of Masters, Don Fum, have made an error himself in holding out the idea that the pipe of Polyphemus' Funnel was large enough to admit the passage of a man's body?

In my almost frenzy I advanced to the mouth of the pipe, and, lowering myself into it, let my body sink as far as it would.

It caught at the shoulders, and after a careful examination I was forced to reach the brain-racking conclusion that my faithful Bulger and I had travelled our last mile together.

There was nothing for us to do but to lie down and die.

Lie down and die? Never! I had noticed in making the descent into the Giants' Well that its side had much the appearance of being walled around by blocks of stone. With Bulger strapped to my back I would slowly climb up from shelf to shelf until my strength failed me, and then I would wait until I thought old Yuliana had come back to gather herbs, and possibly I might make her hear me.

In my despair I sighed and clutched my own arms, and as I did so one of my hands came into contact with something cold and slippery having the feel of

Ingersoll Lockwood

tallow. Taking a pinch of the substance between my thumb and finger, I rubbed it thoughtfully for a moment, and then a ray of hope broke through the awful gloom that enshrouded me so pitilessly. It was black lead—there could be no doubt of it. It had made its way through a crack or crevice in Polyphemus' Funnel, and I had rubbed it off in sliding down the side. With this greasy material to rub on the inside of the pipe to the funnel, and also to besmear myself with, mayhap I might yet slip through into the World within a World!

At any rate, I determined to make the trial, even if I left some of my skin on the flinty rock.

In order to collect my thoughts thoroughly, and that I might proceed step by step in that systematic order so characteristic of all my wonderful exploits, I sat down, and putting my arm around dear Bulger's neck and drawing him up against me, I communed with myself for a good half-hour.

Then all was in readiness for action; and to prove to you, dear friends, how careful Bulger was not to interrupt my train of thought, I have to report to you that although a small animal of the rat family came out from a crevice in the rock while I sat there thinking, as I could see by the light of my tiny wax taper, and had the temerity first to sniff at Bulger's tail and then to give it a playful nip, yet the sagacious animal never budged a hair's breadth.

"Mind hath ordered, now let hands obey!" I exclaimed, as I sprang up and began stripping off my outer garments. This done, I clambered up on the side of the funnel, and began to collect a supply of the black lead, which I deposited near the opening of the pipe. The next thing to do was to get Bulger through the pipe ahead of me. To this end I tied him up in my clothing, bag fashion, and began to lower away.

After paying out sixty-five or seventy feet of the line, he struck bottom, and by his loud barking gave me to understand that it was all right, that I might make the descent myself. Upon hearing his voice, I gave the line a few sharp tugs. He was not slow to comprehend my meaning, and in a moment or so had not only scrambled out of the bag himself, but pulled my clothing loose, so that I might draw the line up again.

My next step was to contrive a way to weight myself when the moment arrived to begin the descent, for I felt sure that I never should be able to arrange it so as to slip through the pipe unless something was pulling at my heels.

Cutting off about ten feet of the rope, I made fast one end of the piece to a long piece of rock, weighing about a hundred pounds. This I laid near the mouth of the pipe ready for use. But now came the most difficult thing of all—it was to draw my shoulders in on my breast and lash them securely in that position, by which plan I expected to reduce my width by at least two good inches.

These two inches thus gained, or, rather, lost, might be the means by which I would be able to slip through the pipe of Polyphemus' Funnel and reach the vast underground passage leading to the World within a World. Putting a noose around my chest, just below my collar bone, I drew my shoulders in as tight as I could bear, and changed the slip knot into a hard one; then having made the other end of the line fast to the side of the funnel, I proceeded to wind myself up as the housewives often do a big sausage to keep it from bursting. This done, I set about rolling in the black lead until I was thoroughly smeared with it.

There was now but one thing more to do before dropping myself into the pipe, and that was to make fast the weight to my feet. It was no easy task, wound up as I was, with my arms lashed down against my body, but by the use of slip knots I finally accomplished the feat, and sitting down put my legs into the pipe and drew a long breath, for I felt as if I was skewered up in a straight jacket.

Bending down, I called out to Bulger. He answered with a yelp of joy that brought fresh vigor to my heart. Now was come the supreme moment which was to witness success or failure. Failure! Oh, what a dread word is that! and yet how often must human lips pronounce it, and in so doing breathe out the sigh in which it ends! Quickly lowering the weight, I wriggled off the edge of the opening, and straightened myself out as I slipped into the pipe.

Had I stopped it like a cork, or was I moving? Yes, down, down, gently, slowly, noiselessly, I went slipping through the pipe to Polyphemus' Funnel. What did I care how that weight caused the line to cut into my ankles? I was moving, I was drawing nearer and nearer to Bulger, whose joyous bark I could hear now and then, nearer to the inner gates of the World within a World!

But woe is me! I suddenly stop, and in spite of all my efforts to start again by twisting, turning, and shaking my body, it refused to sink another inch, and there I stick.

"Oh, Bulger, Bulger," I moan, "faithful friend, if thou couldst but reach me, one tug from thee might save thy little master!"

In a sort of a wild and desperate way I now began to feel about me as well as I could with my hands wedged in so close to my sides, but in a moment or so I had discovered the cause of my coming to such a sudden standstill.

I had struck a portion of the pipe that had a thread to it, like that which encircles a bolt of iron and makes a screw of it, and the thought came to me that if I could only succeed in giving a revolving motion to my body, I would with every turn twist myself farther down toward the end of the pipe.

I could feel that my knuckles and finger tips were being bruised and lacerated by this arduous work, but what cared I for the keen pain that darted from hands to wrists, and wrists to elbows! It was like twisting a screw slowly through a long nut, only the thread in this case was on the nut and the grooves in the screw, and that screw was my poor bruised little body!

All of a sudden, by the swinging of the weight, I could tell that it had passed out at the lower end of the pipe. It was pulling cruelly hard on my tender ankles, but I could twist myself no more; my strength was gone. I was at the point of swooning when I heard Bulger utter a loud yelp, and the next instant there was such a strong tug at my ankles that I sent forth a groan, but that tug saved me!

It was Bulger who had leaped into the air, and catching the rope in his teeth had dragged his little master out of the pipe of Polyphemus' Funnel!

We all fell into the same heap, Bulger, I, and the weight, fully ten feet, and very serious might have been the consequences for me had my fall not been broken by my striking on the pile of my clothing placed directly under the opening; and, dear friends, if you talked until the crack o' doom you could not make me believe that my four-footed brother hadn't placed those clothes there to catch me.

They weren't thrown higgledy-piggledy into a heap either, but were laid one upon the other, the heaviest at the bottom.

Having unwound myself and lighted one of my wax tapers, I made haste to cast away the undergarment with its coating of black lead and resume my clothing; then stooping down, I made an examination of the floor. It was composed of huge blocks of marble of various colors, polished almost as smooth as if the hand of man had wrought the work; and then I knew that I was on Nature's Marble Highway leading to the cities of the under world which Don Fum had mentioned in his book, and I remembered, too, that he had spoken of Nature's Mighty Mosaics, huge fantastic figures on the walls of these lofty corridors, made up of various colored blocks and fragments laid one upon the other as if with design, and not by the wild, tempestuous whims of upbursting forces thousands of years ago, when the earth was in its mad and wayward youth. After a rest of several hours, during which I nursed my torn hands and bruised fingers, Bulger and I were up and off again along this broad and glorious Marble Highway. Strange to say, it was not the inky darkness of the ordinary cavern which filled these magnificent chambers, through which the Marble Highway went winding in stately and massive grandeur; far from it. The gloom was tempered by a faint glow that met us on the way ever and anon, like a ray of twilight gone astray. Anyway, Bulger, I noticed, could see perfectly well; so tying a bit of twine to his collar, I sent him on ahead, convinced that I could have no surer guide.

At times our path would be lighted up for an instant by the bursting-out of a little tongue of flame either on the sides or from the roof of the gallery. I was puzzled for quite a while to tell what it proceeded from; but at last I caught sight of the source, or rather the maker, of this welcome illumination. It proceeded from a lizard-like animal, which, by suddenly uncoiling its tail, had the power to emit this extremely bright flash of phosphorescent light, and in so doing he made a sharp crack, for all the world like the noise of an electric spark. Bulger was delighted with this performance; and on one occasion, not being able to control his feeling, he uttered a sharp bark, whereupon apparently ten thousand of these little torch-bearers snapped their tails at me at the same instant, and filled the vast place with a flash of light of almost lightning-like intensity.

Bulger was so frightened by the result of his applause that he took good care to keep quiet after this.

CHAPTER VII

So heavy with sleep did my eyelids become at last that I knew that it must be night in the outer world, and so we halted, and I stretched myself at full length on that marble floor, which, by the way, was pleasantly warm beneath us; and the air, too, was strangely comforting to the lungs, there being a complete absence of that smell of earth and odor of dampness so common in vast subterranean chambers.

My sleep was long-continued and most refreshing; Bulger was already awake, however, when I sat up and tried to look about me.

He began tugging at the string which I had fastened to his collar as if he wanted to lead me somewhere, so I humored him and followed along after. To my delight he led me straight to a pool of deliciously sweet and cold water. Here we drank our fill, and after a very frugal breakfast on some dried figs set out again on our journey along the Marble Highway. Suddenly, to my more than joy, the faint and uncertain light of the place began to strengthen. Why, it seemed almost as if the day of the upper world were about to break, so delicate were the various hues in which the ever-increasing light clothed itself: then, as if affrighted at its own increasing glory, it would fade away again to almost gloom. Ere many moments again this faint and mysterious glow would return, beginning with the softest yellow, then changing through a dozen different tints, and, like a fickle maid uncertain which to wear, put all aside and don the lily's garb. Bulger and I wandered along the Marble Highway almost afraid to break a stillness so deep that it seemed to me as if I could hear those sportive rays of light in their play against the many-colored rocks arching this mighty corridor.

Now, as the Marble Highway swept around in a graceful curve, a dazzling flood of light burst upon us.

It was sunrise in the World within a World.

Whence came this flood of dazzling light which now caused the sides and arching roof to glow and sparkle as if we had suddenly entered one of Nature's vast storehouses of polished gems? Shading my eyes with my hand I looked about me in order to try and solve the mystery.

It did not take me long to understand it all. Know then, dear friends, that the ceilings, domes, and arched roofs of this underground world were fretted with a metal of greater hardness than any known to us children of sunshine. Its seams ran hither and thither like the veins of gigantic leaves; and at certain hours currents of electricity from some vast internal reservoir of Nature's own building, streamed through these metal traceries until they glowed with a heat so white as to give off the flood of dazzling light of which I have already spoken.

The current never came with a sudden rush or burst, but began gently and timidly, so to speak, as if feeling its way along. Hence the beautiful tints that always preceded sunrise in this lower world, and made it so much like the coming and going of our glorious sunshine.

The Marble Highway now divided, and the two halves of the fork curving away to the right and left enclosed a small but exquisitely ornamented park, or pleasure ground I might call it, provided with seats of some dark wood beautifully polished and carved. This park was ornamented with four fountains, each springing from a crystal basin and spreading out into a feathery spray that glistened like whirling snow in the dazzling white light. As Bulger and I directed our steps toward one of the benches with the intention of taking a good rest, a low growl from him warned me to be on the alert. I gave a second look. A human being was seated on the bench. Beside myself, as I was, with curiosity to come face to face with this inhabitant of the under world, the first we had met, I made a halt, determined to ascertain, if possible, whether he was quite harmless before accosting him.

He was small in stature, and clad entirely in black, a sort of loose, flowing robe much like a Roman toga. His head was bare, and what I could see of it was round, smooth, and rosy, with about as much hair, or rather fuzz, upon it as the head of an infant six weeks old. His face was hidden by a black fan which he carried in his right hand, and the uses of which you will learn later on. His eyes were shielded from the intense glare of the light by a pair of colored glass goggles. As he raised his hand between me and the light I couldn't help catching my breath. I could see right through it: the bones were as clear as amber. And his head, too, was only a little less opaque. Suddenly two words from Don Fum's manuscript flashed through my mind, and I exclaimed joyously,—

"Bulger, we're in the Land of the Transparent Folk!"

At the sound of my voice the little man arose and made a low bow, lowering his fan to his breast where he held it. His baby face was ludicrously sad and solemn.

"Yes, Sir Stranger," said he, in a low, musical voice, "thou art indeed in the Land of the Mikkamenkies (Mica Men), in the Land of the Transparent Folk, called also Goggle Land; but if I should show thee my heart thou wouldst see that I am deeply pained to think that I should have been the first to bid thee welcome, for know, Sir Stranger, that thou speakest with Master Cold Soul the Court Depressor, the saddest man in all Goggle Land, and, by the way, sir, permit me to offer thee a pair of goggles for thyself, and also a pair for thy four-footed companion, for our intense white light would blind thee both in a few days."

I thanked Master Cold Soul very warmly for the goggles, and proceeded to set one pair astride my nose and to tie the other in front of Bulger's eyes. I then in most courteous manner informed Master Cold Soul who I was, and begged him to explain the cause of his great sadness. "Well, thou must know, little baron," said he, after I had taken a seat beside him on the bench, "that we, the loving subjects of Queen Galaxa, whose royal heart is almost run down,—excuse these tears, living as we do in this beautiful world so unlike the one you inhabit, which our wise men tell us is built, strange to say, on the very outside of the earth's crust where it is most exposed to the full sweep of blinding snow, freezing blast, pelting hail, drowning rain, and choking dust,—living as we do, I say, in this vast temple by Nature's own hands builded, where disease is unknown, and where our hearts run down like clocks that may have but one winding, we are prone, alas, to be too happy; to laugh too much; to spend too much time in idle gayety, chattering the time away like thoughtless children amused with baubles, delighted with tinsel nothings. Know then, little baron, that mine is the business to check this gayety, to put an end to this childish glee, to depress our people's spirits, lest they run too high. Hence my garb of inky hue, my rueful countenance, my frequent outflowing of tears, my voice ever attuned to sadness. Excuse me, little baron, my fan slipped then; didst see through me? I would not have thee see my heart to-day, for some way or other I cannot bring it to a slow pace; it is dreadfully unruly."

I assured him that I had not seen through him as yet.

And now, dear friends, I must explain that by the laws of the Mikkamenkies each man, woman, and child must wear in their garments a heart-shaped opening on their breast directly over their hearts, with a corresponding one at the back, so that under certain conditions, when the law allows it, each may have the right to take a look at his neighbor's heart and see exactly how it is beating—whether fast or slow, whether throbbing or leaping, or whether pulsating calmly and naturally. But this privilege is only accorded, as I have said, under certain conditions, hence to shut off inquisitive glances each Mikkamenky is allowed to carry a black fan with which to cover the heart-shaped opening above described, and in this way conceal his or her feelings to a degree. I say to a degree, for I may as well tell you right here that falsehood is unknown, or, more correctly stated, impossible in the land of the Transparent Folk, for the reason that so wondrously clear, limpid, and crystal-like are their eyes that the slightest attempt to say one thing while they are thinking another roils and clouds them as if a drop of milk had fallen into a glass of the purest water.

As I sat gazing at this strange little being seated on the bench there beside me, I recalled a conversation which I had had with a learned Russian at Solvitchegodsk. Said he, speaking of his people, "We are all born with light hair, brilliant eyes, and pale faces, for we have sprung up under the snow." And I thought to myself how delighted, how entranced, he would have been to look upon this curious being, born not under the snow, but far under the surface of the earth, where in these vast chambers of this World within a World, this strange folk had, like plants grown in a dark, deep cellar, gradually parted with all their coloring until their eyes glowed like orbs of pure crystal, until their bones had been bleached to amber clearness, and their blood coursed colorless through colorless veins. While sitting there following out this train of thought, the clear white light suddenly began to flicker and to play fantastic tricks upon the walls by dancing in garbs of ever-changing hues, now brightest yellow, now palest green, now glorious purple, now deepest crimson.

"Ah, little baron!" exclaimed Master Cold Soul, "that was an uncommonly short day. Rise, please."

I made haste to obey, whereupon he touched a spring and the bench opened in the centre, disclosing two very comfortable beds.

"In a few moments night will be upon us," continued the Mikkamenky, "but thou seest that we have not been taken by surprise. I should explain to thee, little baron, that owing to the capricious manner in which our River of Light is apt both to begin and to cease flowing, we are never able to tell how long a day or a night will prove to be. This is what we call twilight. In thy world I suppose day goes out with a terrible bang, for our wise men tell us that nothing can be done in the upper world without making a noise; that your people really love noise; and that the man who makes the greatest noise is considered the greatest man.

"Owing to the fact, little baron, that no one in Goggle Land can tell how long the day will last, or how long it may be necessary to sleep, our laws permit no one to set any exact time when a thing shall be done, or to exact any promise to do this or that on a certain day, for, bless thy soul, that day may not be ten minutes long. Hence we say, 'If to-morrow be over five hours long, come to me at the beginning of the sixth hour;' and we never wish each other a plain good-night, but say, 'Good-night, as long as it lasts.'

"What's more, little baron, as night is apt to come upon us this way unawares, by law all the beds belong to the state; no one is allowed to own his own bed, for when night overtakes him he may be at the other end of the city, and some other subject of Queen Galaxa may be in front of his door, and no matter where night may overtake a Mikkamenky, he is sure to find a bed. There are beds everywhere. By touching a spring they drop from the walls, they pull out like drawers, they are under the tables and divans, in the parks, in the market-place, by the roadside; benches, bins, boxes, barrows, and barrels by pressing a spring may in an instant be transformed into beds. It is the Land of Beds, little baron. But ah! behold, the twilight goes to its end. Good-night as long as it lasts!" and with this Master Cold Soul stretched himself out and began to snore, having first carefully covered up the two holes in the front and back of his garment, so that I shouldn't have a chance to take a peep through him in case I should wake up first. Bulger and I were right glad to lay our limbs on a real bed, although from the way my four-footed brother followed his tail around and around, I could see that he wasn't particularly delighted with the softness of the couch.

CHAPTER VIII

I don't think the darkness lasted over three hours, perhaps it was longer; but Master Cold Soul was obliged to shake me gently ere he could rouse me.

"Now, little baron," said he, after he had wished me a good-morning with the usual "as long as it lasts" tacked to it, "if thou art quite willing, I'll conduct thee to the court of our gracious mistress, Queen Galaxa. Our wise men have often discoursed to her concerning the upper world and the terrible sufferings of its people, exposed as they are to be first frozen by the pitiless cold and then burned by the scorching rays of what they call their sun, and she will no doubt deign to be pleased at sight of thee, although I must warn thee that thou art most uncomely, that thou seemst so black and hard to me as scarcely to be human, but rather a bit of living earth or rock. I greatly fear me that thou wilt make our people extremely vain by comparison. Thy four-footed companion we know well by sight, having often seen his petrified image in the rocks of the dark chambers of our world."

"Master Cold Soul," said I, as we walked along, "when thou gettest to know me better thou wilt find me more comely, and although I shall not be able to show thee my heart, I hope to be able to prove to thee and thine that I have such a thing."

"No doubt, no doubt, little baron," exclaimed Master Cold Soul, "but be not offended. It is not more pleasant for me to tell thee these disagreeable things than it is for thee to hear them, but I am paid to do it and I must earn my wage. Vanity grows apace in our world, and I prick its bubbles whenever I see them."

To my great wonder I now discovered that the world of the Mikkamenkies had its lakes and rivers like our own, only of course they were smaller and mirror-faced, being never visited by the faintest zephyr. To my question as to whether they were peopled with living things, Master Cold Soul informed me that they literally swarmed with the most delicious fish, both in scales and shells.

"But think not, little baron," he added, "that we of Goggle Land have no other food than such as we draw from the water; for in our gardens grow many kinds of delicate vegetables, springing up in a single night almost as light as foam and just as white. But we are small eaters, little baron, and rarely find it necessary to put to death a large shellfish. We merely lay hold of his great claw, which he obligingly drops into our hand, and forthwith sets about growing another."

"But tell me, I pray thee, Master Cold Soul," said I, "where ye find the silk to weave such soft and beautiful stuff as that thy garment is fashioned from?"

"In this under world of ours, little baron," replied Master Cold Soul, "there are many vast recesses not reached by the River of Light, and in these dark chambers flit about huge night moths, like restless spirits forever on the wing, but of course they are not, for we find their eggs glued against the rocky sides of these caverns and collect them carefully. The worms that are hatched from them spin huge cocoons so large that one may not be hidden in my hand, and these unwound give unto our looms all the thread they need."

"And the beautiful wood," I continued, "which I see about me carved and fashioned into so many articles, whence comes it?"

"From the quarries," answered Master Cold Soul.

"Quarries?" I repeated wonderingly.

"Why, yes, little baron," said he, "for we have quarries of wood as no doubt thou hast quarries of stone. Our wise men tell us that thousands and thousands of years ago vast forests grown in your world were in the upheavals and fallings-in of the earth's crust thrust down into ours, the gigantic trunks wedged closely together, and standing bolt upright just as they grew. At least, so we find them when we have dug away the hardened clay that has shut them in these many ages. But see, little baron, we are now entering the city. Yonder is the royal palace—wilt walk with me thither?"

Ah, dear friends, would that I could make you see this beautiful city of the under world just as it showed itself to me then, spread out so gloriously beneath the glittering domes and vaulted corridors, from which poured down upon the exquisitely carved and polished entrances to the living chambers of this happy folk, a flood of white light apparently more dazzling than our noonday sun!

It was a sight so strangely beautiful that many times I paused to gaze upon it. Young and old, all clad in the same gracefully flowing garbs of silk, now purple, now royal blue, and now rich vermilion, were hurrying hither and thither, each armed with the inevitable black fan, and the baby face of each aglow with life and sweet content, while a hundred fountains springing from crystal basins glistened in the dazzling white light, and ten times a hundred flags and gonfalons hung listless but rich in splendor from invisible wires. Strange music came floating along from the gracefully shaped barges with silken awnings, which were gliding noiselessly over the surface of the winding river, the oars stirring the waters until the wake seemed a path through molten silver.

As Bulger and I followed Master Cold Soul along the streets of polished marble, it was not long before a crowd of Mikkamenkies was at our heels, whispering all sorts of uncomplimentary things about us, mingled with not a few fits of suppressed laughter.

The Court Depressor reproved them sternly.

"Cease your ill-timed mirth," said he, "and go about your business. Must I pause and tell you a grewsome tale to check your foolish gayety? Know ye not that all this silly mirth doth quicken your hearts and make them run down just so much sooner?"

At these words of Master Cold Soul they fell back, and put an end to their giggling, but it was only for a moment, and by the time we reached the portal of the royal palace, a still louder and noisier crowd was close behind us.

Master Cold Soul suddenly halted, and drawing forth a huge pocket-handkerchief, began to weep furiously. It was not without its effect, and from that moment I could see that the Mikkamenkies were inclined to take a more serious view of my arrival in their city, although it was only Cold Soul's presence that kept them from bursting out into fits of violent laughter.

Above the portals of the queen's palace there were large openings hewn in the rock for the purpose of admitting light into the royal apartments; but these windows, if they may be called such, were hung with silken curtains of delicate colors, so that the light which entered the throne room was tempered and softened. The room itself was likewise hung with silken stuffs, which gave it a look of Oriental splendor; but never in my travels among strange peoples of far-away lands had my eyes ever rested upon any work of art that equalled the crystal throne upon which sat Galaxa, Queen of the Mikkamenkies.

In the upper world most diligent search had never been able to unearth a piece of rock crystal more than about three feet in diameter; but here in Queen

Galaxa's throne four glorious columns at least fifteen feet in height, and at their base three feet in diameter, shot up in matchless splendor. Their lower parts shut in spangles of gold that glittered with ever-varying hues as a different light fell upon them. The cross pieces and pieces making up the back and arms had been chosen on account of the exquisitely beautiful hair and needle-shaped crystals of other metals which they enclosed. A silken baldachin of rare beauty covered in the throne, and from its edges dropped heavy cords and tassels of rich color and the perfection of human handicraft as to fineness and finish.

At the foot of the throne sat the young princess Crystallina; and standing behind her, and engaged in combing her long silken tresses, was her favorite waiting-maid, Damozel Glow Stone, while around and about, in files and group-wise, stood lords and ladies, courtiers and counsellors, by the dozen.

As Master Cold Soul advanced to salute the queen, a throng of the idlers who had followed at our heels crowded into the anteroom with loud outbursts of laughter. The Court Depressor was greatly incensed, and turning upon the throng he began weeping again with wonderful energy; but I noticed that it was nothing but sound: not a tear fell to obscure the crystal clearness of his eyes. Then he began chanting a sort of song which was intended to have a depressing influence on the wild mirth of the Mikkamenkies. I can only recollect one verse of this solemn chant of the Court Depressor. It ran as follows:—

"Weep, Mikkamenkies, weep, O weep,
For the eyeless man in the City of Light,
For the mouthless man in Plenty's bowers,
For the earless man in Music's realm,
For the noseless man in the Kingdom of flowers,
Weep, Mikkamenkies, weep, O weep!"
But they only laughed the louder, crying out,—

"Nay, Master Cold Soul, we will not weep for them; weep for them thyself." At last Queen Galaxa raised the slender golden wand, tipped with a diamond point, that lay within her hand, and instantly a hush came upon the whole place, while every eye was riveted upon Bulger and me.

CHAPTER IX

Owing to the soft air, the never-varying temperature, and the absence of all noise and dust, the Mikkamenkies, although they die in the end like other folk, yet do they never seem to grow old. Their skin remains soft and free from wrinkles, and their eyes as clear and bright as the crystal of Queen Galaxa's throne.

At the time of our arrival in the Land of the Transparent Folk, Queen Galaxa's heart had almost run down. In about two weeks more it would come quietly and gently to a stop; for, as I have already told you, dear friends, the heart of a Mikkamenky being perfectly visible when the dazzling white light in its full strength was allowed to shine through his body, why, it was a very easy matter for a physician to take a look at the organ of life, and tell almost to the hour when it would exhaust itself—in other words, run down. Galaxa looked every inch a real queen as she half-reclined upon her glorious crystal throne. She was clad in long, flowing silk garments of a right royal purple, and the gems which encircled her neck and wrists would have put to shame the crown jewels of any monarch of the upper world. Her garb had very much the cut and style of the ancient Greek costume, and the gold sandals worn by her added to the resemblance; but the one thing that excited my wonder more than all the others put together was her hair, so long, so fine and silken was it, such a mass of it was there, and so dazzling white was it—not the blue or yellow white that comes of age in our world, but a milk white, a cotton white. And as we drew near, to Bulger's but not to my amazement, her hair began to quiver and rustle and rise, until it buried her whole throne completely out of sight. Of course I knew that, seated as she was upon a throne of glass, it was only necessary to send a gentle current of electricity through her to make her wonderful head of hair stand up in this manner, like the white and filmy tentacles of some gigantic creature of the sea, half-plant, half-animal.

"Rise, little baron," said Queen Galaxa, as I dropped upon my right knee on the lowest step of the throne, "and be welcome to our kingdom. Whilst thou may be pleased to tarry here, my people shall bestir themselves to show thee all that may seem wonderful in thine eyes; for although our wise men have often discussed to us of the upper world, yet art thou its first inhabitant to visit us, and thy wonderful companion is right welcome too. Can he talk, little baron?"

"Not exactly, Queen Galaxa," said I with low obeisance, "yet he can understand me and I him."

"He is quite harmless, is he not?" asked the queen.

You may try to imagine how I felt, dear friends, when as I was about to say, "Perfectly so, royal lady," to my amazement I saw Bulger advance and sniff at the Princess Crystallina and then draw back and show his teeth as she stretched out her hand to caress him.

Bending over him I reproved him in a whisper, and bade him kneel before the queen. This he proceeded to do, saluting her with three very stately bows, at which everybody laughed heartily.

"I would have him come nearer," said the queen, "so that I may lay my hand upon him."

At a sign from me Bulger began to lick his fore-paws very carefully, and then having wiped them on the rug, sprang up the steps of the throne and placed his front feet upon Queen Galaxa's lap.

The fair ruler of the Mikkamenkies was delighted with this sample of Bulger's fine manners, and in order to amuse her still further I proceeded to put Bulger through many of his quaint tricks and curious feats, bidding him "say his prayers," "feign death," "weep for his sweetheart," "count ten," "walk upright," "go lame and cry to tell how it hurts."

Scarcely had he gone half around the circle, feigning lameness, when the damozel Glow Stone began to weep herself, and stooping down commenced to caress Bulger and to kiss his lame foot, caresses which, to my more than surprise, Bulger was not slow in returning, and later too when I bade him choose the maiden he loved best and kiss her hand, he bounded straight toward Glow Stone and bestowed not one but twenty kisses upon her outstretched hands, while the princess Crystallina shrank away in fear and disgust from the "ugly beast," as she termed him.

"Bid him bring my handkerchief to me, little baron," cried Galaxa, throwing it on the floor. I did as the queen commanded, but Bulger refused to obey.

"Thou seest, Queen Galaxa," said I with a low bow, "he refuses to lift the handkerchief without a command from thy royal self," which delicate compliment pleased the lady mightily.

"How comes it, little baron," she asked, "that thou shouldst be of noble lineage and thy brother, as thou callest him, plain Bulger?"

"It comes, royal lady," said I right humbly, "as it often comes in the world which I inhabit, that honors go to them that least deserve them."

"Well, then, little baron," cried Galaxa gayly, "though I be but a petty sovereign compared with thine, yet may small rulers do acts of great justice. Bid thy four-footed brother kneel before us."

At a word from me, Bulger prostrated himself on the steps of Galaxa's crystal throne, and laid his head at her very feet.

Leaning forward she touched him lightly with her golden wand, and exclaimed, "Rise, Lord Bulger, rise! Queen Galaxa seated on her crystal throne bids Lord Bulger rise!"

In an instant Bulger raised himself on his hind feet and laid his head in the queen's lap, while the whole room rang with loud huzzas, and every lady gently clapped her frail and glass-like hands, save the princess Crystallina who feigned to be asleep.

Queen Galaxa now undid a string of pearls from her neck and tied them with her own hands around Lord Bulger's—and so it was that my four-footed brother ceased to be plain Bulger. Then turning to her counsellors of state, Queen Galaxa bade them assign a royal apartment to Lord Bulger and me, and gave strict orders that the severest punishment be at once visited upon any Mikkamenky who should dare to laugh at us or to make disrespectful remarks concerning our dark eyes and skins and weather-beaten appearance, for, as the royal lady said to her people, "Ye might look worse than they were ye compelled to live on the outside instead of the inside of the world, exposed to biting blasts, piercing cold, and clouds of suffocating dust."

By the queen's orders three of the wisest of the Mikkamenkies were selected to attend Bulger and me, look after our wants, explain everything to us—in a word, do all in their power to make our stay in Goggle Land as pleasant as possible.

Their names, as nearly as I can translate them, were Doctor Nebulosus, Sir Amber O'Pake, and Lord Cornucore. I should explain to you, dear friends, the meaning of these names, for you might be inclined to think that Doctor Somewhat Cloudy, Sir Clear-as-Amber; and Lord Heart-of-Horn might indicate that they were more or less muddled in their intellects. Far from it: I have already stated to you they were three of the very wisest men in the Land of the Transparent Folk, and the lack of clearness indicated by their names had reference solely to their eyes.

Now, as you know, the learned men of our upper world have a different look from ordinary folk. They are stoop-shouldered, shaggy-eyebrowed, long-haired, pursed-lipped, near-sighted, shambling-gaited. Well, the only effect that long years of deep study had upon the Mikkamenkies was to rob their beautiful crystal-like eyes of more or less of their clearness.

Now I think you'll understand why these three learned Mikkamenkies were named as they were.

At any rate, they were, in spite of their strange names, three most charming gentlemen; and no matter how many times I might ask the same question over again, they were always ready with an answer quite as polite as the one first given me. They did everything that I had a right possibly to expect them to do. Indeed, there was but one single thing which I would have fain had them do, and that was to let me look through them.

This they most carefully avoided doing; and no matter how warmed up they might become in their descriptions, and no matter how on the alert I was to catch the coveted peep, the inevitable black fan was always in the way.

Naturally, not only they, but all the Transparent Folk, felt a repugnance to have a perfect stranger look through them, and I couldn't blame them for it either. I despaired of ever getting a chance of seeing a human heart beating away for dear life, for all the world just like the swing of a pendulum or the vibration of a balance wheel.

CHAPTER X

Lord Bulger and I were more than pleased with our new friends, Doctor Nebulosus, Sir Amber O'Pake, and Lord Cornucore, although so eager were they to make us thoroughly comfortable, that they overdid the matter at times, and left me scarcely a moment to myself in which to make an entry in my notebook. They were extremely solicitous lest in my ignorance I should set down something wrong about them.

"For," said Sir Amber O'Pake, "now that thou hast found the way to this under world of ours, little baron, I feel assured that we shall have a number of visitors from thy people every year or so, and I have already issued orders to have extra beds made as soon as the wood can be quarried."

Doctor Nebulosus gave me a very interesting account of the various ailments which the Mikkamenkies suffer from. "All sickness among our people, little baron," said he, "is purely mental or emotional; that is, of the mind or feelings. There is no such thing as bodily infirmity among us. Wine and strong drink are unknown in our world, and the food we eat is light and easily digested. We are never exposed to the danger of breathing a dust-laden atmosphere, and while we are an active and industrious people, yet we sleep a great deal; for, as our laws forbid the use of lamps or torches, except for the use of those toiling in the dark chambers, it is not possible for us to ruin our health by turning night into day. We go to bed the very moment the River of Light ceases to flow. The only ailment that ever gives me the least trouble is iburyufrosnia."

"Pray, what is the nature of that ailment?" I asked.

"It is an inclination to be too happy," replied Doctor Nebulosus gravely, "and I regret to say that several of our people attacked with this ailment have shortened their lives by refusing to take my remedies. It usually develops very slowly, beginning with an inclination to giggle, which, after a while, is succeeded by violent fits of laughter.

"For instance, little baron, when thou camest among us, many of our people were attacked with a violent form of iburyufrosnia; and although Master Cold Soul, the Court Depressor, made great efforts to check it, yet he was quite powerless to do so. It spread over the city with remarkable rapidity. Without knowing why, our workmen at their work, our children at their play, our people in doors and out, began to laugh and to be dangerously happy. I made examinations of several of the worst cases, and discovered that at the rate they were beating the hearts of most of them would run down in a single week. It was terrible. A council was hastily held, and it was determined to conceal thee and Lord Bulger from the public view, but happily my skill got the upper hand of the attack."

"Didst increase the number of pills to be taken?" I asked.

"No, little baron," said Doctor Nebulosus; "I increased their size and covered them with a dry powder, which made them extremely difficult to swallow, and in this way compelled those taking them to cease their laughing. But there were a number of cases so violent that they could not be cured in this way. These I ordered to be strapped in at the waist with broad belts, and to have their mouths held pried open with wooden wedges. As thou mayst understand, this made laughing so difficult that they speedily gave it up altogether.

"Ah, little baron," continued the wise doctor with a sigh, "that was a sorry day for the human race when it learned how to laugh. It is my opinion that we owe this useless agitation of our bodies to you people of the upper world. Exposed as ye were to piercing winds and biting frosts, ye contracted the habit of shivering to keep warm, and, little by little, this shivering habit so grew upon you, that ye kept up the shivering whether ye were cold or not; only ye called it by another name. Now, my knowledge of the human body teaches me that this quivering of the flesh is a very wise provision of nature to keep the blood in motion, and in this way to save the human body from perishing from the cold; but why should we quiver when we are happy, little baron? All pleasure is the thought, and yet at the very moment when we should keep our bodies in as perfect repose as possible, we begin this ridiculous shivering. Do we shiver when we look upon the beauties of the River of Light, or listen to sweet music, or gaze upon the loving countenance of our gracious Queen Galaxa? But worse than all, little baron, this senseless quivering and shivering which we call laughter, unlike good, deep, long-drawn, wholesome sighs, empty the lungs of air without filling them again, and thus do we often see these gigglers and laughers fall over in fainting fits, absolutely choked by their own wild and unreasoning action. I have always contended, little baron, that we alone of all animals had the laughing habit, and I am now delighted to have my opinion confirmed by my acquaintance with the wise and dignified Lord Bulger. Observe him. He knows quite as well as we what it is to be pleased, to be amused, to be delighted, but he doesn't think it necessary to have recourse to fits of shivering and shuddering. Through the brightened eye—true window of the soul—I can see how happy he is. I can measure his joy; I can take note of his contentment."

I was delighted with this learned discourse of the gentle Doctor Nebulosus, and made notes of it lest the points of his argument might escape my memory, the more pleased was I in that he proved my faithful Bulger to be so wisely constructed and regulated by nature.

I made particular inquiry of my friends, Sir Amber O'Pake and Lord Cornucore, as to whether Queen Galaxa ever had any trouble in governing her people.

"None whatever," was the answer. "In many a long year has it only been necessary on one or two occasions to summon a Mikkamenky before the magistrate and examine his heart under a strong light. The only punishment allowed by our laws is confinement for a shorter or longer time in one of the dark chambers. The severest sentence ever known to have been passed by one of our magistrates was twelve hours in length. But in all honesty, we must admit, little baron, that falsehood and deception are unknown amongst us for the simple reason that, being transparent, it is impossible for a Mikkamenky to deceive a brother without being caught in the act. Therefore why make the attempt? The very moment one of us begins to say one thing while he is thinking another, his eyes cloud up and betray him, just as the crystal-clear weather glass clouds up at the approach of a storm in the upper world. But this, of course, little baron, is only true of our thoughts. Our laws allow us to hide our feelings by the use of the black fan. No one may look upon another's heart unless its owner wills it. It is a very grave offence for one Mikkamenky to look through another without that one's permission. But as thou wilt readily understand, inasmuch as we are by nature transparent, it is utterly impossible for a marriage to prove an unhappy one, for the reason that when a youth declares his love for a maiden, they both have the right by law to look upon each other's hearts, and in this way they can tell exactly the strength of the love they have for each other." This and many other strange and interesting things did my new friends, Doctor Nebulosus, Sir Amber O'Pake, and Lord Cornucore impart unto me, and right grateful was I to good Queen Galaxa for having chosen them for me. Good friends are better than gold, although we may not think it at the time.

CHAPTER XI

From now on Lord Bulger and I made ourselves perfectly at home among the Mikkamenkies. One of the royal barges was placed at our disposal, and when we grew tired of walking about and gazing at the wonders of this beautiful city of the under world, we stepped aboard our barge and were rowed hither and thither on the glassy river; and if I had not seen it myself I never would have believed that any kind of shellfish could ever be taught to be so obliging as to swim to the surface and offer one of their huge claws for our dinner, politely dropping it in our hand the moment we had laid hold of it. On one of the river banks I noticed a long row of wooden compartments looking very much like a grocer's bins; but you may think how amused Bulger and I were upon coming closer to this long row of little houses to find that they were turtle nests, and that quite a number of the turtles were sitting comfortably in their nests busy laying their eggs—which, let me assure you, were the most dainty tidbits I ever tasted.

I think I informed you that the river flowing through Goggle Land was fairly swarming with delicious fish, the carp and sole being particularly delicate in flavor; and knowing, as I did, what a tender-hearted folk the Mikkamenkies are, I had been not a little puzzled in my mind as to how they had ever been able to summon up courage enough to drive a spear into one of these fish, which were as tame and playful as a lot of kittens or puppies, and followed our barge hither and thither, snapping up the food we tossed to them, and leaping into the air, where they glistened like burnished silver as the white light sparkled on their scales.

But the mystery was solved one day when I saw one of the fishermen decoying a score or more of fish into a sort of pen shut off from the river by a wire netting. Scarcely had he closed the gates when, to my amazement, I saw the fish one after the other come to the surface and float about on their sides, stone dead.

"This, little baron," explained the man in charge, "is the death chamber. Hidden at the bottom of this dark pool lie several electric eels of great size and power, and when our people want a fresh supper of fish we simply open these gates and decoy a shoal of them inside by tossing their favorite food into the water. The executioners are awaiting them, and in a few instants the fish, while enjoying their repast and suspecting no harm, are painlessly put to death, as thou hast seen."

One part of the city of the Transparent Folk which attracted Bulger and me very much was the royal gardens. It was a weird and uncanny place, and upon my first visit I walked through its paths and beneath its arbors upon my toes and with bated breath, as you might steal into some bit of fairy-land, looking anxiously from side to side as if at every step you expected some sprite or goblin to trip you up with a tough spider-web, or brush your cheeks with their cold and satiny wings.

Now, dear friends, you must first be told that with the loss of sunshine and the open air, the flowers and shrubs and vines of this underground world gradually parted with their perfumes and colors, their leaves and petals and stems and tendrils growing paler and paler in hue, like lovelorn maids whose sweethearts had never come back from the war. Month by month the dark greens, the blush pinks, the golden yellows, and the deep blues pined away, longing for the lost sunshine and the wooing breeze they loved so dearly, until at last the transformation was complete, and there they all stood or hung bleached to utter whiteness, like those fantastic clumps of flowers and wreaths of vines which the feathery snow of April builds in the leafless shrubs and trees.

I cannot tell you, dear friends, what a strange feeling came over me as I stepped within this spectral garden where ghost-like vines clung in fantastic forms and figures to the dark trellises, and where tall lilies, whiter than the down of eider, stood bolt upright like spirits doomed to eternal silence, denied even the speech of perfume, and where huge clusters of snowy chrysanthemums, fluffy feathery forms, seemed pressing their soft bodies together like groups of banished celestials in a sort of silent despair as they felt the warmth and glow of sunlight slowly and gradually quitting their souls; where lower down, great roses with snowy petals whiter than the sea-shells hung motionless, bursting open with eager effort, as if listening for some signal that would dissolve the spell put upon them, and give them back the sunshine, and with it their color and their perfume; where lower still beds of violets bleached white as fleecy clouds seemed wrapt in silent sorrow at loss of the heavenly perfume which had been theirs on earth; where, above the lilies' heads shot long, slender, spectral stalks of sunflowers almost invisible, loaded at their ends with clusters of snowy flowers thus suspended like white faces looking down through the silent air, and waiting, waiting for the sunshine that never came; and higher still all over and above these spectral flowers, intwining and inwrapping and falling festoon and garland-wise, crept and ran like unto long lines of escaping phantoms, ghostly vines with ghostly blossoms, bent and twisted and wrapped and coiled into a thousand strange and fantastic forms and figures which the white light with its inky shadows made alive and half human, so that movement and voice alone were needful to make this garden seem peopled with sorrowing sprites banished to these subterranean chambers for strange misdeeds done on earth and condemned to wait ten thousand years ere sunlight and their color and their perfume should be given back to them again.

While strolling through the royal gardens one day, Bulger suddenly gave a low cry and bounded on ahead, as if his eyes had fallen upon the familiar form of some dear friend.

When I came up with him he was crouching beside the damozel Glow Stone who, seated on one of the garden benches, was caressing Bulger's head and ears with one of her soft hands with its filmy-like skin, while the other held its black fan pressed tightly against her bosom.

She looked up at me with her crystal eyes, and smiled faintly as I drew near.

"Thou seest, little baron," she murmured, "Lord Bulger and I have not forgotten each other." Since our presentation at court I had been going through and through my mind in search of some reason for Bulger's sudden affection for damozel Glow Stone, but had found none.

I was the more perplexed as she was but the maid of honor, while the fair princess Crystallina sat on the very steps of the throne.

But I said nothing save to reply that I was greatly pleased to see it and to add that where Bulger's love went, mine was sure to follow.

"Oh, little baron, if I could but believe that!" sighed the fair damozel.

"Thou mayst," said I, "indeed thou mayst."

"Then, if I may, little baron," she replied, "I will, and prithee come and sit beside me here, only till I bid thee, look not through me. Dost promise?"

"I do, fair damozel," was my answer.

"And thou, Lord Bulger, lie there at my feet," she continued, "and keep thy wise eyes fixed upon me and thy keen ears wide open."

"Little baron, if both thine and our worlds were filled with sorrowing hearts, mine would be the heaviest of them all. List! oh, list to the sad, sad tale of the sorrowing maid with the speck in her heart, and, when thou knowest all, give me of thy wisdom."

CHAPTER XII

"Little baron and dear Lord Bulger," began the crystal-eyed damozel, after she had eased her soul of its load of woe by three long and deep, deep sighs, "know then that I am not the damozel Glow Stone, but none other than the royal princess Crystallina herself; that she whose hair I comb should comb mine; that she whom I have served for ten long years should have served me!"

"And to think, O princess," I burst out joyfully, "that my beloved Bulger should have been the first to discover that she who was seated on the steps of the crystal throne was not entitled to the seat; to think that his subtle intellect should have been the first to scent out the wrong that had been done thee; his keen eye the first to go to the bottom of truth's well; but, fair princess, I am bursting with impatience to know how thou thyself didst ever discover the wrong that has been done thee."

"That thou shalt speedily know, little baron," answered Crystallina, "and that thou mayst know all that I know I'll begin at the very beginning: The day I was born there was great rejoicing in the land of the Mikkamenkies, and the people gathered in front of the royal palace and laughed and cried by turns, so happy were they to think they were to be governed by another princess after Queen Galaxa's heart should run down; for, many years ago, a bad king had made them very unhappy, and they had hoped and prayed that no more such would come to reign over them. And pretty soon one of them began to tell the others what he thought the little princess would be like.

"'She will be the fairest that ever sat upon the crystal throne. Her hands and feet will be like pearls tipped with coral; her hair whiter than the river's foam; and from her beautiful eyes will burst the radiance of her pure soul, and her heart, Oh, her heart will be like a little lump of frozen water so clear and so transparent will it be, so like a bit of purest crystal, bright and flawless as a diamond of the first water, and therefore let her be called the princess Crystallina, or the Maid with the Crystal Heart.'

"Forthwith the cry went up: 'Ay, let her be called Crystallina, or the Maid with the Crystal Heart,' and Queen Galaxa heard the cry of her people and sent them word that it should be as they wished—that I should be the Princess Crystallina.

"But, ah me, that I should have lived to tell it! after a few days the nurse came to my royal mother wringing her hands and pouring down a flood of tears.

"Throwing herself on her knees, she whispered to the queen, 'Royal mistress, bid me die rather than tell thee what I know.'

"Being ordered to speak, the nurse informed Queen Galaxa that she had that day for the first time held me up to the light and had discovered that there was a speck in my heart.

"The queen uttered a cry of horror and swooned. When she came to herself she directed that I should be brought to her and held up to the light so that she might see for herself. Alas, too true! there was the speck in my heart sure enough. I was not worthy of the sweet name which her loving people had bestowed upon me. They would turn from me with horror; they would never consent to have me for their queen when the truth should become known. They would not be moved by a mother's prayers: they would turn a deaf ear to every one who should be bold enough to advise them to accept a princess with a speck in her heart, when they had thought they were getting one well deserving of the title they had bestowed upon her.

"Queen Galaxa knew that something must be done at once; that it would be time and labor lost to attempt to reason with the disappointed people, so she set to work thinking up some way out of her trouble. Now, it so happened, little baron, that the very day I had come into the world a babe had been born to one of Queen Galaxa's serving women; and so hastily summoning the woman she ordered her to bring her babe into the royal bed-chamber and leave it there, promising that it should be brought up as my foster-sister. But no sooner had the serving woman gone her way rejoicing than the nurse was ordered to change the children in the cradle, and in a few moments Glow Stone was wrapt in my richly embroidered blanket and I swathed up in her plain coverlets.

"How things went for several years I know not, but one day, ah, how well I recollect it! my little mind was puzzled by hearing Crystallina cry out: 'Nay, nay, dear mamma, 'tis not fair; I like it not. Each day when thou comest to us thou givest Glow Stone ten kisses and me but a single one.' Then would Queen Galaxa smile a sad smile and bestow some bauble upon Crystallina to coax her back to contentment again.

"And so we went on, Crystallina and I, from one year to another until we were little maids well grown, and she sat on the throne and wore royal purple stitched with gold, and I plain white; but still most of the kisses fell to my share. And I marvelled not a little at it, but dared not ask why it was. However, once when I was alone with Queen Galaxa, seated on my cushion in the corner plying my needle and thinking of the sail we were to have on the river that day, suddenly I was startled to see the queen throw herself on her knees in front of me, and to feel her clasp me in her arms and cover my face and head with tears and kisses, as she sobbed and moaned,—

"'O my babe, my lost babe, my blessing and my joy, wilt never, never, never come back to me? Art gone forever? Must I give thee up, oh, must I?'"

"'Nay, Royal Lady,' I stammered in my more than wonder at her words and actions. 'Thou art in a dream. Awake, and see clearly; I am not Crystallina. I am Glow Stone, thy foster-child. I'll hie me straight and bring my royal sister to thee.'

"But she would not let me loose, and for all answer showered more kisses on me till I was well-nigh smothered, so tight she held me pressed against her bosom, while around and over me her long thick tresses fell like a woven mantle.

"And then she told me all—all that I have told thee, little baron, and charged me never to impart it unto any soul in Goggle Land; and I made a solemn promise unto her that I never would."

"And thou hast kept thy word like a true princess as thou art," said I cheerily, "for I am not of thy world, fair Crystallina."

"Now that I have told thee the sad tale of the sorrowing princess with the speck in her heart, little baron," murmured Crystallina, fixing her large and radiant eyes upon me, "there is but one thing more for me to do, and it is to let thee look through me, so that thou mayst know exactly what counsel to give." And so saying the fair princess rose from her seat, and having placed herself in front of me with a flood of white light falling full upon her back, she lowered her black fan and bade me gaze upon the heavy heart which she had carried about with her all these years, and tell her exactly how large the speck was and where it lay, and what color it was.

I was overjoyed to get an opportunity at last to look through one of the Mikkamenkies, and my own heart bounded with satisfaction as I looked and looked upon that mysterious little thing, nay, rather a tiny being, living, breathing, palpitating within her breast; now slow and measured as she dwelt in thought upon her sad fate, now beating faster and faster as the hope bubbled up in her mind that possibly I might be able to counsel her so wisely that an end would come to all her sorrow.

"Well, wise little baron," she murmured anxiously, "what seest thou? Is it very large? In what part is it? Is it black as night or some color less fatal?"

"Take courage, fair princess," said I, "it is very small and lies just beneath the bow on the left side. Nor is it black, but reddish rather, as if a single drop of blood from the veins of thy far distant ancestors had outlived them these thousands of years and hardened there to tell whence thy people came." The princess wept tears of joy upon hearing these comforting words.

"If it had been black," she whispered "I would have lain me down in this bed of violets and never risen more till my people had come to bear me to my grave in the silent burial chamber—unvisited by the River of Light."

At this sad outbreak Bulger whined piteously and licked the princess's hands as he looked up at her with his dark eyes radiant with sympathy.

She was greatly cheered by this message of comfort, and it moved me, too, by its heartiness.

"List, fair princess," said I gravely. "I own the task is not a light one, but hope for the best. I would that we had more time, but as thou knowest Queen Galaxa's heart will soon run down, therefore must we act with despatch as well as wisdom. But first of all must I speak with the queen and gain her consent to act for thee in this matter."

"That, I fear me, she will never grant," moaned Crystallina. "However, thou art so much wiser than I—do as best seems to thee."

"The next thing to be done, fair princess," I added solemnly, "is to show thy heart boldly and fearlessly to thy people."

"Nay, little baron," she exclaimed, rising to her feet, "that may not be, that may not be, for know that our law doth make it treason itself for one of our people to look through a person of royal blood. Oh, no, oh, no, little baron, that may never be!"

"Stay, sweet princess," I urged in gentlest tones, "not so fast. Thou dost not know what I mean by showing thy heart boldly to thy people. Never fear. I will not break the law of the land, and yet they shall look upon the speck within thy heart, and see how small it is and hear what I have to say about it, and thou shalt not even be visible to them."

"O little baron," murmured Crystallina, "if this may only be! I feel they will forgive me. Thou art so wise and thy words carry such strong hope to my poor, heavy heart that I almost"—

"Nay, fair princess," I interrupted, "hope for the best, no more. I am not wise enough to read the future, and from what I know of thy people they seem but little different from mine own. Perchance I may be able to sway them toward my views, and make them cry, 'Long live princess Crystallina!' but I can only promise thee to do my best. Betake thee now to the palace, and scorn not for yet a day or so to take up the golden comb and play the damozel Glow Stone in all humility."

CHAPTER XIII

The first thing I did after the genuine princess Crystallina had left me was to seek out Doctor Nebulosus and learn from him the exact number of hours before the queen's heart would run down.

As he had just been making an examination, he was able to tell the very minute: it was seventeen hours and thirteen minutes, rather a short time you must confess, dear friends, in which to accomplish such an important piece of business as I had in mind. I then made my way directly to the royal palace and demanded a private audience with the Lady of the Crystal Throne.

With the advice of Sir Amber O'Pake and Lord Cornucore she firmly but graciously refused to receive me, giving as an excuse that the excitement that would be sure to follow an interview with the "Man of Coal"—so the Mikkamenkies had named me—would shorten her life at least thirteen minutes.

But I was not to be put off in so unceremonious a manner. Sitting down, I seized a pen and wrote the following words upon a piece of glazed silk:—

"To Galaxa, Queen of the Mikkamenkies, Lady of the Crystal Throne.

"I, Lord Bulger, a Mikkamenkian Noble, Bearer of this, who was the first to discover that the real princess was not sitting on the steps of the Crystal Throne, demand an audience for my Master Baron Sebastian von Troomp, commonly known as 'Little Baron Trump,' and prompted by him I ask, What are thirteen minutes of thy life, O Queen Galaxa, to the long years of sorrow and disappointment in store for thy royal child?"

Taking this letter in his mouth, Bulger sprang away with long and rapid bounds. In a few minutes he was in the presence of the queen, for the guards had fallen back affrighted as they saw him draw near with his dark eyes flashing indignation. Raising himself upon his hind feet, he laid the letter in Galaxa's hands. The moment she had read it she fell into a swoon, and all was stir and commotion in and round about the palace. I was hastily summoned and the audience chamber cleared of every attendant save Doctor Nebulosus, Sir Amber O'Pake, Lord Cornucore, Lord Bulger, and me.

"Send for the damozel Glow Stone," commanded the queen, and when she had appeared, to the amazement of all saving Bulger and me, Galaxa bade her mount the steps of the Crystal Throne, then, having embraced her most tenderly, the queen spoke these words:—

"O faithful Councillors and wise friends from the upper world, this is the real princess Crystallina, whom I have for all these years wickedly and wrongfully kept from her high state and royal privileges. She was born with a speck in her heart, and I feared that it would be useless to ask my people to accept her as my successor."

"Ay, Lady of the Crystal Throne," exclaimed Lord Cornucore, "thou hast wisely done. Thy people would never have received her as Princess Crystallina, for, being by the laws of our land denied the privilege to look for themselves, they never would have believed that this spot in the princess's heart was but a tiny speck like a single hair crystal in the arm of thy magnificent throne. Therefore, O queen, we counsel thee not to imbitter thy last hours by differences with thy loving subjects."

"My Lord Cornucore," said I with a low bow, "I make bold to raise my voice against thine, and I crave permission from Queen Galaxa to parley with her people."

"Forbid it, royal lady!" cried Sir Amber O'Pake savagely, at which Bulger gave a low growl and showed his teeth.

"Queen Galaxa," I added gravely, "a wrong confessed is half redressed. This fair princess, 'tis true, hath a speck in her heart which ill accords with the name bestowed upon her by thy people. Bid me be master until thy heart runs down, and by the Knighthood of all the Trumps I promise thee that thou shalt have three hours of happiness ere thy royal heart has ceased to beat!"

"Be it so, little baron," exclaimed Galaxa joyfully. "I proclaim thee prime minister for the rest of my life." At these words Bulger broke out into a series of glad barks, and, raising upon his hind legs, licked the queen's hand in token of his gratitude, while the fair princess looked a love at me that was too deep to put into words.

"I had now but a few hours to act. The excitement, so Doctor Nebulosus assured me, would shorten the queen's life a full hour."

It had always been my custom to carry about with me a small but excellent magnifying-glass, a double convex lens, for the purpose of making examinations of minute objects, and also for reading inscriptions too fine to be seen with the naked eye. Hastily summoning a skilful metal worker, I instructed him to set the lens in a short tube and to enclose that tube within another, so that I could lengthen it at my pleasure. Then having called together as many of the head men of the nation as the throne room would hold, I requested Lord Cornucore to inform them of the confession which Queen Galaxa had made; namely, that in reality damozel Glow Stone was princess Crystallina and princess Crystallina was damozel Glow Stone.

They were stricken speechless by this piece of information, but when Lord Cornucore went on to tell the whole story and to explain to them why the queen had practised this deception upon them, they broke out into the wildest lamentation, repeating over and over again in piteous tones,—

"A speck in her heart! A speck in her heart! O dire misfortune! O woful day! She never can be our princess if she hath a speck in her heart!" By this time my arrangements were complete. I had placed the princess Crystallina just outside the door of the throne room where she stood concealed behind the thick hangings, and near her I had stationed Doctor Nebulosus with a large circular mirror of burnished silver in his hand. Calling out in a loud voice for silence, I thus addressed the weeping subjects of Queen Galaxa:—

"O Mikkamenkies, Men of Goggle Land, Transparent Folk, I count myself most happy to be among you at this hour and to be permitted, by your gracious queen, to raise my voice in defence of the unfortunate princess with the speck in her heart. Being of noble birth and an inhabitant of another world, it was lawful for me to look through the sorrowing princess, and I have done it. Yes, Mikkamenkies, I have gazed upon her heart; I have seen the speck within it! Give ear, Men of Goggle Land, and you shall know how that speck came there; for it is not, as you doubtless think, a coal-black spot within that fair enclosure, clearer than the columns of Galaxa's throne. Oh, no, Mikkamenkies, a thousand times no: it is a tiny blemish of reddish hue, a drop of princely blood from the upper world, which I inhabit, and this drop in all these countless centuries has coursed through the veins of a thousand kings, and still kept its roseate glow, still remembered the glorious sunshine which called it into being; and now, Men of Goggle Land, lest you think that for some dark purpose of mine own I speak other than the pure and sober truth, behold, I show you the fair Crystallina's heart, in its very life and being as it is, beating and throbbing with hope and fear comingled. Look and judge for yourselves!" And with this I signalled to those on the outside of the palace to carry out my instructions.

In an instant the thick curtains were drawn and the throne room was wrapped in darkness, and at the same moment Doctor Nebulosus, with his mirror, caught the strong, white rays of light and threw them upon Crystallina's body, while I through an opening in the hangings made haste to apply the tube to which the lens had been fitted, and, catching the reflected image of her heart, threw it up in plain and startling view upon the opposite wall of the throne room. Upon seeing how small the speck was and how truthfully I had described it, the Mikkamenkies fell a-weeping for purest joy, and then, as if with one voice, they burst out,—

"Long live the fair princess Crystallina with the ruby speck in her heart! and ten thousand blessings on the head of little Baron Trump and Lord Bulger for saving our land from cruel dissensions!" The people on the outside took up the cry, and in a few moments the whole city was thronged with bands of Queen Galaxa's subjects, singing and dancing and telling of their love for the fair princess with the ruby speck in her heart. I had kept my word—Queen Galaxa would have at least three hours of complete happiness ere her heart ran down.

But suddenly the River of Light began to flicker and dim its flood of brilliant white rays.

Night was coming. Noiselessly, as if by magic, the Mikkamenkies faded from my sight, stealing away in search of beds, and as the gloom crept into the great throne room, some one plucked me gently by the hand and a soft voice whispered,—

"I love! I love thee! Oh, who other than I can tell how I love thee!" and then a grip stronger than that gentle hand seized me by the skirt of my coat and dragged me away slowly, but surely, away, through the darkness, through the gloom, out into the silent streets, ever away until at last that soft voice, choking with a sob, ceased its pleading and gasped, "Farewell, oh, farewell! I dare go no farther!" And so Bulger, in his wisdom, led me on and ever on out of the City of the

Mikkamenkies, out upon the Marble Highway!

CHAPTER XIV

Me, the sorrowing Sebastian, loaded with as heavy a heart as ever a mortal of my size had borne away with him, did the wise Bulger lead along the broad and silent highway, farther and yet farther from the city of the Mikkamenkies, until at last the music of the fountains pattering in their crystal basins died away in the distance and the darkness far behind me. I felt that my wise little brother was right, and so I followed on after, with not a sigh or a syllable to stay him.

But he halted at last, and, as I felt about me, I discovered that I was standing beside one of the richly carved seats that one so often meets with along the Marble Highway. I was quite as foot-weary as I was heart-heavy, and reaching out I touched the spring which I knew would transform the seat into a bed, and clambering upon it with my wise Bulger nestled beside me, I soon fell into a deep and refreshing sleep.

When I awoke and, sitting up, looked back toward Queen Crystallina's capital, I could see the River of Light pouring down its flood of white rays far away in the distance; but only a faint reflection came out to where we had passed the night, and then I knew that my faithful companion had led me to the very uttermost limit of the Mikkamenky domain before he had halted. Yes, sure enough, for, as I raised my eyes, there towering above the bed stood the slender crystal column which marked the end of Goggle Land, and upon its face I read the extract from a royal decree forbidding a Mikkamenky to overstep this limit under pain of incurring the queen's most serious displeasure.

Before me was darkness and uncertainty; behind me lay the fair Kingdom of the Transparent Folk yet in sight, lighted up like a long line of happy homes in which the fires were blazing bright and warm on the hearthstones.

Did I turn back? Did I hesitate? No. I could see a pair of speaking eyes fixed upon me, and could hear a low whine of impatience coaxing me along.

Stooping down, I fastened a bit of silken cord taken from the bed to Bulger's collar and bade him lead the way.

It was a long while before the light of Queen Crystallina's city faded away entirely, and even when it ceased to be of any service in making known to me the grandeur and beauty of the vast underground passage, I could still see it glitter like a silver star away, away behind me.

But it disappeared at last, and then I felt that I had parted forever with the dear little princess with the speck in her heart.

Bulger didn't seem to have the slightest difficulty in keeping in the centre of the Marble Highway, and never allowed the leading string to slack up for a moment. However, it was by no means a tramp through utter darkness, for the lizards of which I have already spoken, aroused by the sound of my footfalls, snapped their tails and lighted up their tiny flash torches in eager attempts to discover whence the noise proceeded, and what sort of a being it was that had invaded their silent domains. We had covered possibly two leagues when suddenly a low and mysterious voice, as soft and gentle as if it had dropped from the clear, starry heavens of my own beautiful world, reached my ear.

"Sebastian! Sebastian!" it murmured. Before I could stop to think, I uttered a cry of wonder, and the noise of my voice seemed to awaken ten thousand of the tiny living flash lights inhabiting the cracks and crevices of the vast arched corridor, flooding it for a moment or so with a soft and roseate radiance.

"Sebastian! Sebastian!" again murmured the mellow and echo-like voice, coming from the very walls of rock beside me.

Hastily drawing near to the spot whence the words seemed to come, I laid my ear against the smooth face of the rock. Again the same soft-sighing voice pronounced my name so clearly and so close beside me that I reached out to grasp Crystallina's hand, for hers was the voice,—the same low, sweet voice that had told me of her sorrow in the Spectral Garden; but there was no one there. In reaching out, however, I had passed my left hand along the face of the wall, and it had marked the presence of a round smooth opening in its rocky face, an opening about the size of a rain-water pipe in the upper world.

Instantly it flashed upon my mind that through some whim of nature this opening extended for leagues back towards the city of the Mikkamenkies through the miles of solid rock, and opened in the very Throne Room of the Princess Crystallina.

Yes, I was right, for after a moment or so again the same low, sweet voice came through the speaking-tube of nature's own making and fell upon my eager ear.

I waited until it had ceased, and setting my mouth in front of the opening I murmured in strong but gentle tones,—

"Farewell, dear Princess Crystallina. Bulger and the little baron both bid thee a long farewell!" and then raising Bulger in my arms, I bade him weep for his royal friend whom he would never see again.

He gave a long, low, piteous cry, half-whine, half-howl, and then I listened for Crystallina's voice. It was not long in coming.

"Farewell, dear Bulger; farewell, dear Sebastian! Crystallina will never forget you until her poor heart with the speck in it runs down and the Crystal Throne knows her no more." Poor Bulger! It now became my turn to tear him from this spot, for Crystallina's voice, sounding thus unexpectedly in his ears, had aroused all the deep affection which he had so ruthlessly smothered in order to bring his little master to his senses and free him from the charm of Crystallina's grace and beauty. But in vain. All my strength, all my entreaties, were powerless to move him from the place.

Evidently Crystallina had heard me pleading with Bulger and had imagined that now I would waver and stand irresolute.

"Heed dear Bulger's prayer, O beloved," she pleaded, "and turn back, turn back to thy disconsolate Crystallina, whom thou madest so happy for a brief moment! Turn back! Oh, turn back!" Bulger now began to whine and cry most piteously. I felt that something must be done at once, or the most direful consequences might ensue—that Bulger, crazed by the sweet tones of Crystallina's voice, might break away from me and dart away in mad race back to the city of the Mikkamenkies, back to the fair young queen of the Crystal Throne.

It became necessary for me to resort to trick and artifice to save my dear little brother from his own loving heart. Drawing his head up against my body and covering his eyes with my left arm, I quickly unloosened my neckerchief, and thrusting it into this wonderful speaking-tube closed it effectively.

And thus I saved my faithful Bulger from himself, thus I closed his ears to the music of Crystallina's voice; but it was not until after a good hour's waiting that he could bring himself to believe that his beloved friend would speak no more.

After several hours more of journeying along the Marble Highway a speck of light caught my eye, far on ahead, and I redoubled my pace to reach it quickly. I was soon rewarded for my trouble by entering a wonderful chamber, circular in form, with a domed roof. In the centre of this fair temple of the underground world sprang a glorious fountain with a mighty rush of waters which brought with them such a phosphorescence that this vast round chamber was lighted up with a pale yellow light in which the countless crystals of the roof and sides sparkled magnificently.

Here we passed the night, or what I called the night, refreshing ourselves with food which I had brought from the Kingdom of the Mikkamenkies, and drinking and bathing in the wonderful fountain which leaped into the air with a rush and a whir, and filled it with a strange and fitful radiance. Upon awaking both Bulger and I felt greatly refreshed both in body and mind, and we made haste to seek out the lofty portal opening upon the Marble Highway, and were soon trudging along it again. Hour after hour we kept on our feet, for something told me that we could not be far away from the confines of some other domain of this World within a World; and this inward prompting of mine proved to be correct, for Bulger suddenly gave a joyful bark and began to caper about as much as to say,—

"O little master, if thou only hadst my keen scent, thou wouldst know that we are drawing near to human habitations of some kind!"

Sure enough, in a few moments a faint light came creeping in beneath the mighty arches of the broad corridor, and every instant it gathered in strength until now I could see clearly about me, and then all of a sudden I caught sight of the source of this shy and unsteady light. There in front of me towered two gigantic candelabra of carved and chased and polished silver, both crowned with a hundred lights, one on each side of the Marble Highway—not the dull, soft flames of oil or wax, but the white tongues of fire produced by ignited gas escaping from the chemist's retort.

It was marvellous, it was magnificent, and I stood looking up at these great clusters of tongues of flames, spellbound by the glorious illumination thus set in silent majesty at this gateway to some city of the under World.

Bulger's warning growl brought me to myself, but I must end this chapter here, dear friends, and halt to collect my thoughts before I proceed to tell you what I saw after passing this glorious gateway illumined by these two gigantic candelabra of solid silver.

CHAPTER XV

O great Don Fum, Master of all Masters, what do I not owe thee for having made known unto me the existence of this wonderful World within a World! Would that I had been a worker in metal! I would not have passed the glorious portal at which I had halted without having set in deep intaglio upon its silver columns the full name of the most glorious scholar whom the world has ever known. Bulger had warned me that this gateway was guarded, and therefore I entered it cautiously, taking care to peer into the dark corners lest I might be a target for some invisible enemy to hurl a weapon at.

No sooner had I passed the gateway than three curious little beings of about my own height threw themselves swiftly and silently across the pathway. They wore short jackets, knee-breeches, and leggings reaching to their ankles, but no hats or shoes, and their clothes were profusely decorated with beautiful silver buttons.

Their hands and feet and heads seemed much too large for their little bodies and pipe-stemmy legs, and gave them an uncanny and brownie look, which was greatly increased by the staring and glassy expression of their large, round eyes. When I first caught sight of them they had hold of hands, but now they stood each with his pair stretched out toward Bulger and me, waving them strangely in the air and agitating their long fingers as if they were endeavoring to set a spell upon us.

I imagined that I could feel a sensation of drowsiness creeping over me and made haste to call out:—

"Nay, good people, do not strive to set a spell upon me. I am the illustrious explorer from the upper world,—Sebastian von Troomp,—and come to you with most peaceful intent."

But they paid no heed to my words, merely advancing a few inches and with outstretched hands continued to beat and claw the air, pausing only to signal to each other by touching each other's hands or different parts of each other's bodies. I was deeply perplexed by their actions, and took a step or two forward when instantly they fell back the same distance.

"All men are brothers," I exclaimed in a loud tone, "and carry the same shaped hearts in their breasts. Why do you fear me? You are thrice my number and in your own home. I pray you stand fast and speak to me!"

As I was pronouncing these words, they kept jerking their heads back as if the sound of my voice were smiting them in the face. It was very strange. Suddenly one of them drew from his pocket a ball of silken cord, and, deftly unrolling it, tossed one end toward me. It flew directly towards me, for its end was weighed with a thin disk of polished silver, as was the end retained in the hand of the thrower. His next move was to open his jacket and apparently press his disk against his bare body right over his heart. I made haste to do the same with mine, holding it firmly in place. This done, he retreated a step or two until the silken cord had been drawn quite taut. Then he paused and stood for several instants without moving a muscle, after which he passed the disk to one of his companions, who, having pressed it against his heart in turn, passed it to the third of the group.

With the quickness of thought the truth now burst upon me: The three brownie-like creatures in front of me were not only blind, but they were deaf and dumb. The one sense upon which they relied, and which in them was of most marvellous keenness, was the sense of feeling. The strange motions of their hands and fingers, so much like the beating and waving of an insect's feelers, were simply to intercept and measure the vibrations of the air set in motion by the movements of my body. Their large round eyes, too, had but the sense of feeling, but so wondrously acute was it that it was almost like the power of sight, enabling them by the vibration of the air upon the balls to tell exactly how near a moving object is to them. Their purpose in throwing the silken cord and silver disk to me was by measuring the beating of my heart and comparing it with their own to determine whether I was human like them.

Judge of my astonishment, dear friends, upon seeing one of their number point to the silver disk and, by means of sign-language, give me to understand that they wanted to feel the heart of the living creature in my company.

Stooping down, I hastened to gratify their curiosity by applying it over my dear Bulger's heart.

At once there was an expression of most comical amazement depicted on their faces as they passed the disk from one to the other and pressed it against different parts of their bodies—now against their breasts, now against their cheeks, and even against their closed eyelids. Of course I knew that their amazement proceeded from the rapid beating of Bulger's heart, and I enjoyed their child-like surprise very much. All expression of fear now vanished from their faces, and I was delighted with the look of sweet temper and good humor that played about their features, now wreathed in smiles.

Slowly and on tip-toe they drew near to Bulger and me and for several minutes amused themselves mightily by running their long, flexible fingers hither and thither over our bodies.

It did not take them long to discover that I was to all intents and purpose a creature of their own kind, but not so with Bulger. Their round faces became seamed and lined with wonder as they made themselves acquainted with his, to them, strange build, and ever and anon as they felt him over would they pause and in lightning-like motions of their fingers on each other's hands and arms and faces exchange thoughts as to the wonderful being which had entered the portal of their city.

No doubt you are dying of impatience, dear friends, to be told something more definite concerning these strange people among whom I had fallen. Well, know, then, that their existence had been darkly hinted at in the manuscript of the Great Master, Don Fum. I say darkly hinted at, for you must bear in mind that Don Fum never visited this World within a World; that his wonderful wisdom enabled him to reason it all out without seeing it, just as the great naturalists of our day, upon finding a single tooth belonging to some gigantic creature which lived thousands of years ago, are able to draw complete pictures of him.

Well, these curious beings whose city Bulger and I had entered are called by two different names in Don Fum's wonderful book. In some places he speaks of them as the Soodopsies, or Make-believe Eyes, and in others as the Formifolk or Ant People. Either name was most appropriate, their large, round, clear eyes being really make-believe ones, for, as I have told you, they had absolutely no sense of sight; while on the other hand, the fact that they were deaf, dumb, and blind, and lived in underground homes, made them well entitled to the name of Ant People. In a few moments the three Soodopsies had succeeded in teaching me the main principles of their pressure-language, so that I was, to their great delight, enabled to answer a number of their questions.

But think not, dear friends, that these very wise and active little folk, skilled in so many arts, have no other language than one consisting of pressures of different degree, made by their finger-tips upon each other's bodies. They had a most beautiful language, so rich that they were able to express the most difficult thoughts, to give utterance to the most varied emotions; in short, a language quite the equal of ours in all respects save one—it contained absolutely no word that could give them the faintest notion what color was. This is not to be wondered at, for they themselves neither had nor could have even the faintest conception of what I meant by color, so that when I attempted to make them understand that our stars were bright points in the sky, they asked me if they would prick my finger if I should press upon one of them. But you doubtless are anxious to know how the Formifolk can possibly make use of any other language than that of pressures. Well, I will tell you. Every Soodopsy carried at his girdle a little blank-book, if I may so term it, the covers being of thin silver plates variously carved and chased as the owner's taste may prompt. The leaves of this book also consist of thin sheets of silver not much thicker than our tin-foil; also fastened to his girdle by a silken cord hangs a silver pen or, rather, a stylus. Now, when a Soodopsy wishes to say something to one of his people, something too difficult to express by pressures of the finger-tips, he simply turns over a leaf of the silver against the inside of either cover, both of which are slightly padded, and taking up his stylus proceeds to write out what he wishes to say; and this done he deftly tears the leaf out and hands it to his companion, who taking it and turning it over, runs the wonderfully sensitive tips of his fingers over the raised writing and reads it with the greatest ease; only of course he reads from right to left instead of from left to light, as it was written. So, hereafter, when I repeat my conversations with the Formifolk, you will understand how they were conducted.

CHAPTER XVI

Although thousands and thousands of years had gone by since the Formifolk had, by constant exposure to the flicker and glare of the burning gas which their ancestors had discovered and made use of to illumine their underground world, gradually lost their sense of sight, and then in consequence of the deep and awful silence that forever reigned about them had also lost their sense of hearing and naturally thereafter their power of speech, yet, marvellous to relate, they still kept within their minds dim and shadowy traditions of the upper world, and the "mighty lamp," as they called the sun, which burned for twelve hours and then went out, leaving the world in darkness until the spirits of the air could trim it again. And, strange to say, many of the unreal things of the upper world had been by the workings of their minds transformed into realities, while the realities had become the merest cobwebs of the brain. For instance, the shadows cast by our bodies in the sunlight and forever following at our heels they had come to think were actual creatures, our doubles, so to speak, and that on account of these "dancing spectres," as they called them, which dogged our footsteps for our life long, sitting like mar-joys at our feasts, it was utterly impossible for the people of the upper world to be entirely happy as they were, and it occurred to them at once that I must have such a double following at my heels, so several times they suddenly joined hands, and, forming a circle about me, gradually closed up with intent to lay hold of the dancing spectre. This they did, too, after I had assured them that what they had in mind was the mere shadow cast by a person walking in the light. But as they had absolutely no idea of the nature of light, I only had my trouble for my pains.

Nor did they give over making every now and then the most frantic and laughable efforts to catch the little dancing gentleman who, as they were bound to think, was quietly trudging along at my heels, but who, so they informed me, was far quicker in his motions than any escaping water or falling object. Finally, they held one of their silent but very excited powwows, during which the thousand lightning-like pressures and tappings which they made upon each other's bodies gave the spectator the idea that they were three deaf and dumb schoolboys engaged in a scrimmage over a bag of marbles, and then they informed me that they had resolved to permit Bulger and me to enter their city provided I would give them the word of a nobleman that I would restrain my nimble-footed double from doing them any harm.

I made them a most solemn promise that he should behave himself. Whereupon they greeted both Bulger and me as brothers, stroking our hair, patting our heads, and kissing me on the cheeks, and, what was more, they told us their names, which were Long Thumbs, Square Nose, and Shaggy Brows.

All this time I had been every now and then casting anxious glances on ahead of me, for I was dying of impatience to enter the marvellous city of the Ant People.

I say marvellous, dear friends, for though many had been the wonderful things I had seen in my lifetime in the far-away corners of the upper world, yet here was a sight which, as it gradually unfolded itself before my eyes, shackled my very heart and caused me to gasp for breath. It was with no little surprise at the very outset that I discovered that the walls and floor of the beautiful passage through which the Soodopsies were leading Bulger and me were of pure silver, the former being composed of polished panels ornamented with finely executed chasings and carvings, and the latter, as had in fact all the floors and streets and passages of the city having upon their polished surfaces slightly raised characters which I will explain later. But as one passage opened into another, and then four or more all centred in a vast circular chamber which we traversed with our three silent guides only to enter chambers and corridors of greater size and beauty, all brilliantly lighted by rows of the same glorious candelabra upholding clusters of tongues of flame—I could compare the scene to nothing save a series of magnificent ball-rooms and banquet-halls, out of which the happy guests had been suddenly driven by the deep and awful rumble of an earthquake shock, the lights having been left burning.

Now the scene began to change. Long Thumbs, who was leading the way, and in whose large palm my little hand lay completely lost, suddenly turned to the right and led me up an arched way. I saw that we were crossing a bridge over a stream as black and sluggish as Lethe itself.

But such a bridge! Never had my eye rested upon so light and airy a span, springing from bank to bank; not the plain and solid work of the stone-mason, but the fair and cunning result of the metal worker's skill, like the labor of love, delicate, yet strong, and almost too beautiful for use.

Two rows of silver lamps of exquisite workmanship crowned its gracefully arching sides, and when we stood upon its highest bend, Long Thumbs halted and wrote upon his tablet: "Now, little baron, we are about to enter the dwelling-place of our people. Thy head is large, and there is, no doubt, much of wisdom stored away in thy brain. Make such use of it as not to disturb the perfect happiness of our nation, for no doubt many of our people will be suspicious of thee, and for the first time in thousands of years a Soodopsy will lay him down to sleep, and in his dreams feel the touch of the dancing spectre of the upper world." I promised Long Thumbs that he should have no reason to be dissatisfied with me, and then making an excuse that I was a-weary, I feasted my eyes for several moments upon the glorious scene spread out before me.

It was the city of the Formifolk in all its splendor—a splendor, alas, unseen by, unknown to, the very people dwelling in it, for to them its silver walls and arches, its endless rows of glorious candelabra uplifting their countless clusters of never-dying jets of flame, its exquisitely carved and chiselled portals and gateways, its graceful chairs and settees and beds and couches and tables and lamps and basins and ewers and thousands of articles of furniture all in purest silver, hammered or wrought by the cunning hands of their ancestors while they still were possessed of the power of sight, could only be known to these, their descendants, by the sole sense of feeling.

From the lofty ceilings of corridors and archways, from the jutting ornaments of the house-fronts, from cornice and coping, from the four sides of columns, and from the corners of cupolas and minarets, here and there and everywhere hung silver lamps of more than Oriental beauty of form and finish, all with their never-dying tongues of flame sending forth a soft though unsteady light to fall upon sightless eyes!

But yet these countless flames, by the aid of which I was enabled to gaze upon the splendor of this city of silver palaces, were life if not light to the Soodopsies, for they warmed these vast subterranean depths and filled them with a deliciously soft and strangely balmy air.

And yet to think that Bulger and I were the only two living creatures to be able to look upon this scene of almost celestial beauty and radiance!

It made me sad, and plunged me into such a fit of deep abstraction that it required a second gentle tug of Long Thumbs' hand to bring me to myself.

As we crossed the bridge and entered the city proper, I was delighted to note that the streets and open squares were ornamented with hundred of statues all in solid silver, and that they represented specimens of a race of great beauty of person; and then it occurred to me how fortunate it was that the Soodopsies could not gaze upon these images of their ancestors and thus become living witnesses of their own woful falling-away from the former physical grace of their race.

Now, like human ants that they were, the Formifolk began to swarm forth from their dwellings on every side of the city, and my keen ear caught the low shuffling sound of their bare feet over the silver streets as they closed in about us, their arms flashing in the light and their faces lined with strange emotions as they learned of the arrival among them of two creatures from the upper world. They were all clad, men and women alike, in silk garments of a chestnut brown, and I at once concluded that they drew this material from the same sources as the Mikkamenkies, for, dear friends, you must not get an idea that the Formifolk were not well deserving of the name which Don Fum had bestowed upon them. They were genuine human ants and, except when sleeping, always at work.

It was true that since their blindness had come upon them they had not been able to add a single column or archway to the Silver City, but in all the ordinary concerns of life they were quite as industrious as ever, chasing, carving, chiselling, planting, weaving, knitting, and doing a thousand and one things that you and I with our two good eyes would find it hard to accomplish.

I had made known to Long Thumbs the fact that Bulger and I were both very tired and weary from our long tramp, and that we craved to have some refreshment set before us, and then to be permitted to go to rest at once, promising that after we had had several hours' good sleep we would take the greatest pleasure in being presented to the worthy inhabitants of the Silver City.

It was astonishing with what rapidity this request of mine spread from man to man. Long Thumbs made it known to two at the same time, and these two to four, and these four to eight, and these eight to sixteen, and so on. You see it wouldn't take long at that rate to tell a million.

Like magic the Formifolk disappeared from the streets, and in a sort of orderly confusion faded from my sight. Bulger and I were right glad to be conducted to a silver bed-chamber, where the traveller's every want seemed to be anticipated. The only thing that bothered us was, we had not been accustomed to keep the light burning upon going to bed, and this made us both a little wakeful at first; but we were too tired to let it keep us from dropping off after a few moments, for the mattress was soft and springy enough to satisfy any one, and I'm sure that no one could have complained that the house wasn't quiet enough.

CHAPTER XVII

I can't tell you, dear friends, exactly how long Bulger and I slept, but it must have been a good while, for when I was awakened I felt thoroughly refreshed. I say awakened, for I was awakened by a gentle tapping on the back of my hand—six taps.

At first I thought I was dreaming, but, upon rubbing my eyes, I saw standing by the side of my bed one of the Soodopsies who, feeling me stir, took up his tablet and wrote as follows:—

"My name is Tap Hard. I am a clock. There is a score of us. We keep the time for our people by counting the swing of the pendulum in the Time House. It swings about as fast as we breathe. There are one hundred breaths to a minute and one hundred minutes to an hour. Our day is divided into six hours' worktime and six hours' sleeptime. It is now the rising hour. If thou wilt be pleased to rise, one of our people from the Health House will rub all the tired out of thy limbs."

I touched Tap Hard's heart to thank him, and made haste to scramble out of bed. Now, for the first time, I looked about the silver chamber in which I had slept. On silver shelves lay silver combs and silver shears and silver knives; on a silver stand stood a silver ewer within a silver basin; on silver pegs hung silken towels, while spread upon the silver floor lay soft, silken rugs, and above and around on ceiling and walls the tongues of flame were a thousand times repeated in the panels of burnished silver.

I had made trial of all sorts of Oriental rubber and bath attendants in my day, but the silent little Soodopsy who laved and rubbed and tapped and stroked me exceeded them all in dexterity, added to which was a new charm, for I was not obliged to listen to long and senseless tales of adventure and intrigue, but was left quite alone to my own thoughts. Bulger was also treated to a sponging and a rubbing—a luxury which he had not enjoyed since we had left Castle Trump.

My toilet was no sooner completed than Long Thumbs made his appearance to inquire after my health and to superintend the serving of my breakfast, which consisted of a piece of most delicate boiled fish flanked with oysters of delicious flavor, and trimmed with slices of those monstrous mushrooms which I had eaten among the Mikkamenkies, the whole served in a beautiful silver dish on a silver tray with silver eating utensils.

Remembering the strange way in which the fish were caught and killed in the Land of the Mikkamenkies, I was curious to know how the Soodopsies managed it, for I knew enough of them to know that the sensation of anything struggling for its life in their hands would suffice to throw them into fits of great suffering, to fill their gentle hearts with nameless terror.

"At the end of one of the many corridors leading out of our city," explained Long Thumbs, "there is a rocky chamber which was called by our ancestors Uphaslok, or the Death Hole, because any being which breathes its air for a few moments is sure to die. So they closed it up forever, leaving only a small pipe projecting through the door; but, strange to say, those who breathe this air suffer no pain whatever, but presently drop off into a pleasant dream, and, unless they be rescued, would, of course, never wake again. Now, as our laws forbid us to cause any pain to the most insignificant creature, it occurred to our ancestors that by means of a long pipe they could turn this poisoned air into the river whenever they wanted a supply of fish for food. This they did, and, strange to say, the moment the fish felt the gas bubbling into the river, they at once swam up to the mouth of the pipe, and struggled with each other for a chance to catch the deadly bubbles as they left its mouth, so pleasant a sensation do they cause as they gradually plunge, the creature breathing them into his last sleep. And in this way it is we are enabled to feed upon the fish in our river, without breaking the law of the land."

I began to understand that I had fallen in with a very original and interesting folk, but Bulger was not altogether pleased with them, for several reasons, as I soon observed. In the first place he couldn't accustom himself to the cold and glassy look of their eyes, and in the next he was a bit jealous of their wonderfully keen scent—a sense which with them was so strong that they invariably gave signs of being conscious of Bulger's approach even before I could see him, and always turned their faces in the direction in which he was coming.

You will remember, dear friends, that I mentioned the fact that the Formifolk went barefoot, and that their feet as well as their hands seemed altogether too large for their bodies, and I wish to add, that while Bulger and I were being led through the long corridors and winding passages on our way into the City of

Silver, the three Soodopsies frequently half halted and seemed to be feeling on the floor for something with the balls of their feet. I thought no more about it, until Bulger and I started out for our first stroll through their wonderful town, when, to my great delight, I made the discovery that the numbers of the houses, the names of the occupants, the names of the streets, as well as all signboards, so to speak, and all guide-posts were in slightly raised letters on the floors and pavements, and then the truth dawned upon me, that Long Thumbs and his companions were simply halting now and then to read the names of the streets with the balls of their feet, in order to know if they were taking the right road.

Ay, more than this, dear friends, the first time Bulger and I passed through one of the open squares of the City of Silver, you may imagine my satisfaction upon the discovery that the silver pavements were literally covered with the writings of the Soodopsy authors in raised characters.

Now, in Don Fum's wonderful book he had, in his masterly manner, given me the key to the language of the Formifolk, so that with very slight effort I was able to make the additional discovery that some of the streets were given up to the writers of history, and some to story writers, while others were filled with the learned works of philosophers, and others still contained many thousands of lines from the best poets which the nation had produced.

And I had very little difficulty in discovering which were the favorite poems of the Soodopsies, for, as you may readily suppose, these were polished like a silver mirror by the shuffling of the many thankful feet over their sweet and soulful lines.

I noticed that the writings of the philosophers in this, as in my own world, found few readers, for the raised letters were, in many cases, tarnished and black from lack of soles trampling over them in search of wisdom.

Somewhat later, when I had become acquainted with Velvet Soles, the daughter of Long Thumbs, a gracious little being as full of inward light as she was blind to the outer world, and she invited me to "come for a read," I had a hard task of it in persuading her that I could not remove what she called my ridiculous "foot boxes" and join her in enjoying some of her favorite poems. It was to me a delicious pastime to accompany this happy little maiden when she "went for a read," to walk beside her and watch the ever-varying expression of her beautiful face as the soles of her tiny feet pressed the words of love and hope and joy, and her heart expanded, and she clasped her hands in attitudes of blissful enjoyment, seemingly just as deep and fervent as if the blessed sunlight rested on her brow, and her eyes were drinking in the glory of a summer sunset. O dwellers in the upper world with the light streaming into the windows of your souls, with your ears open to the music of pipe and flute and violin, and to the sweeter music of the voice of love, how much more have ye than she, and yet how rarely are ye as happy, how rarely do ye know that sweet contentment which, as in this case, came from within?

"Go to the ant; consider her ways, and be wise, which, having no guide, overseer, or ruler, provideth her meat in the summer and gathereth her food in the harvest."

In a short time the Formifolk seemed to become quite accustomed to having Bulger and me among them, and they apparently "touched hands" with me in quite as friendly a fashion as if I had been one of them.

One day Long Thumbs conducted me to the house of the most aged and learned of the Soodopsies, Barrel Brow by name.

He received me very cordially, although I interrupted him at his studies, for, as I entered his apartment, he was in the act of reading four different books at the same time: two were lying on the floor, and he was perusing their raised characters with the soles of his feet, and two others were set up on a frame in front of him and he was deciphering them with the tips of his fingers.

But when informed who I was he stopped work at once and taking up his tablets, asked me a number of questions concerning the upper world, of which he had, however, no very exalted opinion.

"You people," said he, "if I understand correctly the ancient writings of those of our nation who still preserved certain traditions of the upper world, are endowed with several senses which are utterly lacking in us, I am happy to say, for if I understand correctly ye have in the first place a sense which ye call hearing, a most troublesome sense, for by means of it ye are being constantly disturbed and annoyed by vibrations of the air coming from afar. Now, they can be of no possible good to you. Ye might as well have a sense that would inform you what was going on in the moon. Therefore, my conclusion is, that the sense of hearing only serves to distract and weaken the brain.

"Another sense that ye are possessed of," continued Barrel Brow, "ye call the sense of sight—a power even more useless and distracting than hearing, for the reason that it enables you to know things which it is utterly bootless to know, such as what your next door neighbors may be doing, how the mountains are acting on the other side of your rivers, how your sky, as ye call it, might feel if you could touch it with your fingers, which ye can't do, however; how soon rain will fall, which is a useless piece of knowledge if ye have roofs to cover you, as I suppose ye have; but the most ridiculous use which ye make of this sense of sight is the manufacture of what ye call pictures, by means of which ye seem to take the greatest pleasure in deceiving this very sense of which ye are so very proud. If I understand correctly these pictures, if felt of, are quite as smooth as that panel there, but so cunningly do ye draw the lines and lay in the colors, whatever they may be, that ye really succeed in deceiving yourselves and stand for hours in front of one of these bits of trickery when ye might, if ye chose, feast your eyes, as ye call it, upon the very thing which the trickster has imitated. Now, as life is much shorter in the upper world than in ours, it seems very strange to me that ye should wish to waste it in this foolish manner. Then, there is another thing, little baron," continued the learned Barrel Brow, "which I wish to mention. It is this: The people of the upper world pride themselves very much upon what they term the power of speech, which, if I understand correctly, is a faculty they have of expressing their thoughts to each other by violently expelling the air from their lungs, and that this air, rushing into the ventilators of the brain, which ye call ears, produces a sensation of sound as ye term it, and in this way one of thy people standing at one end of the town might make his wishes known to another standing at the other end. Now, thou wilt pardon my thinking so, little baron, but this seems to me to be not a whit above the brute creature, which, opening its vast jaws, thus sets the air in motion in calling its young or breathing defiance at an enemy. And if I understand correctly, little baron, so proud are thy people of this power of speech that they insist upon making use of it at all times and upon all occasions, and, strange to say, these 'talkers' can always find plenty of people to open their ears to these vibrations of the air, although the effect is so wearying to the brain that in the end they invariably fall asleep. But if I understand correctly, the women are even fonder of displaying their skill in thus puffing out the air from their lungs than the men are; but, that not satisfied with this superior power of puffing out the words, they actually have recourse to a potent herb which they steep in boiling water and drink as hot as possible on account of its effect in loosening the tongue and allowing the talker to do more puffing than she could otherwise.

"But all this, little baron," continued the learned Barrel Brow, "might be overlooked and regarded in the light of mere amusement were it not for the fact, if I understand correctly, that brain ventilators being of different sizes in different persons, the consequence is that these puffs of air which ye use to make known your thoughts to each other produce different effects upon different persons, and the result is, that the people of the upper world spend half their time repeating the puffs which they have already sent out, and that even then thou canst rarely find two people who will agree exactly as to the number, kind, strength, and meaning of the puffs blown into each other's brain ventilators, and that therefore has it become necessary to provide what ye call judges to settle these disputes which often last for lifetimes, the two parties spending their entire fortunes hiring witnesses to come before these judges and imitate the sound which the air made when it was set in motion years ago by the angry puffs of the two parties. I sincerely trust, little baron," wrote the learned Barrel Brow on his tablet of silver, "that when thou returnest to thy people thou wilt make known to them what I have written for thee to-day, for it is never too late to correct a fault, and the longer that fault has lasted the greater the credit for correcting it."

I promised the learned Soodopsy to do as he requested, and then we touched each other on the back of the head, which is the way they say good-by in the land of the Formifolk, a touch on the forehead meaning, "How d'ye do?"

CHAPTER XVIII

And, no doubt, dear friends, you would be glad to hear something about the early history of the Soodopsies: who they were, where they came from, and how they happened to find their way down into the World within a World.

At least, this was the way I felt after I had been presented to the learned Barrel Brow, and so the next time I called upon him I waited patiently for him to finish reading the four books in front of him, and then I said,—

"Be pleased, dear Master, to tell me something concerning the early history of thy people, and to explain to me how they came to make their way down into this underground world."

"Ages and ages ago," wrote the learned Barrel Brow, "my people lived upon the shores of a beautiful land with a vast ocean to the north of it, and in those days they had the same senses as the other people of the upper world. It was a very fair land, indeed, so fair that, in the words of the ancient chronicles, the sun looked in vain for a fairer. Its rivers were deep and broad, its plains were rich and fertile, and its mountains stored full of silver and gold and copper and tin, and so easily mined were these metals that our people became famous as metal workers; so deft in their workmanship that the other nations from far and near came to us for swords and shields and spear heads and suits of armor and table service and armlets and bracelets and, above all, for lamps most gloriously chased and carved to hang in their palaces and temples. And so we were very happy, until one terrible day the great round world gave a twist and we were turned away from the sun, so that its rays went slantingly over our heads and gave us no warmth.

"Ah me, I could weep now," exclaimed the learned Barrel Brow, "after all these centuries, when I think of the cruel fate that overtook my people. In a few months the whole face of our fair land was covered with ice and snow, and our cattle died, and many of our people, too, before they could weave thick cloth to keep their delicate bodies from the pinching cold. But this was not all; the great blue ocean which had until then dashed its warm waves and white foam up against our shores now breathed its icy breath full upon us, driving into our cellars to escape its fury; and in a few brief months, to our horror, there came drifting down upon us fields and mountains of ice, which the tempestuous waters cast up against our shores with deafening crash. To remain there meant death, swift and terrible, so the command was given to abandon homes and firesides and escape to the southward, and this most of them did. But it so happened that several hundred families belonging to the metal-working guilds, who knew the underground passages to the mines as foresters know the pathless wood, had taken refuge in the vast underground caverns with all the goods they could carry. Poor deluded creatures! they thought that this sudden coming of the winter blast, of the blinding snow and vast floating fields of ice, was but a freak of nature, and that in a few months the old warmth and the old sunshine would come back again.

"Alas, months went by and their supply of food was almost exhausted and the entrances to the mines were closed by gigantic blocks of ice cemented into one great mass by the snow which the gray clouds had sifted down upon them. There was now no escape that way. Their only hope was to make their way underground to some portal to the upper world.

"So, with lighted torches but with hearts plunged in the darkness of despair, they kept on their way, when one day, or one night, they knew not which, their leaders suddenly came upon a broad street of marble opened by nature's own hands. It was skirted by a softly flowing river that swarmed with fish in scales and shells and skin, and here our people halted to eat and drink and rest, and while one of their number was striking his flint on one occasion to make a fire to cook a meal, to his surprise and delight a tongue of flame darted up from the rocky floor and continued to burn, giving light and warmth to them.

"As they had brought their tools—their drills and chisels and files and gravers and blow-pipes—with them in their carts and wagons, they made haste to fit a pipe to this opening in the rock and set up a cluster of lights. With food and water and warmth and light their hearts grew lighter, especially as they soon discovered that in many of the vast caverns gigantic mushrooms grew in the wildest profusion.

"The wisest of them," continued the learned Barrel Brow, "at once made up their minds that there must be reservoirs of this gas farther along on this beautiful Marble Highway, so, day by day, they pushed farther into this World within a World, halting every now and then to set up a lighthouse as they called it.

"After advancing several leagues the exploring party, upon lighting a cluster of gas jets, were stricken almost speechless with wonder at finding themselves upon the very sill of a towering portal opening into a succession of vast chambers, some with flat ceiling, some arched, some domed, upon the floors and walls of which lay and hung inexhaustible quantities of pure silver. Those magnificent caverns were in reality nature's vast storehouses of the glorious white metal, and our people made haste to set up clusters of gas jets here and there, so that they might view the wondrous treasure-house.

"Here they determined to remain, for here was food and water in never-failing supplies, and here they would have light and warmth, and here they could forget their miseries by working at their calling, using the precious metal with lavish hand to build them living-chambers, and to fashion the thousand and one things necessary for every-day life. So great was their delight as metal-workers to come upon this exhaustless supply of pure silver that they could hardly sleep until they had set up clusters of gas jets throughout these vast caverns, for, no doubt, little baron, thou hast already guessed that this is the spot I am telling thee of; that right here it was where our people halted to build the City of Silver.

"But one thought troubled them and that was where to find needful clothing, for the old was fast falling into shreds and tatters, when, to their delight, they came upon a bed of mineral wool and with this they managed to weave some cloth. Although it was rather stiff and harsh, yet it was better than none.

"While exploring a new cavern onc day, one of my wise ancestors saw a large night moth alight near him, and, gently loosening some of its eggs, he carried them home, more as a curiosity than aught else.

"Imagine how rejoiced he was, however, to see one of the worms which hatched out set to work spinning a cocoon of silk half as big as his fist. There was great feasting and merry-making among our people upon hearing of this glad news, and it was not very long before many a silver shuttle was rattling in a silver loom, and the soft bodies of our people were warmly and comfortably clad. Now, long periods of time went by, which, cut up into your months, would have made many, many years. Our people had everything but sunlight, and this, of course, those who were born in the under world knew nothing about and therefore did not miss.

"But, as was to be expected, great changes gradually took place in our people. To their inexpressible grief, they noticed that as they busied themselves beautifying their new homes by erecting arches and bridges and terraces, and lining them with glorious candelabra and statues, all in cast and wrought or hammered silver, their sight was gradually failing them, and that in not a very great length of time they should be totally blind.

"This result, little baron," continued the learned Barrel Brow, "was very natural, for the sense of sight was in reality created for sunlight; for as thou no doubt knowest, all the fish that swim in our rivers have no eyes, having no need of them. It happened just as they had expected—in a few generations more our people discovered that their eyes could no longer see things as thou dost, but yet they could feel them if they were not too far away, just as I can feel thy presence now and tell where thou sittest, and how tall thou art, and how broad thou art, and whether thou movest to right or left, forward or backward, but I cannot tell exactly how thou art made until I reach out and touch thee; then I know all; yes, far better than thou canst know, for our sense of feeling is keener than thy so-called sight. One of my people can feel a grain or roughness upon a silver mirror which to thy eyes seems smoother than glass. Well, strange to relate, and yet not strange, our ancestors with the going-out of their sense of sight also felt their sense of hearing on the wane. Our ears, as thou callest them, having nothing more to listen to, for eternal silence, as thou knowest, reigns in this under world, became as useless to us as the tail of the pollywog would be to the full-grown frog; and of course with the loss of our sense of hearing our children were soon unable to learn to talk, and in a certain lapse of time we came to merit full well our new name of Formifolk, or Ant People, for we were now blind and deaf and dumb.

"It is long, very, very long, little baron," continued the learned Soodopsy, "since all recollection of sunlight, of color, of sound, died out of our minds. To-day my people don't even know the names of these things, and thou wouldst have as much chance of success wert thou to attempt to tell them what light or sound is as thou wouldst have if thou shouldst try to explain to a savage that there is nothing under the world to hold it up, and yet it doesn't fall. But if thou shouldst lay several pieces of metal in a row and ask one of my people to tell thee what they were, he would try the weight of each and feel its grain carefully, possibly smell them or touch his tongue to them, and then he would make answer: 'That is gold; that is silver; that is copper; that is lead; that is tin; that is iron.'

"But thou wouldst say, 'They all are differently colored; canst not perceive that?'

"'I know not what thou meanest by color,' he would reply. 'But mark me: now I hide them all beneath this silken kerchief, and still by touching them with my finger tips I can tell what metal each one is. If thou canst do it, then art thou as good a man as I.'

"What sayest now, little baron?" asked the learned Barrel Brow, while his face was wreathed in a smile of triumph; "dost think thou wouldst be as good a man as this Soodopsy?"

"Nay, indeed I do not, wise Master," wrote I upon my silver tablet; "and I thank thee for all thou has told me and taught me, and I ask leave, O Barrel Brow, to come again and converse with thee."

"That thou mayest, little baron," traced the learned Soodopsy upon his silver tablet; and then as I turned to leave his chamber he reached quickly after me and touched me with a bent forefinger, which meant return.

"Thy pardon, little baron," he wrote, "but thou art leaving my study without thy faithful Bulger; am I not right?"

I was astounded, for indeed he was right, and though without the sense of sight he had seen more than I with two good eyes wide open. There lay Bulger fast asleep on a silken-covered hassock.

Our silent conversation had so wearied him that he had sailed off into the Land of Nod on the wings of a dream.

He hung his head and looked very shame-faced when my call aroused him and he discovered that I had actually reached the doorway without his knowing it.

CHAPTER XIX

The longer I stayed among the Soodopsies the more did I become convinced that they were the happiest, the lightest hearted, the most contented human beings that I had met in all my travels. If it were possible for the links of a long chain suspended over a chasm to be living, thinking beings for a short while, it seems to me they would hang together in the most perfect accord, for each link would discover that he was no better than his neighbor, and that the welfare of all the other links depended upon him and his upon theirs. So it was with the Formifolk, having no sense of sight they knew no such thing as envy, and all hands were alike when reached out for a greeting.

I was amazed at times to see how they could feel my approach when I would be ten or fifteen feet away from them, and I often amused myself by trying to steal by one of them in the street. But no, it was impossible; a hand would invariably be held out for a greeting. Little by little, they got over their distrust of me, and made up their minds that I had told them the truth when I said that no dancing spectre was forever following at my heels. One of the most interesting sights was to see a group of Soodopsy children at play, building houses with silver blocks, or playing a game very much like our dominoes. I noticed that they kept no tally, such wonderful memories had they that it was quite unnecessary.

At first the children were so frightened upon feeling of me that they fled with terror pictured upon their little faces. Their parents explained to me that I made very much the same impression upon them as if I should feel of a person whose skin was as rough as a sea urchin's.

When at last I succeeded in coaxing several of them to my side, I was astounded to see one little fellow who had by chance pressed his tiny hand against my watch pocket spring away from me terror-stricken. He had felt it tick and didn't stop running until he had reached his mother's side.

His wonderful tale that the little baron carried some strange animal around in his pocket soon caused a crowd to collect about me, and it was some time before I could persuade even the parents that the watch was not alive and that it was not the little animal's heart which they felt beating.

On one occasion, when a little Soodopsy was sitting on my lap with its tiny arm twined affectionately around my neck, I happened to make some remark to Bulger, when, to my amazement, the child sprang out of my arms and darted away with a look of terror upon his little face.

What had I done to him?

Why, it seems that by the merest chance his tiny hand had been pressed against my throat, and that he had been terrified by feeling the strange vibration caused by my voice. Immediately the report was spread about that the little baron carried another little baron around in his throat, that any one could feel him, if I would only consent. It took me a long while to convince them that what they felt was not another little baron, but merely the vibration caused by my expelling my breath in a way peculiar to the people of the upper world. But all the same, I was obliged to say many hundreds of useless things to Bulger in order to give their little hands a chance to feel something so wonderful.

From the little I have told you about the names of the Formifolk, dear friends, you have no doubt understood that their names took their rise from some physical quality, defect, or peculiarity. Besides the names I have already mentioned, I remember Sharp Chin, Long Nose, Silk Ears, Smooth Palms, Big Knuckle, Nail Off, Hammer Fist, Soft Touch, Hole-in-Cheek, or Hole-in-chin (Dimple), Crooked Hair (Cowlick), and so on, and so on.

But, to my amazement, one day, when asking the name of a young girl whose long and delicate fingers had attracted my attention, I was informed that her name was Singing Fingers, or, possibly, I might translate it Music Fingers.

I had noticed that the Soodopsies had some idea of music, for the children often amused themselves dancing, and, while so engaged, beat time with their finger tips on each other's cheeks or foreheads.

But I was completely in the dark as to what they meant by Singing Fingers, or why the young girl should have been so named; hence was I greatly pleased to hear the maiden's mother ask me whether I would like to feel one of her daughter's songs, as she termed it. Upon my acquiescing, the mother approached me and proceeded to roll up the sleeves of my coat until she had laid my arms bare to the elbow, then she took my arms and clasped them across my breast one above the other.

Bulger watched the proceeding with somewhat of displeasure in his eyes; he had half an idea that these silent people might play some hurtful trick upon his little master. But my smile soon disarmed his suspicion.

Singing Fingers now drew near, and as her sweet face with its sightless eyes turned full upon me I could hardly keep back the tears.

And yet, why grieve for any one who seemed to be so perfectly happy? A smile played around her dainty little mouth, disclosing her tiny silvery white teeth like so many real pearls, and her bosom rose and fell quickly, sending forth a faint breathing sound. She looked so like a radiant child of some other world that before I thought, I cried out,—

"Speak, Oh, speak, beautiful child!"

In an instant she drew back affrighted, for the sudden vibration of the air had startled her; but I reached out and touched her hand to give her to understand that she need fear nothing, and then she drew near to me again. Suddenly her beautiful hands with their long, frail, delicate fingers were lifted into the air, and she began to sway her body and to wave her hands in gentle and graceful motions as if keeping time with some music. Gradually she drew nearer to me, and ever and anon her silken finger tips touched my hands or arms as if they were a keyboard and she was about to begin to execute a soft and dainty bit of music; and I noticed that her fingers had some delightful perfume upon them. Now fast and faster the gentle taps rain upon me with rhythmic regularity. They soothe me, they thrill me, they reach my heart as if they were the sweet notes of a flute or the soft tones of a singer's voice. The maiden is really singing to me! It seems to me that I can understand what she is saying, or, rather, thinking, as her dainty finger tips fairly fly hither and thither, and I can hear her low breathing grow louder and louder. Suddenly she leaves my hands and arms and I feel her gentle tapping on my cheeks and brow. So gently, Oh, so gently and soothingly her fingers touch me that at last they feel like rose leaves dragged across my face. The sensation is so delightful, so like the soft touch of sleep to weary eyes, that I drop off in good earnest, and when, after a moment or so, I opened my eyes there sat the smiling Formifolk waiting for me to awake, and there stood the radiant-visaged Singing Fingers in front of me, child-like, waiting to be commended.

And so you see, dear friends, that it is not so hard to be happy after all if you only set about it in the right way. The Formifolk seemed to have set about it in the right way, judging by results, and they arc the only things we have to judge

by. Some men will fish all day and not have a bite, and some people will try their
whole lives to catch happiness and not get any more than a nibble. They don't use
the right kind of bait. Let 'em try a kind act, a live one.

There was something I wanted to ask of the learned Barrel Brow, so the next
call I made on him I put this question to him:—

"Is it possible, learned Master, that thy people have absolutely no guide, no
overseer, no rulers?"

The great scholar of the Formifolk ceased reading the four books which lay
opened before him—one under each hand and one under each foot—as I handed
him my silver tablet.

"Little baron," was his reply, "if there were only a bramble bush big enough for
all you people of the upper world to jump into and if you could only get rid of
your ears too, you would soon be rid of your rulers who oppress you, who prey
upon you; for no one would have any desire to be a ruler if there was no one left
to look at him and if he couldn't hear what the flatterers said about him. Vanity
is the soil that rulers spring from, as the mushrooms spring from the rich loam
of our dark caverns. They pretend that it is the exercise of power that they are so
fond of. Believe them not. It is the gratification of their vanity and nothing else.

"If it were only in thy power to say to every man who itched to be a ruler,—

"'Well and good, brother, a ruler thou shalt be; but bear in mind, weak man, that
when thou hast donned thy gaudy uniform and mounted thy gayly caparisoned
steed, when thou ridest at the head of troop and cavalcade with ten thousand
armed men following thee on foot, as slaves their master, and the plaudits of the
foolish multitude rend the air, no eye shall witness the splendor of thy triumph,
no ear catch a sound of the deafening cheers,' take my word for it, little baron, no
one would want to be a ruler any more.

"Where there are no rulers, little baron," continued the learned Barrel Brow,
"there can be no followers; where there are no followers, there will be no
quarrelling. When it becomes necessary in our nation we form the Great Circle
for deliberation. Each man writes out what he thinks on his tablet. Then the
opinions are read and counted and the majority rules. But we form the Great
Circle only in times of urgent need. Generally speaking, the smaller circles answer
all the purposes; in fact, the family circle is in most cases quite sufficient."

I touched first Barrel Brow's heart in token of my gratitude for the many things
which he had taught me, and then the back of his head to bid him good-night.
You may imagine his and my delight, dear friends, when the wise Bulger raised
himself upon his hind legs, and with his right paw also thanked the learned Barrel
Brow, and then bade him good-night by a light tap on the back of his head.

"Fortunate the traveller," wrote the learned Soodopsy, "attended by so wise and
watchful a companion! True, like a child, he goes on all fours, but by so doing
he brings his heart and his brains on the same level—the only way for a man
to wear them if he would do his fellow-creatures any good. The trouble with
thy people in the upper world, little baron, is that they think too much. They

clasp minds instead of clasping hands; they send messengers with gifts instead of giving themselves. They hire people to dance for them, to sing for them, to be merry for them. They will not be satisfied until they have hired people to help them be sorry, to whom they may say, 'My friend is dead; I loved him. Weep three whole days for him.'"

CHAPTER XX

'Twas the custom in the City of Silver to "touch all around," as it was called, before going to rest. The "touch all around" began in a certain quarter of the city and passed with wonderful rapidity from man to man. Exactly how it was done I never could understand, but the purpose of the mysterious signalling was to make an actual count of all the Formifolk. If a single one were missing, it would be most surely discovered by the time the "touch all around" had been completed. It proceeded with lightning-like rapidity throughout the city, and then, if no return signal was made, the people knew that everyone was in his proper place; that no Soodopsy had lost his way or fallen ill in some unfrequented passage.

I don't think that I had more than dropped off to sleep when I was aroused by Bulger's gentle tugging at my sleeve. Rubbing my eyes, I sat up in bed and listened. Instantly my ear caught that faint, shuffling sound which was always perceptible when any number of the Formifolk were hurrying hither and thither over the polished silver pavement.

I sprang out of bed and rushed to the door, Bulger close at my heels. What a strange sight confronted me! I could compare it to nothing save to the appearance of a large ant hill when some mischievous boy suddenly drops a stone among the crowd of petty, patient, plodding people peacefully pursuing their work.

In an instant all is changed: lines are broken, workmen jostle workmen, order becomes disorder, regularity is changed to confusion. Hither and thither the affrighted creatures rush with waving feelers, seeking for the cause of the mad outburst of terror.

So it was with the Formifolk as I looked out upon them. With outstretched hands and tremulously moving fingers they rushed from side to side, jostling and bumping one another, while a nameless dread was depicted upon their upturned faces. Anon a group would halt, join hands, and begin to exchange thoughts by lightning-like pressures, tappings, and strokes, when others would dash against them, break them apart, and confusion would reign greater than ever.

But gradually I noted that some sort of order seemed to be coming out of the movements of this mad throng. Here and there groups of three and four would form and clasp hands, then these smaller circles would break and form into larger ones, and I noted too that this ever-increasing circle was formed on the outside of the panic-stricken crowd, and as it grew it shut them in so that when a fleeing Soodopsy hurtled up against this steady line, his terror left him at once and he took his place in it. In a few moments the madly pushing, jostling throng had disappeared entirely and the whole city was girt round about by these long, steady lines.

The Great Circle had been formed.

After half an hour the deliberation was completed, and, to my surprise, the Great Circle broke up into squads and companies of fours and sixes and tens, and then each disappeared slowly and steadily with lock step, passing out of the City into the dark or only partially lighted chambers and passages that surrounded it. The search for the missing Soodopsy had been begun.

It was hours before the last squad had returned to the square and the Great Circle had been formed again. Alas! the news was sad indeed. There came no tidings of the missing man. He was lost forever; and with clasped hands and slow and heavy step the grieving Formifolk made their way back to their homes, where the sighing women and children were awaiting their coming. As Bulger and I went back to bed again, it almost seemed to me as if I could hear at times the deep and long-drawn sighs that escaped from the gentle breasts of the sorrowing Soodopsies. I noticed a very touching thing on the following day. It was that every man, woman, and child in the City of Silver grieved for the lost Soodopsy as if he were actually brother to each of them. Love was not as with us, in the upper world, a thing bestowed upon those in whom we see our own faces repeated and in whose voices we heard our own ring out again, sweet and clear as in our childhood; in other words, a love almost of our very selves. Oh, no! while it was true that a mother's touch was most tender to her own child, yet no little hand stretched out to her went without its caress. She was mother to them all; to her they were all beautiful, and as their little frocks were all woven in the same loom, there never could come into her mind a temptation to feel whether a rich neighbor's child was playing with hers, and that therefore it ought to receive a more loving caress. In that portion of the city where the children had their playgrounds the silver pavement was in some places marked off with raised lines and letters, something after the manner of our hop scotch, for the purpose of a game which was very popular with the little Soodopsies. Its name is hard to translate, but it meant something like "Little Bogyman," and many an hour had Bulger and I stood there watching these silent little gnomes at play, fascinated by the wonderful skill which they would display in feigning the drawing near of the Little Bogyman, their hiding from him, his stealthy approach, the increasing danger, the attack, the escape, the new dangers, wild flight, and mad pursuit. Fancy, therefore, my astonishment one morning to note that Bulger was coaxing me thither, although the place was quite deserted, the children being all at their lessons.

But, as it was a rule of mine always to humor Bulger's whims, I went patiently along.

In a moment, as we came to the spot where the pavement was marked off and inscribed as I have explained, he halted and with an anxious whine began to play the game of "The Little Bogyman," turning every now and then to see what effect his actions had upon me.

He made no mistakes. As he entered each compartment, he rested his paw upon the raised letters as he had so often seen the children do with their little bare feet, and then mimicked with wonderful fidelity their actions, beginning with the first scent of danger and ending with mad terror at the close pursuit of the bogyman.

I was more than surprised; I was bewildered by this piece of mimicry on Bulger's part. To my mind it boded some terrible accident to him, for I have a superstitious notion that great danger to an animal's life gives him for the moment an almost human intelligence. It is nature caring for her own.

But all of a sudden the real truth in this case burst upon me: it was not my dear little brother giving me to understand that some peril was threatening him, but that some danger was hanging over my head, the more real in that it was unseen and unsuspected by me.

I called him to me and rewarded him with a caress. He was overjoyed to note that I had apparently understood him. I now made haste to seek out Barrel Brow. He was surprised to feel my salutation. In a moment or so I had told him all. Nor was he slow in detecting my excitement. He, no doubt, felt that in the changed character of my handwriting.

"Calm thyself, little baron," he wrote. "The wise Bulger has told thee the truth. Thy life is in danger. I had resolved to send for thee this very day to warn thee of it: to bid thee quit the land of the Formifolk in all haste, for the notion has spread among our people that it was the dancing spectre at thy heels which caused the death of the gentle Pouting Lip, who disappeared so mysteriously the other day. I therefore counsel thee that thou make ready at once and quit our city to-morrow before the clocks rouse the people from their sleep."

I thanked Barrel Brow, and promised that I would heed his advice, although I confessed to him that I would fain have bided a few weeks longer, there were so many things in and about the wonderful City of Silver that I had not seen. But I owed it to the dear hearts of my own world to take the best care of my life, insignificant though it might appear to me.

Then, again, I felt that it would be madness to attempt to reason with the Soodopsies. To them the dancing spectre at my heels was a real being of flesh and blood, although they had not been able to seize him, and it was really natural for them to suspect that we had made away with Pouting Lip.

Calling out to Bulger to follow me, I left Barrel Brow's home, resolved to make one more round of the wonderful city, and then pack up some food and clothing and be all ready for a start before the clocks began their tapping.

I should explain, dear friends, that, as happens in all cities, the people of this one imagined at times that they hadn't quite elbow room enough, and hence they surveyed other chambers, and set up new candelabra within them, in order to chase the cold and dampness away, and make them fit for human habitations.

In the last one which they had in this way annexed to their fair city, fitting it with a silver doorway and tiling the floor with polished plates of the same beautiful metal, they had discovered a hard mound apparently of rock in one corner, and had resolved that they would come some day with their drills and picks and begin the task of removing this mound.

A strange inclination came upon me to visit this new chamber in order to inspect the work of these eyeless workmen, and see how far they had proceeded with their task of transforming a cold and rocky vault into a bright, warm, healthy habitation.

Imagine my surprise to hear Bulger utter a low growl as we reached the entrance, and I put out my hand to swing the door open, for the Soodopsies were not at work there that day, and the place was as silent as a tomb.

Glancing through the grating, a sight met my gaze which caused my flesh to creep and my hair to stiffen. What think ye was it? Why, the mound in the corner was rocking and swaying, and from underneath one end issued a loud and angry hissing. I'm no coward, if I do say it myself, but this was just a little too much for ordinary or even extraordinary flesh to bear without flinching. I staggered back with a suppressed cry of horror, and was upon the point of breaking into a mad flight, when the thought flashed through my mind that the door was securely fastened, and that there would be no danger in my taking another look at the terrible monster thus caged in this chamber.

A great snake-like head was now lifted from beneath one edge of the mound, on the end of a long, swaying neck. Its great round eyes, big as an ox's, stared with a dull, cold, glassy look from wall to wall, and then, with an awful outburst of hissing, the whole mound was suddenly raised upon four great legs, thick as posts, and ending in terrible claws, and borne rocking and swaying into the centre of the chamber.

What was this terrible monster, and where had it come from?

Why, I saw through it all now at a glance. It was a gigantic tortoise, eight feet long by five wide, at least, and once an inhabitant of the upper world. Thousands and thousands of years ago, by the coming of the awful fields of ice, it had been forced to fly from certain death by crawling down into these underground caverns. Here, chilled and numbed by the dampness and cold, it had fallen asleep, and would have continued to sleep on for other ages to come, had not the industrious Formifolk lighted the clusters of burning jets of gas in the monster's bedroom. Gradually the warmth had penetrated the roof of shell made thicker by earth and layers of broken rock, which the tooth of time had dropped upon it, and reached his great heart, and set it beating again slowly, very slowly, but faster and faster, until he really felt that he had awakened from his long sleep.

By a terrible misfortune, Pouting Lip, the gentle Soodopsy, had happened to be left behind when his brother laborers quit work, and the new silver doors of the chamber had been closed upon him.

Oh, it was terrible to think of, but true it must have been—the poor little

Soodopsy, shut in by his own eyeless folk in this chamber, which he was helping to beautify by his patient skill, had served to satisfy the hunger of this awful monster, after his long ages of fasting.

But why, you ask, dear friends, was all this not discovered when the Great Circle had been formed, and the search was made for him? Simply because the monster, after devouring the lost Soodopsy, retreated to his nest and drew the dirt and crumbled rock up around him with his gigantic flippers, and went to sleep again, as all gorged reptiles do, so that when the searchers entered the new chamber all was as they had left it, the mound of rock, as they had supposed it to be, in the corner undisturbed.

With Bulger at my heels I now turned and ran with such mad haste to Barrel Brow's, that the whole city was thrown into the wildest disorder, for, of course, they had felt me fly past them.

With all the quickness I could command, I wrote an account of what I had witnessed, and when Barrel Brow communicated it to the assembled Soodopsies, a thousand hands flew into the air, in token of mingled fright and wonder, and a wild rush was made for Bulger and me, and we were well-nigh smothered with kisses and caresses.

The moment the excitement had quieted down a little, a Great Circle was immediately formed, and I was honored with a place in it, and when my tablet was passed about, a thousand hands made signs of assent.

My plan was a simple one: it was to make a pipe connection between Uphaslok and the new chamber, and to turn the deadly vapor into the sleeping apartment of the gigantic monster. In this manner his despatch would be a happy one, merely a beginning of another one of his long naps, so far as he would know any thing about it.

This was done at once, care first being taken to make the doors of the new chamber perfectly air tight. I was the first to enter the cavern after the execution of the monster, and found, to my delight, that my estimate of his length and width was correct almost to an inch.

I always had a wonderful eye for dimension and distances.

Seeing Bulger raising himself upon his hind legs, and make an effort to dislodge something from the wall, I drew near to assist him.

Alas! it was dear, gentle, Pouting Lip's tablet. He had been writing upon it, and as the terrible monster advanced upon him, he had reached up and hung it upon a silver pin on the wall. When the Soodopsies read what their poor brother had written, there they all sat down and wrung their hands in silent but awful grief: it ran as follows:—

"O my people! why have ye abandoned me? The air trembles; the whole place is filled with suffocating odor. Must I die? Alas, I fear it! and yet I would so love to feel my dear ones' touches once more! The ground trembles; a stifling breath is puffed into my face; I am wearied, almost fainting, by trying to escape it. I can write no more. Don't grieve too long over me. It was my fault. I stayed behind, when I should have followed. Oh, horrible, horrible! Farewell! I'm going now. A loving touch to all—farewell!"

After waiting a few days for the grief of the Formifolk to lighten a little, I asked them to send a number of their most skilful workmen to assist me in removing the magnificent shell from the dead monster whose body was fed to the fishes. They not only did this, but they also offered to transform the shell into a beautiful boat for me, so that when I resolved to bid them adieu, I might sail away from the City of Silver and not be obliged to trudge along the Marble Highway. The work went on apace. At first the polishers began their task, and in a few days the mighty carapace glowed like a lady's comb. Then the dainty and cunning craftsmen in silver began their part of the work, and ere many days the shell was fitted with a silver prow curiously wrought, like a swan's neck and head, while quaintly carved trimmings ran here and there, and a dainty pair of silver sculls with a silver rudder, beautifully chased, from which ran two little silken ropes, were added to the outfit. I never had seen anything half so rich and rare, and I was as proud of it as a young king of his throne before he finds it is so much like my ship of shell.

At last the day came when I was to bid the gentle Soodopsies a long farewell.

They lined the shore as Bulger and I proceeded to take our place in the bark of shell which sat upon the water like a thing of life.

It was with a great show of dignity that Bulger took his position in the stern with the tiller-ropes in his mouth, ready to pull on either side as I might direct; and setting the silver oars in place, I threw my weight upon them, and away we glided, swiftly and noiselessly, over the surface of the dark and sluggish stream.

In a few moments nothing but a faint glimmer was left to remind us of the wonderful City of Silver, where the silent Formifolk live and love and labor without ever a thought that human beings could be any happier than they. Dear, happy folk, they have solved a mighty problem which we of the upper world are still struggling over.

CHAPTER XXI

I dare say, dear friends, that you are puzzling your brains to think out how it was possible for me to row away from the wonderful city of the Formifolk without running our boat continually ashore. Ah, you forget that the keen-eyed Bulger was at the helm, and that it was not the first time that he had piloted me through darkness impenetrable to my eyes; but more than this: I soon discovered that the plashing of my silver oars kept my little friends, the fire lizards, in a constant state of alarm, and although I couldn't hear the crackling of their tails, yet the tiny flashes of light served to outline the shore admirably. So I pulled away with a will, and down this dark and silent river, for there was a current, although hardly perceptible, Bulger and I were borne along in the beautiful bark of tortoise shell with its prow of carved and burnished silver.

During my sojourn in the Land of the Soodopsies I had one day, while calling upon the learned Barrel Brow, noticed a beautifully carved silver hand-lamp of the Pompeian pattern among his curiosities. I asked him if he knew what it was. He replied that he did, adding that it had doubtless been brought from the upper world by his people, and he begged me to accept it as a keepsake. I did so, and upon leaving the City of Silver, I filled it with fish-oil and fitted a silken wick to it. It was well that I had done so, for after a while the fire lizards disappeared entirely, and Bulger and I would have been left in total darkness, had I not drawn forth my beautiful silver lamp, lighted it, and suspended it from the beak of the silver swan which curved its graceful neck above the bow of our boat.

After lying on my oars long enough to set some food before Bulger and partake of some myself, I again started on my voyage down the silent river, no longer shrouded in impenetrable gloom.

I had not taken over half a dozen strokes, when suddenly one of my oars was almost twisted out of my hand by a vicious tug, from some inhabitant of these dark and sluggish waters. I resolved to quicken my stroke in order to escape another such a wrench, for the silver oars fashioned by the Soodopsies for me were of very delicate make, intended only for very gentle usage. Suddenly another vicious snap was made at my other oar; and this time the animal succeeded in retaining its hold, for I dared not attempt to wrench the oar out of its grip, for fear of breaking it. It was a large crustacean of the crab family, and its milk-white shell gave it a ghost-like look as it struggled about in the black waters, fiercely intent to keep its hold upon the oar. The next instant a similar creature had fastened firmly upon my other oar, and there I sat utterly helpless. But worse than this, the dark waters were now fairly alive with these white armored guards of this underworld stream, each apparently bent upon setting an immediate end to my progress through their domain. They now began a series of furious efforts to lay hold of the sides of my boat with their huge claws, but happily its polished surface made this impossible for them to accomplish.

Up to this moment Bulger had not stirred a muscle or uttered a sound, but now a sharp growl from him told me that something serious had happened at his end of the boat. It was serious indeed, for several of the largest of the fierce crustaceans had laid hold of the rudder and were wrenching it from side to side as if to tear it off. Every attempt of course caused a tug at the tiller-ropes held between Bulger's teeth; but, bracing himself firmly, he resisted their furious efforts as well as he could, and succeeded in saving the rudder for the time being.

All of a sudden our frail bark of shell crashed into some sort of obstruction, and came to a dead standstill. Peering into the darkness, to my horror I saw that the wily enemy had spanned the river with chains made up of living links by each laying hold of his neighbor's claw, the chain thus formed being then rendered almost as strong as steel by the interweaving of their double rows of small hooked legs.

Our advance was not only blocked, but death, an awful death, seemed to be staring us in the face; for what possible hope of escape could there be if Bulger and I should leap into the water, now alive with these fast swimming creatures, whirling their huge claws about in search for some way to get at us. From the brave manner in which Bulger was holding the madly swinging helm, I saw that he was determined not to surrender. But alas, bravery is but a sorry thing for two to fight a thousand with! And yet I had not lost my head—don't think that. True, I was hard pressed; the very dust of the balance, if thicker on their side, might make my scale kick the beam.

I had hauled both oars into the boat by reaching over and beating off the claws fastened upon them, and had up to this moment driven back every one of the fierce creatures which had succeeded in throwing one of his claws over the edge of the boat; but now, to my horror, I felt that our little craft was being slowly but surely drawn stern first toward the river bank. In order to accomplish this, the crustaceans had thrown out a line composed of their bodies gripped together, and had made it fast to the rudder. Not an instant was to be lost!

Once upon the river bank, the fierce creatures would swarm around us by the tens of thousands, drag us down, pinch us to death, and tear us piecemeal!

An idea flashed upon me—it was this: it is folly to attempt to resist these countless swarms of crustaceans by the use of one pair of weak hands, even though they be aided by Bulger's keen and willing teeth. We should, after a brief struggle, go down as the brave man in the sewer went down, when the famished rats leaped upon him from every side at once, or as the stray buffalo goes down when the pack of ravenous wolves closes up its circle about him. If I am to save my life, it must be by striking a blow that will reach every one of these small but fierce enemies at the same instant, and thus paralyze them, or, at least, bewilder them, until I can succeed in making my escape!

Quickly drawing my brace of pistols, I held their muzzles close to the water, and discharged them at the same instant. The effect was terrific. Like a crash of a terrible thunderbolt, the report burst forth and echoed through these vast and silent chambers, until it seemed as if the great vaulted roof of rock had by some awful convulsion of nature been cast roaring and rattling down upon the face of these black and sluggish waters! When the smoke had cleared away, a strange but welcome sight met my gaze. Tens of thousands of the huge crabs floated lifeless upon the surface of the river, with their shells split by the concussion the full length of their bodies.

It proved to have been a masterly stroke on my part, and, dear friends, you will believe me when I tell you that I drew a deep breath as I set my silver oars against the thole-pins, and, having worked my boat clear of the swarms of stunned crustaceans, rowed away for dear life!

Dear life! Ah, yes, dear life, for whose life is not dear to him, even though it be dark and gloomy at times? Is there not always something, or some one, to live for? Is there not always a glimmer of hope that the morrow's sun will go up brighter than it did this morning? Well, anyway, I repeat that I rowed away for dear life, while Bulger held the tiller-ropes and kept our frail bark of polished shell in the middle of the stream.

Whether the air was actually colder, or whether it was merely the natural chill that so often strikes the human heart after it has been beating and throbbing with alternate hope and fear, I couldn't say at the time; but I knew this much, that I suddenly found myself suffering from the cold.

For the first time since my descent into the World within a World, the air nipped my finger-tips; that soft, balmy, June-like atmosphere was gone, and I made haste to put on my fur-trimmed top-coat, which I had not made much use of lately.

At that moment one of my oars struck against some hard substance floating in the waters. I put out my hand to feel of it. To my great surprise it proved to be a lump of ice, and very soon another and another went floating by us.

We were most surely entering a region where it was cold enough to make ice. I was not sorry for this; for, to tell the truth, Bulger and I were both beginning to feel the effects of our long sojourn in the rocky chambers of this under world, whose atmosphere, though soft and warm, yet lacked the elasticity of the open air.

Ice caverns would be a complete change, and the cold air would, no doubt, send our blood tingling through our veins just as if we were out a-sleighing in the upper world on a winter's night, when the stars twinkle over our heads and the snow crystals creak beneath our runners.

Soon now huge icicles began to dot the roof of rock that spanned the river, and shafts and columns of ice dimly visible along the shore seemed to be standing there like silent sentries, watching our boat as it threaded its way through the ever-narrowing channel. And now, too, a faint glow of light reached us from I knew not where, so that by straining my eyes I could see that the river had taken a sweep, and entered a vast cavern with roof and walls of ice fretted and carved into fantastic depths and niches and shelves and cornices, with here and there shapes so fanciful that it seemed to me I had entered some vast hall of statuary, where hero and warrior, nymph and maiden, shepherd and bird-catcher, filled these shelves and niches in glorious array. Farther advance by water was impossible, for the blocks of ice, knitted together like a floe, closed the river completely. I therefore determined to make a landing—draw my boat upon the shore, and continue my journey on foot.

The mysterious light which up to this moment had shed its pale glimmer like an arctic night upon the roofs and walls of ice of these silent chambers now began to strengthen so that Bulger and I had no difficulty in picking our way along the shore. In fact, we crossed and recrossed the river itself when the whim seized us, for it now went winding on ahead of us, like a broad ribbon of ice through caverns and corridors.

Suddenly I came to a halt and stood as motionless as the fantastic forms of ice surrounding me. What could it mean? Were my eyes weakened by my long sojourn in the World within a World, playing me cruel tricks? Surely there can be no mistake! I whispered to myself. That light yonder which pours its glorious effulgence upon those spires and pinnacles, those towers and turrets of ice, is the sunshine of the upper world! Can it be that my marvellous underground journey is ended, that I stand upon the threshold of the upper world once more?

Bulger, too, recognizes this flood of sunshine, and breaking out into a fit of joyous barking, dashes on ahead, to be the first one to feel its gentle warmth after our long journey through the dark and silent passages of the World within a World.

But I dare not trust my eyes, and fearing lest he should fall into some ambush or meet with some dread accident, I called him back to me.

Together we hurry along as rapidly as possible. Now I note that we are drawing near to the end of the vast corridor through which we have been making our way for some time, and that we stand upon the portal of a mighty subterranean region lighted with real sunlight. It stretches away as far as the eye can reach, and so high is the roof that spans this vast under world that I cannot see whether it be of ice or not. All that I can see is that through one of its sloping sides there streams a mighty torrent of sunlight, which pours its splendor with unstinting hand upon the wide highways, the broad terraces, the sheer parapets, and the sloping banks which diversify this ice world. Can it be that one side of this mighty mountain which nature has here hollowed out and set like a peaked roof over this vast subterranean region, is a gigantic window of ice itself through which the sunlight of the outer world streams in this grand way like a silent cataract of light, like a deluge of sunshine? No, this could not be; for now upon a second look I saw that this flood of light thus streaming through the side of the mountain came through it like a mighty pencil of rays, and striking the opposite walls with its brilliancy a hundred-fold increased, rebounded in a thousand directions, flooding the whole region with its effulgence and dying away in faint and pearl-like glimmer in the vast approach where I had first noted it.

And therefore I understood that nature must have set a gigantic lens, twice a thousand feet or more in diameter, in the sloping side of this hollow mountain—a perfect lens of purest rock crystal, which, gathering in its mysterious bosom the sunlight of the outer world, threw it—intensely radiant and dazzling white—into the gloomy depths of this World within a World, so that when the sun went up out there, it went up in here as well, but became cold as it was beautiful, bringing no warmth, no other cheer save light, to this subterranean region which for thousands of centuries had lain locked in the crystal embrace of frozen lakes and brooks and rivers and torrents and waterfalls, once bubbling and flowing and rushing headlong through fair lands of the upper world, but suddenly checked in their course by some bursting forth of mighty pent-up forces, and turned downward into these icy depths condemned to everlasting rest and silence, their crystals locked in a sleep that never would know an awaking, mocked in their dreams by this mysterious sunlight that came with the smile and the fair, winsome look of the real, and yet was so powerless to set them free as once it did when the springtime came in the upper world. All these thoughts and many others besides flitted through my mind as I stood looking up at that mighty lens in its setting of mightier rock.

And so deeply impressed was I by the sight of such a great flood of sunlight pouring through this gigantic bull's eye which nature had set in the rocky side of the hollow mountain peak and illumining this under world, that the longer I gazed upon the wonderful spectacle the more firmly inthralled my senses became by it.

The deep silence, the deliciously pure air, the ever-varying tints of the light as the mighty ice columns acting the part of prisms, literally filled those vast chambers with the rainbow's glorious glow, imparted unto the spell resting upon me such unearthly power that it might have held me there until my limbs hardened into icy crystals and my eyes looked out with a frozen stare, had not the ever-watchful Bulger given a gentle tug at the skirt of my coat and aroused me from my inthralling meditation.

CHAPTER XXII

Scarcely had I advanced a hundred yards beyond the portal where I had halted when happening to turn my eyes to the other side, a sight met them which sent a thrill of wonder and delight through my form. There upon the highest terrace stood a palace of ice, its slender minarets, its high-lifted towers, its rounded turrets, its spacious platform, and its broad flights of steps all glittering in the sunlight as if gem-studded and jewel-set.

It was a spectacle to stir the most indifferent heart, let alone one so full of ardor and buoyancy as mine. But ah, dear friends, even admitting that I can succeed in awakening in your minds even a faint conception of the beauty of this ice palace, as the sunlight fell full upon it at that moment, how can I ever hope to give you an idea of the unearthly beauty of this palace of ice and its glorious surroundings when the moon went up in the outer world at a later hour and its pale, mysterious light was poured through the mighty lens in the mountain side, and fell with celestial shimmer upon these walls of ice?

But the one thought that oppressed me now was: Can this beautiful abode be without a tenant, without a living soul within its wonderful halls and chambers? Or, may not its dwellers, overtaken by the pitiless cold, sit with wide-opened eyes and icy glare, stark as marble in chairs of ice, white frosted hair pressed against icy cushions, and hands stiffened around crystal cups filled with frozen wine of topaz hue, while the harper's fingers cling cramped to the wires stiff as the wires themselves, and the last tones of the singer's voice lie in feathery crystals of frozen breath white at his feet?

Come what may, I resolved to lift the crystal knocker that might hang on the outer door of this palace of ice and awaken the castellan, if his slumber were not that of death. In a few moments I had crossed the level space between me and the first terrace, which it would be necessary for me to scale in order to reach the second and then the third upon which stood the palace of ice.

Imagine my more than surprise upon finding myself now at the foot of a magnificent flight of steps, hewn into the ice with a master hand, and leading to the terrace above.

Springing lightly up this flight with Bulger close at my heels, I suddenly set eyes upon two of the quaintest-looking human beings that I ever remembered seeing in all my travels. They looked for all the world like two big animated snowballs, being clad from top to toe in garments made of snow-white fleece, their skull-caps likewise of white fur, leaving only their faces visible. In his right hand each of them carried a very prettily shaped flint axe, mounted upon a helve of polished bone.

Striding up to me and swinging their axes over my head in altogether too close proximity to my poll to be particularly pleasant, one of them cries out,—

"Halt, sir! Unless his frigid Majesty Gelidus, King of the Koltykwerps, awaits thy coming, his guards will, at a signal from us, roll a few thousand tons of ice down upon thee if thou darest proceed another step. Therefore, stand fast and tell us who thou art and whether thou art expected."

"Gentlemen," said I, "kindly lower those axes of yours and I will convince you that his frigid Majesty hath nothing to dread in me, for I am none other than the very small but very noble and very famous Sebastian von Troomp, commonly known as 'Little Baron Trump.'"

"Never heard of thee in all my life," said both of the guards as with one voice.

"But I have of you, gentlemen," I continued,—for now I recollected what the learned Don Fum had said about the frozen land of the Koltykwerps, or Cold Bodies,—"and as proof of my peaceful intent, like a true knight I now offer you my hand, and beg that you will conduct me into the presence of his frigid Majesty."

No sooner had the guard standing next me drawn off his glove and grasped my hand, than he let it loose again with a cry of fright.

"Zounds! Man, art thou on fire? Why, thy hand burned me like the flame of a lamp!"

"Why, no, my friend," said I quietly; "that's my ordinary temperature."

"And thy companion?"

"Hath even a warmer heart than I have," was my reply.

"Well, our word for it, little baron," exclaimed one of the guards with a chuckle, "there will be no place for thee except in the meat quarry. Possibly after thou hast been cooled off for a week or so, his frigid Majesty will be able to have thee about!"

This was not a very cheerful prospect, for I had no particular desire to be laid away in the royal ice-box for a week or so. Anyway, the only thing to be done was to insist upon being conducted at once into the presence of the King of the

Koltykwerps, and abide by his decision.

One of the guards having saluted me by presenting his battle-axe in real military style, faced about and began to ascend the grand staircase with intent to announce my arrival to his frigid Majesty, while the other informed me that he would conduct me as far as the perron of the palace.

I was wonderstruck with the beauty of the three staircases leading up to the ice palace. Massive balustrades with curiously carved balusters springing from towering pedestals, crowned with beautiful lamps, all, all, I say, all and everything, to the crystal-clear sides of the lamps themselves, was fashioned from blocks of ice. It proved to be a good climb to the top of the third terrace, and I was not put out when the guard solemnly lowered his battle-axe of flint to bring me to a standstill.

The sun in the upper world was, no doubt, nearing the horizon, for a deep and beautiful twilight suddenly sank upon the icy dominions of King Gelidus, and, to my surprise and delight, through the great slabs of crystal-clear ice which served for windows to the palace, streamed a soft radiance as if a thousand wax tapers were burning in the chambers and galleries in-doors. It was a sight to gladden the eyes of any mortal; but if I had been spellbound by the beauty of its exterior, how shall I tell you, dear friends, of the curious splendor of the interior of Gelidus' palace of ice, as it burst upon me when I had crossed its threshold?

Hallway led into hallway, chamber opened into chamber, through portals gracefully arched, and winding staircases climbed to upper rooms, while hanging from lofty ceilings or resting on graceful pedestals, were a thousand alabaster lamps, shedding light and perfume upon this glorious home of his frigid Majesty Gelidus, King of the Koltykwerps. Long rows of retainers, all in snow-white fur, lined the wide hallway, as the guards conducted Bulger and me into the palace and bowed in silence as we passed.

To my more than wonder, I saw that the inner rooms were most sumptuously furnished, chairs and divans being scattered here and there, all covered with superb skins of white fur, while the floor, too, was carpeted with them, and as the soft radiance of the alabaster lamps fell upon these magnificent pelts and set ten thousand jewels in the walls and ceilings of ice, I was ready to admit that I had never seen anything half so beautiful. And yet I was still outside the throne-room of his frigid Majesty!

At length we came to one end of a broad hallway which seemed shut off from the rest of the palace by a wall thickly incrusted with strings of great diamonds, each as big as a goose-egg, extending from the ceiling to the floor, and turning back the shimmer of the lamps with such a flood of crystalline radiance that my eyes involuntarily closed before it.

Think of my amazement when the two guards, laying hold of this wall of jewels, as I deemed it, drew it to the right and left till there was room for me to pass. What I had taken for a wall of jewels was but a curtain made up of round bits of ice strung upon strings and hanging like a shower of diamonds there before me, as they glittered in the light of the lamps each side of them.

I now stood in the throne-room of his frigid Majesty, the King of the Koltykwerps. Now I realized that what I had seen elsewhere in his palace of ice was in reality but a sample of its magnificence, for here the splendor of King Gelidus' castle burst upon me in its fullest strength. Imagine a great round chamber lighted with the soft flames of perfumed oil, streaming from a hundred alabaster lamps, the walls lined with broad divans covered with snow-white pelts, the floors thickly carpeted with the same glorious rugs, while on one side, glittering in the shimmer of the hundred massive lamps, stands the icy throne of the King of the Koltykwerps, decked with snow-white skins, and he upon it, with Schneeboule, his fair daughter, sitting at his feet, and all around and about him, group-wise, a hundred Koltykwerps, the king, the princess, and the courtiers all clad in skins whiter than the driven snow, and you, dear friends, will have some faint idea of the splendor of the scene which burst upon me as the two guards drew aside the strands of ice jewels at the end of the hallway in the palace of ice!

Like all his subjects, King Gelidus looked out through the round window of his fur hood, just as a big good-natured boy does through his skating-cap.

The Koltykwerps were not much taller than I, but were very stocky built, so that when broadened out by their thick fur suits they really took on at times the appearance of animated snowballs. It would be hard for the fingers of the deftest hand to draw faces fuller of kindliness and good nature than those of the Koltykwerps. Their small, honest gray eyes sparkled with a boniform glint, and so broad were their smiles that they were only about half visible through the round holes of their fur hoods. I was delighted with them from the very start, and the more so when I heard King Gelidus cry out in a cheery voice: "A right crisp and cold welcome to our icy court, little baron; but from what our people tell us, thou carriest a pair of hands so hot that we beg thee to take a few days to cool off before thou touchest palms with any of the Koltykwerps, and we also beg thee to be careful and not to lean against any of our richly carved panels, or to slide down any of our highly polished railings, or to handle the strands of our jewels, or sit down for any length of time on the front steps of our palace. And we make the same request of thy four-footed companion, who is said to be of even a warmer disposition than thou."

I bowed and kissed my hand to his frigid Majesty, and assured him that I should make every effort to lower my temperature as speedily as possible, and, in the mean time, that I should be extremely careful not to come into contact with any of the artistic carving of his palace of ice.

As I pronounced these words, the whole company began to clap their hands; and as they did so, a cold shiver ran down my back, for there was a sound, methought, very much like the rattling of dry bones to that applause, but I took good care not to let King Gelidus notice my fright.

His frigid Majesty now presented me to his daughter Schneeboule, a pretty little maid of about sixteen crystal winters, with cheeks round as apples, and as deeply dimpled as the furrows of a cross-bun. Her eyes twinkled as she looked upon Bulger and me, and turning to her frigid papa, she asked for leave to touch the tip end of my thumb, which being done, she gave a squeaky little scream and began to blow on her tiny finger as if I had blistered it.

King Gelidus also presented me to several of his court favorites, all men of the coldest blood in the nation. Their names were Jellikin, Phrostyphiz, Icikul, and Glacierbhoy. They were all dreadfully slow thinkers when you questioned them very closely upon any subject.

It didn't take me very long to discover this. In fact, they requested me to be less warm in my manner, and not to ask them any posers, as they invariably found that deep thought caused a rise in their temperature.

This was, to be honest about it, very annoying to me; for you know, dear friends, what a loadstone my mind is, never asleep, always in a quiver like a mariner's compass, pointing this way and that, in search of the polar star of wisdom.

Upon making known my trouble to his frigid Majesty, King Gelidus, he most gracefully ordered one of his trusty attendants to conduct me to the triple walled ice-cell of a certain Koltykwerp by the name of Bullibrain, that is, literally, "Boiling Brain," a man who had been born with a hot head, and consequently with a very active brain. For fifty years King Gelidus had been doing his very best to refrigerate this subject of his, but without success. As I was just bursting with impatience to ask a whole string of questions concerning the Koltykwerps, you may imagine how delighted I was to make the acquaintance of Bullibrain, or Lord Hot Head as he was called among the Koltykwerps; but, dear friends, you must excuse me if I make this the end of a chapter and stop here for a brief rest.

CHAPTER XXIII

Lord Bullibrain was never allowed to set foot inside the palace of ice. King Gelidus, backed by the opinion of his favorites, still indulged the belief that he would be able in the end to refrigerate him. True, he had been many years at the task, so that it had now become a sort of hobby of his, and almost daily did his frigid Majesty pay a visit to his hot-headed subject and test his temperature by pressing a small ball of ice against his temples. To King Gelidus' mind, a man of so high a temperature was a continual menace to the peace and quiet of his kingdom. What if Lord Hot Head in a dream should wander forth some night and fall asleep with his back against one of the walls of the ice palace? Might he not melt away enough of it to throw the whole glorious fabric into a slump and slush of débris? It was terrible to think of, when he did think of it, and he thought of it quite often.

But Bullibrain had no terrors for me, nor for Bulger either; in fact, Bulger was delighted to be stroked by a warm hand, and he and Bullibrain and I soon became the very best of friends; but his frigid Majesty was so alarmed when he heard of this friendship, that he was seized with quite a spasm of warmth, for, thought he, the united heat of three hot heads might work some terrible harm to the welfare of his people. So he issued the coldest kind of a decree carved on a tablet of ice, that Bullibrain and I should on no one day pass more than a half-hour together; that we should never touch palm to palm, sleep in the same room, eat from the same dish, or sit on the same divan.

These regulations were annoying, but I followed them to the letter; and when King Gelidus saw how careful I was to yield the strictest obedience to his decree, he conceived a genuine affection for me and sent several magnificent pelts to the ice-house, which had been assigned to Bulger and me, for, of course, it would not have been safe for us to lodge in the palace itself, but his frigid Majesty held out the flattering prospect that the very moment Bulger and I should become properly refrigerated, apartments in the palace would be assigned to us, and, in fact, that I should be permitted to eat at the royal table.

Who are the Koltykwerps? Where did these strange folk come from? How did they ever find their way down into this World of Eternal Frost? And, above all, where do they get their food and clothing from? These were a few of the questions which I was so impatient to have answered that my temperature was raised a whole degree, and I was obliged to sleep with only one single pelt between me and my divan of crystal ice.

For a man bred and born in so cold a country as the land of the Koltykwerps, Bullibrain had an extremely quick and active mind. On account of his rapid heart-beat, and the consequent high temperature of his body, he was not able to do his writing on slabs of ice as other learned Koltykwerps had done, for it would not have been a pleasant thing for him to see a poem which he had just finished literally melt away in his hands, without so much as leaving an ink-stain behind, so he had been obliged, with King Gelidus' permission, to do his writing on thin tablets of alabaster.

Before he began to talk to me about the progenitors of the Koltykwerps, he showed me a map of the country in the upper world once inhabited by them, and traced for me the course they had sailed upon abandoning that country, and described the beautiful shores they had landed upon in their search for a new home. I saw at a glance that it was Greenland which Bullibrain was thus unconsciously describing; and knowing as I did that in past ages Greenland had been a land of blue skies, warm winds, green meadows, and fertile valleys, before moving mountains of ice came down from the North and crushed all life out of it, I listened with breathless interest to his wonderful tales of its beautiful lakes, nestled at the foot of vine-clad mountains, all of which Bullibrain now looked upon in fair visions inherited from his ancestors. And I also knew that it must have been the Arctic Ocean which had been traversed by the ships of the Koltykwerps, who had then landed upon the, in those days, sunny shores of Northern Russia.

But the mountains of ice could sail too, and they followed the fleeing

Koltykwerps like mighty monsters, dashing themselves with terrible roar and crash upon the peaceful shores, which they soon transformed into a wilderness of berg, of glacier, and of floe.

Only a handful of the Koltykwerps survived; and these, in their dumb despair taking refuge in the clefts and caverns of the North Urals, could from their hiding-places look upon one of the strangest sights that had ever greeted human eyes. So rapid had been the advance of these mighty masses of ice, crashing against the mountain sides and rending the very rocks in their fury, that the air gave up its warmth, and the sun was powerless to give it back again. The animals of the wild wood and the beasts of the field, overtaken in their flight, perished as they ran and stood there stark and stiff, with heads uptossed and muscles knotted. Them by the thousands and ten times thousands the crushed crystals of the pursuing floods caught up like moss and leaves in a mountain torrent and packed in every cave and cavern on the way, tearing broader and loftier portals into these subterranean chambers, so that they might do their work the better!

"And these, then, O Bullibrain, are your meat quarries," I exclaimed, "whence ye draw your daily food?"

"Even so, little baron," replied the hot-headed Koltykwerp, "and not only our food, but the skins which serve us so admirably for clothing in this cold, under ground world, and the oil, too, which burns in our beautiful alabaster lamps, besides a hundred other things, such as bone for helves and handles, horn for needles and buttons and eating utensils, wool for the weaving of our under-garments, and magnificent pelts of bear and seal and walrus, which, laid upon our benches and divans of crystal ice, transform them into beds and couches which even an inhabitant of thy world might envy."

"But, O Bullibrain," I cried out, "have ye not almost exhausted these supplies? Will not death from starvation soon stare ye all in the face in these deep and icy caverns of the under world, visited by the sun's light yet unwarmed by it?"

"Nay, little baron," answered Bullibrain with a smile almost as warm as one of my own; "let not that thought give thee a moment's alarm, for we have as yet barely raised the lid of this ice-box of nature's packing. We are not large eaters any way," continued Lord Hot Head, "for while it is true that we are not indolent people, for his frigid Majesty's palace and our dwellings need constant repair, and new hatchets and axes must be chipped out in the flint quarries and new lamps carved and new garments woven, yet it is also true that we take life rather easy. We have no enemies to slay, no quarrels to settle, no gold to fight over, no land to drive our fellow-creatures from and fence in; nor can we be ill, if we were willing to be, for in this pure, cold, crisp air disease would try in vain to sow her poison germs; hence, needing no doctors, we have none, as we have no lawyers either, or merchants to sell us what belongs to us already. His frigid Majesty is an excellent king. I never read of a better one. I doubt that his like exists in the upper world. Always cool headed, no thought of conquest, no dreams of power, no longings for empty pomp and show ever enter his mind. Since the day his father died and we set the great Koltykwerp crown of crystal ice upon his cool brow, his temperature has never risen but a half a degree, and that was only for a brief hour or so, and was occasioned by a mad proposal of one of his councillors, who claimed that he had discovered an explosive compound, something like the gunpowder of thy world, I fancy, by which he could shatter the glorious window of rock crystal set in the mountain dome of our under world and let in the warm sunshine."

"Did his frigid Majesty Gelidus put this daring Koltykwerp to death?" I asked.

"Oh, dear, no," replied Bullibrain; "he merely ordered him to be refrigerated for so many hours a day until all his feverish projects had been chilled to death; for no doubt, little baron, a man of thy deep learning knows full well that all the ills which thy world suffers from are the children of fevered brains, of minds made restless and visionary by the high temperature of the blood which gallops through the approaches to the dome of thought, stirring up wild dreams and visions as thy sun lifts the poisonous vapor from the stagnant pool."

The more I listened to Bullibrain the more I liked him. The fact of the matter is, I preferred to sit in his narrow cell with its plain walls of ice lighted up by a single alabaster lamp and converse with him to loitering in the splendid throne-room of his frigid Majesty King Gelidus; but Bulger had discovered that the pelts of Princess Schneeboule's divan were much thicker, softer, and warmer than the single one allowed Lord Hot Head, and therefore he preferred spending his time with her; but fearing lest he might get into mischief, I didn't dare to leave him alone with the princess too long at a time.

CHAPTER XXIV

At the time of Bulger's and my arrival in the land of the Koltykwerps the Princess Schneeboule was about fifteen years of age, and I must say that rarely had it been my good fortune to make the acquaintance of such a sweet-tempered, lovable little creature. She flitted about the ice palace like a beam of sunlight, and there was nothing of the spoiled child about her, although a bit mischievous at times.

Her voice was as full of music as a skylark's, and it was not many days before she and I had become the best friends in the world.

Now, you must know, dear friends, that according to the law of the Koltykwerps, a princess is left absolutely free to choose her own husband, and his frigid Majesty was very anxious that Schneeboule should pick hers out as soon as possible. Moreover, the law of the land gave her perfect freedom to choose a husband of high or low degree, provided he was young enough. The way in which a Koltykwerp princess was required to make known her preference was to press a kiss upon the cheek of the young man whom she might settle upon. This ennobled him at once, and he became the heir apparent to the throne of ice, and entitled to sit on its steps until he should be crowned king.

Now, his frigid Majesty was delighted to see this friendship spring up between Schneeboule and me, for he hoped to make use of my influence to bring her to set the necessary kiss on some youth's cheek before I took my departure from the cold Kingdom of the Koltykwerps. I gave him the word of a nobleman that I would do my best to carry out his wishes.

With Schneeboule for a guide, Bulger and I often went for walks through the splendid ice grottos of her father's kingdom, selecting days when the sunlight of the outer world poured strongest through the mighty lens set in the side of the mountain. Then these grottos took on a splendor that my poor tongue is powerless to describe. Their crystal mazes glittered as if their walls were set with massive jewels most wonderfully cut and polished, and as if their ceilings were fretted with gems so peerless that all the gold of the upper world would fall far short of paying for them. Here, there, and everywhere the skill of the Koltykwerps had carved and chiselled graceful flights of steps, broad landings with majestic columns, and winding corridors lined with long rows of statues, single and group-wise; and ever and anon the visitor came upon a terrace where, seated upon a fur-covered divan, he might look out upon the bewildering beauty of King Gelidus' icy domains, arch touching arch and dome springing from dome, while over and above all, through the gigantic lens in its granite setting, a mile above our heads, streamed a flood of glorious sunlight, lighting up this World within a World with a radiance so grand and so complete as to seem to be a sun of a far greater splendor than the one that warmed the upper world and bathed it in so many gorgeous hues at morn and eve. Hardly a day went by now that the princess of the Koltykwerps did not surprise either Bulger or me with some gift or other.

To tell the truth, dear friends, although my Russian coat was fur-trimmed, yet I began to feel the need of warmer garments after a week's sojourn in the icy domain of King Gelidus, and I think Schneeboule must have heard my teeth chattering, for one morning, upon entering the Palace of Ice, I was delighted to be presented with a full suit of fur precisely similar to the one worn by King Gelidus himself.

Nor was Bulger forgotten by the loving little Princess, for with her own hands she had knitted him a blanket of the softest wool, which she belted so snugly around his body and tied so tightly around his neck that henceforth he felt perfectly comfortable in the chill air of the home of the Koltykwerps.

One day the Princess Schneeboule said to me,—

"Oh, come, little baron, come to my favorite grotto, now that the sun's rays are bright within it; there shalt thou see a wonder."

"A wonder, Princess Schneeboule?"

"Yes, little baron, a wonder," she repeated: "the Little Man with the Frozen Smile."

"Little Man with the Frozen Smile?" I echoed.

"Come and see, come and see, little baron!" cried Schneeboule, hurrying on ahead.

In a few moments we had reached the grotto and bounded into it with the Princess leading the way.

Suddenly she halted in front of a magnificent block of crystal ice, clear as polished glass, and cried out,—

"There, look! There is the Little Man with the Frozen Smile!"

Even now, as the thought of that moment comes over me, I feel something of the thrill of half fear, half joy, as my eyes fell upon the little creature shut in that superb block of ice, himself a part of it, himself its heart, its contents, its mystery. There, in its centre, in easy posture, with wide opened eyes, and with what might be called a smile upon its face—that is a glint of kindliness and affection in its strange eyes with their overhanging brows, sat a small animal of the chimpanzee race. He had possibly been asleep when the icy flood struck him, dreaming of beautiful trees bending beneath purple fruit, of cloudless skies above and a coral beach below, and death had come to him so quickly that he had become a brother to this block of ice while the happy dream was still in his thoughts.

It was wonderful, it was more than wonderful! Spellbound by the strange spectacle, I stood there, I know not how long, with my eyes looking into his. At last Schneeboule's voice aroused me:

"Ha! ha!" she laughed; "look, little baron, Bulger is trying to kiss his poor dead brother."

In truth, Bulger did have his nose pressed firmly against the block of ice in his effort to scent the strange animal imprisoned in that crystal cell—so near, and yet so far beyond the reach of his keen scent.

"Well, little baron," cried Schneeboule, "did I not speak truly? Have I not shown thee the Little Man with the Frozen Smile?"

"Indeed thou hast, fair princess," was my reply; "and I cannot tell thee how grateful I am to thee for having done so."

Then, as she plucked me by the sleeve, I pleaded, "Nay, gentle Schneeboule, not yet, not yet, let me bide a bit longer. The Little Man with the Frozen Smile seems to beg me not to go. I can almost imagine that I hear him whisper: 'O little baron, break open the crystal cell of my prison and take me with thee back to the world of sunshine, back to the land of the orange-tree, where the soft warm winds used to rock me to sleep in the cradle of the swaying boughs, while the wise and watchful patriarch of our flock stood guard over us all.'"

Schneeboule's big, round, gray eyes filled with tears at these words.

"Would that he were alive, little baron," she murmured, "and that I could give him some of my happiness to pay him back for all the long years he has been spending in his icy prison."

In a few moments Schneeboule took me by the hand and led me away from the great block of ice with its silent prisoner. My heart was very heavy, and both Schneeboule and Bulger did their utmost to divert me, but all to no purpose.

Leaving the princess at the portal of the palace, I went to my dwelling which was ablaze with the soft glow of its alabaster lamps, and there I found a beautiful new pelt spread over my divan, a new gift from King Gelidus. But I could take no pleasure in it. My thoughts were all with the Little Man with the Frozen Smile locked in the icy embrace of that crystal mould, which, in its cold irony, let him seem to be so free and unfettered and yet held him in such vise-like grip. After a while I dismissed my serving people and laid me down for the night with my dear Bulger nestled against my breast. But I could not sleep. All night long those strange eyes with their uncanny glint followed me about, pleading strong but silent for me to come again, for me to soften my heart like a child of the sunshine that I was, to shatter his crystal dungeon, and set him loose, to bear him away from the icy domain of the Koltykwerps out into the warm air of the upper world. What was I dreaming about? Was he not dead? Had not his spirit left his body thousands and thousands of years ago? Why should I let such wild thoughts vex my mind? What good would come of it? None, none whatever. I was a reasonable creature, I must not give lodgment within my brain to such silly ideas.

The Little Man with the Frozen Smile had been, through almost playful fate, laid away in a beautiful tomb. I must not disturb it. No doubt in his lifetime he had been the pet of a noble manor, brought to the Northland from some sunny clime by master of powerful argosy. Let him rest in peace. I must not dare to mar the beauty of his crystal tomb, so gloriously transparent!

I was even sorry that Schneeboule had led me into her beautiful grotto, and resolved to go thither no more.

What poor weak creatures are we, so fertile in good resolutions and yet so unfruitful of results, planting whole acres with fair promises, but when the tender shoots pierce the ground turning our back upon the crop as if it didn't belong to us!

CHAPTER XXV

Not only had I been unable to sleep, but by my tossing about I had kept poor dear Bulger awake so that when morning came we both looked haggard enough. I felt as if I had been through a fit of sickness, and no doubt he did too. At any rate I had no appetite for the heavy meat diet of the Koltykwerps, and seeing me refuse my breakfast, Bulger did likewise.

I had promised Schneeboule to come early to the palace, for she had a number of questions which she wished to ask me concerning the upper world.

"Good-morning, little baron," she cried in her sweetest tones as I entered the throne-room. "Didst sleep well last night on the new pelt which papa sent thee?" I was about to make a reply when Schneeboule's hand coming in contact with mine,—for we had both removed our gloves in order to shake hands,—she uttered a piercing scream, and drawing back stood there blowing her breath on her right palm as she exclaimed, again and again,—

"Firebrand! Firebrand!"

In an instant King Gelidus and a group of his councillors drew near, and, pulling over their gloves, one after the other laid his hand in mine.

"Glowing coals!" cried his frigid Majesty.

"Tongue of flame!" roared Phrostyphiz.

"Boiling water!" groaned Glacierbhoy.

"Red hot!" hissed Icikul.

"Thou must leave the palace at once," half pleaded King Gelidus. "It would simply he madness for me to permit such a firebrand to remain within the walls of the royal residence. The intense heat of thy body would be sure to melt a hole in its walls ere the sun goes down."

The royal councillors again drew off their gloves and laid hands upon poor Bulger, when a second alarm, even wilder than the first, was sent up and we were hastily escorted back to our lodging-house.

No doubt, dear friends, you will be somewhat mystified upon reading these words, but the explanation is easy: Owing to worriment and lack of sleep, Bulger and I had awaked in a highly feverish condition, and to the Koltykwerps we had really seemed to be almost on fire, but our fever left us toward night; hearing which, King Gelidus sent for us and did all in his power to entertain us with song and dance, in both of which, Schneeboule was very skilled. Finding that his frigid Majesty was in such a rosy humor, if I may be allowed to speak that way of a person whose face was almost as white as the alabaster lamps over his head, I determined to ask him for permission to cleave asunder the icy cell of the Little Man with the Frozen Smile, and ascertain if possible from the collar, which, made up apparently of gold and silver coin was clasped around his neck, to whom he had belonged and where his home had been.

No sooner had I proferred my request, than I noticed that the white face of the royal Gelidus parted with its smile and took on a terribly icy look.

Methought I could look through the tip of his nose as though an icicle, and methought, too, that his ears shone in the light of the alabaster lamps like sheets of crystal ice, and that his voice as he spoke puffed into my face like the first flakes of a coming snowstorm.

I quickly repented me of my rash action. But it was too late and I determined to stand by it.

"Little baron," spoke royal Gelidus in icy tones, "never a heart beat in a kingly breast that was purer and colder than mine, freer from the warmth of selfishness, with not a single hot corner for ire or anger to nestle in, or for weakness or folly to make their hiding-places. For thousands of years my people have inhabited this icy domain and breathed this pure cold air, and never yet hath one desired to strike an axe of flint into the walls of that crystal prison. However, little baron, there may be some warm corner in my heart wherein cold and limpid wisdom may not be at home. Therefore, come to me to-morrow for my answer, meanwhile I'll take council with the coolest brains and coldest hearts about me. If they see no harm in thy request, thou mayst crack open the crystal gates that have for so many centuries shut the manlike creature in his silent cell, and take him forth in order to study the mystic words graven on his collar; but upon the strict condition that in cleaving open his house of crystal my quarry men so apply their wedges of flint as to break the block into two equal pieces, that when thou hast read what may be there, the two parts be closed upon the little man again, edge fitting edge, like a perfect mould, so exactly that to the eye no sign of line or joint be visible. Dost promise, little baron, that this shall be as to our royal will, it seems meet that it should be?"

I promised most solemnly that the crystal cell of the Little Man with the Frozen Smile should be opened and closed exactly as his frigid Majesty had directed.

It would be hard for me to tell you, dear friends, how happy I went to rest that night upon my icy divan, and how as the tiny flame of my alabaster lamp shed its soft glow upon the walls of ice, I lay there turning over in my mind the strange and mysterious pleasure which was soon to fall to my lot when the quarry men of King Gelidus should set their wedges of flint in this glorious block of ice and cleave it asunder.

Even Don Fum, Master of Masters, had never dreamed of receiving a message from the people who lived in the very childhood of the world, and in anticipation already I enjoyed the splendid triumph which would be mine when I came to lecture before learned societies upon the mysterious lettering on the curious collar clasping the neck of the Little Man with the Frozen Smile.

Imagine my anguish then, dear friends, upon receiving a message from King Gelidus the next day that his councillors had with one voice decreed against the opening of the crystal prison which stood in Schneeboule's grotto!

I was as if smitten with some sudden and awful ailment. I had never felt until that moment how keen the tooth of disappointment could be. I shivered first with a chill that made me brother to the Koltykwerps, and then I burned with a fever so raging that a wild rumor spread through Gelidus' icy domain that I was setting fire to the very walls and roof. With wild outcries, and faces drawn with nameless dread, the subjects of his frigid Majesty rushed pell mell up the wide flights of stairs leading to the palace of ice, and pleaded for the king to show himself.

In cold and frigid majesty, Gelidus walked out upon the platform and listened to the prayers of his people.

"We shall burn," they cried; "our beautiful homes will fall about our ears. These crystal steps will melt away, and all these fair columns and arches and statues and pedestals will turn to water and empty themselves into the lower caverns of the earth. The great window of our sky will fall with awful crash upon our heads, putting an end forever to this fair domain of crystal splendor. O Gelidus, haste thee, haste thee, ere it be too late, let the little baron have his way before bitter disappointment transforms his body and limbs into tongues of flame to lick up this magnificent palace in a single night, and dash its thousand alabaster lamps to the ground, a heap of sheards, no fragment matching its brother fragment, but all a wretched mass of worthless matter!"

King Gelidus and his frosty councillors saw that it would be useless to attempt to reason with the people, and therefore turning toward them, he coldly waved his chilly right hand, and with an icy smile spoke frostily as follows,—

"Go, Koltykwerps to your homes, and be happy. What think you, have I a heated brain, doth my heart steam with foolishness, that you should think me capable of wishing harm to the tiniest Koltykwerp that spins his top of ice in my fair kingdom? Go to your homes, I say; the little baron is already cooling off, for he hath my full consent to cleave asunder the crystal prison of the Little Man with the Frozen Smile. There is nothing be frightened about, my children. So eat hearty suppers and sleep soundly to-night, for my royal word for it, by to-morrow morning the little baron will cease to be the least bit dangerous to the peace and welfare of our icy kingdom. A cold good-night to you all."

In a short half hour the panic-stricken Koltykwerps were all back in their homes again, and when a messenger came from King Gelidus to measure my temperature he found such a great improvement that he opened his chilly heart and sent me a beautiful present from his treasure house, to wit: A small block of ice, clearer than any gem I had ever seen, in the heart of which lay a glorious red rose in fullest bloom, each velvet petal opened out eagerly. Upon consulting my diary I found that it was just six months to a day since I had left Castle Trump and the loved ones sheltered by its time-worn tiles, and cold as was the covering of this thrice beautiful child of the upper world I clasped it to my breast and shed tears.

And this was the way it came about, dear friends, that King Gelidus and his frosty councillors were brought to give their consent to my cleaving asunder the icy prison wherein lay the Little Man with the Frozen Smile.

CHAPTER XXVI

Bulger and I had little appetite for the dainty breakfast of stewed sweetbreads which the Koltykwerps set before us the next morning, for I knew, and he half suspected, that something important was going to happen, being nothing less than the cleaving asunder of the crystal cell which had held the little chimpanzee a prisoner for so many centuries.

Walking beside the merry Princess Schneeboule, who was delighted to know that his frigid Majesty, her father, had at last yielded to my wishes, Bulger and I set out for the beautiful ice grotto; behind us walked Phrostyphiz and Glacierbhoy with instructions from the king to supervise the cleaving asunder of the block of ice; and after them came four of King Gelidus' quarry men, two bearing flint axes with helves of polished bone, and two carrying the flint wedges to be used in the work.

We soon entered Schneeboule's grotto, and the task was at once entered upon.

It seemed to me I could almost see the Little Man with the Frozen Smile wink his eyelids as the quarry men set their wedges in place and began to mark the line of fracture; but, of course, dear friends, you know what an imagination I have, especially when I get worked up over anything. So you must take what I say sometimes with a grain of salt, although as a rule, you may accept my statements with child-like confidence.

With such wonderful skill did the Koltykwerpian quarry men use their axes and wedges that in a few moments, to my great delight, the huge block of ice fell asunder in perfect halves, in one of which the little manlike creature lay on his side like a casting in a mould.

I made haste to lift him out and wrap him a soft pelt, which I had brought along for that purpose, and then I turned to retrace my steps to my chamber, where I intended to begin at once my study of whatever inscriptions should be found upon his curious collar.

"Remember little baron," said Glacierbhoy, "by express command of his frigid Majesty, the Little Man with the Frozen Smile must be returned to his crystal cell to-morrow morning at this very hour."

I bowed assent, and then, having accompanied Princess Schneeboule as far as the bottom of the grand staircase leading to the ice palace, I turned away and was soon in the privacy of my own apartment.

Now came for me one of the bitterest disappointments of my life; but I submitted with a good grace, for it was fit punishment visited upon me for my foolish vanity in striving to unearth some older record of the human race than had yet been done by any of the great searchers and philosophers, not even excepting that Master of Masters, Don Strephalofidgeguaneriusfum!

Know then, dear friends, that the quaint collar, made up of gold and silver coins, or disks, cunningly linked together, which encircled the animal's neck, contained not a single word or letter of any language, the undersides being quite blank, and the upper merely having roughly carved outlines of an object which might possibly have been intended for the sun.

Wrapping the animal up in the soft pelt, I laid him away in a corner of my divan and betook myself to the palace of his frigid Majesty, where I frankly informed King Gelidus of my great disappointment in not finding some few words or even a single word of a language unknown to the wisest heads of the upper world.

Schneeboule was so touched by my sadness that, had I not skilfully kept out of her way, I verily believe she would have thrown her arms around my neck and imprinted upon my cheek the kiss which would have made me the king of the Koltykwerps; but I had no longing to spend the rest of my life in the icy domains of his frigid Majesty, even though my brow would be crowned with the cold crown of the Koltykwerps. If I had been an old man, with slow and feeble pulse, it would have been very different; but my heart was too warm and my blood too hot to fill such a position with agreeableness to myself or satisfaction to the people of this icy under world. So I kept the little princess busy enough, I can assure you, first with songs, then with dance, and then with story-telling.

That night King Gelidus ordered a magnificent fête to be held in my honor. Five hundred more alabaster lamps were lighted, and the royal divans were laid with the richest pelts in the palace, and after the dancing and singing had ended, frozen tidbits from the royal kitchen were passed around on alabaster salvers, and Bulger and I ate until our teeth ached.

It was late when we reached our own apartment, and so full were my thoughts of the beautiful sights which we had gazed upon in the throne-room, that I had quite forgotten about the poor Little Man with the Frozen Smile whom I had covered up and tucked away on my divan; but Bulger had not been so hard-hearted.

Twenty times during the evening he had given me a sly tug at my sleeve as much as to say,——

"Come, little master, let's hurry back; dost not remember that we left my poor little frozen brother tucked away in that icy chamber all alone by himself?" I was very weary and I fell off to sleep almost immediately, and yet I had an indistinct recollection that Bulger was not in his place against my breast. I remembered feeling for him, but that's all. It never flashed upon me that he had gone and lain down beside the poor little stranger, whom I had so unfeelingly lifted from his last resting-place, and yet such must have been the case, for about midnight, it seemed to me, I was awakened by a gentle tugging at my sleeve.

It was my faithful Bulger, but, half awake and half asleep as I was, I merely thought that he was only asking for a caress, as was often his wont when he fell a-thinking about home, so I reached out and stroked his head several times and dropped off again.

But the tugging began anew, and this time 'twas more vigorous and with it came an impatient whine which meant,——

"Come, come, little master, rouse thee; dost suppose I would break thy rest unless there were good reasons for it?" I didn't need a third reminder, but with a single bound landed on my feet, and reaching out for one of the tiny tapers which the Koltykwerps make use of as lighters, I carried the flames from the single lamp burning on the wall to the three others hanging here and there.

The icy walls of my chamber were now ablaze with light. There sat Bulger on the fur-covered divan, beside the place where the Little Man with the Frozen Smile lay hidden under the pelt. His tail was wagging nervously, and his large, lustrous eyes were fixed first upon me and then upon the covering of his dead brother with an expression I never remembered having seen in them before, and then with a sudden movement he laid hold of the pelt and, drawing it aside, showed me, what think you, dear friends, what, I ask in a tone half whisper, half gasp, for now years after I still can feel that wonderful thrill which I felt then? Why, it was alive! That ape-like creature had come to life after his sleep of thousands of years in that narrow, crystal cell! Bulger had lain down beside his frozen brother and warmed him back to life again!

Oh, it was wondrously wonderful to see that pair of little eyes, beadlike in brightness, look up and blink at me; and then to hear that low, moaning voice, so human-like, as if it whimpered, with a shake and a shiver,—

"Oh, how cold it is! how very cold it is! Where's the sun? Where's the soft warm wind, and where are the cloudless skies so blue, oh so beautifully blue, that used to hang over my head?"

Bidding Bulger lie down again beside him and snuggle up as close as possible, I made haste to cover them both with the softest skins I could find.

In a few moments there came from underneath the pile a low, contented cry of "Coojah! Coojah! Coojah!" followed by a curious addition sounding like "Fuff! Fuff! Fuff!" so I put them all together and named the strange new comer to the icy domain of King Gelidus—Fuffcoojah!

Sleep any more that night? Not a wink. The same joy came over me that I used to feel on Christmas morning long ago when Kris Kringle brought me some wonderful bit of mechanism moved by a secret spring—for I always scorned to accept ordinary toys like ordinary children; and oh, how I longed for the morning, when it would be time for me to bundle up the Little Man—no longer him with the Frozen Smile, but Fuffcoojah, the Live Boy from Faraway, with his curious little face screwed up into such a funny look—and carry him to the palace.

How delighted Schneeboule will be! thought I, and King Gelidus too, how he will unbend from his frigid majesty as he watches the antics of Fuffcoojah, and how pleased all the dignified Koltykwerpians, including even Phrostyphiz and Glacierbhoy, will be when I tell them that the Little Man with the Frozen Smile has come to life again!

What crowds of Koltykwerps, men, women and children, will rush up the long flights of steps leading to the Ice Palace, begging and entreating King Gelidus to let them have just a little look at Fuffcoojah, the little man set free from his icy cell by the famous traveller, Baron Sebastian von Troomp!

CHAPTER XXVII

It all turned out just as I had thought it would! The moment it became known that the Little Man with the Frozen Smile had actually come to life, the wildest excitement prevailed in every part of the icy domain of his frigid Majesty. I was astounded at the change in the actions of the Koltykwerps. They moved more quickly, they talked faster, they made more gestures than I had ever seen them do before. In some cases, you will hardly believe it, dear friends, I actually noticed a faint glow in the cold cheeks of a few of them.

I had hoped to be able to bundle Fuffcoojah up warmly and make my escape to the ice palace before the people learned of his coming to life, but in vain. When I made my appearance at the door, there was a large crowd of Koltykwerps pushing and pulling in front of my quarters.

Most of them were good-natured, and cried out,—

"Show him to us, little baron, show us the Little Man with the Frozen Smile whom thou hast brought to life. Let us look upon his face!"

"Nay, nay, Koltykwerps!" I exclaimed, "it must not be! His frigid Majesty must be the first to look upon Fuffcoojah's face. Room, room for the noble guest of royal Gelidus! In the name of his frigid Majesty give way and let me pass!"

The Koltykwerps showed no inclination to obey. To such a pitch of excitement had they worked themselves up that only upon seeing Bulger advance upon them with flashing eye and teeth laid bare, did they reach the conclusion that my brave companion was in no mood to be trifled with.

Thwarted in their wild desire to get a peep at Fuffcoojah, the Koltykwerps now began to rail at me as I passed them by on my way to the ice palace.

"Oho, Master magician! Ha, ha, Prince of the Black Art! Boo, boo, little wizard! Have a care, wily necromancer, see to it that thou dost not practise any of thy tricks of enchantment upon us!" I was glad when the axe-bearer saw my plight and hurried forward to extricate me from the crowd of angry people.

King Gelidus met me at the portal of his ice palace, and at his heels came Princess Schneeboule, who could hardly wait for her turn to take a look at the curious living creature which I unwrapped just enough to let her see its nose.

The instant Fuffcoojah set eyes upon the sweet face of the Koltykwerpian princess, he stretched out his little arm as a child might to its mother. This sudden show of affection caused Schneeboule the liveliest pleasure, and quickly drawing off one of her gloves she reached out and stroked the animal's head, but at the touch of those, to him, icy little fingers he uttered a low wail and drew back underneath the warm pelt in which he was snugly wrapped.

Poor Schneeboule! she gave a sigh as she saw him do this, but it didn't prevent her from coming every minute or so and lifting one end of the pelt just enough to take another look at Fuffcoojah, who, while he never failed to cuddle up closer to me at sight of the princess, yet invariably thrust out one of his black paws from under the pelt for Schneeboule to shake. While seated on the divan nearest the throne, I observed that Phrostyphiz and Glacierbhoy were holding a whispered conference with his frigid Majesty. At once I guessed the subject of their conversation.

Rising to my feet, I made a sign that I wished to address the king, and when he had nodded his head with stern and icy dignity, I began to speak. You know, dear friends, how eloquent I can be when the mood is upon me. Well, standing there almost upon the steps of King Gelidus' throne of ice, I proceeded to defend myself against the charge of being a master of the black art. I will not tell you all I said, but this was my ending:

"May it please your frigid Majesty!

"Here beside me stands the only magician in the case, and the only art, the only trick or charm which was exercised by him was that sweet power we call love.

When first he set eyes upon his four-footed brother locked in the crystal cell of Schneeboule's Grotto, he pressed his nose again and again against its icy wall in vain attempt to know his kinsman, and turned away with a cry of sorrow to find that his keen scent could not penetrate to him. I cannot tell you how great was his joy when I laid Fuffcoojah stiff and stark upon my divan, for I knew not then the scheme ripening in Bulger's mind. But later, all was plain enough. The loving dog leaves his master's breast and carries his true and tender heart over to where Fuffcoojah lies, raises the pelt, crawls in beside him, and presses his warm breast firm and hard against his brother's ice-locked heart, and warms him into life again, then wakes me and tells me what he hath done.

"This, Royal Gelidus and most noble Koltykwerps, is the only art that hath been used to bring Fuffcoojah back to life again, and to call it black is to slander the sunshine, rail at the lily, and call the sweet breath of heaven a vile and detestable thing!"

When I had ended my speech I saw that Schneeboule had been weeping, and that several of her tears stopped in their course down her cheeks hung there sparkling like tiny diamonds in the soft light of the alabaster lamps, where the chill air of Gelidus' palace had turned them into ice.

And therefore when his frigid Majesty said that my words had touched his heart, and bade me ask for a gift from his hand, I said,—

"O cold king of this fair icy domain, let those tears that now hang like tiny jewels on Schneeboule's cheeks be brushed into an alabaster box and given to me. I covet no other guerdon!"

"Even if I did not love thee, little baron," cried King Gelidus with an icy smile, "I would be persuaded; but loving makes easy believing. Go, Phrostyphiz, and bid one of the princess's women brush those tiny jewels that hang on Schneeboule's cheek into an alabaster cup and bestow them upon the little baron."

Scarcely had this been done when Fuffcoojah thrust his head out from under the pelt and, fixing his eyes pleadingly upon me, thrust out his tongue and opened and shut his mouth with a faint, smacking noise. Quick as a flash it dawned upon me that these signs meant that Fuffcoojah was hungry!

And then, as I suddenly remembered that the Koltykwerps were strictly a meat-eating people, that only meat was to be had in their chill domain, quarried almost like marble itself from nature's great refrigerators, a gasp escaped my lips, and I whispered,—

"Oh, he must die! He must die!" My words had not missed the keen ears of Princess Schneeboule.

"Speak, little baron," she cried, "why, why, must little Fuffcoojah die? What dost mean by such a saying?" And when King Gelidus and Schneeboule had heard me voice my fear that he would die rather than feed on meat, they both became very heavy-hearted.

"Poor little Fuffcoojah!" moaned the princess, "can it be possible that he must be carried back so soon to his crystal cell in my grotto?"

"Bid the master of my meat quarries approach the throne," cried King Gelidus suddenly, in a voice of icy dignity.

This important functionary soon made his appearance.

Turning to me, the king bade me explain the case to him. This I did in a few words, when, to the great joy of all present the master of the meat quarries spoke as follows:—

"Little baron, if that's the only trouble, give thyself no further uneasiness, for I shall at once send one of my men to thee with a supply of most delicious nuts."

"Delicious nuts?" I repeated in a tone of amazement.

"Why, yes, little baron, I have a goodly supply on hand. Know, then, that hardly a day goes by that my men don't come upon some fine specimen of the family of gnawers, most generally squirrels, in whose cheek-pouches we invariably find from one to half a dozen dainty nuts stowed away. It has always been my custom to lay these aside, and so I have to inform thee that if Fuffcoojah should live to be a hundred years old I or my successor could guarantee to keep him supplied with food."

These words lifted a terrible load off my heart, for now, at least, Fuffcoojah would not die of starvation.

For a few days everything went well. The Koltykwerps became quite satisfied in their own minds that I had not been practising the black art in the chilly kingdom of his frigid Majesty, and each and every one of them became greatly attached to the curious little creature with the droll little face and droller manner.

But it seemed as if we were no sooner out of one trouble than we were plumped into another, for now Fuffcoojah began to object to the attendant selected to look after him by King Gelidus.

The man was about ten degrees too cold-blooded for him, and ere long it was only necessary for the Koltykwerp to approach Fuff,—as we called him for short,—in order to throw him into convulsions of shivering and to cause him to utter pitiable cries of discontent, which only ceased upon my appearing and comforting him by my caresses.

I now set to work to devise some way to make Fuff's life more agreeable to him, for everybody seemed to hold me responsible for his well being. Ten times a day came messengers from King Gelidus or from Princess Schneeboule to ask how he was getting on, and whether we were keeping him warm enough, whether he had all he wanted to eat, whether he had pelts enough on his bed. Nor was it an unusual thing to have a score or more Koltykwerpian mothers call at my quarters during a single day with advice enough to last a month, and therefore was it that, with a view to providing him with a warmer room to sleep in, I ordered a divan fitted up for him in a smaller chamber opening into mine, upon the walls of which I directed half a dozen of the largest lamps to be hung.

The consequence was that the walls began to melt, hearing of which, consternation spread throughout the icy domain of his frigid Majesty, for to the mind of a Koltykwerp heat powerful enough to melt ice was something terrible.

It was like the dread of earthquake shock to us, or the fear of flood or flame. It was something that filled their hearts with such terror that in their dreams they saw the solid walls of the ice palace melt asunder and fall with a crash. They could not bear it, and so King Gelidus put forth the decree that if there were no other way to keep Fuffcoojah alive, then must he die.

Hearing this, an awful grief came upon poor Schneeboule's heart, for she had learned to love little Fuff very dearly, and it set a knife in her breast to think of losing him.

"Never, never," she cried, "shall I be able to set foot within my grotto if Fuffcoojah is put back into his crystal prison again, with his frozen smile on his face as once used to be." And seeking out her royal father she threw herself at his knees and spoke as follows:—

"O heart of ice! O frigid Majesty, let not thy child die of grief. There is an easy way out of all our trouble with dear little Fuffcoojah."

"Speak, beloved Schneeboule," answered King Gelidus, "let me hear what it is."

"Why, cold heart," said the princess, "the little baron hath plenty of warmth stored away in his body, he hath enough for both himself and Fuffcoojah into the bargain. Therefore, frigid father, command that a deep, warm hood be made to the little baron's coat, and that Fuffcoojah be placed therein and be borne about by the little baron wherever he goeth. He will soon grow accustomed to the slender burden and note it no more."

"It shall be as thou wishest," replied the king of the Koltykwerps; and calling his trusty councillor, Glacierbhoy, he directed him to summon me at once to the throne-room. When I heard this terrible order issue from the icy lips of King Gelidus my heart sank within me, and yet I dared not disobey, I dared not murmur, for I it was who had cleft asunder the crystal prison of the Little Man with the Frozen Smile; I who had made it possible for Bulger to warm him back to life again. Oh, poor, vain, weak, foolish boy that I had been, what was to become of me now?

CHAPTER XXVIII

Ah, little princess, how easy was it for thee to say that I would soon grow accustomed to the slender burden and note it no more? How prone are we to call light the burdens which we lay upon the shoulders of others for our own benefit? True, Fuffcoojah was not as long as a horse, nor as broad as an ox, and when in accordance with the king's decree the hood had been completed and the little animal was stowed away therein, close against my back so as to get a goodly share of the warmth of my body, it seemed to me that Schneeboule was right, that I would soon become accustomed to the load and note it no more. And so it seemed the second and the third day, but not on the fourth; for on that day the little load appeared to have gained somewhat in weight, and although I was quick to feign that it was not so when Princess Schneeboule quizzed me saying,—

"There, little baron, did I not tell thee that thou wouldst soon forget that Fuffcoojah slept upon thy shoulders?" yet in my heart I felt that he really had grown a mite heavier.

On the fifth day Bulger and I were bidden to a merry-making at the palace of ice, and as I rose from my divan to betake me thither, methought I was strangely heavy-hearted, and so did Bulger, for he made several efforts to draw a smile, or a cheery tone, from me, but in vain.

Suddenly I realized that there was a weight pressing against my back, no, not a heavy weight, but a weight all the same, and then I whispered to myself, "Why, if I am going to a merry-making, I'll cast it off!" and then I wakened from my deep abstraction and murmured,—

"How strange that I should have forgotten that Fuffcoojah was in my hood?" And so I went to the merry-making with Fuffcoojah nestled between my shoulders, and the Koltykwerps laughed at the little baron and his child, as they called him, and drew near and raised the flap and peeped in at the curious creature within the hood, and when Fuffcoojah felt their icy breaths, he buried his nose in the fur and sighed and whimpered. Then, for a moment, when the Princess Schneeboule came and sat beside me and praised me for my readiness to carry out her wishes, and thanked me so sweetly for my goodness to her, I forgot all about the little load laid upon me, and I ate the frozen tidbits from the royal kitchen, and laughed and joked with Lords Phrostyphiz and Glacierbhoy, just as had been my wont before Gelidus had decreed that Fuffcoojah should make his bed on my shoulders.

But when the fête was over and I stepped from the broad portal of the ice-palace and looked up at the mighty lens set in the mountain side, through which the moonlight of the outer world was streaming in subdued but glorious splendor, I suddenly felt my legs bend under me, I staggered from right to left, I clutched at shadows, I was, it seemed to me, about to be crushed beneath a terrible burden. I quickened my pace, I broke into a run, I threw my arms into the air as if I would cast off the weight that was smothering me. And so I came to my lodging puffing, panting, gasping.

"Why, what a fool am I!" was my first word when I had got my breath; "it's only little Fuffcoojah on my back, stowed away in my fur hood. I must be beside myself to have thought that a great monster was seated there and that he was gradually pressing me down, crushing the life out of me by degrees, flattening me to the very ground, and I not able to escape from his terrible embrace or to squirm out from under his awful limbs wrapt around my neck and body!"

All night long this monster was clinging to me, and urging me to a faster pace, up and down, across and around, I knew not where, on bootless errands, ending only to begin again, on searches after nothing hidden nowhere, trying a thousand lids and finding every one locked, returning home only to go forth again, up and away and out on interminable highways vanishing in a point far on ahead, with that grievous burden forever on my shoulders growing heavier and heavier, till it seemed that I must go down with it into the dust. But no, it knew full well that it must not ride me to the death, so when I was ready to drop, it threw off part of its weight to give me courage to begin again. When the morning came my pulse was galloping and my cheeks were on fire. I could feel the blood pounding against my temples, and it was natural that my face should be crimsoned over with the flush of fever. Half in a daze I walked forth toward the grand staircase leading up to the ice palace, when suddenly I was startled by a fearful scream. I halted and looked up, when another and another burst upon my ears.

The terrified Koltykwerps were fleeing before me in every direction, shrieking as they fled,—

"Fly, fly, brothers, the little baron is burning, the little baron is burning, fly, brothers, fly!"

In a few moments terror had seized upon every living creature in the icy domain of King Gelidus. They fled from me in mad haste, taking refuge in the distant caverns and corridors, filling the air with their wild outcries, no one being brave enough to halt and take a second look. My inflamed countenance filled them with such awful terror that they could only tear along and cry,—

"Fly, brothers, fly; the little baron is burning, the little baron is burning!"

With Bulger at my heels, I turned and sprang up the staircase with the intention of seeking out King Gelidus, and explaining the matter to him.

But he, too, had fled, and with him every sentinel and serving man, every courtier and councillor. The palace was as still as death. I hastened through its silent corridors calling out,—

"Schneeboule! Princess Schneeboule! Surely thou art not afraid of me? Turn back, I will not harm thee, I'm not burning! Turn back, oh, turn back!"

With this, I reached the throne-room; not a living creature was to be seen; the vast chamber was as still as death. I staggered to a divan, and pillowing my poor aching head on a cushion, I fell into a sound and refreshing sleep.

When I awoke, I rubbed my eyes and looked about me, and at first I thought that I was still alone in the great round chamber with its walls of ice; but no, there on the divan sat Schneeboule, and she smiled and said in mock displeasure,—

"Thou art not a very watchful nurse, little baron, for in thy sleep thou didst squeeze Fuffcoojah so tightly against a cushion, that he crawled out from thy hood and nestled in my arms."

"In thy arms, Schneeboule?" I exclaimed breathlessly, for I feared for the worst, and springing up I drew aside the soft pelt which she had wrapped around Fuffcoojah, and there he lay, dead! Poor little beast, he had been so happy to crawl into the arms of one he loved so dearly, and had cuddled up closer and closer to her in search of greater warmth; but only to come nearer and nearer to a heart that could not warm him; and so the insidious chill of death, which bringeth sweet and pleasant drowsiness with it, had stole over him and he had died.

And Schneeboule's tears, freezing as they fell, now showered like a gentle hail of tiny gems upon the little dead beast, no longer Fuffcoojah, but once again the Little Man with the Frozen Smile. Presently the Koltykwerps recovered from their senseless fear, and first one by one, and then group-wise, they returned to their homes, King Gelidus and his court coming back too, to the fair palace which they had abandoned in their wild fright when the cry had gone up that the little baron was burning.

Everybody was sorry to hear that Fuffcoojah had died the second time, and many were the frozen tears that dropped from the chilly cheeks of the Koltykwerps as they looked upon the Little Man with the Frozen Smile as he lay on the white pelt beside the Princess Schneeboule.

That day we bore him back to the ice grotto, and having laid him in the hollow moulded by his body in the crystal block, it was closed again so skilfully by the king's quarrymen that no eye was keen enough to note where the cleavage had been. And the same uncanny glint was in his eyes, and when the Koltykwerps saw this their icy hearts felt a cold shiver of satisfaction, for not only was the Little Man with the Frozen Smile back in his crystal cell again, but all the fears and dreadful fancies which his coming to life again had given rise to were past and gone forever, and peace and quiet and sweet contentment reigned throughout the icy realm of his frigid Majesty Gelidus, King of the Koltykwerps!

Now nothing remained to make his cold heart crack with joy but to see his beloved child Schneeboule make choice of a husband. And he had not long to wait, for one day upon entering the palace she saw a youth lying at the foot of the stairway overcome with sleep. In one hand he held an alabaster lamp, and in the other a new wick which he was about to fit into it, for the youth was a lamp-trimmer in the ice palace of King Gelidus; and when the Princess Schneeboule saw him lying there overcome with sleep, she stooped and kissed him on the cheek, and passed on without another thought about the matter, one way or the other.

And the kiss froze on the cheek of the lamp-trimmer, where Schneeboule had pressed it.

Presently King Gelidus came tramping into the hallway with his breath white upon his beard, and he saw the youth lying there, and the frozen kiss on his cheek, and he bade Glacierbhoy scrape the delicate frost crystals from the youth's face with a blade of polished horn.

"What hast there, father of mine?" asked the princess, when she saw him bearing the blade of horn along so carefully.

"A kiss which someone pressed upon the cheek of one of my lamp-trimmers, now lying on the staircase overcome with sleep," replied King Gelidus, in ringing, icy tones.

"Why, father of mine," exclaimed Princess Schneeboule, "now that thou speakest of it, I really believe the kiss is mine, for I recollect kissing someone as I entered the palace, I was deep in thought, but no doubt the youth pleased me as he lay there, asleep with lamp in one hand and wick in the other."

And that lamp-trimmer trimmed no more lamps in the ice palace of his frigid Majesty Gelidus, King of the Koltykwerps.

No doubt he made Schneeboule a very good husband, and I'm quite sure that she made him a good wife. I would have been glad to tarry for the nuptial feast, but that was out of the question. I had stayed too long already.

CHAPTER XXIX

As Bullibrain had once remarked, when there are many doors it's a wise man who knows which is the right one to open; and this I found to be the case when I attempted to take my departure from the icy domain of his frigid Majesty, Gelidus, King of the Koltykwerps, for there was a baker's dozen of galleries, in each of which, upon exploring it, I came, after a tramp of half a mile or so, up against a lofty gate of solid ice, curiously carved and fitting the end of the gallery as a cork does a bottle.

No doubt you are wondering why I didn't make my way out of the Koltykwerpian kingdom by following the river: for the very good reason that it went no farther than King Gelidus's domain, emptying into a vast reservoir which apparently had a subterranean outlet, for its thick covering of ice always remained at the same height.

The king's quarrymen were ordered to hew an opening through whichever door I should point out as the one that I wished to pass through, but I was informed by Phrostyphiz that according to the law of the land but one door could be opened during any one year, so that if I found my way blocked and turned back again it would mean a delay of twelve months. Bullibrain, with all his wisdom, was powerless to assist me, although I was half inclined to think that he might have done so had he been permitted to investigate the secret records of the kingdom, carved upon huge tablets of ice, and stored away in the vaults of the palace.

The fact of the matter is King Gelidus was so desirous of having me assist at the marriage feast of Princess Schneeboule, that he threw every obstacle in my way that he could, without openly showing his hand. And Schneeboule herself by the dancing of her clear gray eyes gave me to understand that she, too, was hoping that I would make a mistake when I came to point out the door which I wanted opened.

Bulger saw that I was in trouble, but couldn't comprehend clearly what that trouble was. He kept his eyes fastened upon me, however, watching my every movement, hoping, no doubt, to solve the mystery.

While sitting one day lost in thought over the very serious problem which I found myself called upon to solve, an idea struck me: I had noticed that in the meat-quarries, the workmen often made use of sounding-rods, which were long pieces of polished bone, ending in flint tips. A Koltykwerpian quarryman by dexterously twisting this rod, was able to bore a hole six feet deep or more into the solid bed of ice when desirous of ascertaining the position of a carcass in the meat quarry, and it occurred to me that by piercing the portals of ice which closed their various corridors I have spoken of, possibly Bulger's keen scent might recognize that current of air which would have in it the odor of earth and rock; in other words, make choice for me of the portal which opened on that corridor leading away from the icy domain of King Gelidus and not merely into some outlying chamber of his kingdom.

His frigid Majesty could not object to such experiments, for the law only forbade the hewing of openings large enough for the hewer to pass through.

King Gelidus and half a dozen of his courtiers, looking stern and frigid and conversing in freezing tones, were present to see the experiment tried. Methought their icy lips clacked together with satisfaction when, at my request, one portal after another was pierced, but Bulger, after sniffing at the hole, turned away with a bewildered look in his eyes as if he didn't half understand why I was ordering him to thrust his warm nose into such cold places.

And so we tramped from corridor to corridor, until the quarrymen began to show signs of fatigue, and the sounding-rod turned slower and slower in their hands.

Phrostyphiz blinked his cold gray eyes as much as to say, "Little baron, thou must bide with us for another year!" But I merely turned to the quarrymen, and ordered them to pierce one more portal of ice ere we abandoned the task for the day. They went at the work of piercing the eleventh door with the pace of pack-mules up a mountain-side. But at last the sounding-rod bored a way through, and at a wave of my hand the quarrymen fell back. In an instant Bulger had his nose at the hole, and took three or four quick, nervous sniffs, ending with a long, deep-drawn one, and then breaking out into a string of sharp, jerky, joyful barks, he began scratching furiously at the bottom of the portal.

"Your frigid Majesty," said I, with a low and stately bend of my body such as only those born to the manner can make, "by this portal, at the coming of to-morrow's sun, I shall pass from your Majesty's icy dominion!" And when Phrostyphiz and Glacierbhoy heard these words of mine uttered so loftily, their eyes gleamed cold as steel, and they followed the King in silence back to the palace of ice. Schneeboule met them in the grand hallway; and when she had looked upon their faces she began to weep, for she loved me and she loved Bulger too, and her cold little heart could not bear the thought of our going.

King Gelidus, however, soon recovered his spirits, and ordered a feast with song and dance in honor of Bulger, who during the festivities sat on the highest divan with the softest pelt beneath him; and so many were the frozen tidbits which the Koltykwerps presented to him during the progress of the feast, that I grew alarmed lest he might overload his stomach and not be in a fit condition to make the early start on our journey, of which I had given notice to the Koltykwerpian monarch. But his good sense saved him from doing so foolish a thing; in fact, I was greatly amused to see that, while he accepted every tidbit handed to him, and solemnly went through the motions of chewing it, yet watching his chance, he slyly dropped it out of his mouth and flirted it aside with his paw. Thus was spent our last night at the icy court of his frigid Majesty, and on the morrow the Koltykwerps collected in great crowds on the different terraces to say good-by. I pressed a kiss on the cheek of Princess Schneeboule, and when it had turned to ice crystals, one of her men brushed it into an alabaster box.

Prince Chillychops, the former lamp-trimmer, was on hand with the rest of the Koltykwerpian nobles, but I flattered myself that Schneeboule loved me better than she did him. However, I wished him joy, and gripped his cold palm with such warmth that he stood blowing it for a whole minute. When we reached the lofty portal we found that the quarrymen had already hewn a passage through it, and near by I observed a pile of massive blocks of ice, crystal clear.

These, when Bulger and I should pass through the opening, were to be used in walling it up again; and when I saw this pile of blocks, and remembered the solid workmanship of the Koltykwerpian quarrymen, the thought flitted through my mind: Suppose Bulger hath not chosen wisely, what use would there be in turning back, for my own weak hands would be powerless against a wall built of such blocks, and knock I ever so loud, how could the sound ever traverse this long and winding corridor and reach the ear of a Koltykwerp? "No," said I to myself, "if Bulger hath not chosen wisely, it will be good-by to both upper and under worlds." And then, bearing an alabaster lamp in one hand and in the other holding the cord which I had tied to Bulger's collar, I stepped through the narrow passage hewn by the quarrymen, and turned my back forever on the cold dominion of Gelidus, King of the Koltykwerps. Once I halted and looked back. I could see nothing, but I could hear the sharp click of the flint axes as the quarrymen closed up the door that shut me out from so many cold but loving hearts. And then I drew a long breath and went on my way again.

And that was the last I ever saw of the Koltykwerps save in day dream or night vision.

CHAPTER XXX

Had my hand at that moment not grasped a cord tied to the neck of my wise and keen-eyed Bulger, I really believe I would have come to a halt, faced about, retraced my steps, and begged the inhabitants of this crystal realm to admit me once more into the cold kingdom where Gelidus held his icy court; for a sudden fit of depression came upon me as the chilly air struck against my cheeks and I saw the deep darkness made visible by the tiny flame of my alabaster lamp.

Cold though it might be, I would have sunshine in the icy land of the Koltykwerps, but now how could I tell what fate awaited me?

Luckily, I had asked the captain of the meat quarries to allow me to retain one of his sounding-rods with its flint point, for I feared lest in descending some icy declivity I might fall and bruise, or even break, a limb.

I was determined to advance cautiously along this icy passage, shrouded as it was in impenetrable gloom, and so different from the broad and polished pavement of the Marble Highway; and hence, hanging the lamp about my neck, I proceeded to make use of the sounding-rod as an alpenstock, for which purposes it was admirably adapted. Suddenly Bulger halted, gave a low whine of warning, and turned back. In an instant I knew that there was danger ahead, and letting myself drop on my hands and knees crawled carefully along to make an investigation of the dangerous spot in our route signalled by the watchful Bulger.

It was only too true: we stood apparently upon the very edge of a sheer parapet, how high I had no way of ascertaining, but I was unable to reach any bottom with the sounding-rod.

What was to be done? Turn back?

It was not yet too late, the Koltykwerpian quarrymen could not have completed their task in so short a time, they would hear my knock, they would tear down their wall of ice, and Gelidus and Schneeboule would welcome us back to their ice palace with a cold, but honest satisfaction.

As I sat there plunged in thought, I half unconsciously began to twirl the sounding-rod around until I had sunk it half its length into the floor of ice, and then reaching out I encircled Bulger with my arm and drew him up against me as was my wont when preparing for profound meditation.

I had scarcely done so when the ice beneath me gave one of those sharp, clear, cracking noises so unlike the sound made by the breaking of any other substance; and thereupon I felt the crystal mass on which Bulger and I were sitting tremble and vibrate for an instant, and then, with a sudden downward cant, break away from the mass behind it and begin to move!

Instinctively a sense of my awful peril prompted me to cling to the sounding-rod which I had sunk drill-like into the ice. Luckily it was between my legs, and quick as a flash I intwined them around it, assuming a Turkish sitting posture, while my left arm was wrapped tightly around Bulger's body.

I don't know how it was done, done as it was all in an instant; but there I sat now firmly saddled, so to speak, upon that crystal monster's back, as with a creak and a crash it snapped the crystal links which bound it to the wall of ice and plunged headlong down the glassy slope.

In my fright I had dropped my lamp, and now the deep gloom of this under world inwrapped me. But no, it was not so, for as the escaping block of ice creaked and craunched its way along, the two cold crystal surfaces gave forth a weird glimmer of phosphorescent light which made the flying mass seem like a monstrous living thing, out of whose thousand eyes were darting tongues of flame as it rushed madly along, now gaining speed upon striking a steeper stretch of way, now fouling with some obstruction and dashing against the rocky sides of the corridor, and sending a shower of crystals sparkling and glittering in the black air!

Anon the escaping block comes upon a gentle slope, and with the low music of crushing crystals slips softly along in its flight as if mounted upon runners of polished steel, and then with a sudden dip it glides upon a sharper descent and fairly leaps into the air as it bounds along, hissing over the slippery roadway, and leaving a train of fire behind it. And now it strikes a stretch of way piled here and there with clumps and blocks of ice.

With a mad fury it springs upon the lesser ones with a growl of rage, grinding them to powder, which, like showers of icy foam, it hurls upon Bulger and me seated on its back. But some of the blocks resist its terrible onslaught and our mighty steed is hurled from side to side with crash and creak, as it drives its crystal corners fiercely against the jutting rocks, leaving marks of its white flesh on these black heads of adamant.

It seems an hour since the crystal monster broke away, and yet ever downward he threads his wild flight, butting, bumping, jostling, veering, staggering along, bearing Bulger and me to the lowest level of the World within a World.

Will he never end his mad flight?

Is there no way for me to curb him?

Must he fly until he has ground his very body to such a thinness that the next obstruction will shatter it into ten thousand pieces, and hurl Bulger and me to death?

As these thoughts are flitting through my mind, the flying mass takes one last mad plunge which lands it on an almost level stretch of roadway, and by the different sound given out by the sliding block, I know that we have left the regions of ice behind us, and that our crystal sledge is gliding gently along over a track of polished marble.

But, mile after mile, it still glides along, gently, softly, silently, and then I dare to think that our lives are saved.

But so terrible had been the strain, so fearful the anxiety, so exhausting the effort necessary to hold my place on the block of ice, and keep my beloved Bulger from slipping out of my arms, that I fell backward into a dead faint as the gliding mass came, at last, to a standstill. I think I must have lain there a good half hour or so; for when I came to myself Bulger's frantic joy told me that he had been terribly wrought up over me, and the moment I opened my eyes he began to shower caresses on my hands and face in most lover-like style. Dear, grateful heart, he felt that he owed his life this time to his little master, and he wanted me to understand how thankful he was.

The moment Bulger's nerves had recovered from the shock occasioned by my prolonged faint, I reached for my repeater and touched its spring.

It registered one hour and a half since we had stepped through the icy portal of King Gelidus' domain. Allowing a half-hour for the time I lay unconscious, it showed that our mad descent on the back of the crystal monster had lasted quite a full hour, and reckoning the average speed of the escaping mass of ice to have been a mile and a half a minute, that we were now in the neighborhood of ninety miles away from the cold kingdom where Gelidus sat on his icy throne, and Princess Schneeboule at his feet with Chillychops beside her.

It was with great difficulty that I could rise to my feet, so stiffened were my joints and knotted my muscles after that terrible ride, every instant of which I expected to be dashed to pieces against projecting rocks, or torn to shreds by being caught between the fleeing monster of ice and the gigantic icicles hanging from the ceiling like the shining teeth of some huge creature of this under world.

But could it be, dear friends, that Bulger and I had only escaped a quick and merciful ending to be brought face to face with a death ten times more terrible, in that it was to be slow and gradual, denied even the poor boon of looking upon each other, for darkness impenetrable was folded about us and silence so deep that my ears ached in their longing for some sound to break it. And yet there was something in the sound of my own voice that startled me when I used it: it seemed as if the awful stillness were angered at being disturbed by it, and smote it back into my teeth.

Where are we? This was the question I put to myself, and then in my mind I strove to recall every word which I had read in the musty pages of Don Fum's manuscript concerning the World within a World; but I could recollect nothing to enlighten me, not a word to give me hope or cheer, and I was about to cry out in utter despair when, happening to raise my eyes and look off in the distance, I saw what seemed to me to be a jack-a-lantern dancing along on the ground.

It was a strange and fantastic sight in this region of inky darkness, and for a moment I stood watching it with bated breath and wide-opened eyes; but no, it could not be a will-with-the-wisp, for now the faint and uncertain glimmer had increased to a mild but steady glow, reaching away off in the distance like a long line of dying camp-fires seen through an enveloping mist.

But in a moment's time this wide encircling ring of light had so increased in brightness that it looked for all the world like a break o' day in the land o' sunshine, and here and there where its mild effulgence overcame the darkness of this subterranean region, I caught sight of walls and arches and columns of snow-white marble. And then as I called to mind Don Fum's mysterious reference to "sunrise in the lower world," I swung my hat and gave a loud cry of joy, while Bulger waked the echoes of these spacious caverns by his barking. I tell you, dear friends, not until you have been in just such a plight can you know just how such a rescue feels.

And now, no doubt, you are a bit anxious to know what sort of a sunrise could possibly take place in this under world miles below our own.

Well, when you have travelled as many miles as I have, and seen as many wonders as I have, you'll be ready to admit that wonders are quite as commonplace as commonplace itself. Know, then, that this vast region of the World within a World was girt round about by a broad and placid stream whose waters swarmed with vast numbers of gigantic radiate animals, such as polyps, sea-urchins, Portuguese men-of-war, sea-anemones, and the like; that these transparent creatures, which had the power of emitting light, after lying dormant for twelve hours, gradually unfolded their bodies and tentacles, and rose toward the surface of these calm and limpid waters, increasing by degrees their mysterious radiance, until they had chased the darkness from the vast caverns opening upon the banks of the river, and lighted up this under world with a soft effulgence somewhat brighter than the rays of our full moon. For twelve hours these weird lanterns of the stream made it day for this nether world, and then, as they gradually shrank together and sank out of sight, their expiring fires glowed with all the multicolored radiance of our fairest twilight, and the night, blacker than Stygian darkness, came back again. But now 'twas full daylight, and bidding Bulger follow me I walked in silent wonder along the banks of this glowing stream, which, like a band of mysterious fire, as far as my eye could reach went circling around the white marble mouths of these vast underground chambers.

CHAPTER XXXI

With every turn in the winding way that skirted the white shores of this wonderful stream, its swarms of light-emitting animals lent it a new beauty; for as the day advanced—if I may so express it—they lifted their glowing bodies nearer and nearer to the surface, until now the river shone like molten silver; and as the sheer walls of rock on the opposite bank held set in them vast slabs of mica, the effect was that these gigantic natural mirrors reflected the glowing stream with startling fidelity, and threw the flood of soft light in dazzling shimmer against the fantastic portals of the white marble caverns on this side of the stream. It was a scene never to forget, and again and again I paused in silent wonder to feast my eyes upon some newly discovered beauty. Now, for the first, I noted that every white marble basin of cove and inlet was filled with a different glow, according to the nature of the tiny phosphorescent animals which happened to fill its waters,— one being a delicate pink, another a glorious red, the third a deep rich purple, the fourth a soft blue, the fifth a golden yellow, and so on, the charm of each tint being greatly enhanced by the snowy whiteness of these marble basins, through which long lines of curious fish scaled in hues of polished gold and silver swam slowly along, turning up their glorious sides to catch the full splendor of the light reflected from the mica mirrors. And now the chilly breath of King Gelidus' domain no longer filled the air. I stood in the tropics of the under world, so to speak; and but one thing was lacking to make my enjoyment of this fairy region complete, and that was some one to share it with me.

True, Bulger had an idea of its beauty, for he testified his happiness at being once more in a warm land by executing some mad capers for my amusement, and by scampering along the shore of the glowing river and barking at the stately fish as they slowly fanned the water with their many colored fins; but I must admit that I longed for the Princess Schneeboule to keep me company. But it was a rash wish; for the warm air would have thrown her into convulsions of fear, and she would have preferred to meet her death in the cool river rather than attempt to breathe such a fiery atmosphere. By this time I had advanced several miles along the white shores of the glowing stream, and, feeling somewhat fatigued, I was about to sit down on the jutting edge of a natural bench of rock, which seemed almost placed on the river banks by human hands for human forms to rest upon and watch the wonderful play of tints and hues in this wide sweeping inlet, when, to my amazement, I saw that a human creature was already sitting there.

His eyes were fixed upon the water, and methought that his face, which was gentle and placid, wore a tired look. Certainly he was plunged into such deep meditation that he either took or feigned to take no notice of my approach. Bulger was inclined to dash forward and attract his attention by a string of earsplitting barks, but I shook my head. This wanderer along the glowing stream of day wore rather a graceful cloak-like garment, woven of some substance that shimmered in the light, and so I concluded that it must be mineral wool. His head was bare, and so were his legs to the knees, his feet being shod with white metal sandals tied on with what looked like leathern thongs. All in all, he had a friendly though somewhat peculiar look about him, and his attitude struck me as being that of a person either plunged into deep thought, or possibly listening for some anxiously expected signal. At any rate, accustomed as I was to meet all sorts of people on my travels in the four corners of the globe, I determined to make bold enough to interrupt the gentleman's meditations and wish him good-morrow.

"Whom have I the pleasure of meeting in this beautiful section of the World within a World?"

The man looked at me in a dazed sort of way and replied,—

"I really don't know, I'm happy to say."

"But, sir, thy name!" I insisted.

"Forgot it years ago," was his remarkable answer.

"But surely, sir," I exclaimed rather testily, "thou art not the sole inhabitant of this beautiful under world,—thou hast kinsman, wife, family?"

"Ay, gentle stranger," he replied in slow and measured tones, "there are people farther along the shore, and they are good, dear souls, although I have forgotten their names, and I have, too, a very faint recollection that two of those people are sons of mine. Stop! no, their names are gone from me too, I forgot them the day my own name slipped from my mind!" and as he uttered these words he threw his head back with a sudden jerk and I heard a strange click inside of it, as if something had slipped from its place, and that instant a mysterious expression used by that Master of Masters, Don Fum, flashed through my mind.

Rattlebrains! Yes, that was it; and now I felt sure that I was standing in the presence of one of the curious folk inhabiting the World within a World, to whom Don Fum had given the strange name of Rattlebrains, or Happy Forgetters.

I was so delighted that I could barely keep myself from rushing up to this gentle-visaged and mild-mannered person, whose head had just given forth the sharp click, and grasping him by the hand. But I feared to shock him by such a friendly greeting, and so I contented myself with crying out,—

"Sir, thou seest before thee none other than the famous traveller, Baron Sebastian von Troomp!" but to my great amazement and greater chagrin he simply turned his strange eyes, with the far-away look, upon me for an instant, and then resumed his contemplation of the beautifully tinted sheet of water, as if I hadn't opened my mouth. It was the most extraordinary treatment that I had experienced since my descent into the under world, and I was upon the point of resenting it, as became a true knight and especially a von Troomp, when Don Fum's brief description of the Rattlebrains, or Happy Forgetters, flitted through my mind.

Said he, "By the exercise of their strong wills they have been busy for ages striving to unload their brains of the to them now useless stock of knowledge accumulated by their ancestors, and the natural consequence has been that the brains of these curious folk, who call themselves the Happy Forgetters, relieved of all labor and strain of thought, have absolutely shrunken rather than increased in size, so that with many of the Happy Forgetters their brains are like the shrivelled kernel of a last year's nut and give forth a sharp click when they move their heads suddenly with a jerk, as is often their wont, for they take great pride in proving to the listener that they deserve the name of Rattlebrain.

"Nor do I need remind thee, O reader," concluded Don Fum, in his celebrated work on the "World within a World," "that the chiefest among the Happy Forgetters is the man whose head gives forth the loudest and sharpest click; for he it is who has forgotten most."

You can have but a faint idea, dear friends, of my delight at the prospect of spending some time among these curious people—people who look with absolute dread upon knowledge as the one thing necessary to get rid of before happiness can enter the human heart.

No joy can equal the Happy Forgetter's when, upon clasping a friend's hand, he finds that he has forgotten his very name; and no day is well spent in this land at the close of which the inhabitant may not exclaim,—

"This day I succeeded in forgetting something that I knew yesterday!"

At last the Happy Forgetter rose from his seat and calmly walked away, without so much as wishing me good-day; but I was resolved not to be so easily gotten rid of, so I called after him in a loud voice, and Bulger, following my example, raised a racket at his heels, whereupon he faced about and remarked,—

"Beg pardon, I had quite forgotten thee, I'm happy to say, and thy name too, I've forgotten that; let me see, Art thou a radiate?" (One of the animals in the water.) I was more than half inclined to lose my temper at this slur, classing me, a back-boned animal, with a mere jelly-fish; but under all the circumstances I thought it best to control myself, for I could well imagine that from the size of my head and the utter absence of all click inside of it, I was not destined to be a very welcome visitor among the Happy Forgetters; and therefore, swallowing my injured feelings, I made a very low bow, and begged this curious gentleman to be kind enough to conduct me to his people—among whom I wished to abide for a few days.

CHAPTER XXXII

The Happy Forgetter pursued his way calmly along the winding path that skirted the glowing river, apparently, and no doubt really, unconscious of the fact that Bulger and I were following close at his heels. After half an hour or so of this silent tramp, he suddenly came to a standstill, and with his placid countenance turned toward the light seemed to be so far away in thought that for several moments I hesitated to address him. But as there were no signs of his showing any disposition to come to himself, I made bold to ask him the cause of the delay.

"I'm happy to say," he remarked, without so much as deigning to turn his head, "that I've forgotten which of these two roads leads to the homes of our people."

Well, this was a pleasant outlook to be sure, and, I don't know what we should have done had not Bulger solved the difficulty for us by making choice of one of the paths and dashing on ahead with a bark of encouragement for us to follow.

When I assured the Happy Forgetter that he need have no fear as to the wisdom of the choice, he gave a start of almost horror at the information; for you must know, dear friends, that the Happy Forgetter has more dread of knowledge than we have of ignorance. To him it is the mother of all discontent, the source of all unhappiness, the cause of all the dreadful ills that have come upon the world, and the people in it.

"The world," said one of the Happy Forgetters to me sadly, "was perfectly happy once, and man had no name for his brother, and yet he loved him even as the turtle-dove loves his mate, although he has no names to call her by. But, alas, one day this happiness came to an end, for a strange malady broke out among the people. They were seized with a wild desire to invent names for things; even many names for the same thing, and different ways of doing the same thing. This strange passion so grew upon them that they spent their lives in making them in every possible way harder to live. They built different roads to the same place, they made different clothes for different days, and different dishes for different feasts. To each child they gave two, three, and even four different names; and different shoes were fashioned for different feet, and one family was no longer satisfied with one drinking-gourd. Did they stop here?

"Nay, they now busied themselves learning how to make different faces to different friends, covering a frown with a smile, and singing gay songs when their hearts were sad. In a few centuries a brother could no longer read a brother's face, and one-half the world went about wondering what the other half was thinking about; hence arose misunderstandings, quarrels, feuds, warfare. Man was no longer content to dwell with his fellow-man in the spacious caverns which kind nature had hollowed out for him, piercing the mountains with winding passages beside which his narrow streets dwindled to merest pathways."

In the Land of the Happy Forgetters care never comes to trouble sleep, nor anxious thought to wear the dread mask of To-morrow!

Happy the day on which this child of nature might exclaim: "Since morn I've forgotten something! I've unloaded my mind! It's one thought lighter than it was!"

He was the happiest of the Happy Forgetters who could honestly say, I know not thy name, nor when thou wast born, not where thou dwellest, nor who thy kinsmen are; I only know that thou art my brother, and that thou wilt not see me suffer if I should forget to eat, or perish of thirst if I forget to drink, and that thou wilt bid me close my eyes if I should forget that I had laid me down to sleep.

Bulger's and my arrival in the Land of the Happy Forgetters filled the hearts of these curious folk with secret dread. At sight of my large head they all began to tremble like children in the dark stricken with fear of bogy or goblin, and with one voice they refused to permit me to sojourn a single brief half-hour among them; but gradually this sudden terror passed off a bit, and after a council held by a few of the younger men, whose brains as yet completely filled their heads, it was determined that I might bide for another day in their land, but that then the revolving door should be opened, and Bulger and I be thrust outside of their domain.

From what Don Fum had written about the Happy Forgetters, I knew only too well that it would be useless for me to attempt to reverse this decree; so I held my peace, except to thank them for this great favor shown me.

The daylight, if I may call it so, now began to wane, or rather the thousands of light-giving creatures swarming in the river now began to draw in their long tentacles, close their flower-like bodies, and slowly sink to the bottom of the stream. I was quite anxious to see whether the Happy Forgetters would make any attempt to light up their cavernous homes, or whether they would simply creep off to bed and sleep out the long hours of pitchy darkness. To my surprise, I now heard the clicking of flints on all sides, and in a moment or so a thousand or more great candles made of mineral wax with asbestos wicks were lighted, and the great chambers of white marble were soon aglow with these soft and steady flames.

The Happy Forgetters were strictly vegetable eaters, feeding upon the various fungous plants growing in these caverns in great profusion, together with a very nutritious and pleasant tasting jelly made from a hardened gum of vegetable origin which abounded in the crevices of certain rocks. There was still another source of food; namely, the nests of certain shellfish, which they built against the face of the rock, just above the surface of the river. These dissolved in boiling water made an excellent broth, very much like the soup from edible birds' nests.

The clothes worn by the Happy Forgetters were entirely woven from mineral wool, which in these caverns gave a long and strong fibre of astonishing softness. The Rattlebrains were tolerably good metal-workers too, but contented themselves with fashioning only such articles as were actually necessary for daily use. Their beds were stuffed with dried seaweed and lichens, and Bulger and I passed a very comfortable night.

As I was forbidden to speak aloud, to ask a question, or to walk abroad unless in company with one of the selectmen, I was not sorry when the moment came for the revolving door to be opened. The Happy Forgetters had been led to believe that Bulger and I were a thousand times more dangerous than scaly monsters or black-winged vampires, and hence they held themselves aloof from us, the children hiding behind their mothers, and the mothers peering through crack and crevice at us.

The size of my head inspired them with a nameless dread, and even the half-a-dozen of the younger and more courageous drew aside instinctively to let me pass.

For the first time in my life I was an object of horror to my fellow-creatures, but I had no hard thoughts against them! Timid children of nature that they were, to them I was as terrible an object as the torch-armed demon of destruction would be to us were he let loose in one of our fair cities of the upper world.

And now the guard of Happy Forgetters had halted in front of what seemed to me to be a huge cask fashioned of solid marble, and set one-half within the white wall of the cavern to which they had led me. But on second glance I saw that there was a row of square holes around its bulge, like those in the top of a capstan.

The Happy Forgetters now disappeared for a moment, and when they joined me again each bore in hand a metal bar, the end of which he set in one of these holes, and then at a signal from the leader the huge half-circle of marble began to turn noiselessly around, exactly like a capstan. As each man's lever came to the wall, he shifted it to the front again. Suddenly, to my amazement, I saw that the great marble cask was hollow, like a sentry box; and you may judge of my feelings, dear friends, upon being politely requested to step inside.

Did I refuse to obey?

Not I. It would have been useless, for was not the whole tribe of Rattlebrains there to lay hands upon me and thrust me in?

So taking off my hat and making a low bow to the little group of Happy Forgetters, I stepped within the hollow cask and Bulger did the same; but not with so good a grace as his master, for, casting an angry glance at the inhospitable dwellers in these chambers of white marble, he growled and laid bare his teeth to show his contempt for them.

Now the great marble cask began to revolve the other way and in a moment it was back in place again.

I heard several sharp clicks as if a number of huge spring latches had snapped into place, and then all was silent as the tomb, and I had almost said as dark too; but no, I could not say that, for I looked out into a low tunnel which ran past the niche in which Bulger and I were standing, and to my more than wonder it was dimly lighted.

I stepped out into it; it was as round as a cannon bore and just high enough for me to stand erect; and now I discovered whence the light proceeded. In the cracks and crevices of its walls grew vast masses of those delicate light-giving fungous rootlets, the glow of which was so strong that I had no difficulty in reading the writing on my tablets; in fact, I stood there for several minutes making entries by the light of these bunches of glowing rootlets.

Then the thought dashed through my mind,—

"Which way shall I turn, to the right or to the left?"

Bulger comprehended the cause of my vacillation and made haste to come to my rescue. After sniffing the air, first in one direction and then in the other, he chose the right hand, and I followed without a thought of questioning his wisdom. Strange to say, he had not advanced more than a few hundred rods before I noticed that there was a strong current of air blowing through the tunnel in the direction Bulger had taken.

Every moment it increased in violence, fairly lifting us from our feet and bearing us along through this narrow bore made by nature's own hands and lighted too by lamps of her own fashioning. The motion of the air through this vast pipe caused bursts of mighty tones as if peeled forth by some gigantic organ played by giant hands. It was strange, but yet I felt no terror as I listened to this unearthly music, although its depth of tone jarred painfully upon my ear-drums.

By the dim light of the luminous rootlets, I could see Bulger just ahead of me, and I was content. No shiver of fear ran down my back, or robbed my limbs of their full power to resist the ever-increasing pressure of the air. But as it grew stronger and stronger, half of my own accord and half because Bulger set the example, I broke into a run. Our pace once quickened it was impossible for me to slow up again. On, on, in a mad race, my feet scarcely touching the bottom of the tunnel, I sped along, while the great pipe through which I was borne on the very wings of the gale sent forth its deep and majestic peal.

There was something strangely and mysteriously exciting in this race, and all that kept me from enjoying it to my full bent was the thought that a sudden increase in the violence of the blast might toss me violently on my face and possibly break an arm for me or injure me in some serious way.

All at once the deep pealing forth of the organ-like tone ceased, and in its stead came the awful sound of rushing water. Before I had time to think, it was upon me, striking me like a terrific blow from some gigantic fist wearing a boxing-glove. The next instant I was caught up like a cork on a mountain torrent, swayed from side to side, twisted, turned, sucked down and cast up again, whirled over and over, tossed and tumbled, rolled along like a wheel, my arms and legs the spokes!

Wonderful to relate, I did not lose consciousness as this terrible current shot me like a stick of timber through a flume, whither I knew not, only that the speed and volume went ever on increasing until at last the tumultuous torrent filled the tunnel, and robbed me of light, of breath, of life, of everything, including my faithful and loving Bulger!

How long it lasted—this fearful ride in the arms of these mad waters, rushing as if for life or death through this narrow bore—I know not; I only know that my ears were suddenly assailed with a mighty whizz and rush of water as through the nozzle of some gigantic hose, and that I was shot out into the glorious sunshine, out into the grand, free, open air of the upper world, and sent flying up toward the dear, blue sky with its flecks of fleecy cloudlets, and Bulger some twenty feet ahead of me, and that then, with a gracefully curved flight through the soft and balmy air of harvest time, we both were gently dropped into a quiet little lake nestled at the foot of a hillside yellow with ripened corn. In a moment or so we had swum ashore. Bulger wanted to halt and shake the water from his thick coat, but I couldn't wait for that. Wet as he was, I clasped him to my heart while he showered caresses on me. But not a word was said, not a sound was uttered. We were both of us too happy to speak, and if you have ever been in that state, dear friends, you know how it feels.

I can't describe it to you.

At this moment some men and boys clad in the garb of the Russian peasant came racing across the fields to see what I was about, no doubt, for I had stripped off my heavy outside clothing, and was spreading it out in the sun to dry.

Upon sight of these red-cheeked children of the upper world I was so overcome with joy that for a minute or so I couldn't get a syllable across my lips, but making a great effort I cried out,—

"Fathers! Brothers! Where am I? Speak! dear souls!"

"In north-eastern Siberia, little soul," replied the eldest of the party, "not far from the banks of the Obi; but whence comest thou? By Saint Nicholas, I believe thou wast spit out of the spouting well! What art thou doing here alone?"

I paid no attention to the question. I was thinking of something else of more importance to me, to wit: my splendid achievement, the marvellous underground journey I had just completed, fully five hundred miles in length, passing completely under the Ural Mountains! After a short stay at the nearest village, I engaged the best guide that was to be had, and crossing the Urals by the pass in the most direct line, re-entered Russia and made haste to join the first government train on its way to St. Petersburg.

Having despatched an avant courier with letters to my beloved parents, informing them of my good health and whereabouts, I passed several weeks very pleasantly in the Russian capital, and then by easy stages set out for home.

The elder baron came as far as Riga to meet me, and brought me the best of news from Castle Trump, that my dear mother was in perfect health, and that she and every man, woman, and child in and about the castle were anxiously waiting to give me a real German welcome back home again. And here, dear friends, mit herzlichen Grüsse, Bulger and I take our leave of you.

Other Works Published by the
East India Publishing Company

A Tale of Two Cities
Charles Dickens

Great Expectations
Charles Dickens

Oliver Twist
Charles Dickens

Dubliners
James Joyce

The Pilgrim's Progress
John Bunyan

A Modest Proposal
Jonathan Swift

Three Months in the Southern States
Arthur Fremantle

Heart of Darkness
Joseph Conrad

Julius Caesar
William Shakespeare

The Red Badge of Courage
Stephen Crane

www.eastindiapublishing.com